A Woman of Courage

Also by J.H. Fletcher

Dust of the Land
The Governor's House

A Woman of Courage

Courage

J.H. FLETCHER

First Published 2016
First Australian Paperback Edition 2016
ISBN 978 176037170 8

This is a work of fiction. Names, characters, places, and incidents are either the product of the author's imagination or are used fictitiously, and any resemblance to actual persons, living or dead, business establishments, events, or locales is entirely coincidental.

Published by
Harlequin Mira
An imprint of Harlequin Enterprises (Australia) Pty Ltd.
Level 13, 201 Elizabeth St
SYDNEY NSW 2000
AUSTRALIA

® and TM are trademarks of Harlequin Enterprises Limited or its corporate affiliates. Trademarks indicated with ® are registered in Australia, New Zealand and in other countries.

Cataloguing-in-Publication details are available from the National Library of Australia www.librariesaustralia.nla.gov.au

Printed and bound in Australia by Griffin Press

MIX
Paper from
responsible sources
FSC® C009448

This is for Stefan Lang,
with my affectionate admiration

The secret of happiness is freedom.
The secret of freedom is courage.
                              Thucydides

Courage is the key.
                         Hilary Brand

2004

THE BOSS

Hilary Brand had slept for six hours and now, wearing a silk robe and with her hair tied back, was working at the little desk that was one of the built-in features of the cabin. Around her were the barely-audible noises of the corporate jet: the whisper of the air-conditioning, the hum of the twin engines propelling the Airbus south-east at eight hundred kilometres an hour, thirty thousand feet above the earth.

It was Thursday 15 January 2004, five o'clock in the morning Singapore time, and Hilary was on her way home to Sydney after two productive weeks in Asia. She had held positive meetings in Jakarta and Kuala Lumpur. Her address the previous Monday to mark the fourth anniversary of the founding of Singapore's Management University had been praised by Prime Minister Goh himself.

Singapore spelt business and, on this occasion, her address to the university, but she had other reasons for heading to Southeast Asia every year.

Co-director Martha Tan had been born in Singapore thirty-two years before. Her grandfather was shot on Punggol Beach in 1942, one of seventy thousand Chinese civilians murdered by the Japanese 25th Army in the weeks after it occupied the island. Each year Hilary accompanied Martha to the memorial at the

Hong Lim Centre in Chinatown, joining the young woman in paying her respects to the man they had never known.

This pilgrimage was public knowledge, but there was another ritual she had been careful to keep to herself. Only she and Martha knew of the minor heart attack she had suffered four years before: if a heart attack could ever be called minor. By chance she had been in Singapore at the time and had been rushed to the nearby Mount Elizabeth Hospital. She had bounced back as she always did, discharging herself after two days against the advice of the doctors because she felt fine and was too busy to lounge about in a private ward doing nothing. Nevertheless she had been grateful for the hospital's timely assistance and had made a huge donation to buy additional equipment for its coronary care unit.

Ever since that episode she'd arranged an annual check-up at the same hospital. As Martha never failed to point out, she could have done it more simply in Sydney, but Hilary was having none of that.

'They were in at the beginning,' she said, repeating the joke she made every year. 'Seems only fair they should be in at the death.'

Death was not on her agenda but privacy was. 'I am not Haskins Gould,' she said. Once her greatest mate, Haskins had for years been her greatest enemy. 'He loves the limelight. I don't.'

Maybe so but she was one of the most famous women in Australia; have a check-up in a Sydney hospital and the media would be on it in a flash. Next thing the world would be told she was dying; what that would do to the corporation's share price she refused to contemplate.

She had thought of the check-up as routine, no more significant than the work-out with which she started every morning – even on the Airbus she always managed a few bends and stretches in preparation for the excitement and challenges of the day ahead. Unfortunately Tuesday's examination had proved less routine than she would have wished.

The cardiologist had frowned over the test results. 'Too much strain on the heart, Ms Brand. No need for surgery at present but it may become necessary if you don't learn to take things easier.'

Sagacious advice, no doubt, but her first reaction had been there was little she could do about it. 'I have responsibilities,' she said.

'Indeed you do,' he said. 'And the first one should be to your health.'

Not many people could put Hilary Brand in her place like Dr Chang. 'I shall do what I can,' she promised.

'Be sure you mean it,' he said. 'We are not playing games here. If you don't cut down I will not be responsible for the consequences.'

He'd been right, of course. The occasional breathlessness; the dizzy spell she'd had in Jakarta… The episode had lasted no more than a second or two and she had brushed it aside, but Dr Chang had made it clear it would be asking for trouble to go on doing so. She sat, pen motionless in her hand, as she considered the implications of the cardiologist's warning. So many things still to do… But: *I will not be responsible for the consequences.* Had the time come? The time she'd been promising herself for so many years? Was she ready? Was it even possible? The pressures on her seemed to grow more intense every day.

She had two more reasons for returning to Southeast Asia every year, one official, one not. Officially she flew to Penang to spend time with the children in the home she helped finance. It was something she never failed to do and it gave her huge pleasure, but there was another reason for going and it was the most compelling of all. Even Martha knew nothing for certain about it. She might have guessed but Martha was as discreet as a clam.

'I'm off, then,' Hilary had said before leaving for the airport. It was something else she said every year. 'Give you the chance to do some shopping. Catch up with your family. Go to Sentosa. I'll see you in five days' time.'

Everyone deserved a break, right? But this break was special. Dear Lord, so special.

Penang, she thought now, as she thought so often. Eight hundred kilometres north of Singapore, off Malaysia's west coast. Penang, the tropical island of the storybooks and Rumah Kelapa, the house amid the coconuts, with its flowerbeds brilliant with cannas and its views across the tropical sea… Penang, where my heart is.

Had the time arrived for her to do something about it before it was too late? Or had her promises – not only to herself – been only words?

She needed to make up her mind but not now. With Asia thousands of kilometres behind her, Hilary thrust Penang and Dr Chang's warning firmly to the back of her mind and turned her attention, as always, to what lay ahead. The habit of a lifetime. Of a death time?

Sydney was two hours distant; by the time they landed the local time would be ten o'clock in the morning. There would be the usual on-board customs and immigration clearance; the waiting chopper would lift her over the city's snarled streets to the helipad atop her corporate headquarters and to the hundred and one challenges of her normal fifteen-hour day. And to a proper consideration of the choices with which she was now faced.

At least this evening would be different. At eight-thirty her daughters Jennifer and Sara would be joining her for dinner at the Seven Stars Restaurant with its marvellous views across the harbour to the Opera House. Officially it would be a purely social occasion; in practice the meal would be a prelude to the real business, which would be conducted the next day in separate meetings with both of them.

She had phoned them from Singapore. For Jennifer it would mean flying up from Melbourne, so of course she had whined about the inconvenience, as Hilary had known she would. She loved her daughters equally but their temperaments were very different and there were times, she couldn't deny it, when Jennifer was a trial.

'I'd been planning lunch with Tessa at Ricketts Point. I've booked a table…'

Over the years Hilary had learnt how to handle Jennifer's whines. 'It's just that Sara and I will be having dinner together and I thought it would be nice if you could join us. But if it's inconvenient I shall quite understand.'

'What's it all about, anyway?' Jennifer had always been hot on conspiracy theories, even before the phrase had been invented.

'No special reason. I just thought it would be nice for the three of us to have a meal together. But if you can't make it –'

Jennifer would drink boiling oil before she missed out on a family reunion where important matters might be discussed. Hilary was sixty-three, after all, and would have to start planning the family's future some time. There was no chance Jennifer would willingly miss out on a conversation like that although she still managed to get a moan out of it.

'I suppose I can put Tessa off. Although I can't imagine what Davis will say.'

Hilary suspected her detestable son-in-law wouldn't give a hoot where his wife was or what she was doing but that was hardly something she could say to Davis's wife. 'I'll book you into the Amora,' she said.

By contrast Sara, three years younger than Jennifer in years, ten years older in maturity, had simply warned she might be a few minutes late. 'By the time I get home and catch a shower…'

'Take your time. We'll have a drink while we're waiting. Any other news?'

'If you're agreeable I thought I might have a word with Duncan Redgrave if I can get hold of him.'

Duncan Redgrave was one of their top site engineers.

'What about?'

'This new Parramatta mall. The subbies have been telling me he's always dreaming up some excuse to delay paying them.'

'It's his way of keeping the overdraft down. It means a saving on the interest.'

'But they've got to have the cash to pay their workers. And we need to keep them sweet, Hilary.'

'Have a word with him by all means. But the truth is he'll try the same trick again the moment he thinks he can get away with it.'

'We'll just have to keep an eye on him,' Sara said. People called thirty-three-year-old Sara Hilary's clone: the same chestnut hair and green eyes, the same ferocious appetite for life. Now she laughed. 'It's blowing like hell up here.'

'Where are you?'

'On a steel girder thirty floors up.'

Hilary shook her head, smiling to herself and at Sara, once again in what her mother called her truant-playing mode. Her real job was current affairs anchor with Channel 12 News, a station where she had worked for several years before Hilary had bought the company two years before. Hilary had other plans for Sara but in the meantime she was doing an excellent job, more thoughtful and less aggressive than many in her game. It was a style that might not suit Millie Dawlish, the executive producer Hilary had brought in three months before to raise the programme's ratings, but that was all right too.

Construction was a major part of the corporation's business and construction was in Sara's blood. She had no engineering qualifications but whenever she was free she liked to rush off to one or other of their current developments, doing her monkey act around the steel framework with a hundred metres of air beneath her feet, asking endless questions and learning, learning all the time. No other television station would have put up with it but Hilary had never played by the book and since she bought the station she had encouraged Sara's independent ways: the more she knew about the various strands of the corporation's business the more useful she would be down the track. There had been some rumbling from other members of the programme team but Hilary had ignored them.

Sara wasn't afraid to get her hands dirty, either. Thirty floors up... That would be right. The men loved her. Respected her too, which was probably more important. She would make a good CEO when she'd had a few more years experience and had learnt how to deal with ruffians like Haskins Gould, predators who would gulp her down bones and all given half a chance. For that she would need to spend more time in the boardroom and less balancing on steel girders, but that was a transition that so far Sara had been reluctant to make.

Until her conversation with Dr Chang Hilary hadn't cared, believing she had plenty of time to school Sara into what she saw as her future role in the group, but the cardiologist had made it plain that time was a luxury she no longer had.

'The Seven Stars,' Hilary had said. 'Martha's booked a table for eight-thirty tomorrow night. Be with us as soon as you can. And I want you to have breakfast with me at the lodge on Friday morning.'

'I can't. I've got Millie's early-morning conference call.'

'Tell her you'll be late.'

'She won't like it.'

'She can take a hike. One more thing. If you do speak to Duncan Redgrave make sure he knows you have my backing. And don't let him push you around.'

'As if,' Sara said.

There would be just the three of them. They would eat and drink together as mother and daughters should but in their case seldom did. Jennifer would be petulant, suspecting plots, demanding to be told what was going on and unwilling to accept her assurance that nothing was going on at all; Sara would say nothing. Later they would go their several ways; Jennifer to her hotel, Sara to her terrace house in Paddington. Only then would Hilary's chauffeured limousine take her home to Cadogan Lodge, the harbourside mansion on five acres of the most expensive real estate in Australia, and to the sleep that by then she would no doubt richly deserve.

A tap on the cabin door and Martha came in with a tray bearing a silver pot and cream jug and two bone china cups and saucers. Martha had been a director of the company three years now, a trusted friend whom ten years before Hilary had recruited straight from the University of Singapore after Martha had graduated with a master's degree in business management. Hilary had never regretted her choice. With the group's involvement with Hong Kong growing by the day she'd had plans for Martha, too, but now that might no longer be her decision.

'Coffee, Hilary.'

Hilary Brand was the boss and nobody aboard the jet or anywhere else in her business empire was in any doubt about it, but she had never been one for surnames since her days in the Lady

Northcote Farm School almost half a century before, when the staff
had called her nothing else.

'Brand, come here! Brand, if you don't mend your ways it's you
for the fiery pit!'

I'll see you there, Mrs Wilmot. Although in those days she had
been careful not to say it: the sharp edge of a ruler on your knuckles
was a sure-fire lesson in how to hold your tongue.

Those memories would remain with her forever but she had never
used them as an excuse. The future was what mattered; only that.

Martha placed the tray on the side table and poured. The fragrance
of coffee filled the cabin. This was their normal routine when they
were on the road: a ten-minute chat first thing every morning to discuss the agenda for the day.

'We've radioed ahead,' Martha said. 'The helicopter will be waiting and the ground handler is on stand-by. There should be no
delay.' She spoke deferentially; co-director or not Martha was still
in awe of Hilary Brand, a woman who had risen from dirt-poor
beginnings to become a legend not only in Australia but in much
of Asia too.

They talked comfortably together, running through the appointments Hilary had scheduled for the day.

'No trouble booking a table for tonight?' Hilary said.

Top restaurants in Sydney often required an advance booking,
sometimes several weeks ahead, but for Hilary Brand a table would
always be available.

'None,' Martha said.

Hilary drained her second cup of coffee and stood, stretching the
kinks out of her muscles. At a shade under five feet nine she was tall
for a woman, whip lean and handsome, her chestnut hair without a
hint of grey. Her silk robe had been presented to her by the wife of
one of China's top officials; it was emerald green to match her eyes
and embroidered with a phoenix, the Chinese symbol of eternity,
and she wore an emerald and diamond ring on her hand. She had
celebrated her sixty-third birthday two weeks before but looked ten
years younger.

Martha put the two cups back on the tray. 'Home soon, towkay neo,' she said.

Towkay neo: more than a nickname, it was the respectful title Martha had given her early in their relationship. Towkay was the Chinese word for the top man in any business, towkay neo its feminine equivalent. Both phrases meant the boss, the person in command.

Hilary glanced at the clock on the side table. 'I'd better have a shower and get dressed.' She grinned. 'Put on a show for the cameras.'

Not that there were ever many of those. As towkay neo of the Brand Corporation, one of the most prosperous and respected conglomerates in Australia, she had learnt long ago how to keep the paparazzi at bay.

The telephone light flashed its red warning.

Martha picked it up. 'Hello.' She listened and held out the receiver. 'Head Office,' she said. 'Vivienne on scrambler.'

Vivienne Archer was also a company director and Hilary's second in command.

'I wonder what's biting her.' Hilary had had scrambler facilities installed on the Airbus to keep communications confidential; she took the receiver and pressed the red button to activate the electronics.

'I'll leave you to it,' Martha said.

Hilary's iron rule was that she must be alone when the scrambler was on. Martha picked up the tray and went out. Hilary's fingers drummed the desktop as she waited through the wails and hiccups that told her the system was coming to life. When a hot message was coming the delay seemed to last forever and for Vivienne to call her on scrambler when Hilary would be in the office within three hours this one had to be hotter than fire.

'Hilary?'

Vivienne's voice was cool – but then it always was. If a tsunami swallowed Australia's eastern seaboard she would probably report the news in the words of Robert Benchley's famous telegram from

Venice: *Streets flooded. Please advise.* No, it was not Vivienne's tone but the fact she had thought it necessary to phone at all that made Hilary frown. She drew a deep breath and activated another of the basic rules by which she governed her business and her life. It was a quotation from Gilbert and Sullivan: *Quiet calm deliberation disentangles every knot.*

Let's see if we can disentangle this one.

'Good morning, Vivienne; I trust you slept well?'

Hilary Brand without a care in the world, and other useful lies.

'I apologise for phoning you so early –'

'Where's the fire?'

'Right here in this building,' Vivienne said. 'We've heard from Hong Kong.'

'Tell me.' And listened with mounting fury as Vivienne began to convey the message she had received half an hour before.

JENNIFER

1

There were times when Jennifer Lander thought the whole world had it in for her, a feeling made a hundred times worse by what had happened the previous Monday evening.

'We've having dinner with the Hawthorns tonight,' her husband Davis had said that morning as he left for chambers. 'Do you think you might just possibly try to remember this time?' The smile that was not a smile. 'Hmm?'

He was reminding her of a disagreement they'd had the previous week over a lunch party he had never mentioned but insisted she had forgotten. She was well aware how proud Davis was of his razor-edged tongue, so useful to him in the law courts. He liked to keep it well honed, too; from the day he had finally succeeded in putting the wedding ring on her finger – Hilary Brand's elder daughter, what a trophy! – he had sharpened it on her.

She was not stupid; even at the time she'd known Davis was marrying her not for her wit or the body he claimed to admire so much, but because he hoped Hilary Brand might advance his career. It hadn't happened; there had been a falling out – neither Davis nor Mother had ever told her the details – and ever since Davis had seemed to blame her for it.

'I suppose it was always too much to hope you'd be any help but I expected better things from her. She knows the chief justice; she could use her influence if she wanted. I am her son-in-law, after all.'

He was indeed, and made sure everybody knew it, but Hilary had made it clear she wouldn't lift a finger.

'There is nothing I can do for him. He's wrong, in any case. I have no influence with the chief justice. I barely know him.'

Which had not lessened Davis's resentment; from the first he had complained about what he called the conspiracy between mother and daughter to deprive him of his deserts. This happened most frequently when he'd been at the scotch, but it had not been until six months after the wedding that Jennifer discovered the full extent to which alcohol could affect her husband's behaviour.

Davis had been to a barristers' dinner. Wives were not invited and when he got home Jennifer knew she had a problem. He went straight to the liquor cabinet and poured himself a drink. He did not offer her one but brought the bottle with him when he sat down with her and began to talk.

He started off by boasting about his court triumphs and the masterly way he'd outwitted his opponents: she'd heard it all a dozen times before but repetition had never been a problem for Davis Lander. He drank more and, as always, his mood changed. He grew sulky, once again complaining about Hilary's failure to provide the support her son-in-law surely had the right to expect. Finally he became amorous: a familiar progression that, like a brothel's open door, led invariably to sex.

There was nothing she could do; he was her husband and if he wanted her she had to comply, supposedly with joy – all the romantic novels she had read had made that clear. Her mother could have taught her differently but she'd been against the marriage from the beginning. They'd talked only about the mechanics of sex: which she'd known from school, anyway, and the question of obligation had never come up. She felt guilty for not wanting Davis more; she was nowhere near as experienced as some of her friends but in that department, as in every other, marriage had proved a disappointment. She had thought Davis would teach her with affection and tenderness; he had not. She had thought they would be united, a loving couple indifferent to the vicissitudes of a sometimes hostile world; they were not. She had thought their lovemaking would introduce her to a wonderland of delight; her experience so far had been very different – a nightly assault devoid of tenderness or love that left her bruised both in body and spirit.

Perhaps it was her fault, as Davis said, but if so he did nothing to help her perform better. He did not consider her at all. They hadn't been married a month when he had told her he would permit no children. Jennifer had wanted two: a son to grow up strong and protective of his mother and a daughter to be a friend. She had envisaged a lovely time of shared confidences but came quickly to realise that a man as self-focused as her husband would never welcome competition even from his own child.

That night, as his whisky breath engulfed her, she had used his opposition to children as a last line of defence. 'It won't be safe.'

'My angel mustn't worry her pretty head about such things.' He spoke coyly but his hands were not coy at all. 'There are times when love must have its way.'

As indeed it had; if you could call it love.

Two months later she had told him she was pregnant and he had been furious, blaming her for trying to saddle him with a brat he had warned her from the first he would not accept. 'You think I can't see through your stupid schemes? Well, I'll tell you now, I'll not have it.' He had forced her into an abortion. 'You have no one to blame but yourself,' he said.

Jennifer had been devastated and had known she would never get over it. She never had. She no longer thought consciously about the child but her subconscious was aware of an enduring sense of loss and the knowledge that when it had mattered Davis had not been there for her.

She had long given up any thought of coming to love her husband but nevertheless had tried to play her part: she had been dutiful, always there when he wanted her, had attended functions on his arm, had smiled as required. She had been the public face of his marriage but in private they were strangers meeting occasionally in the desert of their lives. A dozen times she had told herself she must leave him, but had never had the courage to do so. Marriage might be another word for unhappiness but was nonetheless a safe harbour; over the years she had got out of the habit of independence and the world outside her prison seemed full of terrors.

Davis enjoyed twisting the knife; now, as he left for work, he was reminding her yet again of the lunch date debacle. 'Let's see if you can get it right tonight,' he said. 'Seven-thirty, and it's important we're not late. Henry is a stickler for punctuality.'

Henry Hawthorn QC was Davis's head of chambers and as close to God as either of them was likely to get in this life, so Jennifer understood how important it was not to offend him in any way.

'I shan't forget,' she said.

'Make sure you don't.'

Jennifer hated it when her husband spoke to her like that but had never been one for the smart comeback. The one time she had tried to stand up to him it hadn't gone well.

'I am not your tea girl,' she had told him.

'I thank God daily for that,' he had said.

As she did so often she told herself to be patient; lots of people were not at their best at the breakfast table. The trouble was Davis had nothing much to say in the evening either. And lately, even more troubling, he'd been coming home late several nights a week. She didn't like to think what that might mean.

She heard the Lexus disappear down the drive. She went upstairs, and did what she did so often: she inspected her reflection in the bathroom mirror.

She had been a pretty child; she still remembered the warm glow when strange women had stopped Mother in the street to compliment her on her daughter's sweet looks. She was thirty-six now, but when she looked in the mirror it was the chocolate-box prettiness she saw, and not the plump face and discontented mouth that looked back at her. Not bad for my age, she thought. Perhaps a kilo or two overweight but she'd read that men liked girls to have a bit of meat on them. To ease her conscience she had even enrolled at the local gym but somehow had never found the time to go. There was always something: friends to meet, the book club and the wives' lunch club to attend and a dozen other activities. But today, she told herself, she would be on her best behaviour. She would visit Miranda's – always a treat – and buy a new dress. Something stylish and distinctive. Never mind the cost: creating the right impression was what mattered.

To Miranda's she went. Halfway there the car started coughing and emitting horrifying quantities of blue smoke and she remembered she was supposed to have taken it in for a service. What with one thing and another it had completely slipped her mind. Not to worry: she got there anyway, and shutting her eyes to the price she bought an outfit that the assistant assured her would wow the most fastidious host.

Jennifer stared doubtfully at her reflection. 'You don't think it's a bit... revealing?'

The well-endowed assistant assured her it was not. 'It is the latest fashion,' she said.

With the bag stowed safely in the car Jennifer phoned Tessa and arranged to meet her for coffee at their favourite rendezvous in Bayside Avenue. There they enjoyed one of the wide range of coffees imported from various parts of the world. Tessa claimed to be an expert on coffee as on everything else and today had decided they would drink an Arabica coffee from Colombia.

'It is divine,' Tessa said. 'Intensely aromatic.'

Jennifer found her friend's pretensions exasperating. In truth she thought it tasted no different from instant coffee. She did not dare say so but her doubts must have shown.

'One needs an educated nose to obtain the full benefit,' Tessa said.

As good as saying Jennifer didn't have one, but once again she warned herself to be patient. Tessa was a friend and friends were important. With Davis the way he was she would be alone without them and Jennifer could imagine no fate more terrible than that. If being patronised was the price she had to pay then pay it she would.

She smiled brightly. 'I'm sure you are right, sweetie.'

To comfort herself she went to the counter and selected one of the café's delicious chocolate cakes.

'So decadent,' she confided to Tessa when she returned to their table. 'You should try one.'

But Tessa, beanpole thin, stuck to toast.

Jennifer got home a little after twelve. She hung up the new out-fit, poached herself an egg for lunch and afterwards put her feet up for an hour, telling herself it was important she should be at her best for the Hawthorns' dinner tonight.

At five o'clock she had a lovely long bath. It was one of life's luxu-ries, she thought, to soak in scented warm water. Afterwards she put on the new outfit and stared dubiously at herself in the mirror. Had she really shown so much cleavage in the shop? She supposed she must have done, but somehow it seemed more noticeable now. She remembered reading advice given by some American woman. *If you got 'em, show 'em.* She was certainly doing that.

Davis would be home any minute. She wondered what he would say about the new dress or whether he would even notice... but time passed and Davis did not come. It was after six now, leaving him little time to shower and change before they had to set out for the Hawthorns. That was bad news; having to rush made him snaky and as always he would blame her for it.

The minutes ticked by. Six-thirty and still no sign of Davis. Something must have happened to him. She hated unexpected hitches, imagining heart attacks, road accidents, even mugging. She had always been burdened with a vivid imagination; it was the curse of her artistic temperament. For an artist she was; before she got married she'd known several and even been in love with one, and over the years many friends had complimented her on the watercolours she displayed every summer at the community art exhibition.

Davis hated her phoning him at work; after an argument a few months back he had categorically forbidden her to do so. But if he didn't come home in the next ten minutes they would be late whatever they did. She mustered her courage and phoned Davis's chambers. There was no answer. With mounting desperation she tried his mobile but it was switched off.

Now it was a quarter to seven. She didn't know what to do. If she went without him he would be furious. She daren't ring the Hawthorns. She knew how important they were to Davis's career and was terrified of saying or doing the wrong thing.

Five to seven. She made up her mind and rang for a taxi.

There were no taxis. It was the busiest time of the evening: what had she expected?

She hated driving at night, especially alone, but knew she had no choice. Did she know the way? Of course she did. Jennifer went out to her car, climbed in and drove down the road, the engine coughing like a bronchial old man.

It was a nightmare journey. She found she was not as sure of the way as she had thought and every time she slowed to check the signposts someone behind her would hoot. She became increasingly flustered. The congestion was horrible, particularly in Toorak Road; more than once she was afraid the poor old car would conk out on her and was terrified she might miss the turning altogether. By the time she arrived in Hopetoun Road she was a nervous wreck, but at least now she was safe. The Hawthorns' house could not be far away. She pressed her foot on the accelerator and the engine coughed and died. She pulled in to the side of the road – at least she managed to do that – and tried to start the car again. The engine did not fire. Tears perilously close, she looked at her watch (the clock on the dashboard didn't work). Seven-forty. Ten minutes late already and the car refused to budge.

'You wretched, beastly thing!' said Jennifer.

Again she tried the starter. Nothing doing.

'I shall have to walk,' she said.

And did so, grimly. Her high heels didn't help but somehow she managed. Luckily her destination was nearby: an imposing sandstone mansion, its entrance flanked by white stone pillars. She walked down the driveway and rang the bell.

'We were afraid you'd got lost,' said Mrs Hawthorn, ever so sweetly. She was looking at Jennifer's new outfit. Or perhaps at what it did not quite conceal. 'Interesting,' she said.

'I had car trouble,' Jennifer said.

Davis, glass in hand, was scowling and she knew she would be in for it later. There were several other people she did not know. All of them staring; all of them waiting.

'I am so sorry,' she said.

Mr Hawthorn looked at his watch. 'Perhaps if we are all here now we might go in.'

They trooped in like sheep, Jennifer not knowing where to look. She tugged surreptitiously at her dress, hoping to lift the bust line a little, but it was too tight and she couldn't shift it. Dratted thing! She wished now she'd not let Miranda's assistant talk her into it. And the price! Davis would go ballistic when he found out.

She found herself sitting next to a man she didn't know but who introduced himself as Anthony Belloc.

'Are you a lawyer, too, Mr Belloc?'

'I'm a businessman.'

'I have often wanted to ask,' Jennifer said brightly. 'What exactly does a businessman do?'

Anthony Belloc laughed loud and long. 'We try to make money, Mrs Lander.'

'And how do you do that exactly?'

'I have an interest in a number of companies.'

'Just like my mother. And do you make lots and lots of lovely money like she does? Not that I see any of it, unfortunately.' It was her turn to laugh; it might have been the joke of the year.

'I try,' he said.

Jennifer often wished she'd married a businessman. Davis made pots of money – they had a holiday home in the Whitsundays as well as the lovely house in Brighton – and that was what she'd always wanted, but the idea of the law had always bored her. Having your hands on the money itself seemed far more exciting.

Mr Belloc was a delightful dinner companion, both charming and handsome, with neatly groomed dark hair. She guessed he was in his early fifties, which she had always thought the ideal age for a man, mature yet young enough to be interesting, and he was wearing a beautifully made suit. He looked like a million dollars. A million dollars that was now inspecting her with frank admiration. Jennifer's new outfit no longer embarrassed her. Mr Belloc's smile made her feel young again, and desirable, and she loved it.

She had never had a nicer meal. Afterwards she could not have said what they ate or even what they talked about but during dessert he had said there was something he would like to discuss with her and she, sipping her second or was it third glass of wine, had given him her telephone number. Of course nothing would come of it, she would make sure of that, but it was an unfamiliar experience and she welcomed it, especially since Davis always made her feel like a middle-aged frump with her best years behind her.

It was enough to make anyone rebellious; she was not even *forty*, and Anthony Belloc's appreciative eye showed she still had what it took to please a man. She felt excited and a little breathless, like a teenager on her first date.

The party broke up at ten o'clock. She went through the motions, offering her host and hostess extravagant thanks for *a wonderful, truly memorable* evening. She kissed the air beside Mrs Hawthorn's cheek, fluttered her fingers at Anthony Belloc and followed Davis into a black and rainy night. Then there was hell to pay.

'Where is your car?'

Her ears singing with wine and excitement, she laughed. She felt braver than she had for years. 'It broke down. I had to walk.'

'I suppose you never took it in for a service?'

'I had things to do.'

'And why were you so late?'

Ignoring the rain she stopped and glared at him. 'I waited for you. I was ready at six o'clock but you never came –'

'For heaven's sake, Jennifer! I told you before I left this morning that I would meet you here.'

Careless of the other guests who were also leaving, she raised her voice. 'You did no such thing.'

Davis gritted his teeth. 'Stop making an exhibition of yourself.'

'I am not making an exhibition of myself. You said to be sure I was ready. You said nothing about meeting you here.'

Some of the guests were listening to what promised to be an out and out slanging match. There were smiles.

'Get in the car.'

Jennifer sensed an advantage. 'If you open the door for me I shall.'

He did so, slamming it as soon as she was seated. The tyres screeched as he took off. He drove down the drive and turned right into Hopetoun Road with a violence that pressed Jennifer back in her seat.

'Are you trying to kill us?'

He did not answer. They passed her car parked forlornly at the side of the road. They drove home in a fanged silence that did not last beyond the front door. Davis strode to the phone and rang for her car to be towed in. Then he turned on her. 'Are you trying to ruin us? You arrive late wearing a dress like that…'

'What is wrong with my dress?'

'It makes you look like a trollop. And then behaving the way you did at dinner –'

'I am going to bed,' Jennifer said and headed for the stairs.

'I have not finished talking to you.' Thunder roared beyond the window as he followed her into the bedroom. Thunder in the street; thunder in the house. He snatched up a hand mirror and thrust it in front of her. 'Look at yourself! You turn up late and half naked at what I told you was an important dinner…'

That was what had annoyed him. He wanted her to be a mouse and mice did not wear dresses like that. Suddenly she was glad she'd had the courage to wear it. A gesture of defiance, she thought. No wonder he's so mad. 'You never told me –'

'Of course I did!'

Over and over the same arid ground, flinging words like grenades, getting nowhere.

'And letting Anthony Belloc come on to you the way you did,' Davis said. 'Anthony Belloc, of all people.'

Until tonight she had never heard of Anthony Belloc.

'What do you mean, Anthony Belloc of all people?'

'Anthony Belloc is a crook,' Davis said.

'He is a gentleman and a successful businessman.'

'A businessman? Is that what he told you?' He laughed. 'He's a corporate raider. Otherwise known as a vulture.'

'Then why was he there tonight?'

'Because he's a client,' Davis said. 'Henry Hawthorn is defending him in a civil suit. Might even win. But everybody knows he couldn't lie straight in bed.'

'If he's a client it's just as well I was polite to him.'

Davis did not answer; at that moment she would not have cared if he had. 'I am going to bed,' she said again.

And did so, this time without argument.

2

By breakfast the next morning she had come up with a few things she might have said to him had she thought of them in time.

Where were you earlier last night? And why was your phone switched off? To say nothing of other questions she knew she would never have the courage to ask: *Why did you have to go straight from the office, in any case? And how come you were wearing a different shirt from the one you had on when you left the house in the morning?*

She had a bath, taking her time about it and thinking about the dinner party. She told herself of course she wouldn't hear anything: Anthony's remark had been one of those insincere things one said to complete strangers at dinner parties. She wasn't sure she wanted him to call, anyway. Yet when the phone rang at half-past nine she couldn't wait to pick it up.

'Hello?'

It was only the garage saying they had retrieved her car and would be working on it today.

When Davis came home that evening she was afraid he might start off again about the night before but he ignored her. Situation normal; he often pretended she wasn't there, and certainly hadn't laid a finger on her for years. She had long since ceased to think about that loss; it was just another aspect of the loneliness that had been a feature of her life as long as she could remember. Her sister Sara was too tied up in her career to have time for anyone else. They had nothing in common, in any case; Jennifer had seen her on the box only the other day and remembered how unattractive she'd looked. Sharp nose, sharp eyes, sharp voice: Sara's usual current affairs appearance, eviscerating her latest victim. Of course Sara had taken after their mother and Mother was hopeless, rushing endlessly from one meeting to the next, from one country to the next, concerned only with the power and wealth she shared with no one, like a wicked dragon guarding a golden treasure.

Jennifer had never been interested in the business or anything to do with it. Her ambition had always been to have a nice house, a husband and children. And money, of course. It was what most women wanted, surely? She'd missed out on the children but the rest she had. She should have been happy.

In her heart she knew she was anything but; she often felt she had nothing at all. Her husband despised her. She suspected her friends and even the cleaning lady did the same. They lived in a nice house but it wasn't hers; even her car was not in her name. Davis kept her on a tight leash financially, checking her credit card statement every month and complaining if he thought she was spending too much. Mother could have given her a modest allowance. It would have made her life brighter and easier but of course there was no hope of that. When was the last time Mother had given a thought to her firstborn child?

3

Two days after the Hawthorns' dinner party Jennifer was thinking of getting ready for bed when the telephone rang.

Davis took the call. 'Hello?' He listened. 'I'll get her.' He held out the receiver to her. 'Your mother wants you.'

'But… She's overseas.'

Davis stared at her down his long nose. He spoke as though to the village idiot. 'Yes, Jennifer. She is overseas. And now she wants to talk to you.'

'What does she want?' Again her imagination was in overdrive. 'Is she ill? Has something happened?'

'If you talk to her perhaps you'll find out.'

She took the receiver. 'Hello?'

It was not a long call. After less than five minutes of protests – she even invented an imaginary appointment to justify her initial refusal – and of weakening objections leading inevitably to her final capitulation, she put down the phone. She looked at Davis, who was pretending to be engrossed in his paper but who would have listened to every word.

'She wants me to have dinner with her tomorrow night.'

Davis put down his paper. 'Who wants to have dinner with you tomorrow night?'

'Mother.'

'I didn't know she was coming to Melbourne.'

'She's not.'

'Then I fail to see –'

'She's flying back overnight and wants me to meet her in Sydney.'

'Will she be putting you up?'

'She says she'll book me into a hotel.'

'And paying for it, we trust. Why on earth would she want to see you?'

As though the idea were preposterous.

Jennifer bit her lip. 'She didn't say.'

'Are you going?'

'I told her I was having lunch with Tessa…'

'Are you going?'

It was like being cross-examined in court. 'Do you have to talk to me like that?'

'*Are you going?*'

She knew he didn't care whether she went or not but was annoyed she had not asked his permission first. She stared at him defiantly. 'Yes.'

'Leaving us, no doubt, to pay the airfare.' Davis shook his head and picked up his paper. 'When they made you they forgot the backbone,' he said.

She'd read about women, provoked beyond bearing, who had stabbed their husbands to death.

4

The following morning Jennifer was packing when the phone rang. Her heart went bump.

'Hello?'

Only the garage to let her know the car was ready and could be collected at her convenience. She got a taxi and twenty minutes later was listening to the garage manager giving her the bad news.

'We've managed to patch her up this time, Mrs Lander, but I don't know how much longer we can keep her on the road.'

'What is wrong with it?' She had never understood why men spoke of cars as though they were female and not pieces of machinery. Of course some men thought women were pieces of machinery too.

'Just about everything. She's getting old,' he said and smiled. 'Like the rest of us.'

Not a remark Jennifer welcomed. She signed the grotesquely expensive bill – if Davis didn't like it let him buy her a new car – and drove home.

The phone was ringing as she came into the house.

'Hello?'

For a moment she could not place the voice; then, with a sudden flush of pleasure, she did.

'How nice to hear from you.'

'I was wondering,' Anthony Belloc said, 'whether I could tempt you into having a cup of coffee with me this morning. If you're free?'

'Free as the air.' She laughed. 'I would like that very much.'

A cup of coffee with a friend, she thought as she drove to St Kilda. What possible harm could there be in that?

Yet even as she felt the old excitement of a man showing interest in her, her heart grieved for something real, something she had so foolishly turned her back on, leaving her spirit adrift.

1968–91

MARTIN

Martin Gulliver's mother Anna had been a slave to love, until it turned on her.

Her parents, ignorant louts the pair of them, had liked to fight: each other, mostly. When she was fifteen her father tried to put his hands on her. Anna decided she'd had enough and took off with a bloke called Charlie Moss. That had been early 1967. Charlie was a talker, not much else, but Anna would have loved him if there'd been anything there to love. Loved him, anyway, in the only way that interested him. They were fruit picking up the Murray when she told him she was up the duff. Charlie was out of there quicker than a blowie on meat but she'd already been given the eye by another of the pickers. Clive Jacks didn't care about the baby, seemed to know how to scratch a living and certainly knew how to make her dance, so she moved in with him, no worries.

In 1969 Clive decided the Snowy Mountains was the place to be. Martin was eighteen months old by then but that didn't bother Anna. Besotted, she followed Clive into the high country. He'd told her he'd make a killing working the Hydro, but Clive and work had never been a good mix and in mile-high Cabramurra there was snow and work and not much else. Shortly after Martin's third birthday, Clive went out the door one morning, turned left instead of right and kept going.

Those without a connection to the Hydro couldn't stay in the settlement, so with Clive gone it was a case of find a partner or move out. A month after his departure Martin's mother took up with Dave Anderson. Dave was very different from Clive Jacks, who had pretty much ignored Martin. Dave taught him a lot, including how to look out for himself, and for a few years everything was jake. Then, once again, it all went south.

It was winter 1973 and Martin was nearly six. He'd already discovered wonder: the golden blaze of sunlight on the blinding whiteness of snow; the greens and greys and browns of trees; the blue brilliance of a cloudless sky. Already he was asking how he might catch the colours, make them part of him. And winter meant bitter cold but also snow angels.

Some of the children scoffed. 'No such thing!' they said.

Miss Scott the teacher did her best to put him right. She explained that what he had seen had either been frost patterns on the windows or the sunlight taking fire as it moved across the snow slopes on the other side of the valley, but Martin knew better. He had seen the angels dancing and Dave Anderson had agreed that was what they were.

'I seen 'em flying,' he told him, and winked. 'Straight overhead, like they was all dolled up in golden cloth.'

'Stop encouraging his nonsense,' Mother said, but Dave said you were only young once and where was the harm in it?

One evening as it was getting dark Dave went out of the house to sort out a problem in one of the tunnels. Later that night Martin was woken by a banging on the door and men's voices speaking with an urgency that didn't sound right.

'No! Oh no! Oh my God!'

Mother's voice was half-protest, half-scream, followed by a tempest of weeping. Horror squeezed Martin's throat. He got out of bed and went into the kitchen. The air was stiff with tragedy. Three men were standing helplessly around Mother, who was crumpled in a chair, hands clutching her throat, while Mrs Amos, one of the wives, bent over her.

Later Martin heard what had happened. A charge had gone off prematurely; a section of the roof had come down, with Dave and two others dead underneath it. His loss made Martin weep but turned Mother savage.

'Love,' she said, as though she could spit it out of the body it had gutted. 'Don't believe what they tell you. Let it grab hold of you and it'll rip your heart out. Never forget that.'

Night after night Martin lay in bed and listened to her sobbing, the *thud, thud* of clenched fists on the thin walls of their home. The tears.

In the end the situation grew too much for his mother. Early one morning, the town still sleeping, they sneaked away like thieves, no word of farewell to anyone.

'The world is waiting,' Mother said.

It was a big, unknown world, hostile to a child who had known only the mountains.

'Where we going?'

'Who knows?'

In Cooma Mother got a job in a café and Martin discovered the wonder of paint and colour. He tried to put his feelings on paper, found the miracle of the reds and greens and blues and yellows shouting his secrets.

Mother didn't understand. 'Why don'tcha stop messin' with that nonsense and do somethin' useful?'

He didn't care. His heart and hands trembled with his discovery, the secrets that only he knew. He slopped colour, telling the news of Dave's death, the huddled people, the golden puddle of the down-pouring light, the tragedy he painted not in black but as a scarlet cloud overhanging them, with teeth.

Martin's mother once again packed their bags and set out. Cooma, she explained to Martin, was not right.

'But why?' Martin said.

His mother did not say why.

She made sure Martin went to school – she wanted nothing to do with the authorities, who might have come sniffing otherwise – but didn't like him making friends.

'We're doing all right as we are,' she said. 'We don't want nothin' to tie us down.'

They reached Burra when Martin was fourteen. There was a feeling of the desert and abandonment about it and Mother decided this was it. She landed another job and they rented a cottage on the edge of town. The wind blew all year and the air was full of dust.

Martin was painting seriously now; he saw his future in the explosion of colours that made up his world. He explored the abandoned workings and the creek where long ago families of miners living in holes along the banks had been swept away by raging floods. Their ghosts hung like thunder over Martin's developing imagination and accompanied him when in 1986, at the age of eighteen, he won a scholarship and travelled south to Adelaide.

Five years later he was in Melbourne, close to penniless, still experimenting and battling to find even a hint of acceptance for his work, when he spotted Jennifer Brand at a party.

Afterwards he remembered a swirling kaleidoscope of booze, hash and faces. And Jennifer.

He asked a friend about her. He found out her name and the fact that she had come to the party with some bloke called Walter. Walter, it seemed, was a sook and the friend doubted he would prove much of an obstacle. Jennifer was staying with a sheila called Katie Barnes. In days gone by Katie and Martin had put in some miles together but had parted amicably. Two days later he looked Katie up and met Jennifer for the first time.

He talked her into going out with him. Katie told him to watch it, that Jennifer's mother was both rich and famous.

'Real estate. Shopping malls,' Katie said. 'They say she owns half of WA.'

'Good on her.'

Martin couldn't care less about the rich woman unless she wanted to pay him a fat fortune for his paintings, but more and more he was coming to care for the rich woman's daughter. In no time, or so it seemed, he was in love.

He tried to do the impossible, to paint love as an ecstatic revelation of golden and scarlet light with snow angels filling every corner of the canvas in a blaze of glory.

'That is the future!' He shouted the words into the crimson air, the sun-blazing marvel of being. 'That is going to be our life!'

He went to see Jennifer, panting with the excitement of sharing, of being one, and the ceiling fell in on him.

SARA

1

Sara never woke by inches. The alarm roused her at six o'clock and by ten past she was in her tracksuit and ready to go. Half an hour's brisk jog, a shower and a breakfast of plain yogurt, an apple, a slice of wholegrain bread and coffee. As always, she planned to be shiny clean and at least halfway dressed before the conference call with her executive producer at Channel 12. This was scheduled for seven-thirty, as it was every morning, and gave her just enough time to glance at the news headlines first and wonder once again why Mother was so determined to have dinner with her two daughters tonight. At the Seven Stars too. That would cost her an arm and a leg and Hilary, with more than enough money to buy the restaurant and everyone in it, was not given to throwing her money about for no reason.

As she put on her make-up Sara thought that Mother had always been an enigma. Hilary had always seemed so strong, so remote, even a bit like God when Sara was little. Like God you seldom saw her but knew she was there, powerful and all-knowing. It made you feel safe and warm. It never occurred to you that you were living in a cocoon, that the real world was not the world you knew of big houses, big cars and smiling servants, but you learnt. You discovered clouds could come out of a clear sky, that life could be a challenge, at times even frightening. You had to come to terms with that.

Her sister had never handled it well. Sara was thankful, looking back, that strangers had never stopped to say how pretty she was. That had happened to Jennifer and she had never got over it.

Sara still remembered how Jennifer had clung to Martin Gulliver as though she had never wanted to give him up, doing so only when Davis Lander's ring was safely on her finger – all because she decided in the end that a conventional husband was safer than an impoverished artist. How was she to have known that after years of striving Martin's talent would eventually be recognised? The breakthrough had occurred only twelve months back but from what she'd heard his reputation was growing fast. You could still pick up a Gulliver at a reasonable price but it seemed collectors were beginning to take notice. Jennifer must regret not having stuck to her man, in the best traditions of the romances she had liked to read.

Sara, by contrast, had been in her mid-twenties before she'd felt the need for a serious attachment. She'd had the hots for any number of boys but none had worn well. She'd gone along with all the courtship rituals: had listened wide-eyed to their big talk, had cavorted like a dervish to the crack-a-bang riot of the latest club, had permitted herself to be fumbled in the back seats of cars, but somehow it had all seemed so futile. She was a young woman with a young woman's body and it was that that interested them, not the person who was Sara. Natural enough, she supposed, but she resented it all the same, and being her mother's daughter hadn't helped. Everyone knew Hilary was stinking rich and it had put Sara on her guard, suspecting the boys who came on to her of being the gold diggers that some no doubt were. It made the whole business unreal. She was not offended by the exploring hands but it was almost as though it was not happening at all or at least not to her.

Then out of nowhere her world had changed. What a change that had been.

Well, she thought as she finished her make-up, those days were past. Sad, perhaps, but inevitable; looking back, it was easy to see that now. She told herself it was no longer important. What mattered was the future; only that. She ran down the stairs of her Paddington house, eager to face the day.

The phone rang.

2

Millie Dawlish was a sharp-nosed thrusting woman in her early forties who approached her professional life like a Cossack cutting down serfs. Those to be interviewed were either the enemy to be interrogated, humiliated and hopefully destroyed by Channel 12's ace interviewer, or ratings winners to be massaged for the titillation of the masses. Sara might be the boss's daughter but Millie was self-assertion on steroids and if Sara failed to meet her requirements Millie would be looking for a replacement.

'Confrontation equals good television,' she had said. 'That's what the punters want and that's what they're going to get. I'll be looking for lots of blood on the floor by the time you've finished.'

'What about the truth?' Sara had said.

Millie's sharp eyes scoured Sara's face. 'I hope you and I are not going to have problems,' she said.

Sara hoped so, too. It was a good job and until now she had enjoyed it but her reservations about Millie Dawlish were huge. Aggro for its own sake was often counter-productive.

They spent the best part of an hour talking about what they were going to do on the show that evening: an interview with a government backbencher who might or might not have been involved in sex with a minor; another with a Professor Wilkins who had gone online to claim that a recent series of inter-ethnic rapes was excusable, given the racial vilification tolerated by the authorities; there would be a report on two famous sporting figures who might have taken bribes.

'Juicy stuff tonight,' Millie said. 'Be sure you make the most of it, OK?'

'That professor is a nutcase,' Sara said.

'We know that, sweetie, but he's a handy stick to beat the government with so be sure you give him a soft landing. We tell the punters that racial vilification created the problem: see if you can dig out some old footage to support that scenario. Let Wilkins get his views out.'

'And the pollie and the fourteen-year-old?'

Even over the phone Sara sensed Millie's assassin grin. 'We crucify him.'

Sara wasn't happy about it. She supposed she would have to go along but wasn't happy about that, either. At Nuremberg several of the top Nazis had claimed they had disliked Hitler's policies but had gone along because he'd been the boss. The parallel made her uneasy. If she obeyed Millie's instructions and destroyed a politician on what was no more than hearsay, in what way would she be different from those men? Different in degree, maybe, but in principle identical. Yet if she didn't she might be kissing her career goodbye, because Mother had made it plain from the day she acquired Channel 12 that she had no intention of protecting Sara simply because she was her daughter.

'I won't get in your way,' Hilary had said, 'but I'm not going to push you either.'

Now Sara asked herself whether she was a coward or simply pragmatic. And didn't like the answer.

'I'm not sure about the sports guys,' Millie said. 'There's no percentage in giving sports heroes a hard time.'

'We're saying it's OK if they take bribes?'

'Ratings are what matter. Whether they did what people are saying is beside the point.'

But not, apparently, for the politician.

Fifteen minutes later Sara was just about to leave when the phone rang again. Nothing unusual in that; some mornings Millie was on to her three or four times before she got out the door. She sighed and picked up the receiver.

'Hello?'

It was not Millie. It was Willa from the studio front office.

'Somebody's just phoned for you. An outside call.'

'Can't it wait till I get in?'

'He says he has to go out and wondered if you could ring him back. In fact he asked for your home number but I wouldn't give it to him.'

'Who is it?'

'He said his name was Emil Broussard.'

And the world, suddenly, was still.

'Emil Broussard?' Her voice sounded strange. Small wonder.

'That's what he said. Would that be *the* Emil Broussard?'

'Yes. Yes, it would.'

Emil Broussard back in Australia and wanting her to ring him? Wanting her… Dear God.

3

After university, which she left with first-class honours in both journalism and English literature, Sara got a job as a research assistant with Channel 12's Sydney studios.

She worked hard, grabbed every opportunity that came her way and eventually was given her own show, the weekly arts programme that was the market leader in its field. To begin with it was a provisional arrangement but Sara proved popular with the viewers and had soon carved a permanent niche for herself. In addition, with the network's permission, she had a regular column in two magazines and one newspaper. Everyone in the television world knew that Sara Brand had a stellar career in front of her.

In 1997, at the age of twenty-six, she interviewed Emil Broussard, the fifty-three-year-old Frenchman whose status as a top novelist was matched only by his reputation as an accomplished womaniser, gambler and drinker. He had long been one of Sara's literary favourites.

Sara had done her homework. There was no doubt Emil Broussard was an exceptional man. A reading of his novels, these days written in English and later translated by him into French and German, showed that his command of all three languages was second to none.

She had discovered other interesting facts about him. He disliked publicity, gave few interviews and accepted no awards, although rumour said many had been offered. She thought all these things were admirable yet her first impression of him, standing in the entrance to the interview room, looking around and taking his time about it, was not good. More front than Myers, she thought. Then he looked across the room at her and smiled and something went *ping* inside her.

Sara was well practised in looking at the people she was about to interview. Emil Broussard was a tall man of powerful build with dark and penetrating eyes, the whites unblemished: surprising, if he drank as people said. He was clean-shaven, his still-dark hair clipped close to the scalp. His hands were those of a navvy rather than an artist but with clean nails neatly cut. He was wearing a long-sleeved white shirt that fitted him perfectly, charcoal grey tailored pants and polished black moccasins.

She stood up to greet him, holding out her hand. She gave him her best professional smile but underneath her nerves were jumping. She had interviewed many people during her time with Channel 12 – painters, writers, two arts ministers – but this was the big one. Ever since university she had thought of Emil Broussard as a being set aside from the normal run of talented writers. She knew whole sections of his work by heart.

She knew her lack of objectivity might be a problem. She could have got someone to stand in for her but the arts programme was hers. Broussard was the plum in the pudding and no one else was going to gobble him up. The interview wouldn't be easy – like having a chat with God – but she would handle it somehow.

She had taken a lot of trouble over her preparation. She had read the text of other interviews he had given. Most had been predictable, dealing with his books and his place in the pantheon of international writers. Some had tried to delve into his private life, that scrapyard of women, booze and unsettled debts, but Sara didn't care about that. The man wrote like an angel; as far as she was concerned that was all that mattered. As to the man behind the writer… She doubted she'd be able to find out much about him but would give it a go.

4

The interview was over. It hadn't gone too badly. As she feared, she hadn't been able to get much out of him but at least she'd achieved a small success when she mentioned his Breton background. Then his voice had caught fire.

'I am a child of Brittany. Its landscape and traditions are entirely different from France. They are bred into my body and my blood,' he said. 'If you wish to seek the source of my creativity, do not look at Paris. Look at the menhirs outside Camaret sur Mer. That is where the words come from and the emotions that create them. They are engraved in the stone.'

Now the cameras and microphones were switched off. The crew left. Sara offered Emil the customary drink. He accepted, as was also the custom. They sat and drank together, this famous man seeming to have plenty of time to chat. He smiled at her and she knew he was seeing not the television personality who had interviewed him but the woman. That thought affected her powerfully and his smile made her aware of herself.

Sara had always prided herself on being immune to hero worship. She had been born with a determined streak, what Hilary called a doer. It was a quality that had stood her well in her chosen profession – determined people were not easily wowed – but Emil Broussard had always been out of a different box. Now she felt her body responding to the dark eyes, the smile and pleasantly modulated voice with no more than a hint of a French accent.

'I have to congratulate you on your interview,' he said. 'When will it be shown?'

'Sunday week. Our regular arts programme.'

'I see from the internet that you are also a writer,' he said.

So he too had done his homework. She laughed. 'Having a couple of newspaper columns hardly makes me a writer.'

'Words convey emotions and ideas. It is they who make a writer. I have read some of your work,' he said. 'I would say your columns qualify you admirably as a writer.'

Sara had never expected praise from this man. She shook her head, as close to tongue-tied as made no difference.

'What are your plans?' he said.

From anyone else she might have resented the question but Emil could ask what he liked. 'Carry on as I am, I suppose.'

'Will that teach you much about life? About the human heart?'

'As much as I need to know.'

'There is no limit to what we need to know,' he said.

She would not look at him. She was on a slippery slope and knew it but even with her face lowered she could feel the weight of his eyes, against which she briefly fought a losing battle.

You are not a romantic teen, she told herself furiously. She feared she was losing control of the situation. She needed to put an end to it but could think of nothing to say. I am my own woman, she said in her heart. I do nothing I do not wish to do. I will not look at him. To look at him would be dangerous.

Yet even as she thought it her eyes rose. She looked into his. She saw that they were black, with untold depths. Into which she felt herself falling.

Nothing I do not wish to do, she repeated to herself. But that was the point.

'I have the feeling there were other questions you wished to ask,' he said.

She avoided a direct answer. 'Time is always a problem,' she said.

'All the more important that we should waste as little of it as we can. Which is why I too have a question to ask you.'

Her heart thumped.

'Do you have any leave owing to you?'

'I shall have. Once we've finished recording the present series.'

'When is that?'

'Soon.'

'I would like to think you could spare a couple of weeks, in that case.'

'To do what?'

'I have a house on Hideaway Island in the far north of Queensland. At night I lie in bed and listen to the waves breaking below the window.'

Sara thought the beating of her heart might suffocate her.

'When you're free, come north and I'll show you. There are eagles. If we're lucky we may even see an osprey. And you'll have time to ask the questions you didn't ask in the interview.'

Nothing I do not wish to do, she told herself for the third time. It was madness even to think of going on holiday with a man of his reputation. A guest on her show. But also the greatest of living writers.

'No commitments,' he said, and smiled.

That was nonsense. Go and she *would* be committed.

'I am stifling here,' he said. 'The air is used up. Don't you feel it?'

She had not noticed but now felt it strongly.

'Let us walk,' he said.

She was startled. 'Aren't you supposed to be going to a reception?'

'They won't miss me.'

He was saying he didn't care if they did. She envied such freedom.

'Ideas lose their power indoors,' he told her. 'I think we could both do with fresh air.'

He stood and waited until she stood too.

Come north with me, he had said. *If we're lucky we may even see an osprey.*

I have a good job, she thought. Well paid and responsible. It has taken me four years to get where I am. It would be madness to risk losing that. He said come for two weeks but if I go north who can say when I shall come back?

Yet when he turned away she went with him. They walked out of the interview room and down the escalator to the lobby. Beyond the glass doors the traffic was racing along Macquarie Street.

They went into the street. After the warmth of the Cavendish the evening air was like ice, but she could see that Emil was not a man to give ground to the weather. He squared his shoulders and walked into the bitter wind blowing down the bustling street and she went with him. They passed St Stephens Church. Lights were burning in the parliament building. A belch of diesel as a truck roared past; a taxi blew its horn; there was a hint of sleet in the bitter wind.

'It is warm on my island,' Emil said. 'Very peaceful. At this time of year it is heaven. Most of the time I wear only shorts.'

She was shivering, her dress doing little to keep out the cold. A trickle of icy water ran between her breasts. She was filled with longing for the warmth and peace of the tropics.

It was impossible, of course. She had a career. There was a man on the edge of her life. She did not care as he did, but he was kind, gentle…

'We have to snatch life's offerings,' Emil said. 'If we do not, they do not come back.'

He was saying there were no second chances.

He looked at her, face expressionless. 'What about it?' he said. 'Will you come?'

Such a temptation. Such an impossibility. Say yes and she would be his prisoner, yet she could not bring herself to reject him in words. This man; this wonderful man.

'Phone me in the morning,' she said. 'I'll tell you.'

That night she stood in front of her bedroom mirror and stared at her reflection. A slender face that would harden as it grew older. *Little hatchet face*, her mother had called her. She thought: I am twenty-six, tough, capable, self-confident. There are no glass ceilings for people like me. So why am I swooning over a man old enough to be my father? A man with a track record like Emil Broussard's? He may be a wonderful writer but you live with the man, not his books. Am I so conceited that I imagine I can handle him when so many others have tried and failed? Am I stupid enough even to *think* of chucking up a stellar career and going away with him, like the heroine in a soap opera? I am not that woman. I am not. Yet her own face looked mockingly at her. The image smiled.

She closed her eyes but it was no use. The truth hammered in the darkness. She thought: I am lost.

She had told him to phone her in the morning but instead she phoned him. 'OK,' she said.

So easy: yet it wasn't easy at all. Now she had made up her mind she was excited by the prospect of spending time with this man – but as a true partner, nothing less. She wanted to have him anchor himself inside her, mind and body. She wanted to own him, to have him own her, to be one being. Was it possible to want that and still be herself? She was not inexperienced in the arts of love but had never known a man like this, feelings like this. Emil was worldly-wise and over twice her age. It would be madness to do it but if she did not she knew she would regret it always.

Sara remembered when she was a child a Chinese acquaintance of her mother telling her about *chi*, or *feng shui*, meaning harmony.

'There is Chinese saying,' Mr Chow had said. 'Chi rides the wind.' He also explained to her the importance of the wind. 'In Chinese game of mah-jong, player who draws east wind begins game. Therefore east wind, green dragon, signifies hope and adventure. South wind, red phoenix: danger. West is where sun sets, therefore wind blowing from west, white tiger, means emptiness and death. North wind, dark turtle. Turtle brings opportunity and great rewards. Great perils too.' He laughed. 'North wind gambler's wind,' he said.

Sara took her courage in her hands. She went north, into the land of the dark turtle.

5

The night of her arrival she stood with Emil on the deck of his house and watched the sea. The stars burned in a million points of silver fire while he quoted Yeats to her.

The man's voice rang out above the sound of the tranquil-turning waves. The woman listened, watching the silvery glints of starshine on the water. Emotion drenched her throat in unshed tears, then they both turned and went indoors together. Into the finding place.

Sara remembered how emotion had overwhelmed her. It took her a while to understand that what she was feeling was not love of the place or even of the man but of the world and all those things, known and unknown, that lay out there beyond the world.

Looking back now, she saw their first night together had been the high point of their relationship. Other episodes, descending thick and fast, had destroyed the fulfilment and the joy, had in time destroyed everything.

Emil was away, in Sydney somewhere, and Sara had been swimming. Towel in hand, she came back to the house, walked into the living room and was startled to find herself face to face with a man she had never seen before.

She stared at him. 'Can I help you?'

The intruder was somewhere in his late twenties. He was tall, with formidable shoulders, a tight mouth and hard face. His pale eyes had nobody at home behind them and his skin was so white it might have been bleached.

'It's Broussard I want.'

'Mr Broussard is in Sydney.'

'So you say.'

'I say it because it's true. What do you want, anyway?'

'He'll know what I want.'

Sara did not like the look of this man at all. She was very conscious of herself standing there, as close to naked as made small difference. If he wanted to make trouble she'd have a hard job stopping him. Inside she was terrified but remembered what someone had told her once.

They must never see you're afraid.

She stared resolutely into the pale eyes. 'You'll have to come back another time.'

The blond man smiled and it was not a nice smile. 'Feisty little cow, I'll say that for you.'

He strolled towards her, taking his time. While Sara stood, terrified yet determined to show nothing.

His smile deepened. His eyes stroked every inch of her body. 'Any time you feel like a change of scenery, give me a bell. In the meantime you give Broussard a message. He wants to gamble, he pays his debts, OK? Tell him Mr Albertsen wants his money.' He nodded significantly. 'Polite reminder, that's all this is. If I got to come back, things could get ugly. Know what I mean?'

He reached out suddenly and caressed her cheek. Sara hadn't been expecting it and flinched. He smiled, turned away and went out and across the deck. She heard his whistle as he ran down the steps: a jaunty sound clearly audible above the rumble of the sea. Sara's cheek burned where he had touched it. She felt as though every bone had been drawn from her body. She collapsed onto the settee. It was five minutes before she found the strength to stand. Tottering like an old woman, she went into the bedroom and locked the door behind her. She had known before she joined him that Emil was a gambler but had never bargained on anything like this.

When Emil came back she told him what had happened and how frightened she had been.

'You are too easily scared,' he said.

At that moment she could have killed him.

She tried her hand at a few short stories, was unhappy with them and wanted to throw them out, but Emil said he wanted to read them.

He did so one evening while she sat on the edge of her seat, watching him as he turned the pages. Eventually, without a word, he crossed the room and tossed them in the bin. Then he went back to his chair and poured himself another drink.

Hurt and angry, Sara said nothing, waiting for comments that it became clear he did not intend to make. Finally, also without a word, she got up in her turn, walked to the bin and retrieved her manuscripts. She carried them into the bedroom and put them away in the drawer of the desk she used for her writing. Then she went back into the living room. She sat down. She stared defiantly but said nothing.

'They are very bad,' Emil said. 'I cannot believe how bad.'

Sara said nothing.

'They are an embarrassment. Clearly you have no talent whatsoever.'

He went on and on. She neither moved nor spoke.

'You have nothing to say?'

'Nothing.' She stared him down.

'Butchery of the English language offends me,' he said. 'I suppose I should not expect you to understand that.'

She got up.

'Where are you going?'

'To bed.'

It was a gradual process, his telling her he had meetings with publishers and agents that took him away two or three times a month, but before long he was going away for a week at a time. One night, after he'd phoned to say he would be on the last ferry, midnight came without any sign of him. He will surely phone, she told herself, but he did not. It was a hot night, the house was full of echoes and Sara couldn't sleep. She imagined the taxi crashing on the way to Shute Harbour, Emil in hospital, Emil dead...

Long after the last ferry had docked, too exhausted to care any longer, she stretched out on the settee and went to sleep.

At six-thirty, the dawn sky luminescent beyond the palm trees, she was woken by the sound of someone coming up the steps from the grass. She stood, steeling herself to face disaster, then recognised Emil's footsteps. Relief brought tears but also fury that he should have left her to stew all night without a word.

She opened her mouth to let fly at him but he beat her to it.

'What are you doing, up at this hour?'

She had never seen him in such a rage.

'Checking up on me, are you? Well, you don't own me. I shall come and go as I please!'

This before Sara had said a thing.

Emil paused for breath. Now was Sara's chance. The only way to beat a bully was to stand up to him but she was too tired to bother. She wanted sleep, not a fight. Without a word she turned on her heel, went into the bedroom and closed the door. Even the thought that he might come after her was unimportant. Lack of sleep and Emil's anger had turned the bright morning grey.

It was mid-afternoon when she woke. The house was silent; she didn't know if he was there or not and for the moment didn't care. She put on linen shorts and a loose top and walked on the beach. She thought about the previous night and wondered what Emil had been doing and with whom. She wondered where the two of them were going. Such an inspired artist. Such an impossible man. Without mutual respect they had nothing yet the relationship was still precious to her, despite everything. She would not give it up without a fight. Maybe, she told herself, things would improve.

They did not; they grew worse. Once again he went away, the second time in a fortnight. No word where he was going or when he'd be back. That night she gave up hope. She phoned the studio, was told there would be a job for her but not the one she'd had before: that niche was filled.

'When can we expect you?'

'When you see me. But soon.'

She decided to hang on until Emil returned so that she could tell him to his face that she was leaving him.

'In the meantime I shall drink his whisky,' she told the silent house which was no longer home. 'And serve him right.'

Three days later she changed her mind. Dressed and ready to go, she wrote him a note. Half a dozen lines to mark the grave of a relationship that once she'd hoped might last forever. Twenty minutes later she was at the wharf. The ferry had just arrived, the passengers disembarking. She waited to board.

'Where do you think you're going?' Emil towered menacingly over her.

'I have left you a note,' she said.

She had one foot on the ferry when he grabbed her arm.

'Take your hand off me.' Her eyes blazed with such fury that he stepped back. 'I am leaving you,' Sara told him. 'Where I am going does not matter. I have left a note.'

The crewman swung the gate shut between them and the ferry began to move. Emil shouted after her. 'We have unfinished business, you and I.'

Words like a threat; Sara did not answer. Soon the gap between them was too wide to be bridged by voices but neither moved, each staring at the other's diminishing figure until distance took away the last remnant of what they had once meant to each other.

6

'Give me his number,' Sara said to Willa. While her heart thundered in her chest.

She wrote the number down. She held the piece of paper in her hand and felt Emil Broussard at her side, his breath stirring her hair, his lips and hands moving over her body. After she walked out she had been certain she would never see him again. Sad, but better than the endless pain of remaining with him.

Now, out of the blue, he was back.

She thought she should almost certainly not phone him. She had read that in England the authorities were still wary of opening the ancient plague pits, fearful that the toxins of past days might still linger. She had told herself repeatedly that she was over Emil Broussard. Now she discovered she was less certain of that than she would have wished. If I do not phone, she thought, it will mean he still has power over me. And he does not. Let me say that a thousand times. He does not; does not.

She took a deep breath and dialled the number Willa had given her. It rang and rang and she was about to give up when the receiver lifted.

'Emil Broussard…'

She remembered the voice; she remembered everything, good and bad.

'You were trying to get hold of me?'

'I am sorry. Who is this?'

They'd lived together for a year; he'd asked her to phone him and now was pretending he didn't know who she was? But arrogance had always been Emil's way.

She said: 'You know damn well who it is.'

'Ah yes, now I do indeed. Who else possesses such an instinct for courtesy?'

'Who else has more reason? What do you want, anyway?'

'To speak to you, naturally.'

'Why?'

'I thought it would give us both pleasure to have lunch together today. Revisit old joys, old battles...'

Mockery, too, had always been Emil's way.

'Sorry to disappoint you but I am tied up. The programme, you understand.'

You fool, she thought. Why make excuses? The next thing you'll be apologising to him.

'You disappoint me,' Emil said.

'Why?'

That too she should not have said.

'Is the programme so important?'

'It's my job, Emil.'

'Your job...' Contemptuously he discarded the notion that a job might be important to anyone. 'So the slave loves her chains?'

The perfect trifecta: arrogance, mockery and contempt. All facets of the same impossible personality. How had she put up with this man for so long?

'Thank you for your invitation. Whether I love my chains or not, the fact remains I cannot have lunch with you.'

'I have written my autobiography,' Emil said. 'It contains certain information the world has long wanted to know. Information that I have until now been unwilling to disclose. The purpose of my invitation is to discuss the possibility of your interviewing me about it on your programme.'

Don't be too eager, Sara thought. Make him come to you.

'I'm not sure they'd be interested,' she said. 'It would have to be quite sensational to get them to agree.'

'A man who was offered the Nobel and turned it down? A writer whose last contract was for a million dollars? A writer whose Breton father wanted independence from France so much that he fought for the Nazis in the hope of obtaining it?' She could almost see the snarl. 'Is that sensational enough for your people?'

'Fought for the Nazis?'

No wonder he had kept quiet about his past. Always, in his writing and his life, Emil had known how and when to set the hook. Now, between one instant and the next, it was buried deep.

'Of course I'll discuss it with them,' Sara said. 'But I still can't manage lunch. Not today.'

'Dinner, then?'

'Oh Emil, I'm sorry. I'm tied up tonight as well.' To reject him not once but twice… She took a deep breath and plunged. 'It would be lovely another time.'

'Tomorrow night, then. At nine o'clock. *D'accord*?'

Get her make-up off, nip home, a quick shower and change of clothes: another rushed evening. So what was new?

'*D'accord.*'

'Your address?'

It was a rule in the business that you never gave your address to anyone: but this was *Emil*, she told herself, and rules, just occasionally, were meant to be broken.

She hung up, wondering what she'd let herself in for. I am not going down that path again, she thought, never. Never! But memory could be a traitor, and the question in her mind remained.

EXECUTIONER MODE

It was quarter to eleven when the chopper put down on the landing pad atop the Brand Corporation building. With the rotor still turning Hilary thanked the pilot – something she never forgot – and was out of the door and heading purposefully for the lift that would take her to the executive floor housing her suite of offices and the penthouse that was her home from home when she couldn't spare the time to return to Cadogan Lodge: there had been occasions when she had roosted there for days at a time. The vast bed was regularly aired, the towels and other goodies replenished every week. Handy for entertaining important guests, it was a showcase. The dining room contained numerous examples of early colonial Australian furniture, including an 1840 cedar-wood bookcase provenanced to Dorothea Mackellar. One of the two Opie portraits of Lachlan Macquarie hung on the wall behind Hilary's chair; the other was on display at the State Library of New South Wales. The vast reception area provided a contrast in style. It had two hundred and seventy degree views across the city and an outside balcony from which it was possible to see the length of the harbour from the bridge to the Heads. The furniture was luxurious and modern with a few good paintings: Olsen, Nolan, Boyd. Also a Gulliver, the artist whom Jennifer had loved and whom

Tom Tallis, the curator of her collection, had tipped to become the next big name in the art world. Poor Tom, felled by a stroke a month ago at the age of fifty-five. He was a sad loss, both as curator and friend.

In a glass-fronted cabinet a chambered nautilus shell was an elegant brown and white memento of her first magical visit to Penang. Ah, Penang…

But today Hilary had no time for smiling memories of recent days, so she left the penthouse as soon as she had checked that all was in order there and headed across to her office. Now all her attention was focused on the news that Vivienne Archer had given her three hours earlier. She was in executioner mode and must decide swiftly and unemotionally how to deal with the problem of Hong Kong.

Alerted to Hilary's arrival, Vivienne was waiting in the outer office. 'I've got Desmond on stand-by if you want him,' she said.

Fifty-year-old Desmond Bragg, one of the fat boys' lunch brigade, was aptly named, but knew all there was to know about running a television network. Desmond was CEO of Channel 12 and his office, like Vivienne's, was almost but not quite as substantial as Hilary's own: status was a built-in feature of the Sydney business world, extending even to where you ate your lunch. Hilary despised such nonsense but Desmond insisted it was important. He had told her once that the position of your table at Cavaliers sent a signal to the watchers who was on the rise and who wasn't.

'Should we care?'

'We might. For example, you might think it useful to know that Haskins Gould is back in town.'

'I'd hoped we'd seen the last of him. Where's he been hiding?'

'Zurich is what I hear. Got some deal with the Stanislaus Bank. You remember? They were in with that crowd in the Bahamas.'

'Mortensen Associates? They're as crooked as a dog's hind leg!'

'Naturally. And the buzz is he's got a couple of bottom-of-the-harbour schemes on the go as well.'

'You couldn't keep Haskins down with lead boots,' Hilary had said. Although heaven knew she'd done her best. 'Next time I'll use six-inch nails on the coffin lid.'

'Might be wise,' Desmond had said. 'He was letting fly only yesterday.'

'To you?'

'I was at the next table but Haskins always likes the world to know what he's thinking.'

'What he says he's thinking.'

'This time he meant it.'

Hilary was amused, or sort of. 'Talking about me, was he?'

'Among other things.'

'Nothing complimentary, I'll bet.'

'You'd better believe it.'

'What did he say?'

'He said, and I quote, "I'm gunna bring that effing bitch down if it's the last thing I do."'

'Effing? Did he really say that? Haskins never used to be so delicate in his language, as I recall.'

'They come down hard on language at Cavaliers.'

Hilary smiled. 'That must inhibit him.'

'Something else I heard him say: "I am a lion in ambush."'

Hilary laughed. 'Lion? Haskins? More like hyena, I'd say. Should I be worried?'

'I doubt it. Won't hurt to keep an eye on him, though.'

Hilary would not have been seen dead in Cavaliers, the lunch club where the champagne was imported and your status depended on whether the maître d' condescended to take your order himself, but Desmond was the best in his business so she was prepared to tolerate his ways. In truth he was right: signals in the corporate world were always useful, however you got them.

'I would like Desmond to sit in,' she said now. Hilary turned to the young woman who was standing by her desk, dark eyes alert. 'Morning, Janet. Please ask Mr Bragg to join us in five minutes.

Bring us some coffee and hold all calls until I tell you. Martha, I want you to sit in as well.'

Vivienne and Martha on her heels, she walked into her inner sanctum and closed the door.

'Sit down, the pair of you,' she said. 'Vivienne, you'd better tell us what's going on.'

She listened, fingertips joined, face expressionless, as Vivienne obliged.

It was a sorry saga. Acquiring Channel 12 had meant taking over the contractual baggage that came with it. Part of this had been a deal with the Lennox brothers, a two-man team in Hong Kong who had persuaded Channel 12's previous proprietor they had an in with top Chinese officials that would enable 12 to set up its own operation in mainland China. Do that and they would be making money by the bucketload. Of course there were problems; the brothers had been disarmingly honest about the difficulties they faced in winning approval for a foreign-owned station in China and the time frame in which this could come about but 12's management, which in those days had liked to flex its corporate ego by chucking other people's money around, had gone along for the ride. One of the major considerations, predictably, had been the need for what they called seed money and how it could be used to eliminate what might otherwise be insurmountable problems. Channel 12 had entered into an arrangement to pay the Lennoxes two hundred and fifty grand a month to grease palms in what the brothers claimed was an unavoidable part of the commercial process in the People's Republic.

Hilary had been sceptical about the arrangement but had gone along because the legal costs of breaking the contract would have been gigantic. However, two years on there was still no sign of the promised bonanza and she had appointed Cheu Mun Kwong, a Hong Kong enquiry agent, to initiate enquiries. Now he had emailed a twenty-page report, which Vivienne placed on Hilary's desk.

'You need to read this,' she said.

Hilary looked askance at the bulky document. 'Tell me the gist of it.'

'It's a crock,' Vivienne said.

'What are you saying?'

'I'm saying you're down six million bucks.'

There was a knock on the door.

'Come...'

Janet brought in the coffee. Hilary gave her trademark smile. 'Any chocky biscuits?'

'I'll get some.'

'And another cup for Mr Bragg.'

'You know what I think?' Vivienne said. 'I think the whole thing is a fraud.'

'Can we prove it?'

'Mr Cheu thinks he can.'

'Then maybe we should tell him to do that. And get the police on to it as well,' Hilary said.

'I think there could be a better way,' Martha said.

The other women looked at her.

'How?' Vivienne asked. 'If Hilary is down six million...'

Her voice was not exactly unfriendly but not warm either. It was unsurprising. Hilary said nothing, her eyes moving between her two subordinates. Different though they were, they complemented each other and she had the highest regard for them both. They were both senior directors but only one could expect to step into her shoes when the time came. Maybe neither – that would be Hilary's decision – but a measure of rivalry was inevitable between two such high-flyers.

'But is she?'

'The agent seems to think so, if you read his report.'

'All I am suggesting is there may be a way to turn this loss to our advantage.'

The hint of a curled lip. 'To get our money back? I doubt there's much chance of that.'

'Not recover the money, no. But maybe use the problem to obtain some other benefit?'

'Get back to me on that,' Hilary said.

The door opened; Desmond Bragg was not a man to knock. He came into the room. 'Here I am. What's the problem?'

'Sit down, Desmond. Vivienne, tell him what you've just told us.'

Desmond listened. Physically he was a slob but his mind was a razor. When Vivienne had finished he smiled, teeth sharp in the soft face. 'If it stinks like a skunk…' he said.

Hilary nodded. 'My thoughts exactly.'

'How did Willy Montgomery get himself suckered into a deal like this?' he wondered.

'I don't know and I don't care,' Hilary said. 'What matters is what we do about it.' She pressed the conference button on her telephone. 'Come in please, Janet.'

The dark-eyed young woman opened the door. Hilary handed her the enquiry agent's report. 'Four copies of this document, if you please. Priority and confidential. Quick as you can.' Hilary turned to the others. 'Go through it line by line. I want your recommendations on my desk by eight o'clock tomorrow morning. We'll meet at nine-fifteen and decide what we're going to do. Now, what else is on the agenda?'

'You have a finance committee meeting at three,' Vivienne said.

'Reschedule it to five-thirty. Martha and Vivienne, I want you to stay back so we can talk about what's been happening while I've been away. Desmond, please send me up your report on what Channel 12 has been up to. And copy me your suggestions on the programming schedules for the next three months. Soon as you can, all right? We'll discuss them after tomorrow's meeting.'

They heard the authority in Hilary's voice. After her Asian walk-about, the boss was back and, by the sound of her, ready for war.

Vivienne and Desmond had both adopted Martha's name for her and all used it now.

'Yes, towkay neo.'

TEMPTATION

Jennifer's plane was on time. She retrieved her bag from the carousel and walked out of the terminal, looking hopefully to see if Mother had sent a car for her, but there was nothing. Why would she have expected anything else?

There were plenty of taxis but the trip into town set her back a packet and she knew Davis would not be happy about that. Too bad, she told herself. These days Davis was seldom happy about anything but after her meeting with Anthony Belloc that troubled her less than it might have done before.

The taxi drew in beneath the hotel portico. She paid the driver; a uniformed porter took her case from the boot; she climbed the steps into the imposing entrance hall and walked to the reception desk. Members of the hotel staff smiled politely, waiting to do her bidding. It was a refreshing change from how she was treated at home and she was determined to make the most of it. Anthony Belloc had also treated her with respect and – yes! – a measure of admiration. Having coffee with a friend in the middle of the day was hardly a hanging offence – but Davis would have hated it and the thought pleased her. A delightful rebelliousness stirred her blood as it had not been stirred for a long time.

With her room door closed behind her she sat on the king-sized bed, kicked off her shoes and stared about her with pleasure. She got

up and inspected the marble-tiled bathroom, checked the goodies in
the bar fridge, looked at the magazines displayed on the little desk.

She looked at her watch. Six o'clock. She unpacked; daringly she
raided the fridge and helped herself to a miniature bottle of scotch;
she undressed and snuggled into the luxurious bath robe she had
found hanging in a cupboard; she sipped the whisky from a crystal
goblet as she waited for the bath to fill; she poured in one of the
essences she found on the bathroom shelf; she shed her robe and lay
back in the steaming water. Bliss...

Dreamily drifting, half-asleep, she thought back to that morning's meeting with Anthony Belloc.

He had chosen a side-street coffee bar where she had never been.
She was glad of that; there was little chance of being spotted by anyone
who knew her. She giggled drowsily; she had always had a weak head
for spirits and as a result seldom dared touch them; now the whisky
fumes swirled in her head as she thought what Davis would say if he
had any idea his wife had been consorting over coffee and delicious
cakes with another man – and one of his firm's clients, at that!

The giggle deepened to a laugh. She tipped in the last of the
scotch, telling herself she should have told Anthony what Davis had
called him. *My husband says you're a crook.* She decided he would
have laughed too. He might have asked whether being a crook made
any difference to Jennifer's friendship with him.

'Not *friendship*,' she announced to the steam-filled bathroom.
'More like *lust*.' And laughed even more heartily than before.

It was amazing what a hot bath and a glass of whisky could do.
She thought of her husband without affection. She knew in her
mind she was being unfaithful to him. So what? Exactly what he
deserved. Davis was a bully. Davis did not appreciate her. Anthony
Belloc, on the other hand...

A passing fantasy made her breasts tingle: of Anthony taking her
in his strong arms, naked as she was, and telling her how precious,
how truly wonderful, she was. She did not allow herself to pursue
the vision but it created in her a moisture and warmth that had

nothing to do with the bathwater. Which in any case was beginning to cool.

She got out, towelled herself dry and dabbed herself here and there with perfume. It was strange how the thoughts she'd had in the bath – foolish daydreams with no foundation in the real world – made her fingers more sensitive to the tenderness of her skin. More than that: to the hopes, fears and desires that flowed like blood through the flesh beneath.

She put on the towelling robe, inspected the fridge and found a second whisky miniature. Did she dare? She decided yes, she did. She unscrewed the cap, emptied the contents into a fresh goblet and carried it with her to the armchair closest to the window. It was seven o'clock and would be full daylight for another hour yet she could see lights shining in some of the rooms of an adjacent hotel. She could see no one in those rooms but had no way of knowing whether the occupants, if any, could see her.

A thought struck her, so startling she could barely believe it had entered her head. She wondered what any unseen watchers would think if she stood up now – she did so – went close to the window – she did so – stripped off her towelling robe and stood there in the window for the world to see. Stark naked, free of constraints and unashamed. Defiant. *Here I am. See me for what I am.*

She would never do it, of course. She took a mouthful of scotch and laughed, shaking her head. Never in a million years… Her hand toyed with the towelling belt that secured the robe. One gentle pull… Her fingers tightened.

The telephone rang.

Jennifer paused, caught in the moment that divided fantasy from reality. The tension that until that moment had tightened every sinew relaxed. For an instant she staggered, barely able to stand. Then she turned back into the room and picked up the phone.

'Hello?'

'Good evening, Mrs Lander. Hilary asked me to check that you were safely booked in.'

It was that Chinese woman who worked with her mother. Martha something. 'Please tell *Mrs Brand* I am fine.'

'I shall indeed.'

Jennifer detected something in the voice. Surely the girl was not laughing at her?

'The Seven Stars at eight-thirty,' the Chinese woman said. 'Hilary –' was there the tiniest emphasis on the first name? – 'asks me to say we'll send a car to pick you up. Eight-fifteen. Is that OK?'

'That will be fine.' She spoke clearly, separating each word so the woman would be able to understand. Perhaps the whisky might have had an effect also.

'Are you all right, Mrs Lander? You sound –'

'I am fine,' Jennifer said. 'Perfectly fine.'

And put down the phone.

Nearly did a strip tease in front of half Sydney but nothing to worry about. Just losing my mind, that's all.

Perhaps that second whisky had been a mistake. She decided she would lie on the bed for half an hour to help clear her mind for the evening ahead.

She did so. She dozed – something she had warned herself not to do – and it was ten past eight when she came to with a headache and a foul taste in her dry mouth.

'Damn and blast!' said Jennifer.

She brushed her teeth, which helped a little but not enough. She inspected her unpleasantly red eyes and put in some drops, hoping they would do the trick. She was getting dressed when once again the phone rang.

'Reception here, Mrs Lander. Your car is waiting for you.'

'Tell him I'll be down directly.'

She slapped on make-up, stepped into her dress and forced her feet into too-tight shoes. Ten minutes later than intended, she took the lift to the ground floor.

Sitting in the rear of the big Mercedes – black as night and shining like the moon – she watched as the driver manoeuvred her way through the traffic. A woman driver; trust Mother to do things differently. Jennifer drew a deep breath and tried to collect herself. She asked herself whether she would have the courage to carry out the favour that Anthony Belloc, smiling at her across the coffee-shop table that morning, had asked.

'It's a simple enough question,' he had said. 'A loving daughter's natural concern. Who could take exception to that?'

She had said nothing at the time but now permitted herself a cautious grimace. Who could take exception? Mother could; she had never welcomed anyone prying into her affairs.

The car came down the hill towards the harbour, the sails of the Opera House luminescent in the darkness, and Jennifer had another thought. How typical of Mother not to send someone to meet her at the airport but arrange a car to bring her to the restaurant. Jennifer might have wanted to walk or pop into a shop or two – anything. But no. Mother had to have her way even in this. It wasn't good enough.

Was it the whisky that had given her this sudden feeling of independence? It was certainly an unfamiliar frame of mind for someone who as long as she could remember had been treated as a doormat by just about everybody, but did her new-found courage excite her or scare her half to death? Or both?

Confused and apprehensive, Jennifer sat on the edge of her seat as the vehicle drew to a stop in front of the Seven Stars.

The uniformed driver got out and opened the car door. Jennifer stepped out into the warm night air and saw her sister crossing the car park.

DEFIANCE

1

At the studio Sara spent the morning developing that night's stories. She liked to come in hard at the start of her interviews, pose a question designed to rock the person being interviewed. She always spent time working on that and on a choice of follow-up questions depending on the initial response. She thought of it as polishing her sabre. That night her first interview was with the professor whose recent statements implied that politics could justify rape. She checked out his biography and the sensationalist utterances that over the years had become his trademark. God, he was a snake: but their sort of snake, at least in Millie's view.

'He's by way of being a mate,' Millie said. 'So go easy on him, OK?'

No way, Sara thought. Opinions like that could not possibly be justified. She was not going to let him off the hook, whatever Millie might say. Her opening question laid out the battlefield. *Professor Wilkins, do you believe that murder of the innocent is justifiable?* Whether he answered yes or no, she'd got him. Because rape was murder of the soul, was it not, and could never be justified by any society that had the remotest claim to being civilised. Professor Wilkins, a man, trying to justify the gang rape of Sydney teenagers? She would take him apart.

If Millie didn't like it, tough. Because Leanne, Sara's best friend, had been raped on her way to Sara's fifteenth birthday party. Her attacker had never been caught and Leanne had never recovered. Twelve months later she had walked under a bus.

A tragic accident was what people called it.

Eighteen years later the pain still brought tears to her eyes. Professor Wilkins with his smart-aleck theories, she thought savagely; he wouldn't know what hit him. She was looking forward to that.

2

One of Sara's most useful skills was her ability to compartmental-ise her life. Having taken the professor apart on schedule it was as though he no longer existed and she turned to the sexual antics of the errant politician. By comparison he had an easy ride. Deserv-edly so; a minute before they began the interview Sara had a slip of paper put in front of her saying that the police had established that the girl's accusation had been part of a failed blackmail attempt. Luckily a minute was long enough for quick-thinking Sara to turn the interview around and discuss with the accused-now-victim the vulnerability of public figures to such false accusations and what they could do to protect themselves.

Millie was looking daggers. Tough. Given the circumstances there wasn't much she could say about the politician but she no doubt intended to give her a clip on the ear for the way she had eviscerated the professor, but clips on the ear would have to wait. Within minutes of the programme going off air Sara had shed her make-up and was heading for the exit. The programme and the faces of those she had interviewed were gone.

The traffic was bad but Sara was used to it and knew a few short cuts that got her to her inner city home in fifteen minutes.

It always gave her pleasure to come home and the easing of spirit as she shut the door on the world never failed her. Her terraced house was a haven of peace, doubly precious because peace formed so small a part of her life. From the outside the nineteenth-century building was pleasant but nothing remarkable, with a lacework balustrade masking the upstairs veranda. The interior made up for it: a continuous space that had been suggested by pictures of Chinese properties Sara had seen, one room leading to the next in a continuous flow. She'd installed folding glass partitions so rooms could be segregated if necessary but for the most part these stood open. The polished wood floors provided warmth, the grey and white furniture coolness; colour came from an abstract painting in pink and blue above a fitted wall sofa. Tonight, however, she had no time to luxuriate in the peace and elegance of her precious home. She ran up the open wooden staircase, glancing at the time as she went: eight twenty-five. She stripped off and went naked into the en-suite bathroom. She stood under the shower and let the water flow over her.

FAMILY GET-TOGETHER

1

Hilary reached the restaurant on the dot of eight-thirty. Neither of the girls had arrived but that was all right. One of the penalties of her hyperactive lifestyle was that over the years she had become obsessed with punctuality. Like all obsessions it could be a boring business – the unforgiving minute, Kipling had called it. He'd certainly got that right.

It gave extra pleasure to sitting at the window table with a glass of Tio Pepe in her hand. She savoured the sherry's dryness on her tongue and looked at the harbour in front of her, its spreading waters a glory of liquid fire under the moon, the scalloped roofs of the Opera House sheened with silver light. What kind of life was it when even five minutes' inactivity became so valuable?

I really am getting old, she thought. Yet was she really? At sixty-three there was still time for another life, another way of living. Was she ready for it? Was she brave enough to dare?

She looked at her watch, more precious by far than the gold from which it was made. Twenty to nine and still no sign of either girl.

Sara had a reasonable excuse but Jennifer none.

Hilary sighed. An attentive waiter offered to refill her glass; she shook her head, watching the diminishing navigation lights of a container ship heading down the harbour towards the sea.

There was no getting away from it; Jennifer was thirty-six years old yet remained her problem child. Much loved, always, but the source of much irritation too.

In Hilary's opinion it was a pity she hadn't moved in with Martin Gulliver when she had the chance but Martin had no money and a free-wheeling lifestyle. Jennifer had been scared of that. Davis Lander, on the other hand, had been the epitome of respectability, a society player with the prospect of making serious loot down the track, so Davis Lander it had been. Hilary was convinced Jennifer had made the wrong choice but until Jennifer turned to her for help she did not think it was her place to interfere.

Hilary had been against the marriage and the fancy-pants wedding Jennifer wanted.

'Don't you want to make a good impression on Mrs Lander?'

'Not particularly.' Hilary was unimpressed by old money when it was used simply to shore up the social status of the person who had inherited it.

'You don't want me to get married at all!'

'I want you to be happy. I'm not convinced Davis will make you happy.'

'You've been against him from the first!'

He had talked Jennifer into coming to Hilary with a dodgy scheme for which he hoped to get funding. Hilary had refused and there had been a row.

'The first thing I've ever asked you for and you say no?'

'Hardly the first thing.'

'Name me one!'

Hilary had laughed. 'My dear, you've been asking me for things all your life.'

There were times when Hilary thought Jennifer had never forgiven her for that refusal. For which – Jennifer made sure her mother knew – Davis had blamed her.

It was a sour note. Hilary felt no guilt about it but supposed it might have influenced her decision to allow Jennifer the sort of wedding she craved and which Hilary thought a ridiculous waste of money, the bride in a Givenchy dress with half a mile of white tulle and gardenias in her hair, the ceremony graced by half the legal suits in Sydney including a High Court judge whom Hilary cordially disliked.

And so the good ship Jennifer had sailed off into the sunset with her pompous but well-heeled husband and all her days should have been as rosy as a virgin on the morning after but things hadn't worked out like that.

Hilary was sad for her but her life was too full to waste time trying to mend things that couldn't be mended. What Jennifer needed was an affair: with Martin if he was still available but certainly with someone. No doubt it would cause huge problems but might make her a happier woman. It had certainly worked in her own case, but she did not think her daughter had the courage to do anything as audacious as that. Jennifer had lost the knack of happiness and no one could resolve her problems but herself.

Sara was very different, of course: both more outgoing and more secretive. If she'd had love affairs since Emil Broussard Hilary knew nothing of them. No doubt there had been a few men in her life but Sara was too sensible to get hooked unless that was what she wanted and nowadays children were an optional extra, after all.

Sara had done well at university; she had an instinct for construction and perhaps for business too. Certainly her comments about Duncan Redgrave had been on the money. And now she was something of a star on the television screen. Hilary had watched her before leaving for the restaurant and thought she'd done well. Of course she and Millie Dawlish were chalk and cheese but that might not be such a bad thing.

The lights of the container ship were barely visible now. A stir by the restaurant entrance made her look up in time to see the two girls coming through the doorway together. Before she could prevent herself she glanced at her watch. Eight forty-five; fifteen minutes late. Once again she reminded herself that this was a social occasion and punctuality was unimportant. Tomorrow would be a different matter.

In the event the evening went better than she had dared hope. The food was brilliant, the wine delectable – as it should be, she thought, the price they charged – and the view sensational. Conversation had been light and inconsequential, just right for a mother-and-daughters get-together. There had been no disagreements: as always Sara had been watchful with little to say for herself; Jennifer had been pleasant, with a lightness about her that made her mother wonder whether she had taken a lover after all.

'When are you flying back?' she asked over coffee.

Jennifer sipped her Calvados. 'Tomorrow afternoon.'

'Davis meeting you?'

'He has an important meeting –'

'Come to the office. We'll have a light lunch before you go. I'll have a car take you to the airport.'

2

Hilary always enjoyed coming home to what had to be one of the finest properties in Sydney. She liked to remember, too, how she had acquired it and the bargain it had been. It had come on the market just when she had made up her mind to relocate to the east coast. It had been owned by Ambrose Wylde, a wannabe tycoon who had got in over his head. Hilary had agreed to bail him out, lending him the money he desperately needed with the house as security.

When the market went south in 1987 Ambrose had been unable to keep up the repayments and Hilary had taken over the property shortly before she left to go on the Asian walkabout that had turned out to be the most significant journey she had ever made. Ambrose hadn't been happy but from Hilary's point of view it had been a prince of deals: seventeen years on, Cadogan Lodge was worth at least five times what she'd paid for it.

An agent acting for a Chinese billionaire had made approaches but she had no plans to sell. She owned property all over, from a three-floor Park Avenue apartment in New York to a tower block overlooking London's Hyde Park and a ski lodge in St Moritz but, luxurious though they all were, in the end they were only buildings; Cadogan Lodge she loved. It was the closest she had come to somewhere she could call home, with what she liked to think were the best roses in New South Wales. Of course there was also Rumah Kelapa on its secluded beach with its face turned to the sea, but that she did not own. Rather it owned her.

It was past eleven but she did not feel tired. The next day would be an important one, with all it would mean for their future, but challenge had never intimidated her; it did not do so now.

She poured herself a brandy and took it on to the terrace. She raised her glass to the future, the brandy warming her stomach and her heart. Forget Dr Chang and his gloomy prognostications, she thought. I have so much more to experience in life. I don't have time to worry about dying. Death will take me when it will, as with all of us. In the meantime I shall live every day as I always have: to the full.

1940–56

BEGINNINGS

1

Sixteen years later, when she was on the run, Hilary Brand had told Mike Tulip the long-distance truck driver that it had been the mindless fury of the air raid in the hours before her birth, the cacophony of bomb and shell and the throbbing menace of the bombers' engines, that had called her from the floating darkness of the womb into the darkness of a night riven by the fires of a thousand incendiaries that on 30 December 1940 painted the skies over London with flame.

In those days she hadn't the words to say it like that, but it was how she thought about it. How she remembered.

Whether she was right or wrong about the bombs it was certainly true that if she hadn't been born three weeks earlier than the midwife had expected she would never have been born at all.

She remembered Grandma telling her the same thing over and over again, scowling as though Hilary were somehow to blame, how ever since the blitz began thousands of Londoners had sought nightly refuge in tube stations or air raid shelters; with the nearest station too far to reach after the sirens sounded, Hilary's mum had used the air raid shelter on the corner of Vincent and Argyll Streets. Had Hilary not decided to present herself ahead of schedule she would have been there that night when a direct hit on the shelter killed everyone inside and wrecked every house within a fifty-yard radius.

She could remember three years later with Grandma going on and on about it to that friend of hers. Funny how she had a memory for things so far back but she did; she remembered the conversation clearly.

2

'Took 'em in, didn't I?' said Grandma to her friend Mrs Moss.

'A Christian act, that's what it was,' Mrs Moss said. 'A real Christian act.'

'Didn't 'ave no choice, their place was a write off, but many's the time I've regretted it. Born for trouble, that's what the Good Book tells us,' she said, eyeing three-year-old Hilary with a malevolent eye. 'Born for trouble and she never bin nothin' but. Too old, that's what I am. Too old to bring up someone's bastard kid, even me own daughter's. And now with these doodlebug things... I tell you, Mrs Moss, my nerves is that bad –'

'Wouldn't worry about the doodlebugs, Mrs Brand. Not after that business back in 1940. You know what they say: lightning don't strike in the same place twice.'

'I wouldn't be too sure about that,' Grandma said.

'And the father?' Mrs Moss had heard the story a dozen times but never minded hearing it again; listening to other people's tragedies always made her feel more cheerful about her own.

'The Huns got him, didn't they?' said Grandma. 'Dunkirk. Never even put a ring on her finger.' And scowled at Hilary as though that were her fault too.

'Fancy,' said Mrs Moss. 'Still don't seem right you got to bring 'er up alone.' She not only enjoyed hearing about other people's sorrows; she liked to stir the pot, too, when she had the chance.

'Audrey's workin' nights at Harrisons in Hillingdon Street.'

'Just round the corner? That's handy for 'er.'

'Makin' parts for them Lancaster bombers,' Grandma said.

'Best keep that to yourself, Mrs Brand,' Mrs Moss said. 'Don't want no trouble, do we? You know what they say about careless talk.' She chewed her gums as she thought about what her friend had said. 'Parts for bombers, eh? I'll bet someone's makin' a packet out of that.'

'Maybe, maybe not,' said Grandma, detecting what might be a note of criticism in her friend's voice. 'But if they are, Mrs Moss, I'll tell you this for free. Audrey ain't one of 'em.'

Mrs Moss was willing to be offended in her turn. 'I 'ope you're not suggestin' –'

'Only wish she was, eh?' Grandma elbowed her friend's ribs. 'Mr Snap spared me an extra spot o' tea this week. How about we 'ave a cup, eh?'

'Can't beat a nice cup o' tea,' Mrs Moss said.

3

At four o'clock in the morning of 25 June a doodlebug proved Mrs Moss wrong when it blew Harrison's factory apart, taking half of Hillingdon Street with it.

The Civil Defence workers dragged Audrey out of the wreckage at nine-thirty. She had a broken leg and cuts and abrasions all over but at least she was alive, which was more than you could say for a dozen of her mates.

Grandma visited her in the hospital. 'You was lucky, my girl. Nurse says you'll soon be out and about again.'

'Where's Hilary?'

'At 'ome. Mrs Moss is lookin' after 'er.'

'All right, is she?'

'Screamed all night. I couldn't get a wink of sleep.'

'Was she hurt?'

'Just frightened. Nothin' wrong with her. I tell you, girl, my nerves won't put up with much more of this. Think I might put her in care till you're on your feet again. Just temporary, like. What you say?'

'I wouldn't want nothing like that –'

'Just till you're on your feet again,' Grandma said.

The streets were a mess, debris everywhere and people shuffling, faces white with shock. Smoke from the smouldering ruins made Grandma cough as she walked home.

Can't stand no more, she thought. As for the kid… When this lot is over Audrey will be wanting to settle down. Only natural, innit? What chance will she have of that? Stands to reason, no bloke'll want to be saddled with someone else's brat. There'll be fingers pointin', too, you can bet on it. She won't never 'ave no life. Reckon I'll put Hilary into care anyway, then it'll be up to Audrey what she wants to do about it when she gets out of hospital.

She took young Hilary to the Waifs and Strays shelter in Peckham Road.

"Er mum's in 'ospital,' she said. 'One o' them dratted flyin' bombs. Might be best if someone was to adopt 'er. Best for all concerned.'

I hope I done the right thing, she thought as she walked to the bus stop.

4

'You done what?'

'I did it for the best. I couldn't 'andle 'er by meself, with you in the hospital –'

'I tole you I didn't want that!'

'The best for both of us,' Grandma said. 'You want to find yourself a nice bloke when this lot's over. Stan's dead, Audrey. You got to move on.'

'I'm gunna fetch her.'

'You'd be better off without her. You know that as well as I do.'

'I'm gunna fetch her.'

But the official, oozing sympathy, was rock hard in his determination to carry out what he considered his mission. 'I am sorry, Mrs Brand. The child is no longer here. She was put up for adoption. Her grandmother said –'

'Never mind what she said. I'm her mum and I never give you no permission! I want her back.'

'I'm afraid that won't be possible.'

'You mean you can just steal my child and I got no say?'

'I can assure you everything was done perfectly legally. And it is not the Society's policy to reveal the name of the adopting parents. I can assure you Hilda will be very well looked after.'

'Hilary!'

'Excuse me?'

'Her name ain't Hilda. It's Hilary.'

'So it is. I do beg your pardon.'

'But you won't tell me where she is? Her own mother?'

'I am afraid not.'

IN CARE

1

A time of fear, of being lost. She knows no one and nothing. She understands nothing. She has no idea what is happening to her or why. She goes where she is taken. There are other children. She does not know them. She does not speak.

A girl, bigger than she is, speaks to her. 'Hello.'

She eyes her suspiciously and does not answer. She is wearing her little coat with the buttons. She clutches the bear she's had all her life. They are hers. They, the little frock and her hat, are all she has.

A big hand, not unkind but determined, tries to take the bear from her. She makes a protesting noise, clutching it tight. She hears two grown-ups talking.

'We'd best get rid of that filthy thing.'

'Leave it.'

'But it's unhygienic.'

'Leave it, I said.'

She goes on a train. She does not know what it is. She has never been on a train before or even seen one – not knowingly, anyway. It smells different. It is noisy, like all this new swaying unfamiliar world. Part of her wonders when she will be going home; another part thinks that Mum and Grandma and the house and sleeping in her bed and waking up in the morning to the familiar light through the familiar curtains have all gone and will never be coming back.

After the swaying rattling train there is a stern-faced building behind a low box hedge. The building is of brown brick with lines of windows on either side of a central door. Inside the building are long dark echoing corridors with rooms containing many beds in rows, many children Hilary does not know. Shadow-like she stands in the corner of the room and looks about her. The children are not her friends. She clutches her bear. The bear is her only friend. She does not want to stay here. She decides she will walk home.

She gets fifty yards before she is caught and brought back. She looks up into the red face of the woman who caught her and now lifts her, feet dangling, and shakes her in furious hands. The woman's thin-lipped mouth is round and red with rage.

'Where you think you're going? Running away? Don't you dare try that trick on me! Getting me in trouble! You get back indoors now!'

And carries her back inside the brown brick building and sets her down, sending her on her way with a clip around the head for company.

Eighteen months later she tries again. She is five now so gets further but the result is the same. The hard hand stings.

'Nasty little brat! Bundle of trouble, that's what you are!'

That's it. She does not give up but desists. For now. Maybe the chance will come again, maybe not. If it does she will take it. In the meantime she waits. Time passes.

2

Hilary was nine when she was befriended by Miss Anderson, a student teacher. Miss Anderson, very hot on causes, believed her role was to unearth and nurture hidden talent. She thought she had discovered something in Hilary the other teachers had not: a sense of curiosity and a will to accept challenge.

'That one will take on the world, in time,' Miss Anderson told a friend. 'And win too, I wouldn't wonder.'

She showed Hilary a moth-eaten book containing a picture of an ancient map with funny, old-fashioned writing.

'See what you can make of that.'

Hilary was up to the challenge, although it took some time. That was another of her qualities, Miss Anderson thought. When she wanted something she worried at it until she found the answer.

When Hilary had deciphered the archaic writing she took the book back to the student teacher.

'Have you worked it out?'

'It says: *Here be dragons.*'

'Well done!'

'But what does it mean?'

'In the old days there were unexplored parts of the world. When the people who drew the maps didn't know a particular area that was what they used to write.'

Hilary pondered, frowning. 'I don't get it.'

'Because they thought unknown places might contain dangers: savages and wild beasts.'

'That's just an excuse, isn't it? Like they're saying the reason they don't know something is because it's too dangerous to find out.'

'That's right.'

'I'd like to go to those places,' Hilary said. 'But, miss…'

'What?'

'Are there really dragons?'

'Of course there are.'

'With fire coming out of their mouths?'

'Maybe. Who knows?'

'Cor! You think I'll ever get to see them?'

'I think if you make up your mind you'll be capable of doing anything you want.'

3

'Brand!'

'Yes, miss?'

'Pack up your things, you lucky girl. You're off on an adventure.'

Hilary had learnt to be cautious of Miss Trimble.

'What sort of adventure, miss?'

'You'll find out.'

She and a lot of other kids were taken first on the train to another place. It was much nicer than the Middlemore Home but they weren't there long and afterwards she remembered little about it, just a nurse in a white coat poking her about. She remembered what happened next, though. Again the train. Then...

'Cor!'

It was a big boat with two funnels.

'We going on that?'

'You certainly are.'

'Going where?'

'Across the ocean. All the way to Australia.'

'Is it far?'

'The other side of the world. But you'll like it there. Lots of sunshine. Oranges growing...'

'Will we be able to pick them?'

'As many as you can eat. Come along now.'

4

There were lessons on board, just like in a real school. When she got the chance Hilary escaped to the deck and looked out at the ocean. Every day they had to sing a hymn at the morning service, the boys on one side of the room, the girls on the other. Hilary looked around at the faces – some scared, some lonely, some cheeky with you-can't-do-nuthin-to-me looks. Like her, none of them knew where they were going.

'Thy seas are found around us...'

One of the little ones thought it was *Icy frowns around us* but Katy was only five so you had to make allowances.

'Miss...' A boy with his hand up.

'What is it?'

'The seas and the ocean? Are they the same thing?'

'Don't be stupid! Of course they are.'

'Only asking.'

'Well, don't.'

Miss Hammett was a nasty little thing.

The ocean gave Hilary a funny feeling. It was so big, so mysterious. No way to know what might be out there. Miss Anderson's face floated in her memory. She'd been kind – one of the few. But Miss Anderson was gone. Everything she'd ever known was gone. *Here be dragons...* Right. There were days she was scared but mostly she was thinking, Here we go again. It seemed that all her life she had been moved on. She began to wonder whether she'd ever been a real person at all, but one thing cheered her up and kept her going.

At the home they'd told her Mum was dead. Killed in an air raid – that's what they said. Hilary didn't believe that. She could see Mum's face now. She stood beside her on the *Ormonde's* deck. Together they watched the sea and the smoke blowing back from the ship's funnels. Mum's fingers were warm, wrapped around Hilary's hand. At night she came to her in her bunk amid all the other kids. Hilary smelt her clean-Mum smell; saw her eyes shining in the darkness. Her smile. How could she be dead?

One of these days I shall find her, she told herself. In the meantime... She tried to think of herself as a heroine setting out into the world to do wonderful things. *Here be dragons...*

'I'll kill them,' Hilary told Mum that night in the swaying darkness, the sounds of the sleeping children all around them. 'You see if I don't.'

5

The land was flat and featureless, barely breaking the sea's horizon, but later there were cliffs with sand dunes beyond them, and the dunes glowed red and gold and copper in the sunlight. Not a tree, not a moving thing, no sign of life at all.

Hilary hung on the rail, watching. There it is, she thought. At last. She felt apprehension – yes – but also excitement. A new place. A new life. I'll fight, if I have to. I'll be OK.

There were people all around them when they came ashore. People shouting, rushing this way and that. Confusion.

'Where are we?'

Wherever it was, it was very different from the empty land Hilary had watched from the *Ormonde*'s deck.

'Australia.'

'Where in Australia?'

'Station Pier Melbourne, you stupid child,' nasty Miss Hammett said. 'How many times have I got to tell you?'

'Is this where we're going?' Looking around at the docks, the warehouses, the people.

'You are going to the Lady Northcote Farm School in Bacchus Marsh.'

'Is it nice?'

'You'll find out, won't you? When you get there.'

6

'We'll have no messin',' Captain Barnstable said. 'That's the first lesson you got to learn. Any messin', you're looking at trouble. Get it?' And slammed his big stick on the surface of his desk with a wallop that made the children jump.

Captain Barnstable was a scowl with whiskers, red and ferocious, and a button nose set between eyes the colour of slate.

'You get along with me, we'll be right. Any tricks and I'll grind you to dust. *Get it?*'

It made them wonder what they'd come to. They'd been told they were being taken to a place called Something-Marsh so Hilary had expected they'd be living in some kind of swamp. She couldn't imagine it but there was nothing she could do but sit in the rattle-bang of a worn-out truck for what seemed like hours and try not to think.

'If it's a marsh there'll be frogs,' said a girl called Agnes. 'I like frogs. I had a tadpole in a jam jar once. That grew into a frog.'

'What happened to it?'

'It escaped.'

It was something to cling on to; certainly there wasn't much else.

If there were frogs there might be snakes, Hilary thought. Snakes were a different matter, but she didn't say anything; Agnes was the nervous type, a year younger than she was, and it didn't take much to set her off.

The way things worked out it didn't matter anyway because where they were taken wasn't a marsh or a swamp or anything like that. It was a farm with grass and cows and a horse or two with cottages set well apart from each other, some for girls, others for boys. Captain Barnstable and a woman called Wilmot, who had scragged-back black hair turning grey and arms like hams, were in charge. They ordered them about all the time. The town called Bacchus Marsh was a few miles off and in any case was out of bounds.

'There's a lock-up there,' mean-eyed Mrs Wilmot said. 'Oldest in Australia. With rats. Catch you there, they'll stick you in one of their cells.'

With the rats? Agnes looked scared and no wonder. But the food at Northcote Farm wasn't much and after a week or two they were that hungry that some of the kids were beginning to wonder whether it might be possible to *eat* rats.

'Yuck!' said some, especially the girls.

But others weren't so sure. 'Better'n starving to death,' said Cyril Dabbs, who was little and cocky and liked to make out he was tough.

'More likely they'd eat you,' said Bert Friend, who had no time for Cyril. 'Course, they might be too fussy to do that.'

Which led to words and then a free-for-all and after that, inevitably, to a leathering for the pair of them from Captain Barnstable.

It was all beside the point anyway because the only time they got to themselves was Sunday afternoons and there was no time to get to Bacchus Marsh and back, even if they'd wanted.

Some of the kids were taken there on a Sunday morning to go to church although mostly they had to go to a sort of chapel that had been rigged up in one of the cottages. The ones who'd seen Bacchus Marsh said there was nothing there worth seeing. Even the famous lock-up didn't look like much but Hilary wanted to go anyway.

'We're not supposed to,' Agnes said.

'That's why I want to do it,' Hilary said.

Mrs Wilmot liked to crack knuckles with a sharp-edged ruler. She had Hilary down as a bit of a rebel and was right.

Girls weren't supposed to go out unsupervised but one Sunday afternoon Hilary slipped away and nobody noticed. There were lots of trees with hills blue in the distance. No houses or proper roads or anything like that.

At the end of a forested track she came to a deep gorge with a river, green and shining, at the bottom. She'd never seen anything like it. She stood and marvelled at this scented wonderland of colour: the deep gorge, the grey stone cliffs flecked with orange and brown lichen, with trees growing and the water shining far down; the combined scents of freshness and water and vegetation made her head spin. Not only her head was affected; she felt something close to pain deep inside her, as though a hard and protective layer was being peeled away from her heart. She had big-city memories, of London and Birmingham. Her rare trips to the country had been to a neat and tidy English world. She had never known anywhere like this existed and stared now as though her eyes might fall out. She couldn't hang about too long or she'd be in trouble, yet knew that the images of tumbled rocks and water would stay with her forever. A sense of wonder and excitement had entered her life.

After that she went there when she could. To stand there, the only sound the wind and the calling of birds, was to enter into a special place. It reminded her of Miss Anderson and the funny-shaped words on the old map. *Here be dragons.*

'Maybe they got real dragons down there,' she told the trees that surrounded her, but if the trees knew they weren't saying. It was exciting, though, to think of all the might-bes there were outside the confines of the farm.

'One day I'll get away from that place,' she told the trees. 'Then I'll show them.'

All the same, it wasn't always easy to believe in a future. They'd been told that when they were fifteen they'd be sent away, the boys to do farm work, the girls to be domestics.

'We got any choice?'

Quick as quick, the ruler cracked her knuckles; Mrs Wilmot thought she was cheeky to ask such a thing. 'Choices are not part of your future, Brand. You'll go where you're sent and be thankful for everything Northcote Farm has done for you.'

Hilary thought differently. Like all the children, there were days when she felt abandoned, like she was being punished for something she hadn't done. Yet something in her knew that she was different from the others. She didn't know why, only that she had a force in her the other kids didn't have. She was determined to prove to the world and herself that she was a survivor.

Over the years her awareness of her strength became a forged weapon. She would survive – yes, but much more than that. She would triumph. Somehow; anyhow. People who looked down on her now would learn their mistake.

She discovered a battered board game. Snakes and ladders. She traced the patterns, barely decipherable, on the board: the ladders leading her up and up, the snakes that did all they could to bring her crashing down again. She ground her thumb into the heads of the snakes.

'I'll show them!' she said. 'I'll smash them to pieces. You'll see.'

7

Hilary would not have known when her birthday was had Miss Anderson, back in England, not told her. Not that it made any difference: her fourteenth birthday on the thirtieth of December 1954, like all the earlier ones, passed unacknowledged by anyone.

But at least I know, she thought. At least I know I'm real. In a dump like this, with no feeling of belonging to anyone or anything, that was important.

She studied her reflection in a mirror in what Captain Barnstable called the ablutions block. Her face looked much as it always had; if there were changes she couldn't see them, but in the last year her body had certainly changed.

She shared her secret with her reflection, leaning close so that her breath bloomed on the glass. 'I am a woman,' she said.

Or getting there. She knew it and the boys did too. They weren't allowed to mix with the boys at the farm – Captain Barnstable was hot on that – but at the state school down the road they could. Hilary had found she was good at sport and at the annual school sports meeting she had won the long jump and the hundred yard dash, the only Northcote pupil to win anything, and she had seen some of the older boys watching her. Not because she could run faster than the others, either.

She wasn't sure how she felt about that but supposed she would get used to it in time.

The day after her birthday, the last day of 1954, thirteen-year-old Agnes came to her in tears and said she was dying.

'What?'

Babbling about blood.

'Oh that… Maybe you'd better speak to Mrs Wilmot.'

'I did.'

'What did she say?'

'Told me to sort myself out.'

Bloody cow, Hilary thought. I guess I'm gunna have to explain it to her myself. Somebody better do it.

And did. She'd been lucky, having an older girl tell her about it a year ago. Now she passed the kindness on.

Another year and I'm out of here. Can't come soon enough for me. She remembered the snakes and ladders board and how she'd thought about the world back then. *I'll show them! I'll smash them to pieces. You'll see.*

8

Five days after her fifteenth birthday, Captain Barnstable summoned Hilary to what he called his sanctum.

In the years since Hilary's arrival at the farm the captain's nose had darkened from rose to purple and his hair was grey now instead of brown but his parade ground bark was as formidable as ever.

'I am pleased to tell you, Brand, that we have found a fine situation for you.'

'Thank you, sir.'

Yes sir, no sir, three bags full sir. If she'd learnt anything at Northcote it was how to keep her thoughts hidden from the world. It was a handy skill to have.

'A farm at Koornalla. I know the owners personally. Fine people. Very fine people.'

'Where is Koo – whatever you said the name was, sir?'

The captain practised his best scowl, in case this girl was taking the mickey, a phrase he remembered from his army days. But no, it seemed she really wanted to know.

'It is near Traralgon.'

Hilary was no wiser but thought it might be best to ask no more. I'll find out soon enough, she thought.

'They'll be picking you up at twelve hundred hours. Be sure you're ready.'

Twelve hundred hours… His time in the army had been the high point of the captain's life and he made sure you never forgot it but now she was leaving Hilary found it no longer irritated her like it had. If he wanted to live the rest of his life in combat boots let him get on with it. Saying tooraloo to Agnes was harder but she knew you had to move on. Life wouldn't wait if you wasted time looking over your shoulder.

It was quarter after twelve when a Land Rover arrived to pick her up. The bloke at the wheel said his name was Sid Brackett.

'Is that everything you got?' Looking at the carrier bag that held all her worldly possessions. 'You believe in travelling light.'

'Only because I'm broke.'

'Aren't we all?'

'Except I aim to change it.'

'Not at Pattinsons' you won't.'

'Where?'

'Where you're going.'

Story of my life, Hilary thought. Always heading off somewhere and not knowing where. Something else I'll have to change.

2004

CHANGE OF COURSE

1

On the morning after her dinner with her daughters at the Seven Stars Hilary woke at five. It must have been almost midnight by the time she turned out the light but she'd always managed with less sleep than most and her body and mind were well rested, both of them urging her to get moving.

For a moment she ignored them, lying on her back with eyes turned to the open window of her bedroom. It was still dark and she could just make out the fading stars but knew that over the Heads the eastern sky would be showing the first hint of dawn. Always she liked to do this, preparing herself for whatever challenges the day might bring; this was the time when thought came most readily.

Today Sara was coming to breakfast. The weather was set to be fine and warm so last night Hilary had left a note for Mrs Walsh to lay the table on the terrace. It was a suitable setting for a discussion that one way or another would affect the family, the company's shareholders and its thousands of employees scattered around the globe.

She would have liked to include Jennifer in the conversation but Jennifer had never had any interest in the business. Hilary had already decided to keep her out of the loop for the time being; what she was planning to discuss with her over lunch would give her plenty to think about without that.

She thought about how she should bring up the subject with Sara. Sara was not touchy; like everyone on earth she needed to be handled but handling people was a trick Hilary had learnt when she was a rookie selling real estate forty years back and it had stood her in good stead ever since.

She got out of bed, put on a swimsuit and wrap, grabbed a towel and went out into the morning. The house with all its treasures – among them a Chagall original, a Brancusi statue, an ivory study of the sage Zhang Guo Lao presented to her five years earlier by the Chinese minister of culture – stood silently about her. Barefoot, she crossed the lawn and walked to the end of the jetty, its dew-wet planks cool beneath her feet. The outline of the Heads was dark against the advancing dawn with bright Venus hanging like a jewel in the eastern sky. She dropped her wrap, stretched her arms above her head and dived into the cool dark water.

In the summer it was a pleasure, in the winter something of an ordeal, but whenever she was home Hilary made a point of having an early-morning swim. There was something exhilarating and fulfilling about swimming at night in Sydney Harbour with the city's lights reflecting on the broken surface of the water in coins of gold, silver and red. There was a mooring buoy a hundred metres offshore; she had swum out to it so often that she did not need to work out its direction but swam deliberately, not trying to beat the clock but exulting in the pull of her strong arms, the water parting obediently before her. She touched the buoy, a metal bell with a flashing light on top, and trod water for a moment to test her strength – fine – her heart – at peace – and her breathing – calm and controlled – before heading back to the shore.

I shall miss this, she thought. But the future would be an affirmation of what she wanted most in life and, as with everything, there was a price to pay. No matter, she thought. I shall carry this memory in my heart, together with all the other memories making up the tapestry that has been my life.

She ran lightly up the steps to the jetty, rubbed her head and body with her towel and headed indoors.

An hour later, tarted up – as she told herself – like a ten grand show pony, she sat on the terrace, drinking strong coffee and looking at the view. It was a million-dollar view with the sun now well clear of the horizon and ploughing the sparkling waters of the harbour in furrows of golden light.

She drank more coffee and thought again how she would approach the subject. Ultimately it was a selling job. So what was new? Everything had always been a selling job: selling land, selling herself. Always the huckster. She looked at her watch. Seven-twenty. She and Sara would talk seriously, two women who were colleagues and who happened to be related by blood. That was how Hilary intended to handle things. They would talk and they would see.

2

They had finished breakfast. It hadn't taken long; neither of them was a big eater. Boiled eggs, whole wheat bread, freshly squeezed orange juice, a bowl of fruit, fresh coffee.

Sara pushed back her chair and looked at her mother through the dark glasses that guarded her eyes from the sun. And from anyone trying to read her thoughts, Hilary thought.

'What's all this about, Mother?'

Hilary recognised Sara's interviewing technique. Come in boots and all; put the other person on the defensive. But Hilary was not trapped so easily; she had often found that the oblique approach paid off best. 'I like to sit here at this time of day. Looking at the view and thinking things through. Cool and calm deliberation… You know what I mean?'

'You didn't ask me here to talk about Gilbert and Sullivan,' Sara said.

Hilary smiled and launched a counter-attack of her own. 'How are you hitting it off with Millie Dawlish?'

'OK. I suppose. Why?'

I suppose. Hilary loved that, Sara honest enough to admit doubt.

'Not much calm deliberation with that one,' she said.

'You could say that.'

'Good at her job, though.'

No answer.

'You agree?' Hilary said.

'You approved her appointment. You knew her reputation so I guess you got what you were looking for.'

A plane was climbing into the clear air above the harbour, outward bound from Kingsford Smith. Hilary watched it, hearing the diminishing rumble of its engines, then looked at Sara again. 'You don't approve?'

'She will certainly push up the ratings.'

'But you don't approve?'

'Like I said. If you want top ratings she's very good.'

'But?'

'Do you want a top current affairs programme or top ratings?'

'You don't think we can have both?'

'No.'

'What would you do about it?'

Sara shook her head. 'Not my decision.'

'If it were?'

Another shake. Sara, too, was not easily trapped.

'I've given Millie a free hand,' Hilary said.

'So I gather.'

'And if she takes the programme down market?'

'That would be your call, wouldn't it?'

Hilary kept a straight face but underneath she was smiling. Sara had avoided expressing her opinion on either Millie Dawlish or the programme but it was obvious that what she really wanted was a quality product and already knew that with Millie she wasn't going to get it. She was right.

'Millie's brief is to get us top ratings. That means repositioning the programme in the marketplace.'

'You mean heading down market.'

Now Hilary was remorseless. 'We have no choice. But I also know you'll never be happy unless you're involved with a top-quality product.'

Sara took off her dark glasses and leant across the table, staring at her mother with naked eyes. 'What are you saying to me?'

Now Hilary was running on instinct, as she had so successfully in the past. 'I am saying I can offer you a way out.'

'I think you are trying to manipulate me, towkay neo,' Sara said.

Hilary laughed. 'Not manipulate; suggesting a course of action that I hope will offer you more opportunity and more challenge than you have now.'

'You mean manipulate me.'

Hilary laughed a second time and rang the silver bell beside her plate. 'I'll ask Mrs Walsh to get us fresh coffee and I'll tell you about it.'

3

'When I asked you to have breakfast with me this morning I'd thought we'd be discussing your future role in the corporation. But now something else has come up. We're having problems in Hong Kong,' Hilary said. 'We inherited a situation when we took over Channel 12 and it may have gone sour on us. I would like you to help sort it out.'

'Oh?' Warily, giving nothing away.

'Our enquiry agent in Hong Kong is talking fraud. I think he may be right.' Hilary watched Sara's investigative instincts kick in.

'Tell me about it,' Sara said.

Hilary did. When she had finished Sara sat staring out at the harbour for a spell. Then she looked across the table at her mother and her eyes were sharp. 'They said they could fix up an independent television channel in China? A station owned by foreigners? Given the nature of the Chinese government, how was that ever going to work? No wonder your agent has questions. But what do you want me to do?'

'I want you to go over there with Martha and look into the situation.'

'How can I? The programme –'

'Forget the programme.'

'But what about my interview with Emil?'

'Do it when you come back from Hong Kong. It'll be your swansong.'

'Are you asking me or telling me?'

'You're a premium person. You'll never be happy with a less than premium product. The programme's future the way it is, I believe it's time for you to move on.'

'So you want me to go to Hong Kong with Martha. Why?'

Now was the moment. Hilary drew a deep breath. 'Because I am sixty-three years old. Because I plan to retire very soon and want you to take over from me. Not yet; you're not ready. But in a couple of years.'

The impact of Hilary's words set Sara back in her chair. 'Retire? You? Never!'

'You better believe it.'

'It'll kill the share price!'

'Not if we handle it right. Vivienne has been involved at the top of the operation for ten years. She is more than capable of taking over.'

'But you're still Brand Corporation.'

'So we get the PR boys to build Vivienne up.'

'Will the market buy it?'

'The big players know the score. I might have a chat with one or two of the institutions but I don't foresee any serious trouble.'

'But where do I fit in?'

'Vivienne is fifty-eight. If you accept you would understudy her for two years. It'll mean hard work: harder than anything you've done in your life. But I have every confidence you're up to it.'

'I wish I did,' Sara said.

'I'd be worried if you didn't have doubts but I am certain you have the ability to handle it. And by the time Vivienne retires you'll be ready to step into her shoes. You are more charismatic than Vivienne so you can use that time to build up your public image.'

'But what are you planning to do?'

'Something new. Which will also be challenging in its way.'

Sara stared. 'What are we talking about here?'

Hilary's head shake rejected that. 'We're not talking about me. I want to know if you're willing to go to Hong Kong or not.'

Sara combed her fingers through her hair. 'I'm finding this a bit hard to take in.'

'I'm sure you are,' said Hilary in what she hoped was a sympathetic voice. 'But I need to know, you see.'

'Know when?'

'Pretty well straight away. Hong Kong can't wait.'

'Do I have a choice?'

'Yes. You can stay where you are, doing what you do now, with Millie Dawlish calling the shots. Or you can move on to the big stage.'

'And take my luck?'

'I don't think, properly handled, that luck will come into it.'

Sara drank coffee and looked at her mother across the table. 'If I agree to go to Hong Kong I'll be locked in, shan't I?'

'You will still be free to walk away.'

'But you don't believe I will?'

'That is my hope.'

'Does Vivienne know?'

'Nobody knows. Only you.'

'Was that why you wanted us to have dinner with you last night?'

'No. This doesn't concern Jennifer. She's never been interested in the business.'

'Then why did you drag her up from Melbourne?'

'You are my children. I always like to see you.'

'You're up to something,' Sara said.

Hilary smiled. 'Nothing to do with the business.'

'If there'd just been the two of us we could have discussed it over dinner.'

'It's not something to talk about in a restaurant.'

'No one could have heard us.'

'A directional microphone would pick up every hiccup.'

'What are you saying?'

'Only that I am reasonably well known. There are always people trying to eavesdrop and I've learnt to take precautions. You'll have to do the same, in time.'

'I'll need to think about it,' Sara said after a moment.

'Take as long as you like.' Hilary smiled as she threw Sara the challenge. 'As long as you let me have your answer no later than tomorrow.'

After Sara had left Hilary sat on, staring at the shifting waters of the harbour. Well, I have told her. Now all I can do is wait but one way or the other I am determined. I want Sara to accept the challenge – that is my dearest wish – but if she does not I shall find someone else. After Dr Chang's warning, a change of course is what I shall have. I have no intention of dying in harness. From my earliest days in this country I have always known when it was time to move on.

1956–58

FARM GIRL

1

Hilary had been at Pattinsons' getting on for a year but this was her first stock sale. The transporter ground slowly down the long hill and turned into a stockyard swarming with men and livestock. Trucks lined up at the ramps were discharging sheep into the pens. Blue-shirted stock agents hurried this way and that. The air was thick with dust and loud with the bleating of sheep and bellowing of cattle.

Hilary turned to Tim. 'Quite a mob. Is it always like this?'

She had long got used to the set up back at the farm, even if the stockyard was new. Had got used, too, to Mrs Pattinson treating her like dirt. Tim had told her his mother had been a Whelan, which apparently counted for something in Koornalla, and treated everyone like dirt, including his father and himself.

'All except Brett,' Tim said.

Brett was Tim's older brother and the apple of his mother's eye. Brett was away at college but would be home for Christmas, which was now three weeks away. Tim, tall and rangy, with black hair and a willing smile, was a year older than Hilary and was her friend. Her only friend, unless you counted the dogs.

Before she'd arrived Sid Brackett had warned her to look out for the dogs. 'They're a nasty lot,' he'd told her on the long journey from Bacchus Marsh. 'Give 'em half a chance, they'll take a chew out of you, no worries.'

Sure enough, when they arrived the dogs had crowded around, snarling and showing their teeth, but Hilary had always got on well with dogs and in two minutes had them eating not out of her leg but her hand.

'Wouldn't have believed it if I hadn't seen it meself,' said Sid Brackett.

Jasmine Pattinson had resented Hilary from the first, smelling in the new arrival an unhealthy willingness to stand up for herself. To Mrs Pattinson the ease with which Hilary had won over the dogs was a sign of trouble to come. She was all in favour of having cheap labour to help her around the place but wanted it to be timid and obedient, scared of the dogs and of life. It hadn't taken long for her to find out that in Hilary Brand she'd got something different.

'Too independent by half,' she warned her husband. 'You'll see, we'll have problems with this one.'

Edward Pattinson, who favoured a quiet life and had seen nothing wrong with the new girl, did what he had learnt to do over the years. He said nothing.

It wasn't just the dogs; from the beginning Hilary had shown an interest in the operation of the farm. Whenever she managed to get away from the house – not easy, with all the washing up and laundry and ironing and cleaning and Jasmine's eyes burning holes in her back every inch of the way – she got Tim to explain the bits and pieces of equipment and how they worked.

'What are those things?'

'Drench guns.'

'Tell me about them.'

'They're better than the ones we had before. Their valves were always blocking but these are OK.'

'What do you use them for?'

'To pour drench down the animal's throat. See? They've got a dial to help you select the dose you need.'

He explained how to dose a calf, holding it between your thighs and forcing its mouth open to insert the nozzle of the drench gun. 'Make sure you don't stick your fingers too far back or its molars might get you.'

She wanted to know everything, see everything, and the questions never stopped. 'Why do you need it at all?'

'To get rid of parasites: liver flukes, things like that.'

She came across a tangle of toothed traps in a corner of the shed. 'What are these?'

'Old rabbit traps.'

'You got rabbits here?'

'They're everywhere.'

'I thought that disease with the long name was killing them off.'

'Myxomatosis? It hasn't reached here yet.'

They stood on the high ground with the river glinting silver below them and watched Sid Brackett using a chainsaw to clear willows along the river banks.

'Why's he doing that?'

'Otherwise they'll choke the channel.' Tim grinned at her, shoving his Akubra to the back of his head. 'You ever stop?'

'What?'

'Asking questions.'

'I want to know. What's wrong with that?'

'Nothing's wrong with it. Planning on being a farmer, are you?'

'Not planning on anything. If I'm gunna live here it makes sense to know.'

'Ma won't like it.'

Ma can take a jump. But kept the thought to herself; she didn't know Tim well enough to risk saying it yet.

He stood beside her and looked out at the open country below them, the black shapes of the crossbred Aberdeen Angus cattle moving slowly across the flatland paddocks as they grazed, the sheep scattered on the hillside. There were rabbits too, an army of them.

'I love this land,' Tim said. 'The bunnies are a problem but I doubt I'll ever leave.'

With an elder brother at agricultural college that might prove tricky.

'What's he like?'

'Brett? OK, I guess.' But didn't sound as though he meant it. 'You'll meet him when he comes home for Christmas.'

Hilary heard what he hadn't said. 'And?'

'You'll find out.'

Hmm.

They heard the furious bugling of a bull, frustrated and solitary, penned in its paddock.

'What's his problem?'

'He wants to get at the cows and can't.'

He grinned again and she knew he was eyeing her, breasts firm beneath the plaid shirt, backside smooth and tight in her jeans. Hilary was untroubled. She knew he fancied her but he wasn't the sort to try anything unless he sensed she was willing. She liked him a lot but was not ready for anything more; not now, maybe never, so she never teased him, never flaunted herself, but didn't hide from him either. She was as she was, four weeks short of her sixteenth birthday and on the verge of womanhood, and if she ever felt differently about him she would certainly tell him. In the meantime she didn't think too much about it but was comfortable with the feeling. It was strange, all the same, to know she was desired by a man.

Life was unfolding like a flower and she was eager for whatever it might bring, and for the big world out there waiting. But Pattinsons' would do for the time being; not that she had any choice. Captain Barnstable's last words before she left the home had been to warn her to work hard and cause no trouble.

'And don't even *think* of running away,' he'd said. 'Do that and they'll be down on you like a ton of bricks, so watch it.'

Who *they* were Hilary did not know, nor need to know. In one form or another, *they* and their tons of bricks had been down on her all her life, and she had no plans to let them get at her again. So she worked in the house when she must, on the farm when she could, and today, after Jasmine Pattinson had taken her sour face off to a CWA meeting, Hilary had grabbed the chance to accompany Tim to the stock sale.

A strange world it was, a frenzy of movement with men shouting, cattle bellowing, the singsong patter of the auctioneers nagging the dusty air. There was life here yet Hilary already knew this would never be her world.

2

Brett came home at the beginning of December. Hilary looked at him as he clumped up the steps to the farmhouse veranda, a fleshy youth with a round head and belligerent mouth, rosy with sweat on this hot day, and sensed that with his arrival her life on the farm was about to change.

Not that she had the chance to exchange a word with him at first, Jasmine Pattinson shooing her away like a troublesome border collie before flinging her arms around her firstborn son. For whom, it quickly became apparent, nothing could be too good. And who, Hilary saw, was watching her over his mother's possessive shoulder.

Later that day he came looking for her, as she had guessed he would.

'Who are you?'

She told him.

'Where from?'

She told him.

'Nice to have someone to pretty the place up for a change. God knows it could do with it.'

Hilary saw that Brett was the sort to lay claim to the land and everything on it, herself included. No worries, she thought. At twenty-one Brett was five years older than she was but she foresaw no problem handling him, if the need arose. If she wanted to handle him; because it was flattering, wasn't it, to have a grown man looking at her the way Brett did?

He'd been back a week when there was an evening barbecue to which just about the whole district came, proceeds to several charities.

'We have it every year,' Tim said.

Oil drums had been cut in half lengthways and mounted on metal legs. Now they were filled with glowing charcoal and the night air was rich with the smell of grilling lamb and pork and beef. Andrew Flanagan, who had political ambitions, had donated a piglet which was being spit roasted, the fat sizzling as it dripped into the coals. There were potatoes in their jackets and sweet corn and pumpkin. There were desserts for those who wanted them and most people did. There was the falling-down wreck of an old shed where a bar had been set up. Beer in kegs; brandy; whisky. And rum, plenty of rum. Plenty of customers too. Because it was all for a good cause, wasn't it? Although by the time the evening was half over not everyone could have told you the names of the charities or their own names either.

Laughter and cursing and the odd scuffle and a hint of couples up to their own business in the shadows of the gum trees, and Brett Pattinson, eyes glowing with booze, came looking for Hilary and found her, his intentions plain.

HUNTER GATHERER

1

Brett was smiling. His lips were moist and his mouth full of teeth, large and white. 'How you doing?'

'Great.' But she watched him cautiously. She had no experience with drunks or alcohol but instinct told her he'd been drinking. Told her too that when some men were liquored up they could be dangerous. She had told herself Tim's brother would be easy to handle but now, seeing the glaze in eyes small and set too close together above the big nose, she was less certain.

'You eaten?'

'Not yet.'

'Come and have a drink.'

They strolled over to the ramshackle hut. Hilary saw how men moved away as he walked past but he ignored them.

'What'll it be?'

She hadn't a clue about such things, had never tasted any of them. She pulled words out of the air. 'Beer,' she said. 'Or rum. Whatever.'

'Rum,' Brett said to the bloke behind the bar. 'Two shots.'

'Water with it?'

She saw a look pass between the two men.

'No water,' Brett said. He handed her a glass. 'There you go.'

Its smell reminded her of sugar when it had been left on the stove too long but there was a sharpness to it too that made her eyes smart.

'Is it strong?'

'Drink it and you'll find out.'

She sniffed it doubtfully and its fumes were as hot as fire. 'Maybe I should have said beer,' she said.

'Toss it back,' Brett said. 'That's the way to drink it. Then I'll buy you a beer if you want one.'

She knew he was watching the swell of her breasts beneath her dress as she lifted the glass to her lips. She took the teeniest of sips and was at once overcome with a coughing fit, her eyes filling with tears. Brett laughed and slapped her on the back.

'Tip it in. I told you. That's the only way. Otherwise you're bound to cough when you're not used to it.'

But Hilary sniffed it again even more cautiously than before and shook her head. 'No more for me.'

'But you've hardly touched it,' Brett protested.

'You finish it for me. I've had enough.' Apart from its harshness the rawness of the liquor had made her giddy. How can anyone drink the stuff, she thought, if it does that to you?

Brett was no longer smiling. 'You said you wanted rum,' he said. 'I bought it for you. So you'll drink it if you don't want me to ram it down your bloody throat.'

Her coughing fit was over, her tears gone, and she would not let him intimidate her. She lifted her chin. 'No,' she said. 'Thank you all the same.'

'It's an insult to refuse a drink when it's been bought for you.'

'No insult intended. But I'd be crazy to drink something I don't want.'

'Let me get you a beer, then.'

'No thanks.'

Brett scowled. 'Mum said you were awkward. I'm beginning to see how right she was.'

'Your mother isn't often wrong,' Hilary said.

'Bloody right,' Brett said. He tipped her rum into his own glass and swallowed the lot, wiping his mouth with the back of his hand. 'Come for a stroll.'

Alarm bells. 'I'll give it a miss, thanks.'

His alcoholic breath was a sickness in her face. 'Don't be a spoilsport.' He took hold of her arm with hard fingers, squeezing against the muscle. 'Are you a spoilsport, Hilary Brand?'

She gave a small laugh. 'That depends.'

'On what?'

'On the sport you got in mind.'

She saw anger stirring behind the moist eyes, now reddened by drink. 'You coming or not?'

'Not,' Hilary said.

Brett tightened his grip on her arm. 'And I say you are.'

Her chin came up. His grip was tight enough to hurt but she wouldn't give him the satisfaction of saying so. 'You'll have to drag me,' she said.

She stared into his face, flushed with booze and anger. He had expected her to be easy but she saw he wasn't game to make a fuss in the midst of all these people.

He flung her arm away from him. 'I'll catch you later.' He turned away then looked back at her. 'You'd better believe it, my girl. One of these nights I'll be there. That's what you need, I reckon. The taste of a real man.' He walked away, shouldering his way roughly past other people, every inch of him shouting outrage.

Hilary watched him go. The encounter had left her shaken. Onlookers would have said nothing had happened yet it was not so. *One of these nights I'll be there.*

2

Two days after the party Hilary was helping Sid Brackett clear a blocked drainage pipe in the shed outside the kitchen when Mrs Pattinson poked her head around the door.

'A word with you, missy.'

Hilary exchanged a look with Sid and walked into the kitchen. She went to the sink and rinsed the muck off her hands. There was no towel so she wiped her palms on the back of her jeans.

'Yes, Mrs Pattinson?'

'*Yes, Mrs Pattinson...*' Jasmine Pattinson was ropeable; Hilary had no idea why but would no doubt soon find out. 'I got my eye on you, my girl.'

'Yes, Mrs Pattinson.'

'The other evening, I saw the way you were buttering Brett up –'

'I never –'

'Don't you lie to me. With my own eyes I saw you. Drinking at the bar with him... Drinking rum at your age? What you think you're playing at, eh?'

'He asked me! It wasn't my idea.'

But Mrs Pattinson was not listening. 'You keep your dirty ways to yourself, my girl. My son ain't for the likes of you.'

'I wouldn't take him for free!'

The wrong thing to say; Jasmine Pattinson's face flooded with outraged blood. 'Don't you dare talk to me like that. Now: get back to your work, you idle creature!'

That evening Hilary was sitting with Tim on the crest of the ridge that overlooked the river, cool and shining in the darkening air and cleared now of willows, with the paddocks rising through the gum trees on the far slope. At this time of day, as usual, the hillside was alive with grazing rabbits.

'Your mum's really got it in for me,' Hilary said.

'She's got it in for everyone. It's just her way.'

Hilary was still angry. 'A real mean way, you ask me. I never come on to Brett like she's saying. Never in a million years.'

'Plenty of people saw you there with him.'

She saw that Tim was uncomfortable with the subject and that alarmed her. Tim was her only friend and she didn't want to lose him. 'It was Brett's idea, not mine. I was supposed to say no when he offered me a drink?'

'You know what Mum's like.'

'Too bloody right I know.' She was learning to swear, just a bit, and had found it helped ease her feelings.

'She'll wash your mouth with soap, she hears you talking like that.'

'She can try. Why doesn't your dad stand up to her?'

'He's not a fighter. Mostly he keeps out of the way.'

'When is Brett going back to college, anyway?'

'End of January, I suppose. Why?'

'Just asking. Can't be soon enough for me.' Her eyes glinted sideways at him. 'Can't be *bloody* soon enough for me.'

The problem was her so-called bedroom. It wasn't in the main house and wasn't a real bedroom either: what had been a tack store in one of the sheds had been made over, with a bed and a broken dressing table with a brick under the busted leg. She hadn't thought much of it when she first saw it but at least it was away from Mrs Pattinson's nagging voice. She had got used to it but now had another reason for not liking it much because the door wouldn't lock. It was strong enough but with Brett on the prowl she didn't like the thought that he could force his way in whenever he wanted. He'd not come near her since the party but any day he might try to change that. She found a heavy baulk of timber and used it to jam the door at night.

Just as well. Two days later she woke to hear the door handle turning. She listened, mouth dry, heart pounding. She sat up, bedding clutched to her chest, eyes wide in the darkness. The door rattled but did not give.

'Go away!' Hilary said.

Silence. She waited, palms wet, but nothing happened and eventually she lay down again. It made for uneasy sleeping, though.

Two days later it happened again.

'I told you,' Hilary said. 'Go away. Leave me alone.'

Again nothing happened but Hilary's nerves were as ragged as a swagman's shirt by the time Brett headed back to college.

Jasmine Pattinson liked to take Hilary with her when she went into town, to give her a hand carrying the shopping to the car.

Hilary didn't mind. The bags were usually heavy but she was strong and the trips gave her the opportunity to slip away by herself for half an hour or so while Jasmine was looking at dresses or having a cup of tea with a friend.

One day she came back from town and went looking for Tim. 'I thought of a way to make us some money,' she said.

'Rob the bank?'

'Rabbits. We got the traps and the rabbits and now I've found someone who'll buy them off us.'

'What they offering? Penny a pair?'

'Wilkins the butcher said he'll give us a shilling a brace, provided there's no bruising. And that dealer in Warburton Street said he'll pay a shilling each for good skins.'

'You got it all worked out, haven't you?'

'No point doing it if we can't make money out of it.'

'So how many you reckon we'd catch?'

'A dozen a day, easy. That adds up, Tim.'

'I'll work it out,' Tim said.

'I done it already. A dozen bunnies in good nick will bring us six bob for the meat and twelve for the skins. Eighteen shillings a day, Tim! Maybe a quid some days. That's real money, boy!'

'I never would have thought of it,' Tim said.

'Dragged up the way I was, you'd have thought of it all right.'

Although she thought probably not. Tim was a good boy but not much for thinking things out. No worries, she thought. I'll do the thinking for both of us.

'Better not tell Mum,' he said. 'She knows we're making that sort of dough she'll want it for herself.'

'How many rabbit traps we got?' Hilary asked.

'Maybe twenty.'

'Do they work?'

'Most of them.'

'You know how to use them?'

'Of course.'

'You can show me.'

They heard Jasmine shrieking like a galah from the house. 'Hilareee!'

'I'd best be going,' she said. 'Catch you later, OK?'

'When?'

'After tea. Say seven o'clock?'

'OK.'

That evening Tim showed her what she had to do.

'The trick is knowing where to put the trap,' Tim said. 'And making sure they don't suspect it.'

But first you had to set the trap and with the strong spring that was hard yakka. Hilary tried to do it with her hands, forcing down the top of the trap and latching the plate that held the jaws open, but she wasn't strong enough to manage it. 'How do I do it?'

'Stand on the spring leaf until the jaws are wide enough to latch the plate. But make sure you don't let it snap back.'

'And if it does?'

'Bye bye ankle,' Tim said.

She was a bit nervous the first time but soon got the hang of it. 'Now what?'

'Now we find a place to put it.'

He taught her how to recognise rabbit runs and how to conceal the traps with a square of paper over them that was covered in dirt and leaves to hide them. There was a length of chain with a spike on the end that was driven into the ground so that a snared rabbit couldn't drag the trap down its burrow.

'And then?' she asked.

'Then we leave them and come back in the morning.'

'And count how many we've caught,' Hilary said.

'You got it.'

Hilary put on a bold front. She was not sure it would work but work it did. She and Tim checked the traps every morning and as a rule found rabbits in at least some of them. Hilary learnt to kill the rabbits by giving them a sharp blow to the back of the neck. Afterwards they would gut them and carry them home. They would skin them and stretch the skins over pieces of bent fencing wire. They would take the carcasses to Mr Wilkins the butcher and the skins to Mr Salomon the dealer. The cash mounted up.

'When are we gunna spend it?' Tim asked.

'Take your share when you like. I'm hanging on to mine.' It was the first money she'd ever earned and she wasn't planning to chuck it away.

The business with the rabbits taught her more things than how to catch them. She learnt to kill: not easy at first but she got used to it soon enough. She discovered the importance of planning ahead, making sure she had a market before setting out to harvest the rabbits. She found she had the knack of making money. More than anything, her success gave her confidence in her abilities. 'I am a hunter gatherer,' Hilary said happily, quoting something she'd read back in the home.

'I thought they were black Africans,' Tim said.

'Not me,' Hilary said. 'I'm a white Australian. But I hunt. And,' said she, rattling the tin in which they kept the money, 'I gather. What's not to like about that?'

'You're not an Aussie,' Tim said. 'You're a Pom.'

'I'm an Aussie now.'

3

The seasons passed. The winter was a lean time: in the cold weather the bunnies stayed home and who was to blame them? Spring came again and in the killing fields things started to pick up. By the beginning of summer the tin had two hundred pounds in it.

The news came that Brett would be coming home again for Christmas. Jasmine Pattinson was dancing but Hilary remembered last year and was not prepared to go through all that again.

'I'm out of here,' she told Tim.

Tim was horrified. 'You can't just walk away.'

'Who's to stop me?'

'The government.'

'They'll have to catch me first.'

Tim was doleful. 'I hate to think of you going.'

'You'll be off to ag college anyway in the new year.'

It was true but seemed to give him little consolation. 'I shall miss you,' he said.

'I'll miss you too,' she said. But every instinct was telling her it was once again time to move on.

'Will you write to me?'

'If I can.' But was not too sure about that. She had no idea whether the authorities could make her come back or not but didn't intend to give them the chance. A letter might give them an important clue, if they were looking for her.

She divvied up the cash and gave him half.

'You keep it,' Tim said.

'But it's yours. It's over a hundred quid.'

'You need it more than I do.'

Hilary thought about it, decided Tim was right. 'I'll pay you back when I can,' she said.

Two days later, while it was still dark, she left, walking away down the lane towards the road, and the dogs did not raise a peep. An hour later she hitched a lift on a truck heading west.

2004

BREAKING POINT

1

Jennifer had lunch with her mother in the penthouse adjoining Hilary's office. She had never been there before and was impressed by the furnishings and the paintings on the walls.

'Are these from your collection?'

'Some of my favourites.'

She prowled, looking at each in turn. 'I see you have a Gulliver,' she said. Even saying Martin's name gave her a twinge.

'I have several,' Hilary said. 'I like his work and I hear he is beginning to make a name for himself at last.'

Jennifer had nothing to say to that; she had made a conscious effort to shut Martin out of her life – had been too scared of her husband to do anything else – and knew nothing about Martin's present circumstances.

'Come and eat your lunch,' Hilary said. 'I want to talk to you.'

She'd had food sent up from a neighbouring restaurant: grilled snapper and a green salad.

Their places had been set at one end of the long dining table. Genuine silver cutlery and an immaculate white linen cloth: Mother lived well. For a while they ate in silence, Jennifer picking at her food as she waited for Mother to come out with whatever she wanted to say to her. Finally Hilary put down her knife and fork and studied Jennifer across the table. 'You know Tom Tallis has died?'

For a moment she couldn't place the name, then she clicked: Tom Tallis had been the curator who'd looked after Hilary's art collection. She was sorry to hear he'd died but had never known him, so it was hard to feel too upset about it. She wondered why Mother was telling her this or what she was supposed to say about it. 'I didn't know.'

'Only fifty-two,' Hilary said. 'Came into the gallery in the morning, everything normal, told Lucy he wasn't feeling well, next thing he was lying dead on the floor in front of her. Poor girl, it must have been a terrible shock.'

Jennifer had no idea who Lucy was either. 'I'm sorry,' she said. Not very helpful but what was she supposed to say?

'Vivienne phoned me with the news when I was in Jakarta. I miss him. But the world goes on. I don't have the time or knowledge to manage the collection myself so I need to appoint someone to take Tom's place. Someone who knows Australian art, whose judgment I can trust and who can use the money.'

Jennifer waited, still nibbling at her fish. Mother was hardly likely to be offering her the job so she couldn't imagine why she was hearing this.

Hilary looked at her daughter across the table. 'Someone whose judgment I can trust and who can use the money,' she repeated. 'I was thinking of offering the position to Martin Gulliver.'

It gave Jennifer quite a jolt. She felt an obscure need to defend Martin, although against what she could not have said. 'Why do you think he would want the job?'

'That's why I am asking you. You were close to him once. Do you think he'd be interested?'

'I haven't seen him for years but I doubt he's the sort of person you can buy.'

'I would rather call it offering financial support to an artist I admire.'

Jennifer heard the reprimand in her mother's voice but it was news to her that Hilary admired anyone. 'You'll have to ask him yourself.'

'I shall. But I wanted your opinion.'

'It's thirteen years, Mother. We are different people now. How can I possibly know what he'll say?'

Frustration and defiance had joined hands like twin assassins. She could hardly believe she had said such a thing – and to Mother, of all people – but Davis's behaviour after the party and Anthony Belloc's admiration had changed her. Why, she thought, the chains are off. I am no longer afraid.

'I always hoped you would get together,' Mother said. 'You know that?'

'That wasn't how things worked out, was it? Too late now.'

Hilary said, 'It's never too late if you want something enough.'

From somewhere Jennifer found a brittle laugh. 'I'm a happily married woman, Mother.'

'Married, yes, but you aren't happy.'

'How can you say that?'

'Because it is obvious to anyone who loves you as I do. You haven't been happy since that abortion.'

Shock was a bolt of lightning. 'How do you know about that?'

'My dear, I have always known. Davis is a blabbermouth. He mentioned it to someone, I picked up the rumour and made some enquiries. It's easy enough to find out these things when you have money. It is one of wealth's few advantages.'

'You were spying on me.'

'Not at all. I never thought Davis was right for you. I wanted to be there for you if you needed me, which meant learning as much about your problems as I could. But I also knew it was not my place to interfere.' ·

And she had thought Mother had never cared. 'And now you are thinking of bringing Martin Gulliver back into my life. I never thought of you as a matchmaker, Mother.'

'I am thinking of asking him for my sake and for the collection. You have nothing to do with it. Even if he agrees you don't have to see him unless you choose. After all, when I told you he'd died it took you a minute to remember who Tom Tallis was.'

'If I have nothing to do with it why are we talking about it?'

'Because I wanted to know what you thought.'

2

In the plane heading back to Melbourne Jennifer thought about what Mother had said. She'd told Mother the truth; she had no idea how Martin would react to the idea, if Hilary went ahead with it. How was she supposed to know after so many years? It was so obvious she thought Mother must have had another reason for talking to her about it. That would be Mother: always with the cards close to her chest. But surely she *wasn't* trying to matchmake? Two people who would hardly recognise each other after such a long time? And what would Davis have to say about it? He would cut her into little pieces if he ever caught a hint of such a thing.

She had been so occupied with the implications she had almost forgotten to ask her Anthony Belloc's question but just in time she remembered.

'A friend of mine was asking if you were ill.'

Hilary's expression revealed nothing. 'Who of the people you know would be sufficiently concerned to ask something like that?' Her long fingers played with the broken roll on her plate, her eyes steady across the table.

'I forget.'

'It was not your husband?'

'I would hardly forget him.'

'Much though you would like to,' Hilary said.

'You have no business to say that.'

'Even though it's the truth? You are right; we should never speak the truth, should we? Well, well, if you remember who asked, you can tell them I am very well. In the best of health: isn't that what the doctors are supposed to say?'

It was a strange answer, Jennifer thought. There certainly seemed nothing wrong with her yet something about the way she had reacted to the question had raised a question mark in her mind. And something else she had said, also, shortly before they parted.

'One of the penalties of wealth is that you have always to be on your guard.'

An apology? From *Mother*? Yet what else had it been?

It made her wonder more than ever.

3

Jennifer returned to an empty house. There was a note from the cleaning lady. *Mr Lander said he'd be late. Pie and vegies in fridge.*

No mention when Davis would be home; probably Mrs Harris hadn't known. Jennifer lugged her case upstairs to her bedroom. She put it down and sat on the bed. She was depressed beyond measure; she'd been away only two days but to have no one welcome her home was horrible. The truth was, she told herself, nobody cared about her. No one in this wide world. Darling Daddy had cared; she'd been so little when he and Mother broke up that she hardly remembered them as real parents, but as she got older he'd still taken her out twice a month to have a special afternoon tea at Godfreys, the up-market restaurant off King Street. She had always looked forward to those outings and to the way Daddy had looked at her so fondly across the table. She could remember his voice even now.

'You are my special girl, Jennifer. My beautiful special girl. And don't ever forget it.'

She would never forget how devastated she'd been when she heard of his death, as though one of the main props of her life had vanished.

4

She had a bath. Dressed in a robe, rose pink and covered in pictures of daffodils, she heated up her supper and ate it sitting alone at the kitchen table. She switched on the television to keep her company but there was nothing she fancied so she switched it off again. There were plenty of books but she had never been much of a reader. She leafed through a magazine, looking at pictures of impossibly slender models wearing the latest fashions. By half-past nine she was in bed. There had been no phone calls and Davis had not come home. Lonely and full of resentment she knew she would not sleep, but did. She did not hear Davis come in.

In the morning, after the delights of five-star living in Sydney, it was back to reality: breakfast not with but in the company of a husband who, incarcerated behind his morning paper, barely acknowledged her presence. The cat clawed the rug; the toaster continued to give trouble. Outside the window it was a grey and rainy day, the garden tormented by a gusting wind.

Despite everything that had happened in Sydney – the extraordinary, whisky-fumed episode in the hotel suite before the dinner at the Seven Stars and her lunchtime conversation with Mother – Jennifer was determined to make a final effort to restore her marriage to something like health and her cheery smile nearly cracked her face.

'So nice to be home,' she informed the back page of *The Age*. Which did not reply. 'I had a wonderful time. Such a lovely reunion! Mother is insisting I visit her more often.'

'Why don't you?' Davis said from somewhere behind the paper.

'I think I shall.'

'Good.'

Was that all he cared?

Smoke began to billow from the bread in the toaster.

'Oh God!' Jennifer leapt to her feet. Too late. She slid the charred offering onto a plate which she placed on the table in front of her husband. 'I'm afraid it's caught a bit around the edges.'

'I've no time to eat it anyway.' Davis was on his feet and heading for the door. 'I shall be late tonight.'

'It's not good for you to work so hard.' She gave the expected response. 'We don't want you having a heart attack like Daddy did, do we?'

No answer. Davis was gone, taking the newspaper with him. Jennifer was alone with the burnt toast. She had a sudden and untypical urge to take the toast and the plate it was on and the breakfast things and the *cat* and fling them all against the wall.

She had read a magazine article that said isolation and loneliness might be the cause of what the author called aberrant behaviour. Like smashing up the breakfast things, Jennifer thought. But oh, how deeply satisfying that would be. She could almost taste the thrill of seeing the shards of smashed china crashing to the tiled floor, the smear of ketchup and egg on the wall, of hearing the ritual destruction of her suddenly unbearable life, her failed marriage.

She flung open the kitchen door and rushed into the garden, unable to get there fast enough. The rain was pouring down but she did not care. She stood outside, face raised to the clouds, mouth open to taste not only the rain but the sense that at this moment the equilibrium of her existence was slipping away. Slipping away, crashing like the splintered plates, and she did not care.

Her gown was wet, her fluffy mules saturated. Her hair hung in wet strands over her face and she did not care. Nothing, nothing mattered. Why, she thought in astonishment, I am having a breakdown. That is what it is. I am falling to pieces in the pouring rain in the bedraggled and saturated garden of my husband's multi-million-dollar house and I do not care. Not for the house or my husband or my marriage or anything. My poor, ruined, wasted life.

Tears came, floods of tears to mingle with the flooding rain. She was stifling, unable to breathe. She snatched at the neck of her robe, tearing it open, feeling a button rip free. Better but still not enough. She dragged off the robe and let it fall to the ground. She kicked off her mules. Her nightie next, the one with the embroidered rosebuds, so pretty. So meaningless. She drew a deep breath. Free at last.

Naked, Jennifer Lander stood in her garden and howled at the pouring rain.

5

It was a woman at one remove from reality who an hour later, having bathed and washed her hair, made up her face with meticulous care, buffed her nails and obliterated every thought of the episode in the rain-drenched garden, rang her friend Tessa and suggested they should meet for coffee.

'Eleven o'clock? Our usual place? Good. I'll see you there.'

Jennifer went into the downstairs toilet and inspected her reflection in the mirror. She touched up her lips. She fluffed up her hair. She thought she was looking very well. The cracks were there but hidden now. She was detached. It was true that her equilibrium remained precarious within a precarious world but the crisis was past.

She made no attempt to retrieve her wet clothes from the garden. Let Mrs Harris fetch them; that was her job. There was another thing. The car was unreliable. She would not risk having it break down on her again. She would use a taxi and put it on her card. If Davis queried it she would say she needed new wheels, that she would neither endanger herself nor embarrass him by sticking with the old wreck that should have been put out of its misery five years ago. She imagined herself asking him what people would say, seeing the wife of a senior counsel driving around in a heap of junk.

Oh yes. She felt firm, strong. Under the shower, sluicing away the mud from her feet and warming her chilled and shuddering flesh, she had decided. She would make herself new, emerging not from the fire but the deluge. She would reclaim her life.

6

Tessa frowned, trying to pin down what she sensed was change. 'Have you changed your hairstyle?'

'Not really,' the new Jennifer said.

'I'm sure there's something.'

The coffee arrived. Jennifer had been first at the café and had ordered before her friend had the opportunity to impose her views. Tessa frowned. 'I had thought we might try –'

'Harvested in the Jamaican mountains,' Jennifer said. 'So aromatic. I am sure you will agree.'

It still tasted like instant to her but one-upmanship had become important to her new image.

'It will be interesting to compare,' said Tessa, pursing acid drop lips. Control was Tessa's middle name. Perhaps that was why, having lost out over the coffee, she now said: 'I am so glad you phoned. There is something I have to tell you.'

Having said so much she shut up, waiting for Jennifer to show interest, possibly even alarm. But Jennifer ate cake and sipped coffee and waited.

'I wondered whether I should say anything but then I thought, she is my friend and it is my duty to tell her.' While her eyes watched.

Greedy vulture eyes, Jennifer thought. She knew her own face showed nothing. 'This cake is delicious,' she said, brushing crumbs from smiling lips. 'You really must try some.'

Tessa's mind was on things other than cake. 'Have you heard of Juanita Santos?'

Every woman in Australia had heard of her. Supermodel Juanita was famous.

'I may have done. Portuguese?' Jennifer guessed.

Had Tessa not been determined to be in control she might have shown exasperation. 'She is a model from the Philippines,' she said. 'You must have heard of her.'

'Possibly. As I said. What about her?'

Tessa leant across the table and lowered her voice, the better to share the drama of this great secret. 'I hear Davis has been seen with her.'

'She is probably a client,' Jennifer said.

'Seen several times. Sometimes at night. At Withershins once, I believe.'

Only one of the smartest and most expensive venues in town.

'Thank you,' Jennifer said. She had a sick taste in her mouth and her heart was thundering but she managed a smile, secure behind the distance that since this morning's episode was keeping her safe. 'I am always telling Davis he works too hard.'

'If you say so,' Tessa said. She drank from her cup. 'Do you really like this coffee?'

'It is truly aromatic,' Jennifer said.

Tessa pushed away her cup. Jennifer saw it was still half full.

'To trust is a truly Christian virtue,' Tessa said. 'Provided it is not carried too far.'

'Like all virtues,' Jennifer said and smiled. As a true Christian should. 'I am grateful for your concern. It can't have been easy for you. You are a true friend.' And if I never see you again, she thought with a viciousness that surprised her, it will be too soon. 'Your coffee is cold. I'll order you another cup on the way out.' She raised her hand as Tessa tried to speak. 'No, I insist. I'd love to stay and chat,' she said. 'But unfortunately I have things to do.'

And twiddled affectionate fingers from the taxi as it drove away.

Later, her mind once again in turmoil, it was another story. The naked woman baying at the clouds had learnt belatedly that if she didn't look after her own interests no one else would do it for her. Anger bubbling, she stood in the middle of the living room and looked about her. This was her home. It might be Davis's *house* but it was her *home*. She would permit no one and nothing to destroy that. She had been too tolerant in the past. Too submissive. That would stop. The new Jennifer would put her foot down. She would be strong, her own woman. Juanita Santos indeed... They would see about Juanita Santos.

She picked up the magazine she had been glancing through last night. She turned the pages, looking at the clothes and the models wearing them. Not that one. Not that one. There. She stared at the woman. What was she going to do about it?

She thought of the two occasions she'd met Anthony Belloc and the question he had wanted her to ask Mother. She'd felt uneasy – she had sensed something underhanded about it – but had asked anyway and got nowhere. Mother had fobbed her off with some story but Jennifer had a hunch she'd not told her everything. She didn't know what was missing but if there was something, she wanted to know about it, right? Was she not Mother's daughter? Her elder daughter? Didn't she have the right to know? Didn't she have the right to do what she could to protect her own interests? Very well.

Mouth set, she sat down and drew the phone towards her.

FORWARD INTO THE PAST

1

Sara had texted Millie to say she was having breakfast with her mother and would come straight to the studio afterwards. When she arrived at ten o'clock, her mind seething with everything Hilary had told her, she found Millie pacing like a tigress. Millie was dressed to punch your eyes, a study in scarlet and black: flame-coloured hair, high peaked shoulders on the wide-lapelled black tunic, high-heeled scarlet boots, an expression to make Lucrezia Borgia proud.

'What time do you call this?'

Sara looked at her watch. She smiled pleasantly. 'I make it two minutes after ten, Millie.'

'Why are you late?'

'I told you. I was having breakfast with my mother –'

'Until this hour?' Millie raised her voice. 'I don't care if you were having breakfast with the fucking pope –'

'I doubt he'd be doing that,' Sara said. 'Certainly not supposed to, is he?'

Millie stared at her. Sara stared back. Millie was used to people being frightened of her manner, her ratchet voice, most of all her power. Sara wasn't frightened. She never had been frightened but now, after this morning's talk with Mother, she felt a sense of relief. She was free. She saw that Millie knew it too, without knowing quite what she knew. Sara hadn't decided whether to go along with Mother's proposal and had made up her mind to say nothing for the moment. It didn't bother her; this too was power, to know and stay silent.

'I am here now,' she said. 'Let's get to work, when you're ready. What have we got lined up for today?'

It became the usual pressurised day with Millie putting on her drama queen act. She was intolerable yet Sara admired her almost as much as she despised her: a powerhouse of relentless energy that would drive her programme up the charts. *Her* programme, *her* studio, *her* vision. A force of nature or maybe of hell, she would make money for the company or die in the attempt. You had to admire such energy. Misguided, yes, but try telling her that.

And Mother had to know by tomorrow. Resentment flickered. Another force of nature. But Sara had no time to think about Mother now, or her future. Millie demanded not one hundred per cent but more like five hundred per cent concentration, expecting no less than she was willing to give, and Sara respected her for it. Responded, too, and until eight o'clock that night, with the final credits running, that was her world. An attack dog in an electronic universe.

It was an exhausting business but once again she couldn't afford to ease up. Off with the make-up, then, down in the lift to the garage and up and out into the maelstrom of Sydney traffic. She was putting the key in the door of her house twenty minutes after leaving Channel 12. Up the stairs and into the shower, then make-up, keeping an eye on the clock. Sexy underwear next. What dress to wear? She hesitated, chose one that she had picked up recently at Imogen's, a deep emerald item with some cleavage and embroidered with silver thread. She put it on and studied herself in the mirror. OK. Enough on show to be interesting but not too much. An antique silver necklace to complement the trim in the dress and she was ready.

By five to nine she was downstairs and glancing through the paper. She needed to think around what Mother had said this morning, but not now. Now she had a date. She shook her head as she thought about that.

When she had gone into television people had warned her you never dated people you interviewed; it made life too complicated and could cause all sorts of problems down the track. How right they'd been. She'd known it even at the time yet when Emil had offered she had barely hesitated before heading north with him. A gamble it had certainly proved to be, times of wonder and ecstasy, but many more when she had been tempted to murder him for his arrogance and the contempt with which he had treated her. Finally, when she had at last mustered the strength to break away from him his last words had been to tell her she would come back to him. And now, after a single phone call, she was willing to prove him right? Was she crazy?

'No,' she said aloud. 'He is offering me the possibility of an exclusive interview with a world-famous man who in the past has done everything he could to avoid giving interviews. Why should I not take advantage of his offer?'

The doorbell rang. She went and opened the door.

There had been a light shower and Emil had raindrops shining in his hair. She looked at him, then looked again, hoping she was able to conceal her shock. She had lived with this man for a year, had known every inch of his body. Now a stranger faced her. He stood in the doorway like a withered oak. His face and eyes were yellow and he had lost a lot of weight. This was a shadow of the man she remembered.

'Have you had jaundice?'

He gave her a sardonic smile, shaking his head slowly. 'Not jaundice, no.'

This had always been his way: feeding his ego by giving half answers, forcing her to come to him, but she was no longer willing to play his stupid games.

'Let's go then,' she said with a gaiety she did not feel. 'Where are you taking me?'

The restaurant was full but the tables were well spaced so there was no sense of crush. The table linen was white and spotless and the cutlery genuine silver. Beyond the picture windows the lights of Darling Harbour gleamed in the darkness.

Sara had not believed anyone on earth could make her this nervous but the way she felt now she might have had briars down her back. Again she asked herself what she was doing, having a meal with this man. And such a meal. Oyster soup, escargots in a curry sauce, rack of lamb: Emil was pulling out all the stops but she noticed how he only picked at his food. She reminded herself she was there to discuss the possibilities of an interview, only that, but in her heart knew that was nonsense. She'd known it from the moment she had returned his call the morning before: the lurch of the heart, the tightening of the breath warning that even now she was not totally free of Emil Broussard. I am a sorry case, she thought.

Conscious of his dark eyes watching her, she fought for something to say, remembering how at their first meeting she had also found words hard. 'I have never been here before.'

He nodded but did not speak: which was probably all the inane remark deserved. He was obviously ill yet after his initial rebuff she would not ask him again.

They ate; they shared a bottle of chardonnay; gradually the atmosphere eased.

He told her his latest book, *Snake Country*, had sold over half a million copies in the States. She had known that already but allowed herself to be impressed.

'When did you get back?'

'Two weeks ago.'

'I thought you had settled there.'

He had moved to California shortly after they broke up. Now, after two films and another novel, he was back. Had he returned to Australia because he was ill? Was it serious? It certainly *looked* serious. Was that why he wanted to be interviewed, a man who had done his best to avoid publicity in the past? To place himself and his achievements on record, while he still had time? She had no idea about any of these things.

'The interview,' she said.

'I shall ask my agent to speak to your producer,' he said.

It seemed he might be serious about it, after all. He did not say why it had been necessary for them to meet first nor was she about to ask him. If Channel 12 got the interview that would be justification enough, she thought. Yet it did not explain her challenged breath or the tremors she continued to feel, conscious of his eyes watching her.

A taxi took them to Sara's house.

'Thank you for a lovely evening,' Sara said.

She did not move. Neither did he. Seemingly from nowhere the past had joined the present, laying its quiet hands upon them. Wide-eyed, they looked at each other in the taxi's dim light.

2

Next morning Sara lay in bed and watched through the bedroom's closed curtains the silent coming of the dawn. She listened but at this hour in her side street all was still.

She was later than usual and there would be no time for her early-morning jog yet still she lay and did not move while her mind replayed the events not only of last night but also of that day, so long ago now, when she had first arrived at Emil's beachside house and he had quoted Yeats to her.

That Fergus poem had been the start of it, she thought. The beauty and passion of that first night was what had endured: the joy of possession and being possessed, of being one. Whatever had happened later, that sense of fulfilment had remained. That had been at the root of what had happened last night. Sitting in the taxi, watching each other, that was what prompted her to say: 'Do you fancy a nightcap?'

Emil had not answered but continued to look silently, his eyes intent upon her, until she opened the taxi door and got out. He had followed, not a word spoken. He had paid the driver and they had gone indoors together.

His body was much diminished yet he still bulked large in the living room. She did not ask herself what she had done; she did not think but gestured at the easy chair, waiting until he was seated before fetching glasses and bottles, not thinking at all, barely breathing, and came and sat down and watched him, the drinks on the table that for the moment separated them.

'Johnny Walker Blue?' she said.

It had always been his favourite.

'I'll give it a miss,' he said.

This, from a man who used to drink like there was no tomorrow? Now Sara was certain he must have something seriously wrong with him. But until he was willing to talk about it she would say nothing.

She poured herself a Jägermeister. They sat and looked at each other.

'This television programme you are engaged with,' he said. 'It satisfies you?'

'It's OK.'

He continued to watch her, his yellow features drawn, but with the air of patient observation that she remembered so well. 'But?'

'No buts. It's the best current affairs programme on the box.'

And still he watched. 'My information is that its format is about to change.'

'Is that right?'

She would neither confirm nor deny but he must know someone at Channel 12 to have heard the rumour. That had always been his way. He had remarkable sources of information but would never say what they were.

He waited but she said nothing.

'Always you have been in love with the ideal,' he said. 'Always you expect more than the world can deliver. That is your great strength and weakness. Therefore I question whether your commitment to the programme is as strong as you suggest. If it is indeed the best in its field, why is there need to change the format? Unless the intention is to make it more popular.'

Still she said nothing. Outside the window, tyres screeched as a car roared past: another drunk heading home.

'You are strong,' Emil said. 'I have always known that. The strongest woman I have ever known.'

'Because I walked away from you.'

'Because you thought you had walked away from me. The question is whether making the programme more popular will compromise its quality – as I believe is inevitable – and, if it does, what you intend to do about it.'

'Why should you care?'

'Because you and I have always been custodians of quality, which is the bedrock of civilisation. For people like us compromise is impossible.'

'And that is important?'

'Not important. Essential.'

He reached across the table and took her hand. She could have moved it away but did not. He was still strong, his hand still warm, and his warmth and strength communicated themselves to her fingers and her body. 'We are one,' he said. 'We have always been one. That is why we fight, but in our unity is our strength.'

That was nonsense. One when he had thrown her stories in the bin? When he had abandoned her without explanation for days on end?

Still holding her hand he moved the table out of the way and stood up, drawing her with him. They stood body to body, very close, her hand held by his, her eyes held by his.

'We are prisoners,' he said. 'Prisoners of each other and the ideal.'

He took her other hand in his free hand and lifted them to his cheeks. They stood unmoving. He had released her hands and she could have taken them away but did not.

Prisoners of each other and the ideal.

For a minute longer they stood, Sara feeling the growing tension of nerves and breath. Then his lips were on her throat.

3

Sara slept again and woke at seven o'clock: suddenly her disciplined existence was a shambles. Since breakfast with Hilary she had become a traveller in an unfamiliar country where even the language was foreign to her ears. Phrases like *I am saying I can offer you a way out*; like *I don't care if you were having breakfast with the fucking pope*; like *I don't believe I have ever met a woman who has excited me so much.*

Unfamiliar country indeed.

Was that why she had been so quick to embrace her old lover, to seek refuge from the challenge that Hilary had flung in her lap?

The trauma of Emil's confession was with her still. She had taken it for granted they would make love, yet nothing had happened and eventually he had explained why.

Naked on the bed, she had stared at him in horror. '*Liver cancer?*'

'They diagnosed it in California,' he said.

'Can nothing be done?'

'They told me it was inoperable.'

'Have you sought a second opinion?'

'The specialist who examined me is the best in his field. He told me there was nothing to be done and I believe him. I feel it in myself.'

'How long?' It was a question she had to ask although her lips were so stiff with shock it was hard to speak at all.

A Gallic shrug. 'Three months, perhaps. As a maximum. Quite possibly less. I had thought that with you I might pretend I was whole again. Even if only for an hour. After all, I don't believe I have ever met a woman who excited me so much.' Again the shrug. 'But now I find I am no longer able to do even that. Even with you.'

'Was that why you came back? To make love one last time?'

'Who can say? Our motives are often hidden even from ourselves. I am finding that is especially so now, at the end of my life.'

Sara felt her heart move within her. 'Let me hold you,' she said. And did so, while unshed tears soured her throat. Cautiously she said: 'Is there anything –?'

'What you are doing is enough,' he said. What might have been a smile. 'In any case I doubt even you could achieve that miracle.'

A break in her voice. 'I thought you didn't believe in miracles.'

'You are my miracle,' he said.

4

You are my miracle.

Given Emil's nature that was possibly the most remarkable thing he had ever said to her. Knowing him as she did Sara understood that he was saying that after all the traumas they had shared he really did love her and had returned to Australia so he could be with her at the last. His pride would never let him say it but, yes, that was why he was there.

And Mother wanted her to go to Hong Kong.

Could she abandon him when he might have only weeks to live? The course of her future life might depend on her going. Or not going. After all this time did Emil have the right to disrupt her future in this way? If their positions had been reversed, what would he have done?

She turned to look at him. Emil was sleeping on his back, one arm thrown out. He had lost so much weight, his ribs showing where in the old days there had been muscle. On impulse she reached out and touched his arm very gently so as not to waken him. His flesh was clammy and slack and for the first time the reality struck home. It is true, then, she thought. He really is dying. How can I desert him now?

She eased herself out of bed, taking care not to disturb him. She slipped on a robe and went downstairs. She put coffee to perk, got out a packet of cereal, some eggs and a jug of milk and set the breakfast table. She looked at the wall clock. Seven-twenty; Hilary would either be at work or on her way. She went to the phone, hearing the first sounds of movement from the bedroom. She phoned her mother on her mobile.

'Hilary Brand speaking.'

'Mother? Good morning. Are you in the office?'

'I'm doing some work at home but I'll be going in later. Have you thought about my suggestion?'

'Something has come up,' Sara said. 'Something unexpected.'

'What's that?'

'Emil Broussard.'

'What about him?'

'He's come back. He's with me now.'

5

The phone rang while Sara was in the shower. She grabbed the receiver with a dripping hand.

'Hullo?'

'I didn't know Emil Broussard was an old friend of yours.'

Millie sounded offended, as though Sara had deliberately kept the knowledge from her.

'Until yesterday I hadn't known he was.'

'What happened yesterday?'

No, Sara thought, we are not going to talk about that. Or the outcome, as devastating as it had been unexpected. 'We had dinner together and he said he'd get his agent to speak to you about an interview.'

'She just has. But there's a problem. We'll talk about it when you get in.'

1958–61

RUNAWAY

1

The truck pulled in thirty yards ahead of her, its brake lights red in the darkness, the fumes from its exhaust swirling. Hilary ran after it. When she reached it the driver wound down his window.

'Want a lift?'

'Wouldn't mind.'

'Hop in.'

She couldn't see much of him but his voice sounded OK and she thought she'd risk it. One thing she had learnt about Australia was that it was a long way to anywhere and a lift would certainly help. She climbed into the high cab and closed the door.

'Thanks,' she said.

'No worries.'

The driver put the truck into gear and headed on down the road. Soon they were back up to speed and she sensed him look at her.

'Where you goin'?'

'Melbourne.'

You could get lost in a place the size of Melbourne. She'd only seen it for five minutes, the day she arrived in Australia – Bacchus Marsh and Koornalla were the only places she knew in the whole country – but Koornalla was obviously out and not for quids would she go back to Bacchus Marsh.

'I'm not going to Melbourne. Near but not into the city.'

'Where you going?'

'Adelaide.'

'That'll do.'

He stared at her while his hands guided the big truck along the highway. 'Adelaide's a long way from Melbourne. Where are you really headed?'

'Anywhere away from here,' Hilary said. Her hands tightened into fists. She thought, I've blown it. He'll know I'm on the run. He won't know why but he'll know that much and that from his point of view I could be trouble. He'll pull over and tell me to get out.

He did not pull over. He kept going, hands motionless on the wheel, eyes fixed on the road unwinding ahead of them like a silver ribbon in the headlights. She glanced at what she could see of his profile. As far as she could tell he looked OK; neither old nor young, with a big nose and strong-looking chin.

She thought things would probably be all right. She settled back in her seat, watching the road. There was no other traffic and the truck kept up a steady pace. She could see nothing of the countryside in the darkness. The road kept heading west. In front of them the sky was still dark but looking in the truck's side mirror she could see a lightness behind and knew the dawn was chasing them down the miles.

'You took a chance,' the driver said.

'I know it.' She spoke defensively; she did not like to think of that.

'Plenty of ratbags on the road.'

Hilary said nothing but crossed her fingers in the darkness, hoping he was not one of them.

More silent miles, then he said: 'You on the run?'

'Something like that.'

He said no more. Gradually it grew light: a greyness, first of all, then she began to see the dark shapes of bushes. The branches of a tree stood out against the sky. She glanced cautiously at the driver. She could see him properly now. He was a bit older than she'd thought, with a lined face that would have looked better for a shave and dark hair combed back.

'Look all right, do I?' He must have sensed her examining him.

'You'll do.' She grinned cheekily. She'd been on edge all the way but being able to see him made things easier.

They went through a small town, the streets deserted so early in the morning, then it was back to the countryside. The land was flat and she could see sheep grazing in the paddocks beside the road.

'There's a roadhouse a couple of miles ahead,' the driver said. 'I usually stop there to freshen up. You hungry?'

They pulled in; there were other trucks in the parking lot. Inside a few blokes were feeding their faces, some with their noses in newspapers. They freshened up and ate a cooked breakfast of eggs and sausage and potatoes with tea hot enough to rip the skin off your mouth. He wouldn't let her pay.

'I got money.'

'Next time,' he said.

Then it was the road again.

'What's your name?' the driver asked.

'Maggie,' Hilary said. 'Yours?'

'Mike. Mikhail Tulitsin.'

'Blimey.'

'My granddad was from Russia. Mike Tulip is easier,' he said.

'You're not wrong.'

He looked at her. 'Your name really Maggie?'

'I told you!'

'If you say so. You don't look like a Maggie to me, but I don't blame you, if you're on the run as you say. The blues after you?'

'Could be.'

'Why?'

'I was in a home. They sent me to work on a farm but now I've left.'

'Didn't like farm work?'

'There were other reasons.'

'I can guess.'

'Yeah. Well.'

She slept then, woke with a taste in her mouth.

Mike smiled at her. 'You slept well. Two hours.'

There was more traffic now: cars and the occasional truck.

'Is it much further?'

'A way to go yet,' he said. 'And nothing to see all the way. Dead boring, this stretch. I knew it well, one time.'

'How come?'

'Born here, wasn't I?'

Silence for a while, the big truck eating the miles. They had passed Bordertown some time back and were now heading southwest past the southern fringes of what Mike told her was called the mallee country.

'What's the mallee country?'

'Living death to the ones farming it.'

He told her his dad had been given a slice of it as a soldier settler after World War I and he had grown up with the despair and black furies of a man who had attempted to make a living out of unforgiving land.

'Ma walked out eventually. Said she couldn't take it and who was to blame her? Dad blew his brains out in the end,' Mike said. 'Plenty did. I'll never forgive the bastards did that to them.'

'Neither shall I,' Hilary said.

'So what's your story?'

She told him about the bombs the night she was born and vague memories of her gran and how later she was sent to Australia.

'Maybe they did you a favour. There are worse places.'

'That's not the point. It shouldn't ever have happened, should it? I mean, being sent off like a parcel, without no chance to have a say...'

'What about your mum?'

'I don't remember her.'

'Yet you say you remember the bombs the night you were born?'

'I know it's not possible. Yet somehow I do, all the same.'

The miles passed.

'What you gunna do when you get to Adelaide?' Mike asked.

'Get a job, I suppose.'

'Got a driving licence? Anything that says who you are?'

'No.' She'd never thought about papers or of anything beyond getting away before Brett came back.

'Don't worry. My brother Pyotir – Pete – will fix you up.'

She looked at him with narrowed eyes. 'Doing what?' Because you never knew, did you?

Mike laughed. 'Nothing like that. Cleaning job, maybe.'

'Won't they want identification?'

'Leave it to Pete. Resourceful man, my brother.'

After it got dark they pulled off at another roadhouse. This time Hilary paid for the food.

'You need to hang on to your money,' Mike said but gave in when he saw she'd made up her mind. 'Thanks anyway.'

Both of them slept for a while then headed on down the road, following the steep hill around a nightmare hairpin bend and so down into Adelaide.

'Plenty go off the road there,' Mike said.

She could well believe it.

They pulled into the depot and Mike supervised the off-loading before taking Hilary to see his brother, who it turned out worked for a shop called Leppard's Clothing Emporium at the back of the Metro Cinema in Hindley Street.

The two brothers talked quietly to each other – she couldn't hear a word – before the one called Pete turned to her.

'You want to hide from the police?'

'I want a job.'

'But no papers, eh?'

'No.'

'What happens, someone comes asking questions?'

'Why should they?'

'Depends why they want you.'

'They may not want me at all.'

She was thinking this could be a serious problem. It sounded like the man called Pete was not interested in helping her – why should he, after all? – and she had no idea what she would do if he said no.

Then he smiled. 'We'll fix you up. No worries.'

She felt a ton weight had been lifted off her heart.

'I'll get you a union card,' he said. 'That's easy. But it'll cost you.'

'How much?'

'Five per cent of your pay in cash, every pay day, to the union bloke.'

'So much?'

'It's worth it; a union card means you can go anywhere and no one will ask questions. Only thing...' He looked stern. 'How old are you?'

'Seventeen.'

'Too young. We'll say you're twenty-one, OK? And I need your real name.'

'Hilary Brand.' She looked shamefaced at Mike, but he smiled.

'I always knew you were no Maggie,' he said.

'But you can get me a job?'

The card was worth more to her than emeralds; for the first time in her life she would have a piece of paper saying who she was. But the best union card in the world was no use without a job to go with it.

'I'll fix you up here, cleaning the store, helping with the unpacking, that sorta thing. That suit you?'

'That's fine,' she said. She didn't even ask what she'd be paid. For the moment she was a beggar and choosing was off the menu.

2

She got the card and the job. She waved Mike goodbye as he drove away in his truck. She got on with the business of living. She cleaned the shop and the store. Occasionally she got to help unpacking goods in the warehouse out the back. Every month she handed over the cash to the union bloke, guessing not all of it would get back to union headquarters and not caring. She had the card in her own name; she felt she was going places at last.

Home was a dilapidated room in a falling-down tenement in an alleyway off Fenn Place. Fine evenings she would stroll down King

William Street looking at the trams and watching the lights shining in the AMP building. At night she lay in bed and listened to the sound of the trains while the streetlights threw garish shadows across the stained walls.

There was an old fireplace in her room. She found a wood yard at the western end of Hindley Street, and when it got around to winter she sneaked over there at night. There were dogs but they didn't bother her. She'd nick a log or two and toast her toes. Luxury. But it was a dead-end job; she didn't know where she was heading but knew it was somewhere other than there.

When he was in town Mike would drop by, take her out for a feed. Good as far as it went but Hilary was restless. She wanted action without knowing what action it was. There were blokes after her because Hilary was a looker, but that wasn't the sort of action she wanted.

Some weekends she'd take the tram to Glenelg, walk along the beach, treat herself to an ice cream or a bag of chips if she felt like it, but the beach didn't satisfy her restlessness. She was looking, no idea what for.

3

She was eighteen. She became mates with a girl called Irish. Irish was a good sort but a bit of a cough drop too. She was in with a bunch of larrikins who called themselves the Hindley Mob and wanted Hilary to join in.

Hilary wasn't sure about that; she'd heard bad things about the Hindley Mob. 'What do you do?'

'Have fun, mostly.'

'Like?'

Irish was a bit vague about that. 'We show people we own the streets, you know?'

What that meant, they terrorised anyone weaker than they were. A shove and crumblies with disapproving faces went into the gutter. Young kids, too. They helped themselves to things in shops; if the owner objected they threatened to break his windows for him.

'And the blues do nothing?'

'I've known one or two end up in Yatala.'

The thought of gaol didn't seem to bother Irish but Hilary wasn't interested in dead ends and could see that Northfields, the women's prison, was the deadest of all dead ends.

One night she was with Irish and a couple of mates in a pub. One of them got into a blue with the bouncer, who was smaller and a lot older. Maybe that should have told Larry something but he'd never been a good listener. Next thing you knew, the little guy had decked Larry, who leapt up steaming only to have it happen again.

They found out later the bouncer was a former champion boxer. You'd never have known it to look at him. It shook Hilary. She walked home alone. It was true what they said, then. Look before you leap.

That night she lay in bed. She watched the streetlights on the bedroom wall and asked herself where she was headed. She needed action like a drug but there had to be better ways than the Hindley Mob. 'Give it a miss, mate,' she told the darkness.

The next evening Mike was in town and took her out to the usual pit-stop café with plenty of grease and the air blue with fag smoke. Hilary had her up-to-the-minute gear on, rolled-up jeans and greased hair in a ponytail. Mike didn't normally have much to say but this time he did.

'Pete was telling me you're in with that Hindley Street mob.'

She sensed criticism. Her shoulder muscles tensed. 'I been thinking about it.'

'I'd give them a miss, I was you.'

She'd already decided that but didn't like being told. Mike was a good bloke but he didn't own her.

'You're not me.'

'That's true.' And talked about other things.

Hilary felt bad, cutting him off like that. 'I need action in my life.'

'Sure you do.'

'They just have fun.'

'Most of them end in shit trouble. You know that. You are too bright to waste your prospects with a bunch of no-hopers but it's your life. None of my business.'

'What prospects? I'm not bright. I got nothing: no background, no education, no future.'

'You're as bright as a button. But when you talk like that I think maybe you're not so bright after all. What you're saying is you don't *remember* your background. But even that is not true.'

'You reckon?'

'You told me about the bombs.'

'Bombs,' she said scornfully. 'Yeah, right.'

'It's a start. And you told me about your gran.'

'I don't remember my mum, though, not properly. I don't know why she sent me away. Why would she have done that, Mike?'

'I thought they told you she was killed in an air raid.'

'That's what they said. But how do I know it's true?'

He took her hand. 'I know this: the past is past. Nothing you can do about it. Life starts today. Haven't you heard that? Not yesterday or last year – today! And as far as education goes, there's a library, right? You know how to read. So read! You're a looker: do the best for yourself and stop making like a widgie.'

She knew he was right. Once again it was time to move on.

She was determined to keep her cleaning job but instead of wasting her evenings took a part-time job waitressing at a café off Rundle Mall.

The customers there were a lot different from the ones she'd known in Hindley Street: office workers and arty types, two blokes always playing chess at a corner table. One night she met someone called Sean Madigan, over from Western Australia on holiday. Sean was the sort who knew how to pick them.

'The cream of the crop, you are,' he told her.

'Quite the talker, aren't you?'

'So they tell me.'

She didn't mind; she quite fancied him, but still talked him into buying the most expensive items on the menu. He knew what she was doing but didn't seem to mind.

'Anything for you, darling.'

He told her she'd have a big future in WA.

She mocked him. 'Sandgroper country? What's there?'

'Big things coming. You'll see.'

'If I ever get there.' Walking on the moon seemed more likely.

'I'm serious.'

'What would I do there?'

'Anything you like. Try selling. You'd be good at that.'

'Me?'

'Why not? You got the looks, the personality…'

It was hard to believe but he seemed to mean it. 'I talk like an ocker.'

'So do something about it.'

Thinking about it afterwards she decided that was what had impressed her most: his being straight enough not to hide the truth. She started to listen to how the café customers talked. At night she practised in front of the mirror.

Two days later Sean was back. After that it was every night, and always wanting to talk to her.

'You make a conquest there,' said Costa, the café owner.

She began to think Costa was right. It could be a nuisance when she was busy but on the whole she decided she liked it.

The café had one of the new television sets. She watched it whenever she had a moment: the idea of someone performing in a studio in Sydney while their picture appeared hundreds of miles away in a café in Adelaide fascinated her.

'How do they do it?'

Nobody seemed to know.

Johnny O'Keefe was on the box, a new medium and a new sound to get the blood and feet jumping.

'That's what I'd like,' Hilary said to Sean.

'Sing?'

'Voice like mine? You got to be kidding.'

'What then?'

'To be able to watch what I like. The music, the stars. People like Johnny O'Keefe. Not this crap.' Because the other programmes were mostly useless.

'You'd need to own your own TV station to choose the shows.'

She thought about it but only for a moment. 'All right then. That's what I'll do.'

'Planning on being a millionaire, are we?'

'Maybe not this week.'

She let Sean walk her home after the café closed. She wouldn't let him through the door but he kissed her and she kissed him back, feeling electricity striking sparks through her body.

'I like you, Hilary. Like you a lot.'

'I like you too.' Although all this was new territory. 'Not much use, though, is it?'

'How come?'

'With you over there and me here? When you going back to Perth?'

'Tomorrow. You could always come over yourself. I mean it. I would love to see you again.'

'Give me your phone number,' she said. 'I ever get over I'll look you up.'

'Don't leave it too long.'

She smiled but kept her mouth shut.

After he'd gone life went back to normal. She missed him more than she'd expected. Cleaning, waitressing, solitary walks on the beach. Solitary nights in her room. That was the point; solitary walks, solitary nights. There was only one person she wanted along and he wasn't there. Sean's absence confirmed his presence. But she had to fill her spare time. She had energy and the union card. She talked to two of the other waitresses and asked if they'd like to earn some extra cash.

'That bloke comes in some evenings? The one with the red hair? He told me he worked for a printers and I got him to run off some handbills for me.'

'How'd you manage that?' asked Madge.

But Hilary only smiled.

'What did the handbills say?' asked Freda.

'Offered to do house cleaning for a fee. I took them round to all the flats and houses in the area.'

'And?'

'I got half a dozen interested. So I thought, if you'd like to give me a hand…'

It was awkward to begin with, both for the team and the customers, but it didn't take them long to get used to it. For a couple of months they were making good money. Then disaster.

The first thing Hilary knew was a young bloke turning up at the café and wanting to see her. She was out the back when Costa came looking for her. She squinted at him round the kitchen door.

'Who is he? I never set eyes on him.'

'Why you ask who is he?' It never took much to set Costa off. 'I dunno, Hilary, no more than you. But I know the type.' He patted his hairy nose. 'He has official stink about him. Afterwards you tell me what's going on, OK?'

Hilary wiped her hands and went out to see the man. 'Help you?'

Cocky face; know-all smile. 'Anywhere we can talk?'

'Only outside.'

'Let's do that, then.'

Hilary followed him out into the street busy with people. 'What's going on?'

'I was going to ask you the same thing.'

He flashed his card. Detective Constable Symons. Bloody hell. Hilary's first thought was that the home had tracked her down. After all this time? She was eighteen, for God's sake. Would she never be rid of them?

She composed her face. 'How can I help you?'

'We've had a complaint.'

'About what?'

'About stolen money. Know anything about it?'

At least it wasn't the home. But relief was tempered with caution. 'I don't know what you're on about.'

'Of course you don't.' His smile said she was a liar, like all the world. 'You been cleaning flats, right?'

'Me and a couple of mates.'

'We've had a complaint money's gone missing.'

'From where?'

He consulted his notebook. 'Forty-three Windsor Lane. Mr and Mrs Thomas. Mean anything to you?'

'That's one of ours, yeah. They saying we nicked something?'

'Forty quid. From a drawer in a bedside locker.'

'Not one of mine. I think Freda does that one. Freda Gale. But she wouldn't nick anything. Straight as a die, Freda.'

'Of course she is. Got an address for her, have you?'

'She works here. But she's not on tonight.'

'Address?'

'No idea.'

'How convenient. When she's on?'

'Tomorrow I think.'

Symons snapped his notebook shut. 'I'll be back.'

He nodded and walked away. Hilary went back into the café. Her foot was barely inside the door before Costa grabbed her.

'Who was that fellow?'

'The police. He wants to talk to Freda.'

'What you tell him? The policeman?'

'I never told him nothing. It's a misunderstanding.'

It had better be, she thought as she went to see Freda after work. Freda, wouldn't you know it, had her boyfriend with her and didn't want to open the door but Hilary kept ringing the bell until she did.

'For Pete's sake, Hilary... I got company, OK?'

'You'll have more company than you want if you don't let me in.'

Freda with a tatty robe dragged about her. Hilary guessed she had nothing on underneath. Fat lot she cared about that.

'The boys in blue been round asking questions.'

'What about?'

'About you. Mr and Mrs Thomas? Forty-three Windsor Lane? They're saying forty quid's gone missing from a drawer.'

Freda went white. 'Oh my God.'

'Tell me you didn't nick it.'

'I was crook so I got a mate of mine to stand in. Girl called Olga. Oh my God.'

'How well you know this Olga?'

Freda's face said it all.

'Any way to get hold of her?'

Freda shook her head. 'She was moving to Queensland. I let her do it as a favour because she needed the dough.'

'Bloody well found it too, didn't she? And you never thought to tell me, did you?'

'What we gunna do?'

'I'll tell you what we're gunna do,' Hilary said. Never mind la-di-da talk; for the moment, at least, ocker was back. 'First thing tomorrow morning you and me are going to see the Thomases and tell them what happened. Hope to God they believe us. And you'd better have forty quid to give them.'

'I don't have forty quid.'

That'd be right. 'Then I'll give it to them and you can pay me back later.'

Mr Thomas was not very nice about it, going on and on about breach of trust and how disappointing it was and how they would tell all their friends what had happened.

'I gave you the chance because I like to encourage initiative. But after this my wife wouldn't have you inside the door.'

'I quite understand, Mr Thomas.' Grovelling was the only option but inside Hilary was spitting tacks.

At least Mr Thomas said he'd withdraw the complaint.

'Beauty!' Freda said as they walked back. 'Off the hook.'

'Off the hook nothing,' Hilary said. 'You still got to pay me my forty quid.'

'Don't keep on about it,' Freda said. 'You'll get it.'

But next day Freda didn't show up to work and when Hilary went and rang her bell the neighbour said she'd moved out.

'If you see her,' Hilary told the neighbour, 'tell her I'll kill her when I catch up with her. My oath I will.'

142   J.H. FLETCHER

She knew it was no good but other than kick the bin as she went back down the stairs there was nothing she could do.

It made you wonder whether Freda had nicked it after all.

Nor was that the end of it. Two evenings later Detective Constable Symons was back.

'Seems the Thomases don't want to pursue the matter,' he said. 'A pity, in my opinion, but there you are. Don't think you're in the clear. I got my eye on you. One step out of line and I'll have you. Got it?'

Hilary as meek as milk. 'Yes, Mr Symons.'

But her thoughts were bloody. I'll strangle the bitch if I ever get hold of her.

Nor was that all. She suspected Symons was the sort to check-up on her. She wasn't sure how he could do it but she wasn't game to risk it and she didn't know where she stood over the business of the home or whether they could do anything about her having done a runner from the Pattinsons. As long as she was in Adelaide she would be at risk but out of sight out of mind once she was gone. If she wasn't around she doubted Symons would bother to follow her up.

She remembered Sean Madigan. The following morning she dug out his phone number and gave him a call. Hearing his voice gave her quite a kick although he didn't sound too pleased with her.

'What time you call this? It's six o'clock in the morning, for God's sake!'

She'd forgotten about the time difference. 'Sorry about that but I wanted you to be the first to know. I'm heading west.'

PASTURES NEW

1

She had thought she'd hitch a lift across the Nullarbor but in the end decided to fly. She'd been lucky with Mike but she wasn't stupid; lots of truckies weren't like him and there was plenty of empty space between Adelaide and Perth. Being screwed on the journey, willingly or heaven forbid unwillingly, was not part of her plan and she had already decided it paid to play the percentages. It would cost her – worked out at sixty-three quid, a fair bite out of her reserves – and she still hadn't repaid Tim his hundred quid, but she was conscious of time passing. She was eighteen years old and so far had got nowhere in her life. No matter. Her union card said she was twenty-two and she told herself that coming to this new place would be the first step along the highway that would lead her to the heights she was determined to scale.

'Watch me,' she said as the tired old Dakota came limping in to land. 'Five years and I'll have my first million.' God knew how but somehow she'd do it. My oath she would.

The plane doors opened.

'Welcome to Perth,' the steward said.

2

She came down the boarding ladder lugging the case that contained all her worldly possessions. She put one foot on the tarmac, looked around her and thought, Bloody hell. She'd known WA was the sticks but *this*... If she'd had the money she'd have hot-footed it straight back to Adelaide. Or Melbourne. Or Timbuktu. Anywhere. I mean, *look* at it, more bush than airport. Someone on the flight had told her Perth Airport had been an aerodrome in the war and by the look of it nothing had changed. Sandgroper country indeed. Mars would have been a better bet.

Worse yet, there was no sign of Sean. That'd be right. Hilary felt a surge of anger. Anger was good; anger gave her the lift she needed. So she'd flown what felt like halfway round the world to find herself stood up in what looked like a desert? Tough. She was there and it was up to her to make the best of it. She strode across the tarmac to the terminal, if that was what it was. The sun was a ball of fire in a sky white with heat. A light wind lifted plumes of sand from the endless plain and she wondered where the hell Perth was in this emptiness.

A car was coming helter-skelter, dust billowing behind it, and she heard the screech and roar of the tormented engine. Standing in the shade of the terminal building Hilary began to smile. Maybe things were going to work out after all.

The car skidded to a stop. The door banged. Sean came running.

'I was afraid I'd miss you.'

'You nearly did.' It gave her a hot feeling just to see him again – yes, she thought, I was right to come – but she was careful to talk as though it hadn't mattered either way.

She climbed aboard. The car was like an oven and a pretty beat-up oven at that but at least it got them there. After the horror start Perth was a pleasant surprise, with gracious buildings on both sides of the Swan River and a bridge that Sean told her was brand new and would be the making of the state.

'Doesn't look like much,' Hilary said.

'It'll open up the south. Just what the place needs.'

There were two immediate problems: where she was going to stay and what she was going to do for a living.

'Stay with me,' Sean said.

'You got a spare room?'

'No need for that.'

'Oh yes there is.' It would have been easy to say yes but it was too soon. Back in Adelaide he'd had the attraction of the unknown; she still fancied him – even more, if anything – but she didn't *know* him, did she? To move in with him would be asking for trouble.

'You can have my bed and I'll sleep on the couch.'

Maybe she'd risk that much. 'Till I find my feet,' she said.

Perhaps it was the time difference or uncertainty over her future or her expectation that Sean would come on to her during the night, maybe all three: whatever it was, she slept badly. Sean did not come on to her but that made her even more uneasy; it might mean he was serious about her and she wasn't ready for that, either. The next morning she dragged herself out of bed, made them some breakfast and set out to conquer the west.

It wasn't easy.

She managed to find herself a room in a boarding house but the landlady was clearly in two minds about letting a room to an unaccompanied woman.

'Four quid a week. Two meals a day and shared facilities. And no fun and games,' she said. 'Anything like that, missy, and you're out the flaming door. OK?'

'There won't be nothing like that.'

'Too right there won't.'

Getting a job wasn't easy either. Being from back east didn't help but after two days she landed some shifts in a lunch bar and café in a side street off St George's Terrace. The pay would cover the rent but not much more and she wondered whether she had been a fool not to settle for a share of Sean's unit, with all that implied. But instinct told her she was better off as she was; she wanted no extra baggage at the start of her search for her first million.

Not that she was likely to make it in her present job. The pay was pretty ordinary and there were no tips: it might be a different part of the continent but it was still Oz. She scoured the Situations Vacant columns. Television had been around the eastern states since the Melbourne Olympics in 1956 but over west it was brand new. There were firms advertising for technicians and installers but when she applied the hairy man who ran the show gave her the old brush off and no error.

'Employ a girl to clamber around on rooftops? In your dreams, darling.'

Laughing as he said it too, which made it ten times worse.

A foot in the door was all she needed. Finding a door that would open for a woman was a tricky business but challenges were meant to be overcome.

3

She met Sean's parents. That was a disaster. Mrs Madigan looked at her like she was a strychnine salad: sweet tomatoes on top, poison underneath. No layabout easterner who couldn't even speak properly was going to lay claim to her Sean.

'You're not Irish, are you? You don't *look* Irish.'

'I had a friend called Irish back in Adelaide,' Hilary said. 'If that helps.'

Mrs Madigan's eyes peeled Hilary's skin; she'd never been one for jokes. A sandwich short of a picnic if you ask me, she thought.

'Your parents living?'

'Wouldn't have a clue, Mrs Madigan. Back at the home they said I was an orphan but they told me lots of things that weren't true, so the fact is I dunno if they're alive or dead.'

Madigan's law: everyone has to have a background. 'I don't understand what you're saying.'

'They shipped me out here when I was a kid. Stuck me in a home then sent me to work on a farm when I was fifteen. Later I moved to Adelaide, met Sean and now I'm here to make me fortune.' She gave Mrs Madigan the sunniest of smiles, which was not returned.

'At least you're Catholic?' Mrs Madigan hoped. Certain things in life were not negotiable.

'I don't think I'm anything much.'

See Mrs Madigan's rattrap mouth now.

4

Hilary took a long hard look at herself. Her looks would be on her side when dealing with a man but not necessarily with another woman. Her figure likewise. Being a woman at all had already proved to be a challenge. Well, she had to live with that but her lack of education and the way she spoke remained problems. She went for a walk by the river. She passed a planing mill. She listened to the screech of machinery and thought that planing off her own rough edges might be a good place to start. She listened to herself talking to the customers in the café and thought that planing was hardly the right word. A hammer and chisel might do a better job.

She'd started back in Adelaide but what with one thing and another it hadn't come to anything. Now she made friends with a waitress, a Pom who'd been in the country five minutes. Unlike Hilary, this one had a cut-glass accent. She listened to her. Every night she repeated what she had done before, standing in front of her little mirror in her room at the boarding house and practising the sounds she'd heard. Her lips shaped a phrase Miss Anderson had taught her in the old Middlemore days.

How now, brown cow, grazing in the green green grass. Sounded more like heow neow to begin with but gradually it got better. Two months of aching jaws and she could have fooled herself. Ay am Lady Lulu. Ay speak laike a membah of the royal family. Though it slipped sometimes. Oi speak loike a member of the royal femly. Bloody hell!

As for education… She visited the library every minute she could spare, took a book at random off the shelf and sat, dictionary at her side, reading and looking up every word she didn't know. In time it did her confidence no end of good. Not only did she pick up knowledge of things she hadn't known before but acquired the knack of talking about them as a lady – no longer a lydy – should.

She thought about the occupations that were most likely to be available to a woman. Eventually she landed a job in sales at an up-market couturier where her still fragile oh-so-posh accent was more appreciated than it might have been in Subiaco. There were snags. She needed to dress the part, which wasn't cheap, and it was cruel on the feet. The pay was nothing to write home about, either, and for months she had only the most menial of jobs. Sweeping the floor, cleaning the windows, vacuuming, hanging up dresses that would have taken a year of her present pay to buy.

'Lousy pay for a lousy job,' she told Sean. 'I've got to be crazy.'

But she wasn't and knew it. She and Sean were an item now, a lot closer than they'd been and likely to get closer yet, but she still refused to move in with him. She was beginning to think she was in love with him but had seen too many examples of how easily things could go wrong. She'd known two girls back in Adelaide who'd got themselves up the duff. In each case the bloke had done a runner and there they were, stuffed in more ways than one. It wasn't going to happen to her.

'All in good time,' she told herself and Sean.

Mind you, it was getting harder to say no and there'd been moments when they'd got very bloody close, but somehow she'd avoided the trap. It really got up Sean's nose. You couldn't blame him, could you? Lots of times he threatened to walk away but she would not give in. Her virtue – whatever that was – was not an issue, but self-preservation was.

During her sessions in the library she'd read something that expressed it better than she could. 'I've got miles to go before I sleep,' she told herself. 'Or even think of sleeping.' All she knew was she was hungry to get from where she was now to somewhere undefined but wonderful. 'I'm on the first step of the highway,' she told herself. 'I'm going to follow it to the end. All the way to the stars, if I can. And no one and nothing is going to stop me.'

5

Independence didn't come cheap; there were weeks when she was pushed to find the rent without dipping into what she thought of her run-away money, what she'd managed to put aside in Adelaide. Somehow she hung on, eating less than a little and then only at the cheapest places. She walked everywhere she could rather than take a bus. Determined to remain independent she wouldn't let Sean buy her meals but she loved the fact that he was always offering. In the nick of time the shop owner relented and let Hilary start selling, with an increased allowance against commissions.

She would never have believed it but she had a flair for it. Within three months she was selling more than any of the other staff; two months more and customers were asking specifically to be served by *that nice Miss Brand.*

'At this rate you could find yourself taking home fifteen pounds a week,' said Mrs Shargey, the shop owner. 'Maybe even twenty, in time.'

It was an unheard-of wage for a woman, especially one of Hilary's age and background. It was nice not to have to watch the pennies so closely for once but she knew that twenty pounds a week, or five times that, would not take her where she wanted to go.

The papers were saying there was a coming boom in property values, as had happened in the eastern states. The Commonwealth Games were scheduled for 1962 and the government was talking up the state's prospects. Not just talk, either. The bridge across the Swan had been a start; now the old Guildford aerodrome where Hilary had landed was being replaced by a new international airport. The stadium was being built and accommodation for the athletes: not the crummy junk Melbourne had provided for the 1956 Olympics but family-type homes that could be sold to investors after the Games were over.

There was a feeling in the air that at long last West Australia was coming into its own. There was talk of mining ventures in the far north; a huge mansion was being built on the banks of the Swan

by a woman called Bella Tucker who people said had struck it rich.
More and more Hilary sensed that the property market was on the
edge of lift off and was determined to be aboard the rocket when it
left the launching pad. More and more she was convinced that her
present job, well paid though it was, was as dead an end as anything
she'd done.

She still went to the library at weekends, and homed in on the
subjects she thought would be the greatest practical value to her –
textbooks on bookkeeping, valuation and building construction.
Also poetry: she'd read that poetry was a way of taking life by
the throat. She liked that, the challenge implicit in tackling both
poetry and life.

Believing in the coming boom it made sense to get in on the
ground floor. She went to see a real estate agent and within the hour
found herself the owner of a block of undeveloped land in a suburb
called Morley Park.

'Morley Park?' Sean said. 'There's nothing there. How much did
you pay, anyway?'

'Hundred and fifty pounds.'

'You're mad! How you gunna pay for it?'

'Five quid a week. I can manage it OK, with the commission.'

'But I thought you wanted to move on?'

'I do.'

'You're around the twist, you know that?'

'You ain't seen nothing yet.'

'Now what you planning?'

She gave him the father and mother of sunny smiles. 'Hang
around, you might find out.'

She went back to the estate agent, who rubbed his hands, thinking she'd come to buy another block.

'Best investment you'll ever make,' he said. But changed his tune
when she said she wanted a job. 'We don't employ women.'

'Then now's the time to start.'

Jack Almond shook his head. 'The customers wouldn't stand
for it.'

'How do you know if you've never tried it?'

'Stands to reason.'

'Maybe some of them would appreciate the friendly female touch.'

'And maybe they wouldn't.'

But she sensed that she was winning.

'Tell you what I'll do,' Hilary said. 'Give me a go and I'll buy another block off you.'

'Commission only?'

'I've got to live, Mr Almond.'

By his expression he was wondering why.

'Ten a week,' he said.

'Make it fifteen.'

'Ten. And think yourself lucky.'

She was in.

She went back to the dress job and resigned.

'You're mad,' Mrs Shargey said, vexed at losing her best sales girl.

'You could be right,' Hilary said.

She needed a real estate licence, not easy for a woman, but Jack Almond had clout and she got it without much hassle. But that was only one of her problems.

Rent; food; paying off the two blocks of land. She needed a car. And she had to look the part. Whichever way you looked at it, ten quid a week would not stretch.

There was only one way she could see how to do it. She thought about it long and hard. She stared at herself in the mirror. 'Do you really love him?'

He was a good bloke; safe. Kind and considerate. OK, his mother was a problem but she wouldn't be marrying her, would she? Because Sean had proposed to her and she had promised him an answer. She certainly fancied him. Was that love? She decided yes, it was. She liked him, too, which was a bonus. They'd get married and he'd help her get where she had to go and they'd be happy, the best of lovers and the best of friends. Give it a go, she urged her reflection. She decided she'd say yes.

She went to him, heart going pit-a-pat. 'You still want to marry me?'

He looked at her, eyes bright with hope. 'You know I do.'

'OK, then.'

Minutes later, his face buried in her breasts, heat like a tidal wave engulfing her, she cried: 'We are going to be happy! So happy!'

6

That might be how they saw it but Mrs Madigan was ropeable.

'You're getting married?' Like they'd said they were going to Zululand.

'That's about the size of it.'

'Have you spoken to Father Devlin?'

'Leave Father Devlin out of it. It's the registry office we're having, not a church do.'

Hilary could read Mrs Madigan like a book. The cow had no doubt been thinking of a nuptial mass with all the trimmings. And now this *creature* from the eastern states had descended on them like one of the seven plagues of Egypt to cheat her of one of a mother's greatest joys... Well, aren't you the unlucky one? Hilary thought.

The reception wasn't much to write home about. Mr Madigan was like Mr Pattinson in one respect – he favoured a quiet life and over the years had learnt to keep his mouth shut, especially when it came to matters involving the church – but he thought it right and proper that they should do something to celebrate the marriage of their only son.

Mrs Madigan was having none of it. 'Signing a piece of paper in a registry office? You call that a marriage?'

'What do you call it?'

'A travesty is what I call it. Far as I'm concerned, they're not wed at all.'

So it came down to a few beers in the pub, with Sean's drinking mates, who had not been invited, trying with some success to get him pissed and Mrs Madigan as welcoming as a Rottweiler with the bellyache.

'Dunno where you're planning to live,' Mrs Madigan said. 'That hole you're in now won't be big enough when the babies start coming.'

'Thought we'd buy a place in Peppermint Grove,' Hilary said. 'What do you reckon?'

Only the snootiest suburb in Perth. Even the idea was enough to set Mrs Madigan's teeth on edge. Peppermint Grove? What nonsense!

'What I reckon is it's time you came down off your high horse and faced reality, like the rest of us,' she said.

'Maybe I'll do that,' Hilary said.

In the meantime, though, there was the honeymoon. There wasn't the time or money for anything fancy but Hilary was determined they should do something to remember the occasion by.

'It is our wedding, after all,' she said.

They went south into the dark forests.

It was a world out of the storybooks, of wolves and trolls, of tales that Hilary remembered from Miss Anderson, the first and so far only human being to kindle her mind with images of mystery and magic. *Here be dragons.* They wandered hand in hand through a cool and misty landscape of mosses and ferns and giant trees pointing their branchless trunks three hundred feet into the achingly blue sky. There were waterfalls and the shy and barely glimpsed animals that watched or moved as silently as spirits through the undergrowth.

Sean cast an appreciative eye at the massive trees. 'Get felling rights in a place like this we could make a fortune,' he said.

Hilary didn't take him seriously. 'Would you want to do that?'

'Too right I would. They're only trees,' Sean said. He glanced at her, sensing disapproval. 'You're the one's always saying how you want to be a millionaire.'

'I do,' Hilary said. 'And I shall be one too. But let's not wreck the place while we're doing it.'

She'd brought a tent and all the bits and pieces they needed for a camping trip.

Sean was his mother's child; anything unconventional made him uneasy. He wasn't too sure what he thought about screwing in a tent when a decent mattress and a bed that didn't squeak seemed to him to make a lot more sense. Also there was the feeling that unless he was careful his new wife might start making decisions that should more properly be made by her husband. As his mother had also reminded him.

'A man is the head of the household. Make sure she understands that. She won't ever respect you otherwise.' Which was funny, coming from Mrs Madigan, she-wolf in residence.

'I reckon we'd be better off in a pub,' he said.

'Plenty of pubs back home,' Hilary said. 'I want this to be something special. Something we'll remember all our days.'

'What if it rains?'

'Won't matter. We've got our tent. A good one: I made sure of that.' She gave him the happy grin that always turned his resolve to mush. 'You and me and the trees… How romantic is that?' She gave him the gentlest of tweaks to remind him what she had in store for him.

Later there was darkness and dying firelight, a light breeze pressing against the outside of the tent while Sean touched her. He had touched her often but this time should have felt different because now, she thought, she was his. Yet in truth she was conscious of drawing back from that reality. What was happening between them was not right: not the doing of it, that of course was as it should be, but the fact that she was unable to lose herself in the moment. The fact that she remained on the outside looking down at the man and woman going through the motions, concentrating on that so that the moment when he gasped and surged against her and collapsed like a perforated bag went almost unnoticed.

Sleep, later, was a problem for her if not for him. She lay and looked up at the ridge of the tent above her and heard the wind's voice and the myriad sounds of the forest and thought of the future and the number of times tonight's episode would be repeated, an endless series of footprints into the unknown.

It will get better. I love him, of course I do. It'll come right in time. But she wondered nevertheless.

She slept for a while and when she woke the light was showing through the canvas. She eased away from the still-sleeping man and went out into the air. She walked barefoot into the forest. Barefoot and, later still, naked as she embraced the stillness and the voice of the undergrowth and the trees rising above, their majesty carved upon the air, the cathedral of the forest in which she knew it was right to worship.

Her cheeks wet with tears she turned and went back to the tent.

2004

AN UNCERTAIN FUTURE

Hilary rang off and walked out on to the terrace while she thought about what Sara had said.

Emil Broussard...

She had thought they'd seen the last of that damn man. Famous writer he might be but at the time she would have seen him dead in the street and been glad of it. Glad? She would have danced on the body after the way he had brought her daughter so close to disaster. She would never forget how traumatised Sara had been when she came back from her foray into the far north. He would have ruined a weaker person. Thank God she'd had the courage to tear herself away from him.

Hilary had understood how Sara had felt. Had not the same thing happened to her? How could she not sympathise when she too had heard the siren song of love, the song that could both destroy and lift you to the heights? Yet the truth was that understanding and sympathy had no relevance. The first and most important lesson of life was that you always had to be prepared to move on, like the basic law of thermodynamics, where the movement was always from hot to cold, never the opposite.

For Sara to use Emil Broussard's unexpected arrival as an excuse not to go to Hong Kong would be the coward's way. At all cost she must prevent that. How she would do it she did not know, only that she must. The success of everything she had striven for all these years was at stake: to establish a dynasty to carry on the work to which she had dedicated her life.

Of course there was no law that said Sara had to take the job. The top of any tree was a lonely place; you had to earn it, yes, but you had to want it too, want it with all your heart – anything less was to invite disaster. Sara had the ability but could she make the necessary sacrifices, putting the company's health before every other consideration?

She sat on the bench and looked across the harbour. A distant factory whistle echoed and the scent of the roses was strong in the morning air. That scent normally gave her huge pleasure but today less so than usual: responsibility had seldom been a burden to her but at this moment she knew she was holding the company's future in her hands and it was heavy.

She got up. She paced across the manicured lawn to the water's edge and back again. And again down. Emil Broussard's return was not the only problem; Sara was insisting on being told why Hilary had decided to move on.

Was there something wrong with the company? With her health? No, there was nothing wrong with the company and she was unwilling to admit there was anything wrong with her health either.

'Why are you doing it, then?'

'Because it is the right time for the company and the right time for me.'

She had refused to say more but it troubled her that Sara had felt the need to ask. If Sara turned her down, who else was there to succeed her in the longer term, after Vivienne too decided to call it a day?

All her life, since she had been in the position to choose her own path, the courage to accept calculated risks had been the governing factor in everything she had done. That lesson she had learnt at the Pattinsons, as she had acknowledged when she helped Tim buy the farm after his brother Brett, who'd inherited when his father died, had been killed by a boar. Courage was the key.

1961–65

UP THE LADDER
AND DOWN THE SNAKE

1

The way Sean went at her in the early days Hilary was amazed she didn't fall pregnant ten times over, but she didn't. Half of her was sorry, half thought it was just as well. A family would be nice but later. In the meantime she had a fortune to make.

She went at it full throttle. In three months she had made a name for herself.

'Can't believe it,' Jack Almond told his wife. 'No sealed roads, no nothing, and she's selling them like there's no tomorrow.'

'How many times do I have to tell you?' said his wife. 'We women can do things you men can't even dream of.'

They'd all wondered how the customers might react to a woman doing a man's job but it seemed Hilary's fluttering eyelashes (to say nothing of her nous and general ability) took care of that. Whatever the reason, she was selling plenty, all sorts of people eager to respond to her sign advertising cheap land.

One bloke tried to give her a hard time. 'How many blocks are you in for, darling?'

'Four so far.' She gave him a look. 'Sweetheart.'

He laughed. 'You must really believe in the product,' he said. 'Why?'

'The roads are coming. The services. When they do, these blocks will all double in price. Or more, most likely.'

'You sold me,' he said. 'But if things go wrong I'll come a-calling.'

'They won't,' Hilary said. 'You come back later but it'll be to buy more and I'll charge you double.'

He bought two blocks.

'That's the way,' Hilary said.

'Are you really in for four?'

'Darn right.'

Because she'd not blown her commission, like most of the sales force. Hilary Brand was going places and didn't care who knew it.

There were hazards in being a woman, as if she hadn't known already. It wasn't long before a potential customer decided he was more interested in the sales lady than the product.

'You're cute,' she said. 'But I wouldn't do that, I was you.'

'Why not?' Laughing, still looking for a feel.

'My husband wouldn't like it.'

'It's not your husband I'm interested in.'

'Of course not. The only thing, he's a boxer. They call him Iron-fist. The last bloke he fought ended up in the hospital. You don't want your face rearranged, do you?'

Which put paid to that but she still sold him a block. Born diplomat, she thought. That's me.

She drove to work a different way every day, door knocking in evenings and weekends, when people were at home. Cheap Land for Sale: it worked like a charm. Long hours and still longer hours. It was paying off but Sean didn't like it.

'A woman's place is in the home,' he said, echoing his mother, who thought there was something indecent about a married woman working anywhere else.

She said as much to Hilary. 'My husband told me to leave my job the day we married. Sean should have told you the same.'

Hilary only smiled but her mother-in-law had not done with her.

'And still no baby,' she said. Again and again she said it; a proper grouser, that one. 'Why did you marry him if you didn't want a home and a family?'

'To save on the rent,' said Hilary.

It was a joke but Mrs Madigan decided she meant it. 'I rue the day my son got involved with you,' she said.

'Sorry about that,' Hilary said. 'We've bought our own house, remember? We're doing all right.'

Three bedrooms, too. Bigger than anything you ever had, Mrs M. On a big block we can develop later.

'For the moment,' Mrs Madigan said.

'That's right.'

For the moment she was forging ahead – not that Mrs Madigan would ever admit that.

Mrs Madigan spoke to Sean and Sean spoke to Hilary.

'Why can't you be nice to her?'

'When is she ever nice to me?'

'I hate rows,' he said.

'It's our marriage, not hers,' she said. 'Why don't you tell her to back off?'

She was beginning to see that Sean wasn't game to do it. It made her uneasy but she refused to acknowledge it. I'll put some ginger into him yet, she thought.

She told herself she loved her husband. She wanted them to be happy together, to have children together, but it would be when they were ready for them, not simply to suit her bloody mother-in-law.

She had no intention of giving up on the real estate business. It felt right, the timing was right, she knew she was good at it, she was convinced that the property business offered her the best chance to find what she had already said was her highway to the stars.

It was *her* husband, *her* future and she would wage war against Mrs Madigan and anyone else who tried to take them from her. Let no one doubt it.

2

She worked harder than ever. Mostly it was to get ahead in her chosen career but there were days when she forced herself to run faster and faster simply to drown out the doubts that were coming more and more to poison her mind.

She *wanted* her husband to be strong, to stand up for them both against his mother's endless nagging. She *wanted* him to tell Mrs Madigan to butt out of their lives – she would never do it voluntarily – but the old hag had done such a good job emasculating her husband and son that Hilary was coming seriously to question whether Sean was up to the job.

'I love you but you must stand up to her too,' she said. 'I can't do it alone.'

'I will.'

But he did not and Hilary's doubts grew stronger by the day.

Sean had no doubts, or so he said. 'We are one. United. Now and always.'

Hilary did not want that. She was coming to see that Sean wanted her to have no will to be anything but his. 'I have to be free.'

She implored him to understand. He did not. He wanted his wife to be a prisoner, which meant being a prisoner of her mother-in-law too.

'I'll drink poison first,' she said.

Increasingly she was having reservations about bringing a child into a marriage where she could not be free but once again Sean had no doubts. He wanted a child and wanted it now. She heard his mother's voice in his constant demands.

'Not yet,' she told him. 'Not yet.'

'Not good enough for you, am I?'

And again she heard his mother's voice.

Dear God, she thought. What am I going to do?

3

Jack Almond was impressed by her performance and said so.

'You mean it?'

'Would I say it if I didn't?'

She took a deep breath and grabbed what she hoped was an opportunity. 'Any chance of a partnership?'

A blank sheet of paper had more expression than Jack Almond then. 'You're here five minutes and you want to talk partnership?'

'I'm good. You just said it.'

'That doesn't mean you're partner material.'

'Why not?'

'Because my wife wouldn't like it. And because I said no.'

'But...'

'Don't push your luck, Hilary.'

'But I am good,' she told Sean that night. 'I'm the best he's got. He told me so himself.'

'What did you expect?' Sean said.

'I expected more.'

'From an old Jew like him? Where you been all your life?'

Things had cooled off between them recently. This had suited Hilary – she had never reached the heights her instinct told her might be scaled if only they got things right – but tonight she needed him, if only to reaffirm her belief in herself and the future.

'Come here, baby...'

Willing him to get it right, clenching her eyes as she fought for the release that she could sense but never quite reach.

'Come on, come on!' Panting. 'Don't stop, Sean! I'll kill you if you stop!'

No good; in her heart she had expected no better. She felt him thrusting more and more frantically, knew he was on the same old surge, unable or unwilling to slow down, to wait for her, but Sean had left her far behind and within no more than two minutes...

'Ah... Ah... Ah...'

It was over.

Her husband lay inert, log heavy, crushing her. He raised his head to look at her. 'Was it good for you?'

Her lips formed a smile. 'Wonderful,' she said.

Later she lay watching the darkness with Sean snoring beside her. 'I'll give it a month,' she told herself.

And did, with the same dusty answer. Again Jack said it. 'Don't push your luck, Hilary...'

'You must have it out with him,' Sean said. 'He knows what you're worth. What are you after, five per cent? That's peanuts! Tell him if he doesn't give it to you you'll move on.'

She thought about it, decided Sean was right. Partner in a real estate business... It would show Mrs Madigan, if nothing else. She had another good week. The commission was great but the prize was no nearer. She thought the air between her and Jack might be a bit cooler than before but decided to give it one more go. *If you still say no I'll have to consider my future.* She tried out the phrase, decided it felt good.

She knocked on Jack's door, went in before he could respond.

She put it to him, polite but firm. 'Five per cent,' she said. 'Just a token.' Now she was the one on the helter-skelter, rushing forward, unable to stop. She brought out her polished phrase. 'If you can't see your way to agreeing, Jack...' She looked at him but his face was giving nothing away. 'I'll have to consider my future.'

And waited.

'Tell you what I'll do,' Jack said.

Her heart leapt, knowing she'd won.

'No need to consider,' Jack said. 'I'll save you the trouble. Finish up Friday.'

'What?'

Best sales person or not, she was out.

Oh my God.

She went home, feeling six inches high.

'He can't do that!' Sean said.

'He's done it.'

'Don't you believe it. It's a try on. Come Friday he'll have you in, tell you he wants you to stay. Why not? You said it yourself: you're the best he's got.'

She worked herself up to believe it. It made sense, didn't it? She knew she was the best; Jack knew it too. Of course he would come round, she was confident of that. Come Friday she went into the office, all smiles.

'Jack wants to see you,' his secretary said.

'I thought he might.'

She went into Jack's office. 'You were looking for me?'

He handed her an envelope. 'I think you'll find that's everything we owe you.'

Hilary felt her future crumbling beneath her feet. 'But…'

Jack's face was implacable. 'I wanted to wish you all the best.'

It was over.

Stunned, she went home through a suddenly hostile world. What would she do now?

4

Mrs Madigan told her soon enough. Triumphant Mrs Madigan thought all her Christmases had come at once. 'Maybe that'll teach you not to be so cocky in future. Now maybe you'll settle down and be a proper wife to my son.'

'In your dreams,' said Hilary. Of course words were cheap.

'We got debts,' Sean said. 'Mortgage on the house; all that land you're paying off. What we going to do?'

Sean had never been an ideas man. No matter. Getting the push had come as a shock but already she was over the worst of it. Funny thing: she'd thought she'd be terrified but it wasn't like that at all. She felt relief. Now she could rely only on herself. She would show them.

'I tell you what I'm going to do,' she said. 'I am going to sleep on it. In the morning I shall start making plans.'

'You just lost your job,' Sean said. 'How you going to sleep after that?'

Hilary only smiled; she would sleep all right. And in bed later, when Sean decided to come on to her, she pushed him away. She had needed him the other day but not now. 'Leave me be, Sean. Like I said, I've got to sleep.'

The next morning she went walkabout. The only business she knew was selling real estate but if she were going to set up her own operation she would need a base. Two days later she found what she was looking for: an empty shop fronting a busy road. She located the agent – luckily not Jack Almond – and found out what the owner wanted for a two-year lease. Based on her sales record with Jack she reckoned she could manage it easily enough. Even so her heart was in her throat when she signed the papers. She'd better not muck up now.

'Of course I won't muck up,' she told herself and the world.

'I need you to help me,' she said to Sean that night.

'How?'

'A paint job.'

Because the inside of the shop looked more like a rubbish tip than a real estate office.

'It'll take a week,' Sean said when he'd seen the place.

'One weekend,' she said. 'We've got to get moving.'

'Can't be done.'

'Get some of your mates to give you a hand.'

He hesitated. 'They'll want to know what's in it for them.'

'A free piss up. But only when it's finished. And make sure they do it properly.'

'You going to help?'

'I've got better things to do.'

'Like what?'

'Like scouring the neighbourhood for deals.'

But to begin with things didn't look too rosy.

Before she'd been working for Jack Almond, a well-regarded local; now she was just a sheila and an easterner at that. She could see blokes asking themselves why they should deal with her.

I should have thought of that, she told herself. She needed a sandgroper on the team.

She'd kept a record of all the sales she'd made, a filing box of cards giving the names, addresses and contact numbers of every

person she'd dealt with. She suspected she had no right to the information but now was not the time to be picky about legal nice-
ties. That night she sat up scouring the names and came up with a
couple she thought might have potential.

She phoned them in turn to see if either might be interested in
coming to work with her but got a dusty answer from both.

'Give up a paying job to come in with a mob no one's ever heard
of?' the first one said. 'You got to be dreaming.'

The second one agreed.

'What you gunna do now?' Sean asked.

'God knows.'

And with the rent to pay every month he'd better let her in on
the secret pretty soon or it would be all over before it had started.

2004

BETRAYAL

1

Friendly but firm, Jennifer had told herself. But when she sat down with Anthony Belloc at the corner table in a different café all her good resolutions flew out of the window. *Flustered* was perhaps a better word to describe the way she was feeling.

She put on her brightest voice while her heart went pit-a-pat. 'I have never been here before.'

'That's why we're here now.'

This man was trying to make use of her and was therefore dangerous. Her life was in a state of flux. The desire she had felt for Anthony at their first meeting; the moment at the window of the hotel when she had come close to behaving so outrageously; the penthouse lunch with Mother telling her she was thinking of offering Martin Gulliver a job, saying *It's never too late if you want something enough*; Davis's contemptuous indifference on her return home and the violence of her reaction; Tessa telling her so gleefully about Juanita Santos; all these things had come together at this moment and with this man. She was driven by an overwhelming need to break through the walls behind which she had been incarcerated so long; if that meant betraying both Mother and herself then so be it.

She shifted on her chair, feeling the flames of her hidden excitement lick higher. One could be burnt by such flames, Jennifer thought, but did not care. If Anthony Belloc were to offer to take her to a hotel at that moment she would go, and gladly. Even a one-night stand would do, she thought. It would not last – she would not want it to last – but for the moment it would offer at least the pretence of love to freshen the desert of her life.

She had never known herself think in such poetic terms; poetry in any form had never appealed to her whereas Mother, she remembered, was always dipping into books of verse. She felt uneasy at the intrusion of such imagery into her thoughts but smiled at this dangerous man whom her husband had called a crook. He was wearing a beautifully made grey suit, a white shirt and what might be a club tie. He looked like a man who got things done. I would like him to do things to me, she thought as she sipped coffee from the cup the waitress had brought.

'You spoke to your mother,' he said. As though he knew for certain that she would have obeyed him.

'At lunch before I left.'

'Anyone else there?'

'No.'

'Good. What did she say?'

The question he had instructed her to ask: What had Hilary been doing going into the Mount Elizabeth Hospital in Singapore less than one week ago?

'How did you know I had?'

'Someone mentioned it to me. Are you saying you didn't?' Only the new Jennifer would have dared ask that.

Hilary's tart response: *'I am not saying that. I was minding my own business. I recommend you do the same.'*

'She admitted she visited the hospital,' Jennifer said.

'We knew that already. A journalist friend of mine is working over there. His girlfriend is a staff nurse at the hospital. She spotted your mother, told him and he tipped me off. What I have to know is what she was doing there.'

'She told me she was visiting the cardiac unit.'

'Does she have something wrong with her heart?'

'Not that I know of.'

'Would she tell you if she had?'

'Probably not.'

'Someone I know mentioned they saw you there so naturally I was concerned.'

'It was a routine check-up. I have one every year. It's a sensible precaution when you reach my age.'

'But everything was all right?'

'I'm still here, aren't I?'

'You are saying it was just a check-up?' Anthony said.

'That's what she claimed,' Jennifer said.

'Do you believe her?'

'No.'

'Why not?'

'Why visit a cardiac unit in Singapore just to have a check-up? Why not do it here?'

'So you think she's hiding something?'

'I'm sure of it.'

'Something serious?'

'Bound to be. Otherwise why Singapore and not here?'

'But she seemed all right in herself?'

Jennifer thought. 'She looked tired,' she said.

'She's just come back from a trip to Asia. You'd expect her to be tired.'

'I suppose so.' But was doubtful.

'Was that all the information you have for me?'

'One more thing. She said she was checking on equipment she donated to the hospital a year or two ago.'

'That stuff doesn't come cheap. Does she make a habit of donating equipment to hospitals?'

'I don't know.'

'I was hoping you would have something more definite,' he said.

'I asked her what you wanted. I've told you what she said. What more do you want?'

'I want to know whether she's got anything seriously wrong with her. Whether she's trying to hide something.'

'Why should you care?'

'Because of the share price,' Anthony said.

'Explain.'

'If we knew for certain there was something seriously wrong with her we could make a killing. An absolute killing.'

Jennifer did not understand. 'How?'

'Because of how the market would react when it found out.'

'You want me to ask her whether she really has something seriously wrong?'

'Of course not!' Even the thought appalled him. 'That's the last thing I want.'

'But that was what you wanted me to find out. If I ask her –'

'Surely you can see that was completely different?' Exasperated nostrils flared as he downed the last of his coffee. 'Then you were the concerned daughter worried about her mother's health. She's told you there's nothing wrong, right?'

'Right.' Dubiously.

'So if you start pushing her about it she'll think you're up to something.'

Jennifer gave him a straight look. She knew now that the only outcome of this meeting was there would be no outcome. She would not think of the hopes she'd had only minutes ago. 'So *you* are up to something,' she said.

He was preoccupied, barely listening to her. 'I'll get my mate to talk to his girlfriend again. Maybe she can dig out the old records, find whether your mother was ever in the hospital for anything more serious than a routine check-up. There has to be something,' he repeated fiercely, his clenched fist tightening on what Jennifer saw was hope. 'None of it makes sense otherwise.'

'So what do you want me to do?'

'Nothing. You've done what I asked.'

'Didn't help much.'

She hoped he would disagree but he did not. 'We can't all be winners,' he said.

In the taxi taking her back to Ricketts Point Jennifer saw the waters of the bay and the smart houses lined up like grenadiers on the other side of the road, things she had seen a thousand times yet now saw as though for the first time. She had travelled into a strange place; now all her recent thoughts and hopes stood with fingers pointing at her in condemnation.

Betrayal. And for what?

She changed her mind about going home to the empty house where there would be nothing to distract her from her sense of guilt. She leant forwards and spoke to the taxi driver.

'I've changed my mind. Take me to Southlands.'

In the complication of shops and different levels and shoppers all more purposeful than she, she walked for a while, looking and not seeing, stunned by all the things she would have permitted to happen but which had not, torn between regret and relief at the futility of her meeting with Anthony Belloc. She had been right; he had been interested in her only to use her. Now he had no further use for her. Suddenly she was shivering with the aftermath of shock and the coldness of the air-conditioned mall and wrapped her arms around her plump and aging body and wondered in despair whether there would be anything more for her in life.

It was in this mood that Jennifer Lander found the exit and paused and looked at the noticeboard strategically placed in the entrance and saw a notice that took the breath from her lungs, announcing an exhibition of Martin Gulliver's paintings at the Lansdowne Gallery, off St Kilda Road.

DECISION TIME

1

On the map it wasn't far from Paddington to Woolloomooloo but with the city in semi-permanent gridlock the journey, especially first thing, seemed to take forever. Fighting her way through Sydney's early-morning mayhem Sara had plenty of time to think about her mother's life and how little she knew about it or her.

The horns of vehicles threatened the smoggy air and she saw there had been an accident at a street intersection, a ute and a car with its side panels stove in, two furious men gesticulating. With one lane blocked the incident would make a thousand people later to the office than they would otherwise have been. Two hundred metres further on Sara had to slam on her brakes as some bastard elbowed his way into her lane, missing her by millimetres. Her horn joined the chorus of all the other horns but the fat neck of the other driver showed no concern.

Serve him right if I rammed him, Sara thought.

Hilary had to put up with none of this: a chauffeur-driven car, a chopper when she needed one, the Airbus for the long haul journeys. Pricey, of course, but how delightful if you had the dough.

Hilary was offering her that, with all the other benefits that came with it, but also a burden whose weight she could not begin to imagine. Hilary, starting with nothing, had thrived on it. Wrong, Sara thought. Mother had started without money or position, yes – with blow-all education, either, or so she always claimed – but she'd always been a winner. From the first she'd had the brains, the will and the courage to follow what she had once told Sara was her highway to the stars. It was a neat phrase but was the daughter capable of following where the mother had gone or would she want to create her own highway? Did she really want to enter an environment where one mistake could cost millions?

Hilary was a walking, talking miracle and where was the percentage in taking over from someone like that? Yet to turn down such a challenge was equally unthinkable. Hilary had paid her the greatest of compliments by believing her capable of assuming the burden and she had a duty to Hilary and herself to prove she was up to the challenge.

She reached the Channel 12 building and drove into the underground parking area: four levels to cater for the people who worked in the fifty-floor building. Two hundred and forty-five metres high, the tallest structure in Sydney. How typical of Hilary that was. Nothing but the best, the highest, the most spectacular would do. In a way it was like a child stacking building blocks one on top of the other. Would she eventually build so high that one misplaced block would bring the rest tumbling down?

No, Sara thought, if that ever happened, which God forbid, it would be a problem for Hilary's successor. Not the most encouraging of thoughts.

As she took the express lift to the fortieth level she thought about her last words with Emil before leaving him forty minutes earlier.

'You've been on to your agent already? I thought you were still asleep.'

'No point wasting time.'

'I haven't said I'll do it.'

'You'll do it.'

His confidence had exasperated her. 'You know how I hate being taken for granted?'

'Of course you'll do it. All the questions you never had time to ask at our first interview?' Now he was mocking her. 'You no longer want to find out the truth about Emil Broussard?'

Of course I do, she thought. That's the problem.

The lift sighed to a stop. In contrast with yesterday the reception area was quiet although the air was still charged with the suppressed energy endemic to the industry. She went to see Millie Dawlish and found her busy with two assistants, an enormous sheaf of papers and, as always, a tongue willing to lash. She would have done a good job in convict times, Sara thought.

Millie looked up as Sara came in and kicked the two assistants out. She waved to the visitor's chair on the other side of her desk. Sara sat.

'Emil Broussard,' Millie said. 'What is it with you and him?'

'We are old friends,' Sara said.

'I've been asking around,' Millie said. 'I gather you were a bit closer than that.'

'At one time. Not any longer.'

'Screwing him, were you?'

Vulgarity could sometimes uncover truth but Sara, knowing Millie Dawlish, was ready for vulgarity and only smiled.

'Have a bust-up?'

'You could say so. I walked out on him.'

'Yet now he not only wants to give us an exclusive – a man who's dodged giving interviews all of his life – but insists he will only do it with you.'

'Amazing, isn't it?'

'Got you back in the sack, has he?'

'Nothing like that.' Although it had been closer than she would have believed possible.

Millie had a death glare when she chose to use it. 'I don't know whether to believe you or not.'

'Believe what you want. Don't you want Channel 12 to have an exclusive interview with one of the world's top writers?'

'A Nobel Prize winner? A lot of our viewers would run a mile.'

'He never won the Nobel.'

'That's right. They say he turned it down; is that right?'

'Maybe that would be one of the things he would be willing to tell us. If we interview him.'

'If you interview him, you mean. His agent was very clear about that. You would be willing to do it, I take it? Your old mate?'

Sara remembered what Millie had said in her early days at the station. 'I'm not sure there would be much blood on the carpet.'

'He's got to have some shameful secrets, sweetie. We all have those.'

Sara thought: His father...

'When would all this be happening?'

'Pretty soon. He wants it as soon as we can draw up the agreement.'

'Does he have any other terms?'

'Just that you do it.'

'You happy with that?'

'Of course I'm not happy. You're too close to him for a really objective interview.'

'Too close to take him apart, you mean?'

Millie's killer glare was suddenly a killer grin. 'How well you know me.'

'Let me know when you've made up your mind,' Sara said.

'Of course. Now, let's see what we've scheduled for tonight.'

2

As soon as she could escape Sara went into her own office. She sat down and thought. She was keen to do the interview, right enough, but Hilary had said this Hong Kong business was urgent. Go to Hong Kong with Martha Tan and interviewing Emil might well be impossible. And how would Millie react when she discovered Sara was moving on? Because Sara knew that whatever Hilary might say there would be no turning back. It was eerily similar to the situation when Emil had invited her to Hideaway Island. No commitments, he had said, but she had known better and been right.

She sent Hilary a text, asking to see her as soon as possible.

Within minutes she had her answer.

Come now.

Hilary and Desmond Bragg were in conference but Janet had been told to send her in as soon as she arrived.

'Give us five minutes, Desmond.'

'Hong Kong,' Sara said as soon as they were alone.

'Yes.'

'You still want me to go?'

'Yes.'

'OK.' An inconsequential word yet of such significance, committing her to a future that was certain to be traumatic and might conceivably prove beyond her ability to handle. 'But there is a problem,' she said.

Hilary's expression did not change. 'Which is?'

'Emil is offering to do an interview with Channel 12 but only if I do it.'

The ghost of a smile. 'Millie has already told me.'

'How am I supposed to do both?'

'Very simple. You go to Hong Kong. When you come back you do the interview. Problem solved.'

'What if he won't wait?'

'I think you'll find he will. But if he won't then we miss out. Hong Kong and what you make of it is worth a hundred interviews with Emil Broussard.'

'To you, perhaps.'

'And to you.'

'Are you so all-knowing?'

'Not at all. But if it hadn't meant that much to you, you would never have agreed to go.'

It was like trying to hack your way through steel plate with a penknife: there was no way to reach her mother behind the implacable exterior, the woman to whom everything was so simple, so clear.

'I loved him, you know.'

'Which makes your courage all the more remarkable. I am thankful you are over it.'

And Sara lost it. 'There are times I think you've never loved anyone in your life.'

'Then you would be wrong.' Hilary's expression softened. She reached across the desk and took Sara's hand in hers. 'I don't want to fight with you. But if you ever sit in this chair you will understand it is a dilemma you have to face every day of your life.'

'That the company comes first.'

'No. To balance your duties between the company and those who are dear to you.'

Sara's eyes smarted, aware if only for a moment that for once in their lives she and her mother had almost succeeded in touching one another.

'Who is going to tell Millie?'

'Desmond will take care of that. Channel 12 is his baby.'

'Does Desmond know?'

'About you? Of course. I told him as soon as I got your text.'

'But I could have been planning to tell you I'd decided to stay with Channel 12.'

'You are too much like me to take the easy choice. You've proved that a dozen times over, even with Broussard. I hated it at the time but now I believe your affair with him was a good thing. You discovered you had the courage to accept the challenge he presented, and the courage to walk away when you saw it was not working. Not many have the strength of purpose to do that.'

'Like Jennifer?'

'I wonder. Until this week I would have agreed with you. Now I'm not so sure.'

'When we saw her the other day she seemed no different to me. Except that she'd been drinking.'

'Which itself was a change. But there was definitely something. I should know. After all –' and again the spectral smile '– I've known her all her life, have I not? And I had the feeling she may be coming to her senses at last. I certainly hope so.'

'You've never liked Davis.'

'I think Davis Lander is a detestable man. He is arrogant and a bully and, as my mother-in-law said to me once, I rue the day he married my daughter.'

Sara was interested. 'Did she really say that to you?'

'Mrs Madigan said it, yes. Jennifer's grandmother, not yours.'

'Why?'

'Lots of reasons. She was fishing, you know.'

'Mrs Madigan?'

'Jennifer. She was looking for answers to a number of questions I did not intend to answer. The interesting thing was that she was willing to ask them, which is more than she would have done once.'

'What questions did she ask?'

But the shutters were up again. 'Nothing that need concern you at the moment.'

'I still want to know why you've decided to move on when the business has been your life.'

'Not all my life,' Hilary said. 'A major part, I grant you. As to my reasons, I'll tell you when I'm ready. Or not, as I decide. Now, let us talk about your upcoming work schedule.'

'I must do tonight's show.'

'Of course. Tomorrow morning I have asked Martha to brief you about Hong Kong. Two hours should be ample. She'll expect you in her office at seven-thirty. Bring an overnight bag and don't forget your passport: you'll be going straight to the aircraft from here. Any queries, sort them out with Martha.'

'You're saying she's in charge.'

'I am.'

It was another test but Sara had no trouble with it. She was the new kid on the block; of course Martha had to be in charge.

'You'll be taking the Airbus.'

'Surely there's no need for that,' Sara said.

'There is every need. It is too big an investment to sit in the hanger when it can be usefully employed, and one of your first lessons is that from now on everything you do will send a message, whether you like it or not.'

'What message will the Airbus send?'

'That you and Martha are speaking with my voice. It should help things along a little.'

'You mean it will give us face?'

'There is a lot of nonsense talked about face but in this instance I think you are right.'

'How long will we be away?'

'Five days should be sufficient.'

'Will it take us so long to deal with the Lennoxes?'

'There are other things you'll be looking at while you're there. Martha has all the details.'

'Five days with only an overnight bag?'

'Buy whatever you need while you're there. Martha will open an account in your name at Shanghai Tang. The quality of their clothes is excellent and the prices reasonable. The company will pay, of course, but be careful. Mr Henderson or one of his assistants check all accounts and he isn't called Eagle Eye for nothing. I'll expect you back here at the weekend but we shall be in daily contact every day you're away.'

'When you said I'd have to work hard I can see you weren't joking.'

'You'd better believe it. Welcome on board,' Hilary said. 'Desmond is mad at me for taking you away from him but he'll get over it. I am glad you made the right decision.'

'I hope you won't regret it.'

'So do I. Now, you'll be wanting to get back to Channel 12, will you not?'

A whirlwind would have been more peaceful.

Back at Channel 12 Millie was waiting and she was as sour as vinegar. 'You're on your bike, then?'

'Seems like it.'

'I knew you wouldn't last. The boss's daughter? You'll be looking for a soft landing, no doubt.'

'If you think I'll be getting that you don't know my mother.'

'I'm not sure anyone really knows your mother, herself included.' Millie ironed the anger off her face. 'Now: Primrose Rice will be taking over from you. Let's get her in and we'll talk about the show...'

A MOMENT TO LOOK BACK

Hilary had a full morning of meetings with more stacked back to back as far as the eye could see but at twelve she had a two-hour breather. She was feeling a bit frazzled. A shower, she decided, that's what I need. That and a few minutes' lie down and some fresh clothes and I shall be like a new woman.

She stood under the sharp double jet, hot and then cold, letting the water hammer down on her head, and indeed felt refreshed by it. She towelled herself dry and added a discreet squirt or two of Mademoiselle. Naked, she stood in front of the full-length heated mirror and stared critically at her reflection. Not how she'd looked at twenty, but two kids and forty-three years later you could hardly expect anything else. Not too bad, all the same. Her tummy was trim, arms and breasts firm, thighs still shapely. Even in her youth she had never been the beauty Sara had grown to be, but she'd had enough about her to draw men to her or at least those she had wanted to be drawn. Tim Pattinson had been the first – dear God, how wonderful to be sixteen again, with all challenges still in front of her – but Sean Madigan had been the one she had married, back in the days when life's adventures had all been before her.

1965–66

MOVING UP

1

Hilary Brand and Associates. Neither Sean nor his mother had liked that. 'My name not good enough for you?'

'Don't be silly. It's just business.'

His expression had shown what he thought of that.

The golden letters, each a foot high, were inscribed boldly over the door to tell the world of her arrival and for the information of customers, but as the drizzly evening closed in with the smell of fried food from the takeaway next door there were no customers and the door was closed.

Inside the smartly carpeted office Hilary Brand was alone. Wearing the smart new clothes she hoped would make her look like the tycoon she was determined to become, she sat in her smart new executive chair at her smart new executive desk in her smart, newly painted office and looked at nothing. The smart new doorbell remained silent. The winter evening brought gusts of chilly rain to splatter the shop window and she knew that unless something changed very soon she was looking down the barrel of disaster. Instead of the queue of eager buyers she had envisaged there had been nobody for over a week. It was 26 June, the rent was due in four days' time and she hadn't the money to pay it. Or to pay for the telephone she knew would be cut off if she didn't settle the account very soon. Or for the electricity. Or for her petrol bill and the registration on her car that would be due at the end of July.

You, she told herself, are on the bones of your arse.

The truth was supposed to make you free but recognising it didn't help unless you could do something about it. But do what? She had the know-how, or at least enough to make a meaningful start on her quest for her first million; she had the premises and the will. Her track record with Jack Almond had given her every reason to be confident of the future yet every day it was becoming more and more obvious that nobody was interested in doing business with a sheila from the eastern states with no local connections.

'We,' she told the antique hatstand the salesman had told her would bring a touch of class to her office, 'are in the shit.'

The trouble was there was blow-all she could do about it; she couldn't change either her gender or her background.

Husband Sean, goaded by his mother, was on her back every day. 'Give it away,' he said. 'Talk sweet to that Mrs Shargey; she might take you back. You were earning good dough at her dress shop before you started getting grand ideas.'

'Thought she was too smart for the rest of us,' she had heard Mrs Madigan say. 'Little Miss Nobody from back east who was gunna take over the town. Now look at her.'

Hilary set her jaw. If all else failed she might have to go to Mrs Shargey and eat humble pie but not until she was down. She wasn't down yet.

She looked out at the rainy darkness. The lights of the take-away were still shining but down the street the wet pavements were empty; nobody would be coming by tonight. She switched off the lights, locked the door behind her and headed home. Without Sean's wages they'd be eating sawdust tonight and not too much of it, either. And didn't he like to tell her so.

He was still after her two or three nights a week. It never lasted long: two minutes, mostly, five if she was lucky. *Wham, bang, thank you ma'am.* Except that with Sean there wasn't too much of the thank you ma'am, either.

Something else to live with, although – with less and less optimism – she was still hoping things would improve.

Next day the skies had cleared and it was a brisk thank-you-for-having-me morning as Hilary walked to work. She turned the corner and saw a young couple waiting outside the shop door. Not even eight o'clock, she thought. They must be keen. And the first customers she'd seen all week. She quickened her pace.

'Sorry to keep you waiting…'

Then she realised she knew them; they had bought a block from her while she was with Jack Almond. Actually two blocks.

'How nice to see you again. How can I help you today?' Unlocking the door, mind scrambling, trying to remember their names. 'Dave and Sandy, isn't it? Dave and Sandy Peterfield?'

She made them coffee; she made a royal fuss of them. Why not? Customers were an endangered species at Hilary Brand and Associates.

She sat at her desk and gave them her million-watt smile. 'Are you looking to buy more land?'

'Not exactly.'

She hadn't expected that. 'Then how can I help you?'

'We've done well out of the blocks you sold us,' Dave Peterfield said.

'Very well,' Sandy said.

'That's good.'

'And we enjoyed doing business with you,' Sandy said.

'We thought you were very efficient. Business like, you know,' said her husband. 'But nice with it.'

'I am sure you haven't come out so early in the morning to pay me all these compliments,' Hilary said. 'Not that I'm complaining.'

'We doubled our money on both blocks,' Dave said.

'More than doubled,' Sandy said. 'And we thought other people must have done the same.'

'The same or better,' Dave said. 'So we thought –'

'We thought we'd like to get in on the property boom,' Sandy said.

'Before it really is a boom,' Dave said.

Hilary looked at them in turn. 'You want to come and work here? Is that what you're saying?'

'If you're willing. We are both local born and bred,' Sandy said. 'We've got loads of contacts.'

'I turn out for the local footy team,' Dave said.

'And I'm involved with the local children's centre. We like to be involved with the community.'

'Which we thought might help,' Dave said.

'I'll be honest with you,' Hilary told them, 'I've no money to pay either of you. I've hardly got a business.'

'You think a local face might help?' said Dave.

'Two faces?' said Sandy.

'You see,' Dave said, 'we have faith in the product and in the future.'

Sandy, who had been a book-keeper before her marriage, agreed to run the office and keep the books, field telephone calls, handle clients. This freed up Hilary and in no time both she and Dave were in the field.

'One thing we must do,' Hilary said.

'What's that?'

Two days later they stood and looked admiringly at the new sign. Hilary Brand, Peterfield and Associates.

'Now we'll show them,' Dave said.

2

They did, and in spades. The deals and the dough began to roll in. The bills were paid, there was money in the bank, everything was looking rosy. But six months later sales started to taper off.

'There's a limit to what we can do in one neighbourhood,' Hilary said. 'It's time to go further afield.'

A week later she came across a big block of land for sale. People said it had been on the market for a while with no one interested, even for the asking price of a hundred quid. Hilary couldn't see why but when she walked across it she soon found out. Twenty yards in and she was in water over her boots. There it was and she could see why it had put buyers off, yet it didn't seem right. The land was not particularly low-lying so she could see no reason why it should be so wet. She went to the Lands Office, met someone called Lance Bettinger, who gave her a hand interpreting what the records showed. He seemed a dinky-di sort of bloke a few years older than she was. Not bad looking, tall and trim with dark hair and an open face. No fool, either; in no time he confirmed what she'd thought, that it was not standing water but run-off that would be cured when the drains for nearby developments were put in.

'And when's that going to be?'

'That's confidential.' But there was a smile in his voice when he said it.

'Let's put it this way,' she said. 'If you were me, would you buy it?'

'You can't expect me to answer a question like that,' he said.

'It would be most unprofessional,' she agreed.

'But property is always good.'

All in all she quite fancied Lance Bettinger. You are a married woman, she reminded herself. But her gonads were not listening.

She went back, parlayed the purchase price down to seventy-five pounds and agreed to pay it off over twelve months. She went back to see Lance Bettinger.

'There's a block going cheap. Really cheap.'

'My sister could always use a quid,' Lance said.

'Consider it done.'

Six months later the drains were in, Hilary's land was as dry as the Gibson Desert and she sold it for a couple of grand.

Not a huge killing but a start.

On the domestic front things weren't so rosy. Sean wasn't comfortable with the idea of his wife earning five and ten times more than he did. Said he felt diminished by it.

'You get the benefit too,' she said.

'Still don't seem right. A man's got his pride.'

So he did; pride and an eight-to-six job in a machine shop. The most he could hope to earn was ten, maybe fifteen a week. Hilary was pulling down somewhere close to eighty.

The established agents hated her. Plenty of them shared what had been Jack Almond's opinion.

'No job for a woman.'

They hated being wrong even more than they hated her.

'She'll trip over her feet one of these days,' they said. 'Let's hope it's soon.'

If things went pear-shaped she knew she could expect no mercy.

FOLLOWING THE HIGHWAY

1

Hilary Brand and Dave Peterfield were sitting in the office. It was Thursday 30 June 1966, the last day of the financial year, and papers were spread on the desk between them as they examined the sales figures Sandy had presented to them that morning.

'One hundred and seventy thousand dollars,' Hilary said.

Seventy thousand for each of them, thirty thousand for Sandy. Decimal currency had been introduced back in February and for most people, although not for Hilary Brand or the Peterfields, it was still a bit of a puzzle working out values in the new money.

Dave sat back in his chair with a pleased expression on his rugged face, rearranged by a decade of footy. 'Pretty damn good, I would say,' he said.

'It's a start. A long way short of good enough, though.'

'Nothing will ever be good enough for you,' Dave said.

He was right. It was the way Hilary was made and she knew it. It made for restless nights and an increasingly toey husband.

Sean was not happy. Their honeymoon in the forests of the south was five years gone and the cracks were beginning to show.

Mrs Madigan wouldn't let up. 'Must be something wrong with her. Take her to the doctor,' she told Sean repeatedly. 'I want a grandson.'

With every month that passed there was less and less chance of that. The passion of the early days was long spent; nowadays Sean hardly touched her from one week to the next. She was growing away from him and he hated it. On the rare occasions he made love to her it was with a barely suppressed anger, as though he wanted to punish more than caress her.

She continued to put up with it. She did not want to admit failure even in this but her mind was increasingly closed to him, her body not yet but getting there. She saw the highway unrolling ahead of her and was determined to follow it to the end. She would have liked him to join her on her journey but knew there was no chance of it. She was beyond him now.

'Driving around I see lots of other agents' For Sale signs,' she told Dave Peterfield. 'Sometimes they sit there for months. I think we should try a new approach.'

She had not forgotten her attempt to get into the television business, when the burly contractor had laughed her out of his office. 'Anyone in your footy club work for television?'

'One bloke's an announcer.'

'Any chance of meeting him?'

'What you got in mind?'

She smiled, dollar signs all over her. 'You'll see.'

When she had been working in Mrs Shargey's fancy-pants dress shop she had told herself she needed allure. Now, when she and Dave sat down over a beer with Boyd Michaels, she with just a hint of cleavage out, she needed it in spades. Luckily she'd had plenty of practice; most of the people she'd been selling to were blokes.

She gave twenty-three-year-old Boyd the full treatment and in no time he was simpering and Hilary moved in for the kill. 'You have a real way with you,' she said. 'I'll bet people buy television sets just to watch you reading the news.'

Boyd did not deny it.

'I reckon you'd be a star in selling, if you ever fancied a change.'

Boyd did not deny it.

'What I want is someone to do a bit of selling for us, right after the news. We'd make it worth his while, obviously.'

Boyd was nervous but interested. 'What would I have to do?'

'Just read this simple message.'

She handed him a piece of paper. He tried it out aloud.

'If any of our viewers have property they'd like to sell, Brand Peterfield have large numbers of keen buyers waiting. This could be your big chance to cash in!'

He looked even more nervous. 'I dunno...'

'The station gets money from its adverts,' Hilary said. 'It relies on it. It'll get money out of this. So what's the difference?'

'I'll speak to the advertising guys. See if they like the idea.'

'What's not to like?' said Hilary.

Dave had his concerns. 'The Land Agents' Supervisory Committee,' he said.

'What about them?'

'They'll crucify you,' he said.

'Why should they do that?'

'Soliciting business from other agencies' clients? That's prohibited, isn't it?'

'We're not soliciting anything from anybody. We're making a general appeal to the public. If clients of other agents choose to reply it's not our fault. In any case we don't know if the station will do it.'

The station would do it all right; its advertising department couldn't wait to get her on board. The agreement was signed and paid for; the first broadcast made. The timing was what made it: not slung in with all the other adverts but in its own slot immediately after the nightly news, when the majority of viewers were watching and no one could miss it.

How the committee would react they still didn't know but it didn't take them long to find out what the station's MD thought about it. He went ballistic, screaming down the phone with Hilary holding the receiver a foot from her ear.

'Giving you priority? What're our other advertisers going to say, eh? I'm closing your slot. If I find you've pulled a fast one you'll be hearing from our solicitors...'

'I have a contract,' she said. 'Signed, sealed and delivered. I've paid you guys a thousand quid for five gigs. You close me down, I'll be the one doing the suing.'

'You've got a *contract*?' Apoplexy was a distinct possibility.

'I have it in front of me now.'

Quiet as a turtle dove, the MD was then.

'I see. You needn't think you'll be getting another one,' he said, trying to be fierce.

'Suit yourself,' Hilary said. 'Our money's good but if you don't want it…'

After that the answers to the adverts rolled in. Dave continued his doomsday scenario that the committee would take away their licences but Hilary, cocky as a rooster, didn't believe it and was right. The committee might not like it but Hilary had exploited a loophole in the rules and they could do nothing. The only come-back was a good one: they had a huge number of enquiries and a good many sales too.

2

Five months later Hilary was driving home after a successful trip south of Fremantle with two more sales under her belt and she decided she'd explore some of the side roads. It was a sunny day with a light breeze off the sea and the sky was throbbing with heat. She was two weeks off her twenty-sixth birthday and she was let-ting rip with 'A Hard Day's Night', one of the Beatles hits she'd first heard during their Aussie tour two years back. She remembered watching her first rock and roller on the box in Adelaide but she'd come a long way since her Johnny O'Keefe days. Her bull-frog voice threatened to crack the windscreen as she crested a hill, the ocean visible in turquoise glimpses to her left, and slammed on the brakes in a slide and smother of dust.

'So there you are,' Hilary said.

The large block stretched up the slope to the right of the road. Thoughts started ticking in her head. Twenty acres, maybe twenty-five; road frontage; views of the sea, at least from further up the hill.

The only building she could see was a tumbledown shack. It would have looked abandoned had it not been for a plume of smoke rising from the tin-pot chimney and shredding on the breeze.

She had lucked on the Wiggins' place. Every estate agent in the west had heard of it and the misanthropic old man who lived there alone with a pack of savage dogs for company. The word was that the property had no power, no running water and no telephone. Those who had seen him said that Walter Wiggins might be ramshackle in body but had a ferocious temper and hated trespassers with a passion. The dogs hated them even worse.

The only way to get hold of Walter Wiggins was to yell from the boundary wire. That set the dogs going but nine times out of ten their owner ignored even that. The tenth time he threatened to set the beasts on anyone setting foot on his land and the only one who had tried it said afterwards he'd been lucky to escape with his life.

Walter Wiggins was impossible. Everyone said so but that was not a word in Hilary's vocabulary. The only gate into the property had a king-sized padlock that by the look of it hadn't been opened in a generation. She thought about it then climbed on the gate's metal frame, stood tall and let fly with a whistle that might have been heard a mile away. The dogs came howling.

Hilary gave them a few seconds to get a good look at her. 'How you going, dogs?'

Their mouths were red, their teeth enormous. Moving carefully so as not to startle them, she climbed down to join them.

3

'You got a nerve,' Walter Wiggins said. 'I'll give you that. Them mutts don't make mates easily.'

The pack leader was nuzzling in Hilary's lap. She patted the shaggy head. 'I've always got on with dogs.'

'I call that one Bradman,' he said.

'Bradman? Like the cricketer?'

'Cause he was always taking a bite out of the Poms. You ain't a Pom, are you?' he said, suddenly fierce.

'No chance,' Hilary said.

She looked around her. It was more rubbish tip than house, with refuse everywhere you looked: tin cans and cardboard boxes and bags full of what smelt like a ten-year supply of kitchen waste. A graveyard of empty bottles. Old Walter was kitted out to match: a shirt that looked like he hadn't had it off in a year, an ancient sweater despite the heat that was more holes than material, a pair of pants that would have put a scarecrow to shame. His mouth was toothless and the lines on his face were more like chasms; looking at the dirt in them Hilary thought you could excavate them and maybe find diamonds. God, you needed a strong nose in her job.

'What you want, anyway?' His voice creaked like he hadn't used it for ten years.

'A cup of tea would be nice,' Hilary said.

'You wha'?'

'Cup of tea. With something nice to put in it.'

She'd found it paid to carry a half bottle of scotch on her travels; it was amazing how often a friendly shot helped sweeten a deal. She produced it now.

Wally wiped his paw over his lips. 'Blimey.'

He got them each a mug of tea that was strong enough to melt glass; as for the state of the mugs, don't even think about it.

If I die of food poisoning it'll be in a good cause, Hilary thought.

She handed over the scotch and watched as Wally took a gulp of tea and then filled his mug.

'You want some?'

'A small one to be sociable,' she said.

A small one was what she got.

'What's your game?' Wally said.

'A grand in your hand,' Hilary said. 'And a stack more later. That's my game.'

'What I got to do to get it?'

'Sell your place to me.'

'I been here all my life.'

'So maybe it's time to move on. Think about it. A grand – non-refundable, by the way – will buy you a house with heating, running water, all mod cons. What's there not to like about that?'

'What about me dogs?'

'They go with you.'

Wally chomped on the idea a bit, slopped more whisky into his mug and swilled it down. While Hilary held her breath.

'Make it two,' he said.

'A grand now. Non-refundable, like I said. Another five when the deal goes through.' She gave him her best smile. 'Plus a crate of scotch to celebrate with.'

'Now you're talking.'

'All I need is your signature.'

She was waltzing all the way home. The land, once it was subdivided and services put in, would be easy to sell. Her mind was doing its calculator bit; she reckoned, all up, she was looking to clear over a hundred grand.

'Maybe more,' she told the sunset. 'Any luck, quite a bit more.'

Now, at last, she was really motoring.

4

'You're trying to steal my son away from me,' Mrs Madigan said. 'That's what it is.'

Hilary was sick of her mother-in-law's endless sniping. 'All I said was I thought it would be nice to move into a bigger place.'

'You've got a house now. What you want a bigger place for? When you got no family?'

'A bit of extra space for when we have one.'

A buffalo would have snorted more quietly. 'That'll be the day,' said Mrs Madigan.

Lord give me strength.

It was a bigger house. A better one too, and a better suburb, a three-bedroom brick house on a double block which might be handy for development later. When once again she decided to move on.

She made a mistake, told Sean her thinking.

'We've hardly settled in and already you're talking of moving? What's wrong with this place?'

Nothing was wrong with it, but it wasn't Peppermint Grove. She remembered telling Mrs Madigan that was where she was heading and the old bitch had sneered. Well, that was still where she was heading; on one of her forays into the area she had even picked out the house she wanted, if it ever came on the market. And Mrs Madigan could sneer all she liked.

5

Sandy stuck her nose around Hilary's door. Hilary was on the phone. She put her hand over the mouthpiece and looked at Sandy enquiringly.

'Abe Raucher on the other line.'

Abe was their lawyer.

'I've got a man here I'd like you to meet,' Abe said.

'Is he buying or selling?'

'Neither. But he has an idea you'll find interesting.'

Hilary was always in the market for interesting ideas. 'When does he want to come round?'

'How about now?'

'I'll be here. What's his name?'

'Haskins Gould.'

1942–66

HASKINS GOULD

He had been born Joseph Haskins Gould in the British colony of Singapore in January 1942, a month before the Japanese arrived. His father had been top gun of an Australian motorcar firm and baby Joseph and his parents had been among the last to escape before the surrender.

He grew up surrounded by the story of that escape: the freighter crowded with over two thousand escapees continuously bombed and machine gunned by Japanese planes yet somehow, miraculously, reaching safety in Australia. As a babe in arms he remembered none of it, which did not stop him in later life boasting how he'd helped two nurses drag a wounded gunner to safety.

'They called me a boy hero,' he said modestly, 'but it was nothing, nothing.'

The first thing the boy hero really remembered was growing up in an arcaded bungalow that might have been transplanted from the tropics they had been in such a hurry to leave, as though a portion of their previous lives had accompanied them into what was to become permanent exile.

His father had been involved in the war effort and later with General Motors and the production of the new Holden motorcar. They were what people in those days called comfortably off but for Haskins that had never been enough. His parents indulged him;

he did what he could to help them do so, taking everything they gave him and always on the lookout for more. He had never been hampered by scruples. He was smart, though, and money drew him like a magnet.

He went to the States and in California discovered the gold mine that was called shopping malls. He did well; he was nifty with a knife in what was acknowledged to be a cut-throat business; he didn't give a damn about the ruined lives he left behind him; and he had the knack of dealing with councillors eager for a sweetener so building permits had presented no problem.

Unfortunately questions were raised about some of his business practices. Some of those he'd bribed were singing like a choir and in 1966, one jump ahead of the authorities, he returned to Australia eager to explore the possibilities and steal anything that wasn't nailed down.

He'd been back a month when a lawyer gave him a name.

NEW VENTURES

1

Hilary sized up her visitor as he walked into her office. Haskins Gould was built like a truck, fists like coconuts. Barely suppressed energy radiated off him like heat.

He looked around her office with a pleased expression. 'Nice,' he said with a hint of an American accent. 'Way too small but nice.'

Hilary saw that being outspoken was a way of life for Haskins Gould. 'At least we agree it's nice,' she said. 'And what can I do for you, Mr Gould?' *Mr Gould*: to put him in his place, gently but definitely.

'More like what I can do for both of us.' Uninvited he sat down on the other side of her desk, stuck his elbows on the desk top and leant forwards, staring into her eyes. 'Malls.'

'I beg your pardon?'

'Shopping malls,' he said again. 'I'm from Sydney originally but I've been two years in California. They are the coming thing there. I'm just off the boat and I been looking around. Bit of a one-horse town, ain't that right? A bit behind the times? I reckon a few malls would fit real well into this fair city. And into a dozen other towns in WA too, if I'm any judge.'

Hilary had acquired a sandgroper's attitude to the rest of the world, Sydney in particular, and didn't relish her town being described as a one-horse anything by some eastern states bum who thought he knew the lot.

'Tell me about them.'

He did. Hilary, no slouch herself when it came to talking a blue streak, recognised an expert when she heard one and was prepared to discount ninety per cent of everything this hybrid Aussie-American wanted to tell her but, as he talked, she found herself growing more and more interested in what he had to say.

'How high is the tallest building in Perth?' he said. 'I'll tell you: it's ten storeys. In California that would be like a hole in the ground. In LA I was building shopping malls eighteen, twenty storeys high.'

'Under one roof?'

'Sure under one roof. Inside there'd be ten, maybe fifteen, levels. Ground floor you put your high-ticket tenants, a supermarket, anything you need to draw the buyers in. Maybe a few restaurants where shoppers can rest their weary feet. Other shops at the higher levels. Outside a parking area and a petrol station.'

'Will locals go for it?'

'All their shopping under one roof? In pleasant surroundings? Why shouldn't they?'

'And the rents?'

'Flat rate plus a percentage of turnover.'

'You say you built them in America?'

'I sure did. It's like a vertical warehouse with individual compartments. It's not hard; you need to be well organised but it's not hard.'

'So why do you need me?'

'Abe was saying you got the land.'

'Or know how to get it, yes. Is that all you want?'

'Two other things. We'll need money and I'll need a free hand to build it.'

'I'm in good with the banks,' Hilary said. 'I reckon I can sweet-talk them into a loan, if I decide to go ahead. But I'm not sure about the free hand.'

'I got my methods,' Haskins said. 'They worked in California; they'll work here. Like I said, I'm a good organiser and that's what makes the difference.'

'You got any plans I can look at? Any photos of work you've done in California?'

'I got some back at the hotel.'

'Bring them down. I'll have a look at them and get back to you.'

'I'll bring them but they stay with me. We can look at them together. Then we'll go and talk to the bank.'

2

Hilary decided to keep Haskins away from Henry Lancaster, scared his brash ways might put the banker off, but when she got back from her meeting she told him all about it.

'Poor Henry! I don't think he could believe his ears. This woman walking into his office, cool as you please, and asking him for a half-million-dollar loan on what – let's face it – is nothing but a piece of empty land.

'"But where is my security?" he asked me. "It's not the land," I told him. "It's the vision. The future. It's an idea whose time has come." I showed him the plans. Photos of similar work you'd done in the States. "You're an ideas man, Mr Lancaster," I said. Buttering him up, you understand? "Well, this is the biggest idea in the retail trade you're ever likely to see." I was that confident. I could see it as clearly as though it was already built: a tower fifteen storeys high crammed with shops and people coming and going.

'"One-stop shopping," I said. "That's how we'll promote it. I'm a great believer in slogans, Mr Lancaster, and I guarantee this one will draw them in. One-stop shopping: the housewives will come running! You can bet your pension on that!" Which was funny because I suppose he was, in a way. Yet they say bankers are so conservative!'

'You got him to see it,' Haskins said. 'That's why. You showed him the vision.'

'I think I did.'

'And he's gonna lend us the money?'

'He is indeed. And before a brick has been laid. Of course I've been dealing with the bank for years and never put a foot wrong. But he still had to stick his oar in, even after he'd said yes. "You know, Mrs Madigan, there are not many women I would do this for. Entrepreneurs of the female gender are an unusual species, I think you will admit. In fact you and Bella Tucker, the iron ore magnate, are the only two I know."'

'But we've got it?' Haskins said.

'Of course I got it.'

He eyed her coldly. 'That's what matters. I don't give a hoot in Hades how you got him to agree, babe. Just so long as you did.'

2004

A NEW DAWN

1

The hall where the exhibition was being held was in a side street but well advertised. A large banner over the building's imposing entrance shouted the name for the world to see. *MARTIN GULLIVER*, the letters two feet high or more.

No one else was about; Jennifer stood at the street corner, hands sweat-clammy, heart racing, and stared at the glass-fronted doorway while she debated whether she dared go in. Her heart said yes; common sense said no. Martin was the past, a long-ago love that thirteen years back she had abandoned for security, status and respectability. How stupid to imagine that Martin might still have the feelings for her that had tumbled from his mouth on that fatal day when she had told him she was marrying Davis Lander. Both of them had shed tears. But the world had moved on; the years had taken their youth but in exchange had at least given Martin the success that in those days it had seemed he might never have.

I was a coward, Jennifer thought. I turned my back because I was afraid. I am afraid still. Of what? That Martin might not be there. That he might be there. He would spurn her: and who could blame him? Even worse: he might not recognise her at all.

Thirteen years.

Her dry mouth swallowed sourness. No. She half turned away, again paused.

If I do not go in I shall once again prove myself the coward I was before. If I do not go in I shall regret it forever.

In a way she could not understand, her will was disconnected from her body as now she walked down the street between the grey and silent buildings, crossed to the entrance and went up the steps to the glass door.

The door creaked as she pushed it open. She went in. And stopped, staring at the paintings hanging around the room.

They were a universe of colour, a battle cry and celebration of golds and greens and reds. A dozen shades of red. The artist had shaped ecstasy and flung it in the face of the observer. A powerful statement by a man she had known yet, it was now obvious, had never known at all.

The colours overwhelmed in their intensity, filling the exhibition room with light. They were too much, too much. Jennifer closed her eyes yet the vibrations remained. She could sense their brilliance; terror could lurk in those violent hues.

'You are supposed to look at them.'

She heard the smile; knew the voice.

'I am drowning, Martin.'

This before she had opened her eyes. *Drowning, and not only in the colours.* Again her heart was thundering. Again her limbs seemed disconnected from her will. Her eyes were pleading as she opened them and looked up at him. Helpless, after so long.

He had always been big but was more solid now, with a little grey in his hair and crow's feet about his eyes, but he was still Martin. Still the man she knew now she had never ceased to love.

'You look like you could do with a cup of coffee,' he said.

The café was just round the corner from the exhibition hall. It was odd; she had thought it would be awkward, sitting with each other after such a long time, but it was not. Chatting was as easy as though they had never parted. Nothing weighty, at least to begin with. What they'd done; what they had not done. No sense at all of skirting around the edges of pain. No pain at all; rather a sense of rediscovery.

No, he had never married. Not exactly celibate but nothing serious. Nothing permanent.

She, still married. Davis was doing well, oh yes. No, they had no children. A nice house in Brighton; a cottage in the Whitsundays.

She did not tell him that her life was consumed by endless failure and futility.

Until Martin, his artist's eyes prising out the secrets she had hidden even from herself, said: 'You are not happy.'

It was not a question.

She stared back at him, trying to muster a show of defiance to conceal her shame. 'You have no right to say that.'

'I have every right,' he said. He leant across the table to wipe the tears from her cheeks but there were many tears and he could not.

'I betrayed you,' she said.

'We betrayed each other.'

'How can you say that?'

'I shouldn't have let you walk away. I should have stopped you.'

The hint of a smile like sunlight through cloud. 'How could you do that?'

'I should have forced you. Dragged you by the hair, if I had to.'

'Dear Martin…' Impulsively she leant forwards and covered his hands with her own. 'That might have been a bit painful.'

'No more painful than it was anyway.'

Which was true.

'But what's the point of talking about it?' she said. 'It's too late. And I have a husband.'

Whom it would not do to underestimate.

'Of course it's too late to talk.'

Jennifer was taken aback; she had not expected him to agree so readily. But Martin had not finished.

'Too late to talk. Now we have to act.'

'Act?' She stared.

'You don't think I'll let you get away again?'

Jennifer unable to speak, knowing he was right.

'I have a boat,' Martin said. 'You know anything about boats?'

Jennifer was stunned by the suddenness of it all, as though all decisions had been taken away from her.

'Boats? No. I have never –'

'Then now is the time to learn.'

2

Jennifer Lander lay on the cushioned berth in the cabin of the little sailing boat, listening to the sound of the water against the hull, feeling the movement as the tightly drawn sails propelled them over the waters of Port Phillip Bay, and watching the reflections of sunlight flowing across the white-painted deck over her head. She was thirty-six no longer. She was plump and middle-aged no longer. She was twenty-two and reed-slim and knew with absolute certainty that none of this could be happening to her.

I am not that type of woman, she told herself. I am not. Yet mingled with incredulity was the warmth and joy of knowing that what had happened had indeed happened and that when the opportunity came she would do it again, do it gladly. At that moment she cared about nothing else, neither Davis nor what her friends – friends? – might say. Nothing else mattered but this, this, this.

I am willing to be his slave, she thought. Oh I love him. I did before, all those years ago, yet somehow never realised until now what I had been missing in my life. She thought of herself when she had really been twenty-two years old. I was such a fool.

3

She saw him at a party. She turned to Katie Barnes, the girlfriend with whom she was staying.

'Who is that?'

'Which one?'

'The tall man in the corner. The one with the beard and the blonde girl in tow.'

Katie looked. She laughed. 'You've certainly got an eye for an alpha male. That is Martin Gulliver.'

She spoke as though the world knew his name but Jennifer had never heard of him. 'Who is Martin Gulliver?'

'He's an artist. He is also the original devil on horseback.' She laughed. 'That's why all the girls want to eat him up.'

'And do they?'

'Some do, some don't.'

'Did you?'

Katie laughed. 'That would be telling.' She took Jennifer's hand. 'Come and meet him.'

Panic stirred. 'No. Leave it.'

'Up to you.'

'Leave it.'

That was the start of it. Two days later he turned up on Katie's doorstep. Up close Martin Gulliver was as tall as a tower, with broad shoulders and an exuberant air that took Jennifer's breath away. Before they had exchanged a word she already knew she had never met anyone like him.

He asked her out and she couldn't wait. She was stifled with shyness, wondering why on earth a man like this should seek her out, thankful only that he had.

'Painting is my life,' he said and that was fine.

He took her first to an art gallery and then back to his room, where he had paintings all over the place, framed and unframed, on the walls and on the floor. The room looked as though it had not seen a broom or duster in years, and that was fine too.

So this was how bohemians lived, she thought, and supposed you could get used even to that, if you had to. He undid her dress and kissed her breasts which no one had ever done and the unexpected sensation swept her like a tidal wave. She let him go no further and thought she'd blown it but she hadn't and they became an item, improbable but accepted by his friends. She knew they assumed they must be sleeping together. It would have embarrassed her once but she found she didn't care what anyone thought, knowing herself, startlingly, to be in love.

4

He took her to more art galleries and exhibitions, showed her paintings by El Greco (weird), Turner (disturbing) and Nicholson (incomprehensible); through him she met other artists and would-be artists, writers and would-be writers.

Yet, Martin apart, it was an environment where she knew she would never be at home. Her longing for respectability was undiminished and respectability was sadly lacking in Martin's life. Her feelings for him remained strong, at least for the time being, but she told herself there could be no long-term future in what for her was an alien world.

Martin told her he was planning a painting trip into the Outback. 'Come with me.'

She gasped, a pulse leaping savagely *down there* when he said it and when he told her about the countryside, harsh, unforgiving and beautiful, the red and green palette of the earth, the mulga scrub, the polished gibber plains flowing like a grey tide, the distant promise of Lake Eyre white as salt beneath an unforgiving sun. The way he spoke made her ache to see it but scared her too. She was frightened of going with him into that landscape, of committing herself to the flame of a relationship that she was uncertain she could handle, this man who might plumb her soul. She wanted safety and knew that with Martin Gulliver, an unknown artist with not a penny to his name, there was no safety to be had.

5

Today she had gone out with him in his sloop and sailed to the far side of Port Phillip Bay, where they had anchored and gone ashore and eaten lunch at a hotel with old-fashioned furnishings, thoroughly delightful, and afterwards had returned on a dying breeze. When they were well offshore but still clear of the main shipping lane they had hove to and made love again. Already she had lost count of the number of times it had happened. Now they were under way again, the breeze had picked up and soon she would be going back to the house and a life that was no longer real to her.

What was to become of her she did not know, nor did she think about it. For the moment the present was everything. She was someone whose life had been a desert but had now become miraculously rich and green and that was enough.

Careless of observers, open to love and life as never before, she went up naked into the cockpit and sat at Martin's side. He smiled at her but made no comment. The sun was strong and she felt it biting into her white shoulders. She looked at his arm, brown and muscled, at the fingers holding the tiller, and there was a quiver deep inside her.

Insatiable, she thought with pleasure. That's me. She quaked with hidden laughter. The sunlight, falling upon her naked body, was full of joy.

She thought of Mother – she had never felt comfortable calling her Hilary – and of Sara who had phoned the previous night to say she was leaving for Hong Kong. 'I wanted to know if there was anything you'd like me to buy for you while I'm over there.'

She hadn't been able to think of a thing but was interested by Sara's news. 'How exciting. A holiday or is Channel 12 sending you?'

'Mother is sending me over there with Martha Tan. It'll be a long way from being a holiday, I fear.'

They had never really got on – she had always thought Sara hard – but felt more kindly towards her at the moment. 'I hope you have a good time and don't work too much.'

Sara had laughed and that had been the end of it. Now, in the middle of Port Phillip Bay, Jennifer wondered what Mother and Sara would make of her new relationship, if they ever found out about it. Mother would be pleased; she had never had any time for

Davis. She hoped Sara might approve as well; she had discovered they had more in common than she had suspected. Like herself and everyone else, she thought, Sara was looking for fulfilment.

'The only difference is,' she said aloud, 'is that now I have found it.'

Although God alone knew how it would work out.

Martin glanced at her but said nothing and she did not explain. Warmed by sunlight and by love, Jennifer smiled.

RAIDING PARTY

1

On its approach to Chek Lap Kok international airport the Airbus flew over the crowded streets of what Martha, pointing over her shoulder, told Sara was Kowloon, the scarcely less crowded ones of the island with the harbour between them shining like a golden shield in the afternoon sunlight.

Sara stared down at the forest of concrete and steel that was the high-rise buildings of Hong Kong and turned to her companion. 'You were telling me Brand Corporation has been involved in some of the construction work in Hong Kong?'

'As member of various local consortiums, yes. It would have been considered inappropriate to give a western company a contract to build a complete building.'

'Too colonial?'

'As you say. The local businessmen would have been unhappy too which could have made difficulties for the government. The logistics might have caused problems as well. We would have had to open our own office here, with staff to supervise, and that would have been very expensive.'

The steward came. 'Make ready for landing, ladies. If you please.'

They raised the backs of their seats, checked their seat belts were fastened and sat waiting as the engine sound died to a whisper. They barely felt the bump of the wheels hitting the tarmac.

The airport buildings were huge and impressive and Sara, first time in Hong Kong, said so.

'We had a hand in building the terminal also,' Martha said.

'How come?'

'Hilary is a friend of the architect.'

'He did her a favour?'

'Not at all. He was impressed with our work on two high-rise buildings in Happy Valley so suggested we should put in a tender. And we won,' Martha said. 'Also the 2ifc, which is Hong Kong's tallest building. Again contact with the architect helped.'

Typical Hilary, Sara thought. Always going for height.

'Again we were members of a consortium. We couldn't do it all ourselves but our work was the best. Everybody said so. We made nothing on the deal but it opened the door to other opportunities.'

'I trust profitable opportunities?'

'Very profitable,' Martha said contentedly.

They cleared immigration and customs. Martha led the way across the arrivals hall, pushing her way through the mob. 'Hong Kong is a very crowded place. Worse than Singapore.' They reached the automatic doors. The shadows were long and a sneak wind was blowing dust down the street. 'The train, the MTR, is fast and clean,' Martha said. 'But I have arranged a limo.'

'More convenient?'

'Certainly, and more comfortable. But I did it to create a good impression. Image is very important,' Martha said.

'Who are we trying to impress?'

'Everybody,' Martha said.

2

Wary of the driver's ears, neither of them mentioned business until they were in Sara's hotel room, with its spectacular views of Victoria Harbour.

'Remind me how we found out about the Lennoxes,' Sara asked.

'Andrea Chan tipped us off. All being well we shall be meeting her tomorrow.'

'Who is Andrea Chan?'

'The senior assistant at Lennox Brothers. At first she was troubled about betraying her employer but when she found that funds intended for China were being diverted elsewhere she felt it her duty to warn us. It wasn't an easy decision for her.'

'The whole thing was hardly ethical,' Sara said. 'Paying these guys to bribe Chinese officials.'

Martha shrugged. 'That's business. Quite simply, we have no choice.'

'And now?'

'Now we are here to find out where the money has gone.'

'So what do we do about it?'

'First we meet with Andrea Chan. We need to discuss the situation with her. Then we can decide what to do.'

'When are we meeting her?'

'I hope tomorrow.'

'You hope? Is nothing arranged?'

'Her time isn't her own. She works for them, remember. There is a Chinese saying: a suspicious man is a dangerous man. When I spoke to her on the telephone two days ago she sounded frightened. It is most important we fit in with her timetable or it could mean bad trouble for her.'

'She might lose her job?'

'Her job is nothing. What I am thinking about is her life.'

Sara was taken aback. 'You're saying they might harm her?'

'Of course. We are talking millions of dollars. In this city people have been murdered for much less.'

That was certainly something to chew on. 'So we are in her hands.'

'Absolutely.'

'What do we do in the meantime?'

'We wait. She has my mobile phone number. Today, maybe tomorrow, she will phone. In the meantime I'll take you shopping. Hong Kong is great for that. And we'll be meeting important people later in the week. Very influential men, so we need to be properly dressed. That way we honour them and ourselves at the same time.'

'What sort of thing should we wear?'

'I'll help you with that,' Martha Tan said.

3

They went to the Pedder Building, to the world-famous establishment called Shanghai Tang.

It was spread over two floors and Aladdin's cave wasn't in it – if you supposed Aladdin to have been Chinese – with brocade-covered walls, red lacquer cabinets and a long table that Martha said was made from huanghuali, the wood of the flowering pear.

'Very rare,' Martha said. 'Very pricey.'

Across the table were draped deceptively casual displays of silks, linens and cashmere, all in the vibrant colours Martha said were the hallmark of Shanghai Tang.

Sara looked doubtfully at a tangerine-coloured cheongsam on a stand. 'I am not sure Chinese clothes go on a westerner.'

'I certainly wouldn't recommend a cheongsam,' Martha said. 'But you are slim and will be suited by other clothes from this designer, elegant clothes that you will be able to carry very well.'

By the time they left they had ordered two dresses each, silk lined, for evening wear. All were in vibrant shades of rose-red and blue and patterned with chrysanthemums, two with short sleeves and two sleeveless. All had high collars.

'Very good choices,' Martha said. 'These dresses are made in the style they call qipao. And the chrysanthemum is traditionally a good luck flower also.'

Sara also ordered two pairs of pants, two blouses and three dresses for daytime use. Martha bought a light summer coat, green cotton and embroidered with silk peonies. Everything would be delivered to the hotel by the following evening.

The store manager herself came to bid them a ceremonial good-bye, smiling and bowing at the door.

'So she should, the money we've spent,' Sara said. 'If we'd stayed much longer we'd have bankrupted the company.'

As it was Eagle Eye would probably have a heart attack when he saw the bill but had Martha not told her they would be meeting influential people whom they would have to impress? Eagle Eye could take a hike.

They ate in the hotel that night.

'What food would you like?' Martha said. 'Western or Cantonese?'

'I think Cantonese,' Sara said. 'When in China…'

'I agree absolutely,' Martha said. 'You want me to order?'

They had the food sent up from the restaurant: pan-fried bird's nest and crispy eel in cinnamon flowers, with sugar peas and Chinese spinach in a garlic sauce. And rice.

'There's always rice in Cantonese cooking,' Martha said.

'You want wine?' Sara asked, then looked at the wine list. 'My God!'

'Import tax makes the prices too much,' Martha said. 'Maybe we should stick to jasmine tea.'

'I would say you're right,' Sara said.

'How are you enjoying the food?'

'The food is exquisite,' said Sara, her chopsticks snaking out to claim another piece of the delicious eel.

She wondered whether Andrea Chan would contact them in the morning. She thought about the risk the Chinese woman was running. Sara had always known you had to be tough in business but the thought of people putting their lives on the line had never occurred to her. I pray she is safe, she thought.

They were getting ready for bed when Martha's telephone rang.

4

'I have to go out,' Martha said.

'At this hour?'

'No need to trouble yourself. I'll go alone.'

'No you won't,' Sara said. 'What's going on? Who was that on the phone?'

'That was Andrea Chan.'

'She is not in any trouble?'

'No, no.'

'Then tell me.'

'She wants to see me.'

'Tonight?'

'Tonight.'

Hilary had put Martha in charge on this trip and Sara had been happy about it. She also understood that Martha wished to protect her boss's daughter, but there were limits. They looked at each other and Sara's eyes were steady.

'We came together. We go together.'

'You'd better put on the clothes you travelled in, then. Where we're going is no place for smart clothes.'

'And where is that?'

'You'll see.'

Rain was misting down when they left the hotel and the streets were shining. Behind them the tower was brilliant with lights which were repeated all the way along Harbour Road. Vessels in the harbour were also lit up while the Kowloon shore was gaudy with neon, red and blue and gold. Cars hooted as they followed each other down streets that formed golden tunnels between the dark shapes of office buildings. Somewhere music blared from a karaoke bar.

Ignoring the rain Martha turned right and set out along Harbour Road. After a hundred yards she turned into a narrow street, then again into another, even narrower, one. Soon the glitter of Harbour Road was behind them. Here the moist air created haloes of light about the street lamps. Another turning led into a narrow lane. Shabby buildings crowded hunch-shouldered on either side. The lane was rutted, water shining in puddles: this was a different world from the luxurious hotels not fifteen minutes' walk away, or the bright lights and jam-packed markets of Kowloon. Martha pressed on purposefully but Sara, lacking any previous knowledge of the city, had lost her sense of direction by the time they arrived at a tiny dilapidated house, little more than a hut, with a single light burning in the window. The stink of waste, animal and human, tainted the air.

Martha stopped. Eyes alert, she turned her head as she stared around and behind her. Sara did the same. The lane, thick with shadows, seemed deserted, yet Sara sensed the night was full of eyes.

Martha knocked on the door of the hut. At once it opened. After the darkness of the lane the light from the kerosene lantern was dazzling. A hand gestured urgently. They went in and the door closed behind them.

The tiny room was sparsely furnished and redolent of cooking oil and garlic. In one corner an old Chinese woman sat in a bamboo chair, her wrinkled face a yellow skull, her slanted eyes cloudy with cataracts. She did not move and seemed unaware of the newcomers' arrival.

The woman who had let them in was very different. About twenty-five, Sara judged, and smartly dressed, she seemed out of place in what was little more than a hovel.

A rattle of Chinese as Martha and the young woman spoke to each other.

Martha turned to Sara. 'This is Andrea Chan,' she said. 'She say she has a flat on the Kowloon side but asked to meet here, at her aunt's place, so there will be less danger of anyone seeing us together.'

'Less danger?' Sara said. 'Not no danger?'

'No one can give one hundred per cent guarantee.'

Sara spoke to Andrea Chan in English. 'I believe you have cautioned us about the activities of your employers. That must have been very difficult for you and we are truly grateful.'

'Nothing,' Andrea said and then turned to Martha, speaking once again in Cantonese. Sara, watching, saw that her lips were trembling. Martha had been right; the young woman was frightened.

'She thinks her bosses are watching her,' Martha translated. She turned back to Andrea Chan. 'Better we speak English,' she commanded.

'Of course. I am sorry.'

'Tell her what you just told me,' Martha said.

'There are bank statements in Lennox offices showing where money has gone,' Andrea said. 'Both Hong Kong and Channel Islands banks. These will provide proof of what has happened to your funds.'

'Then we need to get hold of them,' Sara said.

'Of course. But copying so many statements impossible during office hours. Can be done only at night.'

'You have keys to the offices?'

'Have.'

'So what are you suggesting?'

'We drive there now. You leave me there. Do not wait outside or police may notice and ask questions. Half an hour later you come back. By then I shall have copied all the statements.'

'There will be nobody else there at this hour?'

'There should not be. I hope not.'

'Security? Alarm systems?'

Andrea shook her head but her lower lip was caught in her teeth, her hands were shaking and Sara saw that she was not happy at all.

'Are you certain you want to do this?'

'Only way. I have car. We drive there now. You leave me there, come back in one half-hour, I shall be waiting.'

'Good,' Martha said. 'We agree.'

'No,' Sara said.

The two women looked at her.

'No?' Martha said.

'It is too dangerous.'

'How dangerous, if nobody else is there?'

'You told me Andrea thinks they may suspect her. You said your-self that a suspicious man is a dangerous man. How can we be sure no one is watching us now? What happens if her bosses turn up while she is copying the statements? What do you think they will do to her?'

'Then what do you suggest?'

'I go in with her.'

'Impossible!'

'Not impossible at all,' Sara said. Her certainty was a warm tide. 'It is the only way of ensuring her safety.' She turned to look at Andrea. 'As a citizen of Hong Kong you are more vulnerable. My mother is one of the richest and most powerful women in Australia. She also has influence in Asia. I do not believe they would dare harm us physically if I am with you while you are doing this.'

'Too risky,' Martha said in a decided voice.

'Too risky for me but not for Andrea?'

They stared challengingly at each other for what seemed a full minute before Martha gave ground.

'Then maybe we should all go.'

'Somebody has to look after the car,' Sara said.

'I do not like it,' Martha said.

'None of us likes it,' Sara said. 'But that's the way it has to be.'

5

The building housing the Lennox Brothers offices was dark.

Martha looked at them from the car. 'Half an hour,' she said.

Sara checked her watch. It was five past eleven. 'Agreed.'

The rain was heavier now. The two women watched the car drive away then turned to the building. Andrea Chan produced a key and unlocked the door. Sara's nerves were as tight as wire as she waited for the clamour of an alarm but there was nothing. They stepped inside and Andrea locked the door behind them. The foyer, marble-floored, was a vastness of silence in which their feet echoed like gunfire. Shadows hung dark. Sara listened but all was still. They walked to the bank of lifts and Andrea pressed the call button. The sound of the descending lift was gigantic in the stillness. The lift door opened. They stepped inside; Andrea pressed the button for the fourteenth floor. The lift door closed and the cage swept them skywards.

Sara looked at Andrea. The Chinese woman was beautiful, her ivory skin unblemished. She looked calm now but Sara felt sick with tension.

The lift sighed to a stop. The door opened. They stepped out into darkness. Andrea had brought a torch; they walked down a corridor to the end suite of offices with a glass-panelled door. *Lennox Brothers and Associates.*

Andrea sorted through her keys.

The silence pressed about them and Sara's skin was clammy with sweat.

Come on, come on…

The lock clicked and Andrea opened the door. Sara held her breath. Again there was no alarm.

'Wait here!'

Sara obeyed. Close to running, Andrea went swiftly to a bank of monitors behind a reception desk and pressed a series of switches before coming back. All smiles now.

'OK. I have switched off the alarm.'

She locked the office door. She did not switch on any lights but, guided by the torch, walked confidently into an office that opened off the reception area.

Sara went to follow her then stopped abruptly, blood curdling, as she heard the whir and sigh of a lift moving in what they had thought was an empty building.

1967

AN END AND A BEGINNING

It was a do or die effort, the only way Hilary could think of saving her marriage. With the first shopping mall nearing completion and a hundred other ideas on the drawing board the timing was diabolical but it couldn't be helped. If she didn't do something *now* it would be too late because Sean, backed by an increasingly ferocious Mrs Madigan, had had enough.

Hilary didn't discuss her plan with Sean but did it anyway. Sex had become a rarity between them but she had always been able to get him going when she was in the mood and did so now. And again the following night.

Sean didn't know what was going on. 'Something got into you?' he asked.

'Other than you, you mean?' She smiled. 'No such luck.'

But two months later she had news for him.

'A baby?' Sean said. 'You sure?'

'Aren't you pleased?'

Because although she'd been putting it off for years, although she supposed she'd cheated him by not telling him she'd stopped taking precautions, it was still important that Sean should be pleased about it. Unfortunately the way he reacted made it hard to tell whether he was pleased or not.

'I'd stopped thinking about it, tell you the truth.'

'You can start thinking about it now,' Hilary said.

While Mrs Madigan – who had been bitching for years about the absence of a grandchild – now complained even more bitterly, wouldn't you know it, how Hilary had trapped her darling son all over again.

For the first few months it made no observable difference to Hilary's life at all. She still wrote deals at every opportunity. She drove up and down the coastal strip, north and south of Perth, tying up blocks of land for more development, sweet-talking councils, making deals with builders, never forgetting the new shopping malls that she and Haskins Gould had inked in for all the major towns. She still climbed the scaffolding to check on the progress of their first mall: she had promised the bank six months and it was important they kept to the timetable. Haskins climbed with her, which was unsurprising because Haskins was everywhere, gesticulating, running, above all yelling.

'Get moving – I got a deadline even if you haven't! You wanna be paid, you got to work. OK? So get with it!'

She looked down at what seemed chaos: the air thick with dust with electricians and cables everywhere, plumbers and labourers having to hop over wires waiting to be embedded in the walls, everywhere the roar of drills and voices, the clatter of hammers.

'Those wires… They're not live, are they?' Hilary said.

'Some clown trips over them we'll soon know,' Haskins said.

He couldn't have cared less and Hilary saw what she had already known, that he was not a man to worry about such things.

'And we'll have the unions on our back.'

'Not a chance. Every man jack on this site is self-employed. I spelt it out from the beginning. You want a union, go someplace else. This is a non-union shop.'

'And?'

'And there they are. We pay the best and we'll get the best or I'll know the reason why.' He leapt forwards, clutching the scaffolding by one hand, the other waving frantically. 'Carry it, you lazy bastards! Don't drag it!' A foghorn voice from a giant man. He returned to Hilary's side. 'Jesus!' he said.

'Every construction site I've been on,' Hilary said, 'they've brought in one group of tradesmen and then another. That way there's less confusion.'

'It also takes a hell of a lot longer.'

'How can you keep track of what's going on?'

'Like I told you, I done this sort of thing a dozen times before.'

And, once again, he started yelling.

Haskins's antics were unrelenting but they worked. The mall went up like Jack climbing the beanstalk, the giant at the top being the question that repeated itself endlessly in Hilary's nightmares. Would the shopkeepers buy the concept? She had held endless meetings and most had sounded cautiously interested but words were cheap and so far no one had signed up. Without shops the project was nowhere but everyone was waiting for someone else to take a lead. Hilary sat down with representatives of two major supermarket chains, trying to talk one or other of them into leasing a big chunk of the ground floor, but it was the same story: neither was willing to take the lead, and without a major store being involved the smaller shops would not commit either.

And time, as the bank kept saying, was running out.

'We need action and we need it fast,' said Haskins Gould.

Hilary had kept him out of the talks, afraid his abrasive manner might scare not only the bank but potential tenants. She still wanted it that way but welcomed his input too. 'How did you handle this type of situation in the States?'

'We put sugar on the table.'

'Meaning?'

'We got to offer them something they can't refuse. We tell the big boys we'll discount their rent by fifty per cent for the first twelve months of a five-year lease and twenty-five per cent for the second year but only if they sign up within a couple of weeks. If they ask can they afford it, you say can they afford to be left out of what is going to be the way of shopping for years to come. Those guys will have done their homework. They'll know it worked in the States and will work here. Offer them a discount like that and they'll bite. Tie one of those guys up, the sheep will follow. And if you can get a big name to open the mall when it's ready it'll be us for the stratosphere, baby.'

First things first. Hilary followed Gould's advice and went back to the two big boys, talking discounts, and signed up one of them within a week. The other crowd were miffed at missing out but she told them there'd be plenty of other opportunities since plans for the building of shopping malls were being finalised – *as we speak!* – in every major population centre in the state. A lie but it tended to focus the negotiator's mind.

'On the same terms?'

The men in suits spoke as though that was a reasonable assumption but Hilary laughed. 'That was a once-in-a-lifetime opportunity. Next time it'll be the going rate.'

They didn't like it? Tough.

'The mall has to have a name,' Hilary said to Haskins Gould. 'What are we going to call it?'

'The first one in the state?' Haskins said. 'Maybe the Virgin Centre.'

With Haskins it was hard to know when he was being serious and when he wasn't.

'I doubt that would go down well,' Hilary said.

'I don't know. I know guys who'd pay a big premium to get their hands on a real virgin.'

'Don't they have enough troubles in their lives without that?' she said.

'On the other hand,' he said, 'belly like yours, I guess you don't look that virginal.'

Sometimes he was just begging for a poke in the puss, as she'd heard a Yank say once. 'There is a precedent,' she reminded him.

'I'd say one virgin birth is enough,' Haskins said. 'In any case I'm Jewish, if you've forgotten.'

'So was she.'

They settled on calling it the Majestic Plaza.

'You know anyone who's high profile?' Hilary asked Dave.

'The state premier's chairman of our footy club.'

'If we guarantee him lots of favourable publicity, you reckon he'll open Majestic?'

'Is the Pope a Catholic?'

MOVING ON

1

The Majestic Mall was nearing completion. Now what Haskins Gould called the tarting-up process had begun, the process by which, he said, they would turn a shed into a palace.

'Flowers, chandeliers and sweet background music turned real low but audible, you know?' he told Hilary. 'Classy restrooms. And clean, real clean. We got to make the ladies think it's a privilege to step inside the door. Make love to them, right? Put them in the mood to spend big. That way everyone's happy.'

Hilary went along with what he was saying but for the moment had other things on her mind. She was out to there by now and any thought of scrambling around on scaffolding was long gone.

'It gets much bigger I think I may burst,' she told Sean who, as usual, carried the tale home to Mummy when they next visited the old hag.

'Such a fuss,' Mrs Madigan told her husband. 'You'd think no one had had a baby before. I had four and you never heard me complaining.'

Watching Mr Madigan's expression Hilary saw he had different memories of those days but wisely kept them to himself. She asked herself what she had done to deserve a mother-in-law like this, gift wrapped from the Evil One. By whom Mrs Madigan set such store.

2

At first the premier had been coy about doing the honours but Hilary wooed him ardently over a slap-up meal courtesy of Brand Peterfield and won him round; Kevin Donnelly had a name for being susceptible to good-looking women and good-tasting wine, although, as Hilary said, she was hardly looking her best at the moment.

'More like Colonel Blimp,' she said.

The premier, charming as only an Irishman could be, denied it. 'You are absolutely beautiful,' he said. 'The epitome of Australian motherhood. Whereabouts in Ireland did you say your ancestors came from?'

'Galway,' Hilary said. A bright smile, fingers and toes crossed tight. 'Or so I am led to believe.'

Liar, liar, pants on fire... But all in a good cause, was it not?

'I only hope I don't pop on the day of the opening,' she said to Haskins.

'Hey, wouldn't that be a great idea?' Haskins said. 'Happen during the premier's speech it'll make the front pages, for sure. Television too, if we're lucky. Maybe you should see if you can arrange it. Jump up and down a few times, why don't you?'

Haskins Gould at his best gave added depth to the word *gross*.

3

In the event Hilary made it but only just. The next day she woke Sean early.

'Here we go,' she said.

A long hard day ran into a long and even harder night. She had been both apprehensive and excited, heading to the hospital with Sean sweating like a pig at her side, but after a few hours apprehension – say rather terror that it would never end – was definitely in the ascendancy.

No wonder they call it labour, she thought, as another contraction threatened to tear her voice from her throat. The hardest bloody labour I've ever done. And to think for every one of the billions of human beings on earth some woman has been through this. God help the female race.

The hours had leaden feet but in time they ceased to have meaning. All that was left was pain: on and on and on.

Jennifer was born at three o'clock in the morning while the world outside the hospital windows was dark.

Sean had been at the hospital for a while but had left after an hour, seeing no point hanging about when nothing seemed to be happening. Happy to have an excuse to take a day off work he'd had a few beers with some mates and later kipped out on the settee. He was asleep when Jennifer was born, too far under to hear the phone, so he knew nothing until he rang, bleary eyed, in the morning.

'A girl?' he told the nurse. 'Well, better than nothing, I suppose.'

And could not understand why the stupid cow was so sniffy about what had only been a joke. However, it was a joke he did not repeat to anyone else.

Mrs Madigan paid a call on her daughter-in-law later in the day; no one was going to accuse her of failing to do her duty.

'Looks a bit peaky to me,' she told the new mother. 'You sure there's nothing wrong with her?'

Hilary closed her eyes to shut the old bat out, thinking how you could always rely on Mrs Madigan to come up trumps, whatever the situation. She'll be the best most beautiful most intelligent child in the whole world, Mrs Madigan. So there.

And cuddled the baby close, her overflowing heart warming her like a fire.

Did my mother ever do this to me? Hilary wondered.

4

She certainly had a pair of lungs on her. The way she bellowed, Hilary decided she could hire her out for foghorn duties at a lighthouse. It was also true that having a baby in tow was a complication.

A baby's yelling could be a big turn off when it came to buying or selling a block of land but there was no help for it.

'Now if I were an old-time British aristocrat,' she told Sandy Peterfield, 'I'd have a wet nurse on tap.'

On tap was right; the way Jennifer went at them Hilary began to wonder if she'd have any nipples left by the time she was through. She told Sean so.

'Don't say that,' he said.

Sean had always had a tender spot for Hilary's nipples but the marriage was on the skids and both of them knew it. They didn't talk about it but Mrs Madigan, eyes like a vulture, said it for them. Only to her son – after her remarks about the baby she and Hilary were barely on speaking terms – but she said it.

'A judgment, that's what I call it. It's not as though you was ever properly married anyway.'

She introduced him to Jane Doyle, a nineteen-year-old with an interesting bosom and teeth, mostly nice if you didn't look at them too closely, who sang in the St Ignatius church choir. An Irish Catholic and a fresh young chick: what was there not to like about that?

Sean and Hilary hung on for almost another two years but Jennifer's second birthday was the last straw. Sean failed to appear at the tiny tots party Hilary and Sandy had organised and Hilary later learnt he'd been attending choir practice with Jane Doyle. With Sean's voice if anything worse than hers, it wasn't hard to figure out what that meant.

That night she told Sean she was leaving him and taking Jennifer with her. She knew it was mainly her fault; she worked all the hours God gave and even when she was home it was the same story. A partner should be more than just a sexual object and in the companionship stakes she'd fallen down badly. No wonder Sean had come to feel neglected, but she did not know what she could have done about it. Chalk and cheese, she thought. That's the problem. She'd had such hopes but it seemed even love could fail.

'I'm sorry about it,' she said. 'It doesn't seem possible for a woman to have a career and a marriage.'

'And with you the career has always come first,' said Sean.

She looked at him helplessly, her bags packed and in the car. Sean's nose was out of joint but that was nothing compared with his mother. The day after Hilary and Jennifer had moved into their new flat Mrs Madigan was on the doorstep and Mrs Madigan was in a right old rage.

'Even now you got to do things back to front,' she said.

In Mrs Madigan's book the man made the moves and the woman followed, but it was a book Hilary had never read.

'I am sorry about it,' Hilary said, repeating what she had told Sean. It was true but didn't help.

There were nights when she asked herself where she was going in her life. She knew she was different from most people. Normally it didn't trouble her but now it did. The darkness pressed upon her and there were tears. Her sense of failure was so strong that she feared it would never ease. It was no use saying it was for the best, she thought, even though it was.

A property deal went sour and Hilary knew it was her fault; distracted by her marriage problems she had misjudged the situation. It cost them: not a lot, thankfully, but it was still a blow to the heart. She had an intense hatred of failure in any form and now she'd had two in a row.

'We all put up a blue occasionally,' Dave told her.

It was no consolation. *I will not fail; I must not fail.* It had been her mantra ever since she broke up with Jack Almond. Life was an egg; she had a superstition she would not admit even to herself that the smallest failure could open a crack in the shell leading to ruin. A crack in the teacup… Auden had written a poem about that, hadn't he?

5

She knew she must get on with her life but it wasn't as easy as she'd expected. It was strange; she was the one who had decided to move out yet now she felt she'd been blown off course. Maybe it was the baby, she thought, but immediately felt guilty for thinking it. Of course it was not Jennifer; she hugged her until she squeaked. Jennifer was perfect. No, it was something in her. Whatever it was, the new house was not just unfamiliar; it felt alien. Yet two months later an unexpected phone call poured refreshment on what had been a parched land.

It was eight o'clock at night. The day had not gone well and Hilary was tired and out of sorts. She had been contemplating a long bath in hot scented water and the last thing she needed was to be badgered by intrusive phone calls at this time of the evening.

She snatched up the receiver. 'Yes?'

A man's voice. 'I heard on the grapevine that you and your husband have separated. Is that right?'

She couldn't believe she was hearing this. 'And you are?'

'Lance Bettinger.'

She could not place the name. 'Do I know you?'

'We met in the Lands Office. You were checking on a parcel of land with drainage problems?'

Now she remembered: dark hair and grey eyes, a pleasant man a few years older than she was. He had been very helpful and she had thanked him by letting him have one of the blocks at a dirt cheap price. An attractive man. Her spine, which had been rigid with indignation, relaxed.

'Of course I remember you. What can I do for you?'

'I was wondering if you'd be free to have a drink with me?'

'Tonight?'

'That was my idea.'

Why couldn't he have phoned earlier? She remembered him very well now and going out for a drink with him might have given her just the fillip she needed. 'I can't manage it tonight. I have a young baby and no babysitter and it's too late to arrange someone now.'

She let the words hang out there, hoping he would suggest another time, but he didn't.

'No worries,' he said cheerfully. And rang off.

'Damn and blast,' she told the empty room as she replaced the receiver. 'Very damn and very blast.'

Now she felt worse than ever. Maybe the bath she'd promised herself would revive her spirits. She went into the bathroom, slopped in half a pint of bath lotion – divinely scented but ultra pricey – and turned the taps on full. Steam gushed. She checked on Jennifer – sleeping – went into the bedroom and started taking off her clothes.

The doorbell rang.

Now what?

She was down to pants and bra. She dragged a dressing gown over them and went to answer the door.

'I hope you like red wine,' Lance Bettinger said.

6

A week later Lance turned up out of the blue. She thought he might be lonely so invited him in. They sat in the living room, drank a decorous cup of tea while he talked about birds.

'Into bird watching, are you?' she said.

'Certainly am. Both types. And you?'

'Maybe the ones with feathers.' Truth was she had never thought about it.

'Come spring I like to get out to Rottnest Island. A great place for birds, Rottnest.'

'Plenty there?'

'Stacks of them: curlew sandpipers and dozens of others.'

The name meant nothing to her. 'And these curlew sandpipers are special?'

'You could say so. They're tiny creatures, yet every year they migrate here all the way from Siberia.'

'Why would they do that?'

'Nobody knows.'

Rottnest was not just birds, he said; there were lots of beaches too, and places to eat. Bike tracks: everyone rode bikes because vehicles weren't allowed. You could go swimming.

'Christmas there are stacks of visitors but this time of year it's almost deserted. Only a hundred or so people live there full time so you can have the beaches to yourself. They have quokkas too.'

'Quokkas?'

'Marsupials about the size of cats. Look a bit like kangaroos.'

'Are they special too?'

'About the only place in the world you'll see them. On the mainland cats and foxes have almost wiped them out. They can climb trees.'

A kangaroo in a tree would be something to see.

'How do you get there?'

'Ferry takes half an hour. You could come with me if you were interested.'

'That would be nice.'

'I'll give you a hoy,' he said.

After he had gone she sat and thought. Lance was interesting and pleasant to be with; she thought she could come to fancy him quite a lot. Unfortunately that would be asking for trouble. She had drummed up the courage to ask and he had told her yes, he was married.

'But we broke up six months ago.'

Perhaps, but it was still dangerous territory.

'Will you and your wife be getting together again?'

'No chance.' He said between one day and the next she'd upped sticks and left him. 'No notice, no discussion. She's in north Queensland now.'

'What's she doing there?'

'Living with some cane farmer. They met when he was over for a conference. First thing I knew about it she'd moved out and taken the kids with her.'

'How many have you got?'

Three, he told her: Debbie, aged nine; Charlie seven and Michael, just six.

'You miss them?'

'Very much.'

'It must have been quite a shock. You getting a divorce?'

'We haven't discussed it.'

'Because you can, can't you, after you've been separated a year?'

'Why should I make it easy for her to marry him?'

'Is that what she wants?'

'Maybe. I don't know.'

'Have you asked her?'

Silence.

Dangerous ground indeed but Hilary was reluctant to leave it there. 'Would you take her back if she wanted?'

'After what's she done? Never!'

It was crazy to get involved with him. Yet she did not care. Lance was there now; her feelings for him were now. She would settle for that. The alarm bells could ring as much as they liked; she would not listen.

On the way to inspect a site the next day she thought about it some more. Rebounds from failed relationships, from what she'd heard, mostly ended in disaster. Hopefully not this time but that was all you could say: there was no certainty.

In the meantime Lance had his work at the Lands Office. It was a nine to five job with no earth-shaking future but it suited him. He wasn't ambitious but Hilary's life was a whirlwind.

The lawyers were carrying out the funeral rites of her failed marriage; business and Jennifer were her only concerns now and business was booming. They'd finished their second mall and were well ahead with number three. They had housing developments under way; the meetings with councils and town planners seemed endless. They had employed more staff; Sandy had an assistant now and they'd taken on a couple of draughtsmen and a young woman to give them a hand. They were thinking of employing an architect. Hilary had thirty hours work to get through in every twenty-four but she thrived on it. She and Haskins were twin dynamos; the work was rolling in and the money. They had the world at their feet. The pain of the marriage break-up was mostly behind her and she told herself she was happy.

Jennifer was thriving too. A young woman called Agnes came in every day to look after her when Hilary was at work – to take her with her all the time was impossible – but she was determined not to be one of those women who neglected their children because of their jobs. It took a bit of juggling but she made a point of walking Jennifer in her pushchair every day. Exercise as well as time with her daughter: what was there not to like about that?

Jennifer was a remarkably pretty child. When Hilary did her shopping at the Majestic Plaza – where else? she said to Lance – she always took the child with her and it delighted her how many passers-by, complete strangers, complimented her on Jennifer's looks. Her pretty daughter's existence filled her heart. Surely that should be enough?

What did she need with additional complications in her life? With a married man called Lance Bettinger?

2004

BURGLARS GO TO GAOL

Sara and Andrea stared at each other. The sound of the approaching lift filled the silence. For a moment shock froze them, then Sara came to life in a rush.

'We're burglars: if they catch us they'll put us in gaol! We must hide. Quick!'

Andrea's slant eyes were as round as moons. For an instant she did not react.

The whine of the lift was very loud now.

Sara grabbed her, shaking. 'Where can we hide?'

Andrea came to life. 'In here.'

She grabbed Sara's hand and ran, Sara stumbling after her. There was a small kitchen with toilets beyond.

'In here.'

They crowded into the cubicle and pushed the door to. Breath was in short supply now. They stared at each other, listening. Now the lift was silent. There was no other sound.

A sign was hanging from a hook above the toilet cistern.

OUT OF ORDER

Sara took it down and looked questioningly at the other girl. Who nodded. Sara listened to the silence. She inched open the door, propped the sign open on the tiled floor and closed the door again. Carefully she shot the bolt. They waited, listening.

For what seemed a long time Sara heard nothing. Then came the sound of a telephone lifting; a man's voice.

'Charlie Lennox,' Andrea whispered.

'I came into the office to get some papers and found the security system had been switched off.'

The two women stared at each other in horror.

'The thunderstorm? So if I reset it when I leave it'll be OK? I'll do that then. But maybe you could send someone round to check? Just in case. That's fine.'

The phone went down. There came the sound of a man humming.

Stop messing about, Sara implored him silently. For God's sake… If the security men arrived while they were still there…

Terror renewed itself as they heard the sound of heels approaching on the tiled floor. The sound of Charlie Lennox relieving himself. The gush of a tap as he washed his hands. He went out and a minute later they heard the click of the outer door followed by the sound of the lift going down. Relief made Sara weak. Only now did she realise how she and Andrea had been clutching each other's hands so tightly that it was hard to separate them.

'Let's get out of here,' Andrea whispered.

'Not until we get hold of those papers.'

'We shall have to turn off the alarm again.'

'So let's do it.'

Now they were running. Out of the toilet section, into the office, switch off the alarm, open the desk drawer, grab the file of papers, aware that at any minute the security goons might turn up…

'No time to copy them,' Andrea said.

'Take the whole file,' Sara said.

Andrea opened the door, Sara waiting outside as she reactivated the alarm system. She came out in a rush and locked the door behind her. The two of them turned to summon the lift when they once again heard it on the move. Mesmerised, they watched the winking lights as the monitor above the lift gate charted its progress up the shaft.

If we get out of this place alive it'll be a miracle, Sara thought.

Andrea was breathing fast. 'Down the stairs,' she said.

Their heels echoed in the stairwell as they ran down to the next level. They waited, once again holding hands, until they heard the lift sigh to a stop on the floor above them. The security detail had arrived.

'We'd better get moving,' Sara whispered. 'They've only got to come down one flight...'

No need to finish the sentence.

'They'll hear the lift.'

'We'll keep going this way.'

To be as quiet as possible they took off their shoes and continued down the endless-seeming staircase, bare feet soundless on the cement, until they reached the ground level and the exit into the lobby. Sara opened the door an inch and looked cautiously out. Nothing.

'All clear,' she said.

Andrea unlocked the outer door and they went out into the street, the deserted pavements shining with water after the storm. They heard the diminishing sound of an engine as a car sped down a neighbouring street. They looked in both directions but saw nothing. Where was Martha?

'I know a place we can wait,' Andrea said.

They stood in a narrow passage between two high-rise buildings one block down the street. From there they could see the entrance to the building they had just left. As a hiding place it was far from perfect but would probably do.

'How long?' Andrea asked.

'Another ten minutes.'

Charlie Lennox's unexpected arrival had thrown their schedule into chaos. They waited until, with a cataclysmic crash of thunder, the storm returned. Within seconds the world was water as the rain beat down on their unprotected heads.

ANGELS OF RETRIBUTION

1

'Did you get everything we need?' Martha said.

She had picked them up in the midst of the deluge and driven them both to the hotel. They had crept into the foyer before the bemused eyes of the night staff, who were unaccustomed to accepting drowned rats into their five-star establishment.

Martha, the only presentable one of the three, had summoned help in the form of towels to mop up at least some of the wet.

'Otherwise we shall have them dripping all over the lift floor. And we wouldn't want that, would we?'

Now Sara and Andrea were sharing the massive shower and returning inch by slow inch to the civilised beings they had been two hours earlier.

Civilised burglars? Sara thought. Isn't that something of a contradiction?

But who cared, with hot water and perfumed shower gel to help ease away both the chill and trauma of their adventure?

With Andrea wearing clothes borrowed from Sara – 'I've never been able to afford anything like this,' she said – the three of them spent hours going through agreements; statements from banks in Jersey, the Cayman Islands and Liechtenstein; deposit receipts and copies of emails. They examined each one carefully; they discussed them in detail; they filed them in sequence.

At two o'clock in the morning Martha pushed her chair back from the table where they'd been working. 'You have done well. Enough here to hang the Lennoxes from the top of the 2ifc building.'

They lay down for a while; may even have slept if you could call it sleep when Sara found herself, terrified breath and pounding heart, fleeing down the avenues of nightmare from vast and unknowable figures whose outstretched talons reached out to rend her screaming flesh...

Andrea had to get back to Kowloon, change into her office clothes and office face and present herself at the normal hour for a normal day's work, so she left while it was still dark.

'I am feeling sick,' she said and smiled apologetically. 'Nerves...'

It was hardly surprising yet her face, as grave and beautiful as ever, showed nothing of the night's terrors.

2

They weren't the only ones who'd worked late; lights were burning in the Lennox offices, where Charlie and Damian Lennox were looking into the night's alarms.

'I am not happy,' Charlie said. 'Something doesn't smell right.'

Damian was grumpy. He disliked being phoned by his overassertive brother in the small hours, yanked from his bed and ever-charming companion in response to a crisis that was almost certainly a figment of Charlie's imagination. 'Sounds like a storm in a teacup to me. You said you were here, for God's sake. Did you see anything? Anyone?'

'The security boys say that after I left the alarm was switched off and then on again. Something must have caused it.'

'Power failure, most likely. There was a storm, remember? Did the security people find anything?'

'No, but –'

'I'm going back to bed.' And to the delights of Miss Oh's welcoming body.

But Charlie had opened the filing cabinet. Now he turned to his brother. 'The bank statements file...'

'What about it?'

'It's not here.'

They stared at each other.

'Nobody broke in,' Damian said.

'So someone had a key. And knew how to turn off the alarm.'

Again they stared at each other.

'Andrea Chan,' Charlie said.

'You think she's planning to blackmail us?'

'I don't know. What I do know, we'd better find out fast.'

'A visit from some of our friends?' Damian said.

'My thoughts exactly,' Charlie said. He went and picked up the phone. When he spoke it was in Cantonese.

3

It was eight-thirty in the morning and Sara was feeling pretty sick too, but taking a leaf from Andrea's book, was determined to show nothing. She put on her face, studying herself in the bathroom mirror. Eyes clear, mouth firm. No shadows of the fear she had felt behind the toilet's locked door with Charlie Lennox only metres away. Yet her mind remembered what her face had forgotten and the memory could still bring sweat to her palms. Not only of the traumatic time in the Lennox offices but of what had come later, when two hours earlier Martha Tan had burst into Sara's bedroom to find her in the shower.

'Sara! Sara!'

She emerged from the shower, water streaming, towel tied loosely about her waist. 'What is it?'

'Andrea Chan.'

'What about her?

'Two gangsters paid her a visit an hour ago.'

4

Andrea had been asleep in bed when a violent hammering on the door of her flat woke her. The shock brought her heart into her throat. Luckily the door was double locked but her flat mate was away and she was alone. She crept to the door and looked through the spy hole. Two men were standing very close to the other side of the door with what looked like baseball bats in their hands. The flats on either side of Andrea's place, normally noisy at all hours with shouts and laughter, the clatter of mah-jong tiles, were silent as though the occupants were holding their breath, no one game to ask the two men what they wanted. No one game to come to her aid, if aid were needed.

The taller of the two men must have guessed she would be watching because he smiled, broad lips and broken teeth, and spoke to her in a harsh voice, addressing her through the door in the rough Cantonese spoken by the triads.

'Come out, Chan Zhang Li. Come out. We wish to talk to you.' And he began rhythmically and with increasing violence to beat on the door with the butt end of his bat.

'Come out, Chan Zhang Li! Come out!'

While, behind the flat door, Andrea felt the blood drain from her face.

5

Sara put on one of the day dresses she had bought at Shanghai Tang. She rejoined Martha and they went down to breakfast together. They discussed how they would handle their ten o'clock meeting with the Lennox brothers. They went out into a morning washed clean by the night's rain.

At ten o'clock on the dot a cheongsam-clad woman, snooty-looking as only a young and beautiful Chinese woman could be, ushered them into the Lennox boardroom, carpeted, wood-panelled and with expensive Chinese prints on the walls. She closed the door and they were alone.

They were kept waiting for ten minutes. Martha had warned Sara the brothers might try this tactic.

'It is a way of telling us they have nothing to hide.'

'But they have.'

'Of course. We have the papers, as they will soon discover. Something else they will discover also.'

'What?'

'That we are the angels of retribution.'

Now in the boardroom they did not speak. Martha had warned Sara about this also.

'The room is very likely bugged,' she had said.

Eventually their patience was rewarded. The door opened and the two Lennox brothers came in.

Charlie and Damian Lennox were effusive in their greetings yet their smiles failed to conceal their underlying resentment that the Brand Corporation should have presumed to send these two women to check-up on them. But Sara saw something else too: the wariness of men prepared for trouble. Although now Andrea was out of the way they were no doubt hoping they would be able to ride out any storm.

'You are more than welcome, of course you are,' Charlie Lennox said. 'We are delighted to see you. We only hope you won't feel you've been wasting your time.'

And ours. Which he did not say but clearly implied.

'Hear hear,' said Damian Lennox.

Tweedledum and Tweedledee. They were both fat but Damian was the fatter of the two.

'You'll be wanting to hear how our negotiations have been going in Beijing,' Charlie said.

Martha smiled but said nothing. Sara, taking her cue from Martha, smiled but said nothing.

'It's been a slow and arduous process,' Charlie said.

'As we warned you,' Damian said.

'Indeed yes. We made that very clear,' Charlie said. 'Both to Ms Brand and to Channel 12's previous owners. But we are glad to report progress.'

'Excellent progress,' Damian said.

'I can confidently say that six months, perhaps less, should see our getting a positive response to our negotiations,' Charlie said.

'Almost certainly less,' Damian said.

Sara watched the two faces: genial, a little sweaty, both of them with the expressions of men who could be trusted all the way to the bank. Both of them lying through their teeth. Mr Cheu's damning report had been one hundred per cent correct; the papers she and Andrea Chan had stolen put that beyond doubt.

If I never go through that again it will be too soon, Sara thought. No more cloak and dagger nonsense for me; next time we'll use professionals.

She watched Charlie Lennox's lips shaping his lies and remembered how close she and Andrea had come to being pinched last night. The cops called, a charge of breaking and entering... How good would that have looked? And what would Hilary have said? She could imagine her mother, very much the CEO, tearing strips off her: *The first job I give you and you end up in gaol?*

Thank God it hadn't happened but it would be a long time before she forgot those terror-soaked moments behind the locked toilet door with Charlie Lennox washing his hands not three paces away. And then the security team arriving and the pair of them running barefoot down the endless flights of stairs... The memory made her sweat even now.

Martha interrupted Charlie as he rabbited on about the rosy future that awaited them all. 'We don't have time for all this nonsense. You have the file, Sara?'

Umbrage from Charlie Lennox. 'My dear lady...'

Slowly and carefully Martha laid the first damning document on the table. 'Perhaps you care to explain this?'

Charlie's agreeable smile vanished when he saw what it was: a statement from a bank in the Channel Isles. 'How did you get hold of this?'

Martha smiled but did not answer.

Charlie stared at it, no doubt hoping the figures would disappear. His face paled. Damian's face paled. They looked like a two-man coven of disconcerted ghosts.

'Or this, from a bank in the Cayman Islands?'

'I have seen neither of these statements before,' Charlie said. 'I know nothing about them.'

'Nothing at all,' Damian said.

Their voices were as white as ghosts too.

'Our assistant Andrea Chan handled this side of the operation,' Charlie said. 'I'll call her in.' He snatched up the phone. 'Tell Andrea to get in here at once!' Then listened to the receptionist before slowly replacing the phone. 'She is not in today.' His moistened lips shone. 'I have to say I find this most embarrassing.'

'Not to say suspicious,' Damian said.

'Highly suspicious,' Charlie said.

'We trusted her implicitly, you see.'

'We shall both be heartbroken if there is anything amiss.'

'Or if it became a matter for the police.'

'I was thinking more of the Hong Kong Corruption Commission,' Martha said.

It was like the silence after a bomb blast, everyone watching each other.

'I hope you are not suggesting that we –' Charlie Lennox said.

'We are as concerned as you,' Damian Lennox said.

'When we get hold of Andrea Chan –' Charlie said.

'Our understanding is that two men paid her a visit early this morning,' Martha said.

'We know nothing about our staff's private lives,' said Charlie Lennox.

'We respect their right to privacy,' said Damian Lennox.

'It was not a social call. She reported that the men had threatened her but sensibly she did not let them in. Instead she phoned the police.'

'And?'

'And nothing. When the men heard the sirens they left.'

'How do you know this?'

'Because she told us so.'

'I was not aware you knew her.'

'Now you are.'

In the streets outside the building the morning might be warming up but in the boardroom the atmosphere was glacial. Watching the Lennox brothers' faces Sara saw suspicion harden into certainty.

'That is how you obtained these papers,' Charlie Lennox said. He slapped his open hand on the boardroom table; there was nothing amiable about his expression now. 'You broke in and stole them.'

Martha remained calm. 'We reject any such suggestion,' she said.

'Then how –'

'How does not matter. The fact is we have them.'

'The police will want to speak to Andrea Chan about this,' Charlie Lennox said.

'Your accomplice,' Damian Lennox said. No amiability there either.

Martha glanced at Sara; taking her cue, she joined in the discussion for the first time. 'Andrea flew out of Hong Kong this morning. I went with her to the airport and saw her safely on a flight to Sydney.'

'Andrea Chan will report to Hilary Brand when she gets to Australia,' Martha said. 'She has copies of all the papers. She'll be under the protection of Brand Security from the moment she disembarks. Do not think of trying to intercept her.'

'Surely you cannot imagine we would do such a thing,' Charlie Lennox said.

'Surely not,' protested Damian Lennox.

'Those gangsters didn't call on her by chance,' Martha said. 'We are satisfied you have engaged in systematic fraud. Your actions have cost the Brand Corporation a great deal of money. Now I am asking what you plan to do about it.'

'Fraud?' Charlie very much on his high horse. 'Nonsense! The balances in those statements represent funds set aside for contacts in China –'

'Spare us,' Martha said. 'You owe us six million Australian dollars. Some you sent overseas; some are still here in Hong Kong. We require a clear statement how you plan to repay. Or do you want us to contact the Corruption Commission?'

6

Sara listened on the extension as Martha and Hilary talked. It was a guarded conversation, the habit of caution deeply engrained in both women.

'Any chance of recovery?'

'Maybe fifty per cent,' Martha said.

'And the rest?'

'Hidden in maybe a dozen accounts in many countries. I doubt we'll ever get it back. We can always try but I suspect what we recover will be nowhere near the cost of pursuing them.'

'What do you suggest?' Hilary said. 'The police? I'll get our legal boys on to it as soon as our friend arrives but from what you say we've enough to put them away for years.'

'That's very true,' Martha said. 'But I ask myself, what's the use of locking them up? What's the benefit for us?'

'It would warn others who might be tempted to try the same trick.'

'Maybe it would do that. But in the meantime we lose everything and get nothing back. In any case, while police start investigating there's a good chance they'll grab what cash they can and vanish. For people who've got money, that wouldn't be too hard, would it? No, I think there may be a better way.'

'You think you can turn this around?'

'Maybe yes, maybe no. But definitely worth a try.'

'Riddle time again?' Hilary said.

'No riddles. Absolutely straightforward.'

A long silence while Martha leant forwards on the edge of her seat, body tense like a dog waiting for the rabbit.

'Very well,' Hilary said eventually. 'I'll give you your head on this. But make sure you keep me in the picture, OK? And Martha, we'd better come out on the right side of this. That is important both for the company and for you.'

'I understand, Hilary. I'll get back to you. One or two days, no more. OK?'

She hung up.

'What are we going to do?' Sara asked.

'Speak to the big shots.' Martha saw the confused look on Sara's face. 'When we deal with China,' she said, 'we have to think like they do. That is very important.'

'But you are Chinese too.'

'I am Singaporean. Very different. So I too have to learn. First lesson: respect is very important. Respect for each other. Also getting respect from the outside world. What the Lennox brothers have done, they have cheated foreigners. Worse still, foreigners wishing to invest in China. Wishing to create business in China. Charlie Lennox and his brother lose respect not only for themselves but for China also. It could make the world say China is a bad place to do business and that would be very bad. If we prosecute them and they go to gaol, the whole world will know what happened. Chinese officials won't want us to do anything like that. But if they know what happened and know too we are protecting their good name by *not* prosecuting these men, they will respect us too and reward us for our consideration. That is how China does things,' Martha said.

'So we write off the money –'

'And in return win their respect. I promise you, that will be worth many times what we lose. Oh yes, Sara, that is the right way to handle this.'

'I am glad you are here to teach me these things,' Sara said.

1970

THE ISLAND AND THE JETTY

1

Hilary was cross. Lance had raised the question of Rottnest Island. She had liked the idea of seeing a new and interesting place with a new and interesting man yet so far nothing had come of it. Before Lance had mentioned it she had never given Rottnest a thought but to be given a half-invitation and then to have nothing happen was aggravating.

Write it off to experience, she told herself. She had more than enough to keep her busy; what was she doing, thinking of a relationship with a married man? It was madness.

She went out to yet another meeting. When she came back there was a message on her answering machine.

'Rottnest Island. Saturday suit you?'

Just my luck, she thought. She'd arranged to meet Haskins in Busselton to check progress on the new mall. The feedback had been good but she wanted to see for herself how things were going. She had never cancelled a business meeting before but the mall wasn't going to fly away, was it? It would be no hardship to reschedule to a day in the week.

She left a message on Haskins's answering machine. She returned Lance's call. She said yes.

She arranged for Agnes to come in. On Saturday morning Lance picked her up early and they headed west to Fremantle and the Rottnest ferry.

The sea was calm and blue with the occasional flicker of white from a foam-toppling wave.

'People say you can see blue whales sometimes,' Lance said but today they saw only seagulls squalling and circling in the ferry's wake.

He hired two bicycles. 'I never thought to ask if you can ride,' he said.

'It's been a time.'

She managed, though. They rode through the flat green landscape. There were no hills; the highest point of the island was only 150 feet above sea level. They passed trees that Lance said grew nowhere else. They caught the distant blink of salt lakes shining in the sunshine. They found an isolated beach, as empty as he had promised. The hot sun burned her shoulders; it was a day of magic, with a snack meal at a café whose owner was full of smiles and brought the food to them where they sat beneath an awning on an outside terrace. Afterwards they walked again and saw many birds, including what he told her was the famous curlew sandpiper.

'No quokkas,' she said.

'They are nocturnal.'

They saw a reef heron, though, dark and solitary on a coastal flat of round white stones.

'*The mussel-pooled and heron-priested shore*,' declaimed Hilary, who was having a love affair with Dylan Thomas.

When they got home darkness was tiptoeing gently down, like a quokka out of a tree. On the flat's doorstep he kissed her and she felt her toes quiver.

'Thank you for a perfect day,' she said. And for the perfect end to a perfect day.

2

She discovered she couldn't arrange a time during the week after all. She went through her diary with Sandy. It was obvious she couldn't drive all the way to Busselton, inspect the site, talk with the site engineers and subbies, meet the council officials and drive back again all in one day and there was no way she could be away two weekdays. She phoned Haskins.

'It'll have to be next weekend,' she said.

'I'll arrange for the planning officer to have a site inspection,' Haskins said. 'So make sure you're here too. Don't fuck me up a second time, OK?' No ducking and diving with Haskins Gould; when he wanted to tick you off you got ticked.

'Without fail,' Hilary said.

On Friday Lance rang to ask if she'd like to take in a movie with him the following day.

'I can't. I have to go to Busselton.'

'Another time, then.' He sounded quite cheerful about it. 'How's your week been, anyway?'

'Busy,' she said. 'Jennifer had a bit of a cold too, which didn't help, but she seems to be over the worst of it now.'

'That's good,' he said. A pause while neither spoke. Then: 'Better get moving, I suppose.'

Hilary gave herself a lifeline, throwing out the words before he could hang up.

'I was wondering whether you might like to come down to Busselton with me. If you're free.'

'What about Jennifer?'

'Agnes will look after her.'

It was a brilliant, dew-wet morning when they headed south out of the city. It was one hundred and forty miles to Busselton but seemed further, the road straight and for the most part uninteresting.

'What's in Busselton?' Lance asked.

'You should know,' Hilary said. 'It's your job to know.'

'I know the statistics. I know most of the shoreline blocks have been sold. I'm asking what the place is like. Its ambience.'

'Its ambience?' Hilary repeated. 'My, what smart words you use.'

'Incredible, isn't it? I can read simple sentences too.'

'Busselton has the longest wooden jetty in the southern hemisphere.'

'Wow!'

'It's a major tourist attraction, or so they say. The statistics indicate the town is growing fast.'

'Hence the new mall. How thoughtful of you to provide for the future population.'

'We live to serve,' Hilary said.

'And never a thought for the profit.'

'The idea never entered our heads.'

A huge truck roared past, shaking the car as it headed north.

'There is an old gaol –'

'Wow!'

'Which is said to be haunted.'

'Wow again!'

'Here I am giving you a conducted tour and all you say is wow.'

'But heartfelt, I assure you.'

'The town is the centre of a major wine-growing region.'

'Now you're talking.'

They booked into adjoining rooms at the motel. Hilary freshened up, then went to the site.

Lance said he would explore. 'Maybe pick up some wine,' he said.

The site was the usual bedlam: hammers, drills, concrete mixers, Haskins Gould yelling loud enough to drown the lot of them. Had she not known better Hilary would have been appalled, but Haskins had brought in the malls in Perth and Albany ahead of schedule and she did not doubt he would do the same there.

'Everything under control?' she said.

'I'll be having somebody's arse if it's not,' Haskins said.

It was a Saturday but the shire offices were open until midday. She observed proper protocol, paying court to the appropriate officials. She entertained the mayor to lunch.

'More a public relations exercise than anything else,' she told Lance later.

'Don't knock it. Public relations are important.'

'And it doesn't hurt to keep an eye on things.'

She said no more but one of the subbies had been complaining about Haskins.

'Cuts more corners than a grand prix driver,' the electrician said. He claimed others felt the same but were more cautious about speaking out.

Hilary had faith in Haskins's ability to deliver a project on time but he was a ruthless bastard, no denying it, and ruthless bastards needed to be watched. She had more than a streak of ruthlessness herself but liked to think she was also a straight shooter. With Haskins she wasn't so sure. It was something to tuck away in her mind for future reference, should it be needed.

That evening she and Lance had a pleasant meal in town. It was dark when they left the restaurant. The night was warm and cicadas were singing in the undergrowth.

'Going to show me this famous jetty?' Lance said.

They strolled along the wooden structure and the night was alive with the surge and sigh of the ocean.

'What's out there?' Lance said.

'Nothing till you reach South America.'

'What about Africa?'

She shook her head. 'Further north.'

They stood side by side at the end of the jetty. It was like being on a boat far from shore.

'Three thousand feet,' Lance said. 'Over half a mile.'

It felt a lot more than three thousand feet, Hilary thought. More like three thousand miles. *Alone, alone, all, all alone, alone on a wide wide sea,*' she said.

'We did the Ancient Mariner at school,' he said. 'And you?'

'Poetry wasn't a big feature of our lives at Northcote,' she said.

'But you caught up later.'

'I am still catching up,' she said. 'I'll be catching up all my life.'

They walked slowly back to the motel. Hilary wondered what she would do if he came on to her but he did not. Next morning, after an early breakfast and with the car boot packed with cases of wine, they would be heading back to Perth.

Hilary was finishing her second cup of breakfast coffee when Haskins put in an appearance. She had not been expecting him and raised a questioning eyebrow as she looked at him.

'Trouble?'

'Nothing we can't handle.'

But that was nonsense; Haskins wouldn't be there if there wasn't a problem.

'Coffee?' Hilary said.

'Thanks.'

Lance caught Hilary's glance. 'I'll go and finish packing,' he said.

The coffee came. Haskins gulped noisily.

'Now,' Hilary said. 'What's this all about?'

'I stopped by just to make sure you weren't intending to come down to the site this morning.'

'I wasn't planning to. But it sounds as though maybe I should.'

'I would recommend, strongly recommend, you don't.'

'Something's happened. What is it?'

'Nothing you need to bother your head about.'

Hilary hated to be patronised by this man. By any man. 'Tell me.'

'One of the boys kicked a hole in a live electric cable last night.'

A cold hand clutched Hilary's heart. 'He's not –?'

'Dead? No, he's not.'

'Thank God!'

'Amen to that. We'd have had the damned inspectors all over us if he was.'

'I wasn't thinking of the inspectors,' Hilary said.

'Well, I was. I surely was. We got to keep this project moving and nothing mucks up your schedules quicker than a bunch of damned inspectors.'

'Is he hurt?'

'Shaken but that's all. The story is he was drunk.'

'Our story or the true story?'

'Why, both.' Haskins's innocence would have charmed a death adder.

'You'd better be right,' Hilary said.

Haskins smiled. 'Babe,' he said, 'I'm always right.'

'Is there likely to be any comeback?'

'None. Like I said, he was drunk.'

'So what do you plan to do about it?'

'Pour oil on troubled waters,' Haskins said.

'And you don't want me down there?'

'I want you to stay away.'

Hilary was troubled. 'I shouldn't. But I've a meeting this afternoon. Do I have your word he's OK?'

'My sacred oath, babe.'

3

When he got back on site Haskins called the previous night's shift foreman to his office.

'I think it's time I wised you up to what it means to do business with Haskins Gould,' he said. He stared with merciless eyes at Merv Beale and the foreman, tougher than most, flinched. 'You'd better spell out what happened.'

'It was no one's fault,' Merv said. 'Endless rush, live cables everywhere… It's a miracle it hasn't happened before.'

'I'll decide that,' Haskins said. The chair creaked as he sat down. His massive shoulders were hunched, fists loosely clenched on the desk in front of him. 'So tell me.'

'The late shift had just started. Somehow Bluey Morris tripped over a live cable. It came unhitched and the shock flung him halfway across the floor. It's a miracle he wasn't killed –'

'Late shift comes on when?'

'Ten o'clock.'

'And this accident happened when?'

'About ten-thirty. They came runnin' to me in the store at ten-thirty-five.'

'Ten-thirty, eh? So Morris had been on about half an hour when he fell over the cable?'

'About that.'

'I hear Morris likes a drink.'

'They all do. But he wasn't drunk –'

'You a doctor, Beale?'

'No, of course I'm not a doctor.'

'You didn't check him out, I mean? Breathalyse him, anything like that?'

'No!'

'Then you're not in a position to say whether he was drunk or not, are you?'

'He didn't act like he was drunk.'

'Until he fell over that damn cable. I'll tell you how it was, Beale. He'd had a few drinks before he came on. Not sufficient to make him incapable but enough to impair his judgment, you get me? He stumbled – anyone in that state could do it – next thing you know he's halfway across the floor and lucky to be alive.' Haskins paused, his eyes on the foreman's face. 'On your shift.'

Merv bristled. 'No way you're pinning this on me –'

'Wouldn't dream of it. I mean, a man has a drink too many, how are you to know?' A smile with teeth, like the gates of hell. 'Not a good look, though, is it, and you with a good job here. Doing well too. In fact I've been thinking of giving you a raise. Pity to mess up because some feller should know better comes on shift half-cut.'

They looked at each other.

'Trouble is, we get the inspectors in there's no knowing where their fingers will end up pointing. You get me?' His fingers tapped the desk. 'Morris married, I hear?'

'Wife and three kids,' Merv said.

'Maybe I'd best have a word with him.'

Bluey Morris was prepared to be truculent but was scared too; everyone was scared of Haskins Gould.

'Sorry about what happened but we're always in such a rush. And that cable –'

Haskins held up his hand. 'Nobody's blaming you, Bluey. In fact I just wanted to say how thankful we all are you're not hurt. But you had a fright. We understand that.' He took a cheque out of a drawer and pushed it across the desk. 'Five hundred bucks. Buy something nice for your kids, why don't you? A token of appreciation for all your hard work.'

Bluey Morris turned the cheque in his hands. 'For the kids, you say?'

'That's it.'

'Well… Thanks very much. Much appreciated.'

'My pleasure.'

Haskins tilted his chair against the wall and watched as Morris went out.

Late in the afternoon he phoned Hilary in Perth.

'Done and dusted,' he said.

'What was it all about?'

'Nothing to worry your pretty little head about,' Haskins said.

He knew how much she hated that.

'And if I insist?'

'Sometimes it's best not to know.'

Partners they might be but he was glad he'd talked her out of coming on site. Next thing you knew she'd have wanted to talk to the people involved and he certainly wouldn't have wanted that. Even at the best of times, having a woman under his feet tended to inhibit him. He went back into the mayhem of the work area beyond his office door. He started yelling. 'C'mon, you bastards. Think you're all on holiday, do you? Get moving!'

ROLLER COASTER

1

Once again Lance had taken her by surprise. Now they were sitting on the settee in Hilary's living room. They were not touching but not that far apart either. He leant forward and recharged their glasses. Hilary picked up the bottle and looked appreciatively at the label.

'Margaret River cabernet,' she said. 'Are you a connoisseur?'

'I like a nice drop.' He took a sip and put down his glass. Hilary took a sip and put down her glass.

He looked at her; they looked at each other.

'I like a lot of things,' he said.

Heart beating; she felt like a marsh. 'Give me an example,' she said.

Lance leant slowly forward. Their lips barely touched. He sat back. 'There you go,' he said.

'Is that the best you can do?'

'It's a start.'

A little later his left arm was round her shoulders, his lips were on hers, his right hand had somehow found its way inside her dressing gown, eased up her bra and now was cupping her left breast.

Things were getting out of hand, she hoped. She broke off the kiss. 'This is where I am supposed to say stop it,' she said.

His hand remained where it was. It did not move but the touch of his palm against the tender skin was sending quivers all the way to her toes.

'And if I don't?'

'Then I would have to resort to other strategies.'

'Such as?'

'I could slap your face.'

'That wouldn't be nice.'

'Or I could smile and do nothing.'

'Lie back and think of Queen Victoria?'

'Something like that.'

'That sounds like a lot more fun.'

'It does, doesn't it?'

The hand was moving again. Gently smoothing. Stroking. The quivers were growing more intense, force five on the Richter scale and climbing. Any moment now the walls might come tumbling down. If they hadn't already.

'Are you still feeding the baby?' he said.

'Not for months now.'

'Are they still sore?'

'Maybe a bit tender.'

'I promise I'll be very gentle.'

Later, lying naked on the bed, she watched him put his shoes on.

'I had been planning to have a bath when you arrived,' she said.

'Have one now,' he said.

'Could do.'

She knew she would not. For tonight she would keep the scent and substance of him intact. Awake or sleeping she would lie surrounded by the memory of what had happened. She would relive the taste of him on her lips and in her body. She would kiss the air where he had been.

Next day she was distracted, waiting for a call that did not come. She thought: You fool, you couldn't wait to get your knickers off, could you? He's a man, for God's sake. He's had his fun and moved on. What else did you expect? You bastard, she thought. How dare you fill me and now leave me empty? How dare you? She'd give him a talking to, the next time she saw him. If she ever did.

She went home to the flat that evening. She played with Jennifer, she bathed and fed her, played with her some more, and all the time there was a dull ache in her heart that nothing would shift.

You fool. You nincompoop. You moron. On and on.

The ring of the bell brought her heart to her throat. She was careful not to run to the door. She opened it.

'I've brought Chinese takeaways,' Lance said. 'I hope that's all right.'

Her heart was doing cartwheels. 'I've no wine,' she said.

He put the cardboard boxes in the kitchen. 'Give me five,' he said. And was gone. In no time he was back with a bottle of Sauvignon Blanc and another of brandy.

'Remy Martin,' she said. 'Wow!'

'Think rich,' he said.

'Think bankrupt,' she said.

'What I've been hearing, I don't see that as a problem for you any time soon,' he said.

'What have you been hearing?'

'That in commercial terms Hilary Brand is on the road to big things. And getting there fast too.'

'That would be nice,' she said.

At the end of the evening she turned to him: 'You want to stay over?'

'Would that be wise?'

'No, it wouldn't.' Her eyes grew intense. 'You want to stay over?'

'What's in it for me?'

'Nothing you haven't had already.'

'Offering seconds?'

'You never know your luck.'

'What a splendid idea. But I've no toothbrush.'

'That I can provide.'

'And a razor?'

'That too.'

'You believe in being organised.'

'I believe in hanging on to what I've got,' she said.

'I'll bear that in mind,' he said.

'Make sure you do. But in the meantime...'

2

She was obsessed, no other word for it. She wanted him with a passion she would not have believed possible. More than desire, it was a physical illness that left her body aching. She needed to feel his body on hers, his body in hers. She could have wept with the intensity of her feelings.

They were seeing each other most evenings; then Lance phoned. His voice was taut. 'I won't be able to see you for a few days.'

'Oh?'

'I have to go away. I'll be back at the weekend.'

'I shall miss you,' she said, too proud to ask the questions that were shouting in her mind. *Why? Where are you going? And why can't you tell me?*

She wondered if he might say he loved her. He did not. Neither did she speak but waited, hoping.

'See you,' he said.

At the weekend, he had said. I shall be back at the weekend. It seemed an eternity. Even Dave noticed her preoccupation. 'Not like you at all,' he said.

She told herself to be patient. With patience all would be resolved.

On Thursday she turned up at the office as usual. Tomorrow night, she was thinking. He will be home tomorrow night.

Sandy looked up as Hilary walked in, Sandy with an anxious expression on her face.

'Good morning,' Hilary said, falsely bright. Then saw the woman sitting on the other side of Sandy's desk. Sitting waiting on the other side of Sandy's desk. And knew. No word spoken but she knew.

'This is Mrs Bettinger,' Sandy said.

Sandy knew; of course she did. She knew and Dave knew and all the world knew, didn't it, because Hilary had made no attempt to conceal her feelings. There had been no reason to hide them, had there?

Now this.

'Perhaps you'd like to come in,' she said to Mrs Bettinger.

Quite pretty, she thought. Not as brash as I'd imagined. Not bad at all. While the doom bells rang in her head. She managed somehow to smile as she spoke but was thankful to reach her chair and collapse into it, all strength gone from her legs.

She took a deep breath, willing her shaking limbs to be still. Because this woman was the enemy, was she not? An enemy to be destroyed, if possible, but in any case to be handled with care. With very great care.

'You wanted to see me?'

'You know my husband,' Mrs Bettinger said.

'Indeed I do.'

'Aren't you ashamed?'

She was wearing a little too much make-up, Hilary thought, her lips scarlet and challenging. As was her way of sitting in the chair, leaning forwards with an aggressive expression on her face. It was confrontation, then, and knowing it steadied Hilary's nerves. If this woman thought to browbeat her she was in for a disappointment.

'I was under the impression you had moved to Queensland,' she said.

'Lance is still my husband.'

'I understood you were planning to make another life for yourself. In the cane fields.'

'No business of yours,' Mrs Bettinger said. 'Anyway that's all over now. I'm back.'

'On a visit? Or to stay?'

'I'm here to take back what's rightfully mine,' the woman said. 'I'm here to tell you to keep off. Lance isn't for you.'

I suppose Lance has a say in that.

The words trembled on Hilary's lips but she did not speak. What this woman thought or said did not matter. What Hilary thought and said did not matter. Only Lance could decide. At least she had learnt one thing at the Northcote home. She knew when to keep her mouth shut, her thoughts hidden. Lance would decide.

'Thank you for coming round,' Hilary said. 'For being so frank with me.'

'I mean it,' Lance's wife said. 'Keep off.'

Darkness threatened her. She denied its presence; even at night she refused to accept it yet there it was, hovering at the edges of her mind, waiting to engulf her. The weekend came and went. Lance will phone, she told herself, but he did not. She heard nothing. Pride prevented her trying to contact him but by Tuesday she could bear it no longer. She held the receiver in her hand for a full minute while her thoughts warred with one another. She drew a deep breath. She dialled.

'Lance Bettinger...'

'I am sorry to trouble you,' she said, fighting to keep her voice even. 'We need to talk.'

'Lunchtime,' he said, his voice cool. 'At the Baron. Twelve-thirty.' It was a stranger speaking.

The Baron of Beef was a local pub. They had eaten there before. She had an appointment but that could be changed.

'I'll be there.'

Lance was there first and had taken a table in a corner partly hidden behind an ornate screen the publican claimed he had brought back from Java but that some customers said had come from a Subiaco junk shop. The ambiguity suited the occasion, the denial of what Hilary had believed was love. Perhaps Lance had chosen the table for that reason or – more probably – to ensure they were hidden from the rest of the dining room.

She sat down. She found the conventional words – *How are you going? A bit warm today, isn't it?* – but to look at him across the cloth-covered table, even for the instant she permitted herself, brought a pain so savage that for a moment she doubted she would be able to talk or eat or indeed do anything but endure.

No, she thought, I shall not let him do this to me.

Therefore she forced herself to look at him as the warm tide of an unanticipated emotion flooded through her. She had expected politeness, the hard cold politeness of a stone. She had expected distance, as though Lance were watching her through the wrong end of a telescope. She had not expected tears.

His face was wet, his clenched hands knotted on the table in front of him. Without conscious decision Hilary reached out to cover those hands with her own, aware how indescribably precious they were to her, and realised that after all this was to be a meeting not of dismissal but of shared pain.

'It is the children,' he said.

Now all Hilary could think of was how to ease his suffering. 'I understand,' she said. 'Please...'

'I have a duty to them,' he said.

She tightened her hands on his. 'Don't.'

The four hands clung together in mute acknowledgement of that reality. Hilary sensed the wife smiling in the shadows. The wife who had talked of her rights, her ownership.

'I don't think there is any point in this,' she said. A wry smile, as brittle as sticks. 'I doubt I could eat anything, anyway. We both understand and accept the situation. I shall think of you always with... affection' – she would not mention love, for fear her voice would break – 'I blame you for nothing. You brought me such happiness. Such joy –' her voice creaked after all '– but as we must part, let us part with dignity. Yes?' She stood. She reached out and touched his hands. For the last time. She found the strength to share her love in the brittle smile she gave him. For the last time. She turned and walked away, her senses numb.

So the world ends.

Yet it was not so. Six weeks later the doctor confirmed what she had already suspected. It seemed that in one respect the world was not ending at all but just beginning.

2004

A MEETING WITH A POWERFUL MAN

1

'Everything arranged,' Martha said. She seemed very pleased with herself.

'Tell me what we're talking about,' Sara said.

'We are talking about China. About huge business opportunities for us in China!' Martha was not quite dancing but it was close. Then her happy face sobered. 'If we play our cards right. If things go well for us tonight.'

Sara laughed. 'Always the riddles! Why don't you tell me what you're on about? What's so special about tonight?'

'Tonight we meet Mr Wong Chee-Weng.'

'Who is?'

'A top man. Very important here and in Beijing. He has a lot of influence in China! But the meeting has to be very hush hush. He'll come with his advisers. If things go well this could be a big deal for Brand Corporation!'

'How did you manage to arrange it?'

'Family connection; my second aunt's husband has a cousin in the administration.'

'Does Mr Wong know about the Lennox business?'

'Of course. Otherwise he would not agree to talk.'

'Where are we meeting him?'

'At the Kee Club tonight. Very exclusive, very private. Usually bookings have to be made months ahead but for a man like Wong Chee-Weng all things are possible. We should be there at nine-thirty.'

'Dress?'

'Smartest one you have.'

2

Sara chose a red and blue qipao dress from Shanghai Tang, one with short sleeves. Before they left the hotel Martha had looked at it approvingly.

'Good choice. You look very elegant.'

'Chrysanthemums for luck, right?'

'Right.'

When they arrived they got out of the taxi and Sara looked around her. The Kee Club was situated over the Yung Kee restaurant and from the outside didn't look like much.

'Very discreet,' Martha said.

Inside was a different story: a lounge and bar with private rooms leading off and a dramatic gilt staircase leading to a restaurant on the upper level. Martha spoke to a tuxedo-clad man, very tall and thin, who sneered down his nose at them as though he suspected they had come to the wrong address.

'This private club,' he said. 'Members only.'

Martha was having none of that. 'Mr Boon Kim-Chwee,' she said in English, and followed it up with a volley of Cantonese as hot as fire.

The flunky wilted, his expression changing at once. He led them deferentially across the lounge to the door into what Martha said was called the Red Salon.

'Please be seated,' he said abjectly. 'I shall inform Mr Boon you are here. A drink while you are waiting, perhaps?'

'Champagne!' Martha said. 'And make sure it is imported. None of your local muck!'

'Of course.'

The man fled. Sara stared at this woman who without warning had transmogrified into the late and unlamented Madam Mao of terrible memory.

'What did you say to him?'

Martha smiled contentedly. 'I said: "Turtle dung ferret, you dare address your betters in this way? Learn humility or I shall report you to Mr Boon."'

'It certainly worked. And who is Mr Boon?'

'Alias for Mr Wong Chee-Weng. Famous men, powerful men, often use other names to conceal their true identity.'

'But that waiter knew who he was.'

'Of course he knows,' Martha said. 'Everyone knows. They must. Otherwise how can anyone know how important he is?'

Sara did not try to work out the logic of that. 'When do you think he'll turn up?'

'He's here already, I think. Maybe watching us right now. But important men always arrive late. They like to keep others waiting.'

'To show how important they are,' Sara said.

Martha beamed. 'Now you're beginning to think like a Chinese woman!'

The champagne arrived and they sipped it.

'Very good,' Martha said.

The door opened silently. Almost before they were aware of it Mr Wong had joined them. He was not alone; two other men came with him but there was no mistaking who was in charge.

Wong Chee-Weng was a big man, stout, but his flesh was hard. He was smiling but looked formidable and Sara thought he would grin a lot and they would never know his thoughts.

Mr Wong gave both women a genial smile, sat down and spoke to one of his aides. The man nodded and left the room. Wong turned his attention back to the two women.

'We shall eat,' he said in good English. 'You enjoy Chinese cooking?' he said to Sara.

'Very much.'

'Good, good. My wife is excellent cook. Could have been professional chef.' He laughed and patted his belly. 'As you can see.'

Who had chosen the menu Sara never discovered but the food was indeed excellent: sweet almond soup, abalone with fresh salmon, crabmeat with egg white, Cantonese roasted duck, hor fun with oxtail... The dishes seemed endless, as did the enthusiasm of the diners. But even the best of things had to end and eventually Mr Wong put down his chopsticks, selected a toothpick and sat back in his chair.

'Lennox Brothers,' he said.

He was looking at Sara, so she was the one who answered him. She was aware of Martha watching her; she felt like a schoolgirl facing her first public test.

'We feel humiliated by the Lennox brothers,' she said. 'We allowed them to cheat us. It was a serious error and we wish to express our regret at our foolishness in this matter.'

Mr Wong, hand cupping his mouth, was busy with his toothpick. Eventually he removed both hand and toothpick. 'There is no profit in discussing the past. Especially as I understand you have severed your connection with these men.'

'Absolutely,' Sara said. 'As soon as we found out about it we took action.'

'Forceful action is good when dealing with such men. Valiant in defence of right: that is old Chinese saying.'

'And a very wise one,' Sara said.

'Yet I have read nothing about this regrettable affair in the newspapers.'

Sara said carefully: 'It is our belief that publicity would be in no one's interests.'

Wong nodded. 'Good, good. Tell me, Ms Brand, why does your corporation wish to invest in China? To teach us how to improve, heya? To learn from you?'

His expression was bland, his smile unchanged, but Sara sensed that her reply would prove crucial to what clearly had the potential to be an important relationship.

'I would not presume to think along those lines,' she said. 'This is my first visit to China and I am here to learn, not instruct. Both the

Brand Corporation and I personally are looking for your guidance, Mr Wong, if you would be gracious enough to advise us.'

'You have the authority to speak for the Brand Corporation?'

'In this I do.'

He looked at her for several seconds. 'Why do you wish for this advice? Why should you care?'

'Because anyone with eyes to see knows that China is a coming force in the world. We inherited the Lennox contract from Channel 12's previous owners. The way things worked out it has cost us a lot of money. We do not complain – that is always a risk in business – but of course we regretted it.' Her eyes met his eyes, dark, unreadable. 'I do not regret it now.'

'Why is that?'

'Because it has given me the opportunity to begin to learn what I can about China. It is only a beginning, of course – it would take a dozen lifetimes to know even a fraction of what there is to know – but to begin is important. Was it not Lao Tzu who said the journey of a thousand *li* starts from where one stands? In that sense I am a pilgrim. And who better to instruct me than a man from China?'

If Wong was surprised by her words he did not show it. His response was sharp. 'You hope to learn in order to profit from us?'

Now it was Sara's turn to smile. 'Knowledge is its own reward, Mr Wong. But I like to believe we would all profit from such a relationship.'

Wong looked at her impassively then nodded several times and stood up. 'Thank you, Ms Brand. A most interesting discussion. I trust you enjoyed the poor food.'

'The food was excellent, Mr Wong.' She risked another smile, as among friends. 'Or should I call you Mr Boon?'

His laugh was like a bark. 'You will excuse me now. Pressure of business, you understand.'

'Of course.'

For the first time he turned and spoke to Martha in Chinese, then jerked his head at his two aides who followed him out of the salon.

Sara and Martha looked at each other.

'Did I upset him in some way?' Sara said. 'He said nothing about the future.'

'It went extremely well. You handled it just right. Wong Chee-Weng was pleased.'

'He spoke only to me.'

'Of course. I expected nothing else. You're Hilary Brand's daughter. One day you'll be running the company.'

'Maybe.'

'That is what he expects. What we all expect. Therefore he needed to learn your thinking, just as you needed to learn his.'

'About what?'

'About China. About everything.'

'Then why did he say nothing about the future?'

'That will come.' She shrugged. 'Or not. It will not be his decision. He will report to Beijing and Beijing will decide. But I believe the signs are positive.'

'He said something to you at the end, as he was leaving. What was it?'

'He thanked me for bringing you to meet him. And to say we need concern ourselves no more about the Lennox brothers.'

'Why? Have they left Hong Kong?'

Martha smiled. 'Better not to ask. But if Mr Wong says we need not concern ourselves with the Lennoxes we may be sure he is right. Now we should return to the hotel. I shall tell that waiter to summon a taxi.'

On the way back to the hotel Martha said: 'How did you know the Lao Tzu quotation?'

'In television you learn to prepare yourself for the person you are interviewing. I thought it might be useful. But he did not seem to notice.'

'He noticed. He was very impressed.'

'How do you know?'

'I know. I think everything went very well.'

'But what do we do now? About Mr Wong, I mean?'

'We wait.'

3

They didn't have to wait long. Two days later Sara had a phone call from one of Wong's aides to say that he would like to meet with her and her mother as early as was convenient to discuss matters of mutual interest.

'He wants to speak to Hilary?'

'Of course,' Martha said. 'She is the CEO of Brand. Why should he not wish to speak to her? What I find interesting is that he wishes to include you in the talks also. You must have impressed him very much.'

'And Hilary will certainly want you there as well,' Sara said.

'The Three Musketeers,' Martha said.

When Martha Tan was in her daughter-of-China mode it was easy to forget how familiar she was with western culture but Singapore had been a British colony for over a century after all.

'You're not wrong,' Sara said.

She phoned Hilary.

'Have you sorted out that problem yet?' Straight-to-the-point Hilary.

'Yes. We have it on good authority we shall have no more problems there.'

'And the money?'

'We have recovered some. Not all.'

'Only to be expected, I suppose. Worth suing them?'

'That might prove difficult.'

A pause. The line cracked faintly.

'I see. Anything else?'

'Yes. Something important. I'm flying down tonight. I'll tell you when I see you.'

'Getting on with Martha OK?'

'Very well.'

'Good. I'll speak to you when you get here. Martha's familiar with the procedure when you arrive. Leave it to her. I'll arrange for the chopper to be on stand-by.'

'Any thoughts about Andrea Chan?' Sara said.

'I'll tell you when I see you.'

And rang off. Straight-to-the-point Hilary indeed. Well, at least you knew where you were with her.

'We're going back tonight?' Martha said. 'I'll tell the desk.'

I wonder what happened to the Lennoxes, Sara thought. They had certainly made enemies. Not only had they stolen from Brand; they had made problems for Mr Wong and China. And she suspected Mr Wong was not a forgiving man.

I guess we'll never know what happened, she thought, and resolved she would do everything possible to put them out of her mind. As Martha Tan had said, sometimes it was better not to know.

4

They flew down overnight, slept on the plane and showered and refreshed were in the office first thing. Or at least Sara, still used to television hours, thought of it as first thing but, as Martha had warned her, she found Hilary had been at her desk a full hour before the Airbus put down at Kingsford Smith.

And this could be my future? Sara thought. If I play my cards right and there are no hiccups and all the other mixed metaphors I can think of, I too could be arriving at the office at seven o'clock every morning? I must be out of my cotton-picking mind. To use another well-polished phrase.

Sara and Martha saw Hilary together, with both Vivienne Archer and Desmond Bragg sitting in. Coming down on the plane the two women had discussed how they should go about reporting what had happened. Martha had been nominally in charge when they went to Hong Kong and Sara therefore wanted Martha to report on what had been her mission, but Martha wouldn't have a bar of it.

'Wong Chee-Weng spoke to you, not me. Like it or not, he obviously thinks of you as Hilary's successor and so you are. He wishes to see you with Hilary because he sees you as the future and Chinese people think long term.'

'Even when they come from Singapore?'

Martha smiled. 'Even then. Continuity and future very important in Chinese thought. They think westerners are mistaken in focusing too much on short term and not enough on long.'

'You think he sees me as the long-term future of the company?'

'Of course. And he is right.'

So it was the spokesman for the long term who told the meeting what had happened.

'The Lennox boys,' Desmond Bragg said. 'You say this Wong guy said we don't have to worry about them any more? Why should he say that?'

'In my opinion they are probably dead. No proof but that is what I believe.'

'You're saying he may have had them killed? Jesus! Hard ball, eh?'

'You'd better believe it,' Sara said.

'Which raises a question,' Vivienne Archer said. 'Do we want to get into bed with men we think may be murderers?'

Sara thought Hilary would reply but she did not. She watched Sara and waited for her to answer. Go for it, she thought.

'I think we should, yes. First of all, my suspicions are no more than that. We have no evidence. Also we have no plans to do what the Lennoxes did. We shall keep faith with them and I am quite sure they will then keep faith with us.'

'You hope,' Vivienne said.

'And believe,' Sara said.

Hilary intervened for the first time. 'Martha, your view?'

'I think Sara is right.'

Vivienne was still troubled. 'But what do they want? Or what offer are they planning to make us?'

'We don't know. And unless we continue talking to them we never shall.'

Vivienne appealed to Hilary. 'You want us to deal with a bunch of latter day Mao Zedong thugs?'

'I want us to talk to them,' Hilary said. 'Find out what they want. I want to see what opportunities they can offer us. And that is what we shall do.' She turned to Martha. 'How do we get hold of this man Wong?'

'I have a contact number.'

'Give it to Janet. What is the time difference between here and Hong Kong?'

'This time of year, two hours behind us.'

Hilary looked at the gilt clock on her desk. 'Tell Janet to get him on the line at twelve o'clock.' She looked at Martha. 'Ten o'clock their time. He should be in his office by then, yes?'

'Probably been there several hours by then.'

'It'll give him time to clear his desk.'

Although Wong's desk, like hers, was unlikely to be cleared any time soon.

'A suggestion,' Martha said.

'Yes?'

'When he proposes a time to meet, choose another time and maybe a week later than he says. It's important not to appear too eager.'

'I shall remember,' Hilary said.

'And it will give me time to do that interview with Emil Broussard,' Sara said. 'If you haven't forgotten.'

Hilary looked at her level-eyed. 'I don't forget much,' she said. 'I even remember when I was born.'

Sara had heard that story often enough. She thought it was nonsense but was not foolish enough to say so. 'More than I can say,' she said. 'But I suppose you remember that too.'

'Your birth? Of course I remember it. I remember it very well.'

1970–78

ADDITION TO THE FAMILY

1

The child gave Hilary a hard time even before it was born.

'I reckon I've got a footballer in there,' she told Kirstie MacLeod.

She was really forging ahead now: money in the bank, a big house and now a housekeeper, Kirstie MacLeod, who was also her friend.

It certainly felt like a footballer. Hilary, sick of the way the brat booted her about, took it for granted that the troublemaker was a male child but refused to confirm it.

'All in good time,' she said. 'Anyway, I don't think there can be much doubt.'

Yet in the event she got it wrong. Clearly having made up its mind that it wished to get out into the world the child did so, slipping out into a warm sunny evening two days before Hilary's own birthday.

'A girl?' Hilary said. 'I would never have believed it.' She called it Sara. 'After Abraham's wife.'

'What's Abraham got to do with it?' Kirstie said.

'Not a lot, let's hope.' But had an idea that some of those Old Testament ladies had been as tough as the desert out of which they had emerged. 'Troublemakers the lot of them,' she said. 'And judging by her performance so far this one will be just like them.'

And kissed the downy head, suspecting it would not be long before she would want to strangle it. This time she got it right.

2

Sara was a fighter. She fought with everyone and everything: her mother, her sister and – when she was old enough to go to school – the kids and teachers too.

'She is not cruel or nasty,' Hilary said. 'Just determined.'

She suspected she too had been like that. The way her life had begun she would have got nowhere without determination.

Sara had an enquiring mind: a child of great potential, her form teacher said, but as demanding as gifted children often were.

'She needs challenge,' Miss Barker said. 'Her mind needs to be stretched.'

Challenge was right: Sara provided plenty of that herself without help from anyone else. She ran away twice; fortunately she never got far but somewhere in the recesses of Hilary's mind memory chimed. Hadn't she tried to do the same thing herself? She remembered being carried indoors by a pair of outraged hands, a woman's shrill voice scolding.

Sara was very different from Jennifer, that was for sure. But – a secret Hilary would carry to her grave – it was not so surprising, was it? Not when you remembered they had different fathers, whatever Sara's birth certificate might say. As soon as the divorce from Sean had been finalised she had in any case changed both children's names to Brand, and it was Hilary, Jennifer and Sara Brand who in the June of 1978 travelled to seek adventure in the far north of Australia.

Jennifer accepted the idea without comment but Sara was full of questions.

'Arnhem Land? What's there?'

'That's what we're going to find out.'

'Why does it have that name?'

'It's named for a Dutch ship that explored that part of the coast in the seventeenth century.'

'What was it doing there?'

'I don't know.'

'I shall find out,' Sara said.

Hilary sighed, looking out of the aircraft window. They had barely left Perth and already it had the makings of a long trip.

They were away a fortnight. Hilary acquired new images to add to those she already had. Standing on top of the escarpment called Ubirr Rock, watching the sun rise over the silent green expanse of the Nadab floodplain. The three of them sleeping in a tented camp and waking to the shriek and trumpeting of birds as they greeted the dawn. The two girls looking over the side of the ferry at Cahill's Crossing, staring into the mud-swirled waters of the East Alligator River. Their first spine-tingling sight of crocodiles on the sun-dried mud of the riverbank. So peaceful; so – surely? – harmless; so lethal.

Jennifer looked at them apprehensively. 'Will they really kill you?'

'And gobble you up,' Hilary said. 'You'd better believe it. Don't you go anywhere near them,' she told Sara who looked as though she might be planning to do just that. 'You hear me?'

It was country so remote they felt they must have travelled into a different universe. Everything they saw was new yet as old as the land itself. The black faces, the unearthly sound of what Hilary told them was a didgeridoo, the sense of other-worldliness; even the empty beaches, vast extents of yellow sand that might never have known the imprint of human feet, put there by an unseen hand for them to walk on, on the lip of an ocean that might extend forever.

A guide took them into a succession of rock shelters. They looked at the pictures stencilled on the walls. Many thousands of years old according to the guide, they were manifestations of what he told them were some of the creation figures out of which the land had been formed. There were other pictures too: of fish and possum and wallaby, and they too seemed to take form out of the rock.

They walked out of the shelter into the morning light and the world was bright and shining as though fresh-minted for their especial joy. On such a day it was a privilege to be alive and each night, eyes wide in the darkness, Hilary relived that day's enchantment: the sounds and silences; the calling of birds and humped backs of dolphins; the images setting fire to the stone within the rock shelters; the all-pervading sense of magic filling heart and mind with wonder.

The day before they left, their guide, perhaps conscious of the deference that Hilary's experiences had roused in her, took her to see a woman of the Yolngu people who, he said, used pigments she made from bush plants to create paintings depicting the past and present of her people, the rainbow serpent of the Dreaming and Ulamina, the starfish man and his stolen canoe.

The power and authenticity of the paintings struck Hilary at once. She bought two and arranged for them to be crated and sent to her in Perth. When they arrived she took them out and looked at them. She invited Kirstie MacLeod to look at them too, to share in the excitement.

Kirstie looked at them with something like resentment. A nice woman, but not one given to intellectual challenge. 'What kind of pictures are they, anyway?'

'I got them up north.'

'Oh well then.' As though nothing good ever came from what Kirstie no doubt considered heathen regions. 'What you going to do with them?'

'I shall look at them and remember my time up there. It was like visiting another world.'

'I dare say,' Kirstie said. 'Me, I'll be happy to stick with the world I got, thanks very much.'

1984–86

A SEARCH FOR ROOTS

1

Back in the wheeler-dealer world she had made her own Hilary
prospered beyond her wildest imaginings yet amid the tumult and
excitement of her success the echoes of all she had seen and felt in
Arnhem Land remained. Again and again she stood in front of the
two paintings of the Yolngu woman and shared the heritage that
she sensed in the fire and wonder of their mysterious images.

'Dunno what you see in them,' said Kirstie MacLeod.

'I see the roots of the past.' The words came from nowhere but set
Hilary thinking. 'They'll be the start of my collection.'

Because it occurred to her that a collection of Australiana,
Aboriginal as well as western, might help provide a substitute for
the roots she presently lacked.

'Most people have parents, grandparents, family they can look
back to. People who give them a sense of who they are. I don't have
that. All I know is I am an Australian. By collecting these things I
shall be creating my own past.'

'I dunno how pictures like them two will do that,' Kirstie said,
'but I suppose you know what you're doing.'

She clearly had doubts about that, but Hilary had none. She
had recreated herself from the penniless and ignorant child she had

been to what she was now. She was still doing it and, as she had told Lance Bettinger, would continue to do so all her life.

She would need help from someone who knew what he or she was talking about. She would speak to the boss of the Western Australia Art Gallery and see if he could recommend someone. She also needed someone to do a detection job for her. She had been brought up to believe she had no family, that both her parents were dead. But were they? What she remembered of those early days was that she had been told a heap of lies.

At a reception hosted by the premier she had met Bella Tucker, the legendary owner of Desire, the palatial house overlooking the Swan River, and of vast pastoral and mining interests in the far north. Hilary phoned Bella and asked if she could recommend the name of an enquiry agent who might look into the matter for her.

'Try Gayle Hastings,' Bella Tucker said. 'If you mention my name she may be able to help you.'

Hilary was in Sydney – nowadays she was spending more and more time there and beginning to think of moving there permanently – but the following morning she phoned Gayle Hastings in Perth, and she agreed to fly over the following day.

'I'll send a car to meet you,' Hilary said.

Later the following afternoon they sat down in the privacy of Hilary's office.

2

The enquiry agent was little and neat and all business. Her features were nondescript, which Hilary supposed might be useful in Gayle Hastings's line of work. She sat on the other side of Hilary's desk, wrote notes with a gold pencil in a leather-bound notebook and said she would look into things.

'I have agents in the UK,' she said. 'I'll get them digging as well. As soon as I have something I shall get back to you.'

'You will want a deposit,' Hilary said.

'Time for that later,' Gayle Hastings said. She rose to her feet. 'I'll see myself out.'

She walked to the door, footsteps silent on the Wilton carpet, and was gone. She left so little impression on the air it was hard to believe she had been there at all, yet Hilary recognised efficiency when she saw it and thought Gayle Hastings would do a good job.

She picked up her phone. 'Get hold of Sotheby's WA office. The fine art dealers, that's right. I want to speak to a man called Tom Tallis.'

They agreed to meet the following week when Hilary would be back in Perth. She met him not at the office but in the Peppermint Grove house she had bought three years before, with its views between specimen trees to the sunlit ocean.

Tom Tallis was not in the least like Gayle Hastings but equally impressive in his own way. Breaking her own rule of not pre-judging people she hadn't met she had decided Tom Tallis would either be young, extravagantly dressed with a flamboyant bow tie and the widest of wide lapels on a hairy jacket, or tall, haughty and patronising, theatrical in an Oscar Wilde-type cloak and determined to put this wealthy philistine in her place.

Both images were as wrong as they could be.

Tom Tallis turned out to be tall and lean, formally dressed in a dark suit and tie, with grey hair cut short and a high tanned forehead. He looked like a man who spent time in the open air, possibly a tennis player: which, as Hilary later discovered, was exactly what he was. None of which mattered. What was important was that the head of the art gallery had told her he was one of the leading authorities on Australian art. 'Anyone from Augustus Earle to John Blackman,' the chairman had said, 'he's your man.'

Hilary hadn't heard of either Augustus Earle or John Blackman but hoped he was right about Tom Tallis's expertise. Over coffee she explained her thinking.

'I find that very interesting,' he said. 'I believe every nation's art defines not only its history but its attitude to the world and its place in civilisation. In that sense it forms the heritage of us all.'

'Not only western civilisation,' Hilary said. 'I have a couple of Aboriginal paintings I would like you to see.'

She had them hanging in the living room. He stood and studied them silently for several minutes before turning to her. 'You bought these from a dealer?'

'From the artist.'

'Did you have anyone to advise you?'

'They were among a selection the artist showed me. I picked out a couple that I particularly liked.'

'You chose well. You obviously have a natural flair.'

She lifted her chin at him. 'For an ignoramus?'

The comment clearly did not faze him. 'For anyone.' He pointed. 'Such energy... They almost leap off the wall at you. Aboriginal art is the coming thing and I have come across a number of Aboriginal artists but I have not seen many as lively as these. A woman, you say? What did you say her name was?'

'I didn't. She did me a favour by agreeing to see me.'

'So you are not willing to give me her name?'

'Not without her permission.'

'How did you meet her?'

'When I was on holiday in Arnhem Land.'

They returned to the terrace and to a renewed pot of coffee.

'I understand you are planning to build up a collection of modern Australian art and are looking for a curator,' Tom Tallis said.

'An adviser initially. Perhaps a curator later on, when the collection takes shape.'

'And you are wondering whether to offer me the job?'

'Provided I believe we can work well together.'

'How much latitude would I have?'

'To make recommendations? Unlimited.'

'And to buy? At auction, for example?'

'Later, perhaps, but only when I'm sure we're on the same wavelength.'

'You are planning to invest in Australian art. Is that what you're saying?'

'Not quite. I intend to build the finest collection of Australiana that money can buy. Not to sell but to say to the world this is Australia's heritage. This is who we are.'

'It'll cost you.'

'Of course it will cost me. But that is what I want. My only question is whether you are the man to help me or whether I must look elsewhere.'

'Just paintings?'

'Everything. Paintings, books, journals, maps, photographs, artefacts, anything that will help to demonstrate our roots.'

As a means of establishing roots for a woman who had always been conscious of their lack, it would be a start. And hopefully Gayle Hastings would find the rest.

FOUND AGAIN, LOST AGAIN

1

'We've managed to locate your mother,' Gayle Hastings said.

Hilary's hand tightened on the telephone. She felt relief but also apprehension.

'Where?'

'North of Sydney.'

'What? Are you sure?'

'Absolutely sure.'

'I was expecting you to say she was in London.'

'Not for forty years. After the war she married an Aussie soldier and came back with him. She's lived here ever since.'

Now apprehension took another form. 'Have you spoken to her? Is she well?'

'My agent spoke to her,' Gayle Hastings said. 'She reports that considering her age your mother seemed very well. Very well physically.'

'Physically?' Hilary said.

'Apparently there is some dementia. She is living in a home.'

With Mum now well into her seventies Hilary should have thought of that possibility but had not. 'Has the agent told her about me?'

'Not yet. I thought I should discuss the situation with you first.'

'What situation is that?'

'She has three children by her second husband.'

'I suspect she and my father may never have married,' Hilary said. 'That would explain why I ended up in a home. If that was the case he would have been her first husband. But I do not see that as a problem.'

'I understand there are several grandchildren.'

That too was to be expected – almost inevitable, one might say – yet still it was a knife turning in her heart.

'Your point being?' Hilary asked.

'We do not know how she will react to having you come back into her life. It is getting on for half a century, after all.'

'You're saying she may not recognise me.'

'The world moves on; people change. And you were very young when you were taken away.'

Of course she wouldn't recognise her; she wasn't foolish enough to think she might. But she thought if she explained...

She hadn't reckoned on dementia. Or the effect her unexpected arrival might have on an old, sick woman, on the old woman's family. Thinking about it, Hilary saw that she had been no more than a milestone on the road of her mother's life. Had she the right to disrupt what little remained?

So often she had envisaged the tears and joys of reunion, the healing for them both after so long. But now?

All this needed to be thought through; Gayle Hastings had been right to do nothing before speaking to her first.

'Let me have her address,' she said. 'I'll get back to you.'

2

The home was in a small coastal town on the central coast of New South Wales. Hilary flew in by chopper.

'This shouldn't take long,' she told the pilot. 'Expect me back in two hours.'

She took a taxi to the home. It was a nice-looking place standing in its own grounds on a bluff overlooking the sea. She had spoken by telephone to the matron before leaving Sydney so she was expected. Eager Mrs Hegwood, eyes round and bright as sovereigns, made much of Hilary – 'It is not every day we are visited by such a celebrity,' she said – and sent a nurse, pert and plump, to escort their famous visitor to Mrs Jinks's room.

The nurse, all bust and bum, led the way along a concrete path past a succession of individual chalets, each fronted by a paved area with a chair placed just so and with a window looking seawards across an expanse of lawn. There were beds of flowers that had somehow survived the sea winds and beyond them a high wire fence.

'In case any of them tries to wander off,' the pert nurse said. 'Some do, from time to time. You a friend?'

'I knew her a long time ago,' Hilary said.

'I doubt she'll remember you,' the nurse said. 'Poor soul doesn't know which side is up any more.'

'Does her family visit her?'

'Her daughter comes from time to time. But it's not easy. There's no real communication.' The nurse was not too proud to grab the visiting celebrity's arm. 'There she is. Enjoying the sunshine.'

Mrs Jinks was sitting on her outside chair and staring at the ocean. Or perhaps just staring. A suet face above a body like a half-filled sack. She had scanty white hair with the scalp showing and Hilary would never have known her.

'Don't you go catching cold, Mrs Jinks,' the nurse shouted. 'Deaf,' she said to Hilary. And again shouted in a bruising, jovial voice. 'Got a visitor for you.'

But Mrs Jinks continued to stare seawards. Hilary was unused to feeling helpless but did so now. Never in a million years would she be able to relate this sad wreckage of a woman to her vague impressions of the warm and loving being from whom she had been stolen a lifetime back. Never in a million years. Yet if she felt helpless she was not intimidated; the day had not dawned when she would be that.

'Good day, Mrs Jinks.'

For the first time the old woman turned her head and looked at her.

'Hello, Alice.'

'Her daughter,' the nurse said.

'Long time since I seen you,' Mrs Jinks – *Mum?* – said. 'Why don't you come more often? Too much trouble for you to be bothered, I suppose.'

The voice was English but rang no bells.

'This isn't Alice,' the nurse said. 'This is a visitor kindly come to see you.'

'Stop it,' Mrs Jinks said. 'You think I don't know me own daughter? Stop telling me lies. She lies all the time,' she said to Hilary, whom shock had rendered speechless. 'Come to take me home, have you?'

'Now don't you go getting yourself in a state,' the nurse said. 'There's a dear.'

Despite the aggressive bust she seemed kindly enough but it was clearly hopeless. As she had said, communication was impossible.

'They come into my room at night and steal my money,' Mrs Jinks confided.

Belief suspended, Hilary rested her hand gently on the old woman's shoulder. To touch her seemed so strange, as though by doing so she might bridge the lost years. But there was nothing there. Nothing and no one. Her mother, if this was indeed her mother, did not exist.

'I'll come and see you again,' Hilary said. And fled, lips closed tight on horror, as behind her Mrs Jinks began to shout.

'Can't wait to get away, can you? Your own mother.'

Dear God.

'Don't be distressed,' the nurse said, hurrying to keep up. 'The poor old soul doesn't know what she's saying. It's sad when they get like that. But it's not as though you're family, after all.'

Hilary sat in shock as the helicopter buzzed her back to the city. The face like grey dough, the senile rage, had been a painful experience but did not erase her early childhood memories: the kindly arms, the smell of home. For the first time in years she was close to weeping at the loss of the two lives that should have grown together but instead had been so cruelly ripped apart. With the near tears came anger and a hardening resolve to do whatever it took to ensure that the same wickedness was never imposed on any child again. It was impossible to protect all children everywhere but even one saved would be better than none.

When she was back in her office she telephoned Gayle Hastings.

'No need to take your enquiries any further. Just send me your account. I appreciate all you've done.'

She put down the phone and thought again about the old woman she had seen that day. Would she visit her again? The woman called Mrs Jinks? There was no point but she thought she might, all the same. We have only one mother, after all. As for the half-sister whose existence she had only just discovered... Hilary had always wanted to find her roots but that woman was a stranger. They knew nothing of each other, would have nothing to say to each other. There was no feeling of belonging. If she'd been a Catholic she might have lit a candle but as it was... Leave it.

1987–88

CATACLYSM

1

They had been good years, challenging and exciting, in which Hilary's fortune had multiplied many times. What she had renamed the Brand Corporation had grown with it. Brand Peterfield was still bringing in the dollars with the Peterfields still running it, but it was now a small player in a vastly greater operation.

It was October 1987 and the market was going crazy, roaring up and up with never an end in sight. Up and up. Everyone from the prime minister to the office clerk was on the train pounding up the track to the country of the blessed.

Hilary went along for the ride like the rest of the world but unlike the rest of the world kept her eye on the track and her hand on the brake.

For months she and her advisers had been planning a move on Channel 12, the television company she'd coveted for years. At long last it looked as though a takeover might be a goer but she wasn't aiming to do it with too much borrowed money. Owing billions might work fine for some but Hilary had always believed in keeping her feet on the ground. Also it seemed to her the property market, still rising strongly, was beginning to look vulnerable. She decided it was time to offload.

'You crazy?' Haskins Gould's buzz-saw voice mirrored his disbelief. 'Things are just getting going.'

Maybe he was right but she didn't think so. They owned twenty-three shopping malls across the state and Hilary wanted out. 'So make me an offer, you think like that.'

He couldn't wait. Two weeks' intense negotiations and Haskins took over the malls; Hilary hung on to the undeveloped land. She let him think she was sacrificing her heart's blood by selling him the malls; in fact she was glad to see them go. When you did a development you handed over the keys, banked the cheque and moved on, but malls were a business. The returns looked good but the hassles – with tenants and self-important council officers – were never-ending. Maintenance could be a problem too. Everything had to be spotless; the shoppers wouldn't notice if it was but would be quick to move on if standards started slipping.

Haskins was leveraged out of sight to buy the malls but that wasn't Hilary's problem. She was liquid, millions in the bank as she waited for the Channel 12 deal to come to the boil.

It was as close to a done deal as you could get. Then, all of a sudden, it was not. At the eleventh hour a cowboy called Willy Montgomery came in with an offer for the shares that left the Brand Corporation floundering in the dust.

'I always knew he had more ambition than sense,' Hilary said. 'But a billion bucks? Even I never dreamt he'd come up with something as crazy as that.'

All the same she sat down with the accountants to see if they could make any sense of it. They went through the offer line by line but they all agreed that at that price the takeover was not a starter.

'Unload our holding,' Hilary said. 'The way Willy's pushed up the share price we'll make a killing anyway.'

So they would. Hilary still lacked her television station but she wasn't sentimental. She couldn't see how Willy could make a go of it with that level of debt hanging round his neck. If she was right there might be other chances down the track.

'And at a better price too.'

2

5 October: share prices surging. 9 October: the market still rising. 12 October: up again. Euphoria! Yet there were straws in the wind for those who wished to see them. The US was jittery, with sharp falls in the second half of the week, yet by Friday 16 October confidence was still high despite wild storms having closed the London markets, with dealers in their twenties eyeing the happy prospect of buying a second Ferrari to accompany the first. Haskins was bouncing like a pea on a griddle, boasting to Hilary that his malls were up more than ten per cent from the price he'd paid her such a short time ago.

'You missed out, doll! But fortune favours the brave, ain't that right? And you can't say I didn't warn you.'

Then Monday 19 October, and Chicken Little was proved right when across the world, first in Hong Kong, then in Europe and the States, the sky fell in. By the end of October the Australian market was down over forty per cent.

3

In early November Hilary was alive financially, even flourishing. All the same, the shock was huge.

She sat in her twentieth floor office at the antique desk that she'd bought in London two years earlier. It had cost a fortune. And what was it? A trinket; a statement of what she had become. A property mogul. It meant nothing. She was what she had always been: a woman, with the blood and guts of a woman. Only that. The rest... Trappings.

She had escaped the October bloodbath unscathed yet knew how close she had come to losing everything.

'Dumb luck,' she told the silent air. 'That's all it was.'

Again she remembered how in the moment of her birth she had come so close to death. Luck then; luck now.

It didn't seem enough. She thought it was time to reinvent herself. The market would be down the gurgler for months now, possibly for years. It would give her an opportunity to draw in fresh air, see new places, hear new songs. She would come back refreshed, stronger and more determined than ever. But where should she go?

She paced to and fro around the office, stopped in front of the painting facing her desk: a jungle scene by Blackman with bamboos and ferns and mystery, a rippling stream running through it and fading at last into the distance. It had entranced her from the first.

That was what she would do. She would go to Asia. She would discover the mystery of temples deep in the forest, follow jungle paths and hidden waterways, embrace renewal in the artefacts of the past.

4

Of course it was not as easy as that.

She still had a business; she could not simply abandon it. Also she was in the throes of negotiating to take over a magnificent property on Sydney Harbour from its bankrupt owner. Her mother had died six months earlier so she no longer needed to visit her at the home where she had spent her last years but she had finally decided to move the corporate headquarters from Perth to the commercial hub of the east coast.

She was satisfied that her deputy would be more than capable of running the show in her absence – she would keep in regular touch and would always be available to fly back if needed – but in the last few days she had become aware of a significant problem that would have to be sorted before she could think of going anywhere.

There were also the girls. Jennifer was nineteen, Sara three years younger. Neither was living at home: Jennifer was at secretarial college in Victoria, Sara at boarding school in Bunbury. It was important that she should discuss her plans with them both.

She had hoped Jennifer would go to university but she wasn't academically inclined and secretarial college had seemed the best alternative. She had chosen Melbourne because a friend was going there and they would be company for each other. Hilary had wondered how Jennifer would make out – she had never shown the toughness of character to be truly independent – yet she had survived well. Now she showed no concern that her mother might be disappearing off the radar for several months.

'Or maybe longer,' Hilary said.

'What do you plan to do?'

'If I knew the answer I'd tell you.'

Which seemed to satisfy Jennifer. Certainly she asked no further questions. They had always been something of an enigma to each other.

When she talked to Sara in Bunbury she found her younger child a lot more inquisitive.

Mother and daughter sat at a window table in a Victoria Street café and looked out at the arcaded shops and overhanging trees on the other side of the road. Traffic passed to and fro as they ate individual fruit pies and drank: coffee for Hilary, a banana smoothie for Sara.

'The pies are good,' Hilary said.

'They're home made.'

'And taste like it.'

'Looks like I'll be in the hockey team next year,' Sara said.

'That's nice. How are the studies?'

'Good.'

Sara did not elaborate but Hilary knew she was telling the truth; she made it her business to keep an eye on her children's academic progress. Coming from an educationally underprivileged background that would always be a matter of great importance to her and the school head had told her Sara was one of their brightest pupils.

'Any thoughts what you want to do when you leave school?'

'I'd like to get involved in the media. Television.'

'I missed out on Channel 12,' Hilary said.

Sara slurped her drink; the window rattled as a large truck powered past. 'Are you disappointed?'

'I was at the time. But the way things worked out I was lucky. It meant we were able to ride out the storm.'

'Was it that bad?'

'It still is. We haven't seen the end of it, not by a long chalk.'

'Is that why you're going away?'

'Partly.'

Sara thought for a while before answering. 'Are you hoping to find out things?'

'Yes.'

'About yourself?'

'Mainly, yes.' Sara's adult awareness never ceased to amaze her. 'I suppose you could say about life generally.'

'Where are you going?'

'Southeast Asia. Apart from that I don't know at this stage.'

'Going walkabout?'

'Something like that.'

'How long will you be away?'

'However long it takes. Six months. Maybe longer.'

'But you'll keep in touch?'

'Every week.'

'When are you leaving?'

'As soon as I can.'

'What's keeping you?'

'There's a problem at work.'

'Serious problem?'

'Unfortunately yes. But I'll sort it out.'

'I wish I had your self-confidence,' Sara said.

'You'll be fine,' her mother said.

5

The problem was serious indeed because Haskins Gould had been cheating her. Systematically, over several years, he had been siphoning off development funds to play the stock market in his own name – and he'd made millions from it, at least on paper: millions that weren't his. Hilary would never have found out had the market not crashed. But it had and Haskins had been caught, unable to repay what he still insisted had only been a loan. Now she and Brand Corporation were out two and a half million.

'A loan, for God's sake!' Haskins tried to look fierce, missed by a mile. 'No need to get your knickers in a knot. I'll pay it back.'

'Of course you will,' said Hilary. She waited a beat. 'When?'

He spread his arms like a drowning man. 'Soon as I can.'

'And how, exactly?'

Haskins hated to be pinned down. 'Listen, Hilary, it's the market. You know that. As soon as things pick up again –'

'No.'

'Whadda you mean?'

'I mean I am not prepared to wait.'

'Don't come hard-nosed on me,' he said. 'What do you expect me to do?'

'I expect you to find the money and pay back what you've misappropriated.'

'Misappropriated? What the hell d'you mean by that?'

'I mean stolen. As in theft.'

Hilary's glare would have flayed the skin from a man less brazen faced than Haskins Gould. The money mattered but what really hurt was her loss of faith in a man she had thought she could trust. Yet at another level of her mind she knew she was not surprised; Haskins had always sailed close to the edge. Knowing that, Hilary was furious: not that Haskins had tried to do her down but that she had been trusting enough to let him. She would never forgive either of them for that. She remembered what the sub-contractor had said when they'd been building the Busselton Mall. *Cuts more corners than a grand prix driver.* How right he had been.

'I mean I want my money and I want it now.'

'I haven't got it.'

'Then find it. I'll give you six weeks.'

'Do me a favour! How am I supposed to find two and a half million in six weeks?'

'You've got assets. That mansion in Point Piper. Sell it.'

'The market like it is? I'll be lucky to get half what I paid for it!'

'That's not my problem.'

Haskins was incoherent, huge hands flailing, spit flying. 'That's right. Kick a man when he's down. What kind of bitch are you, anyway?'

'A bitch who wants her money back.'

He would have killed her if he could. His shoulders hunched. 'You sure know how to make an enemy, Hilary.'

He had frightened many in his time but Hilary was not so easily scared. 'You did that, Haskins, when you broke our trust.'

'That right? Then I'll tell you something else. You'll get your money. But I'll be back. And I shall make it my business to bring you down, Hilary. You can take that to the bank!'

'I can hardly wait,' she said. Contempt larded her voice.

She never knew how he managed it but somehow he came up with the money with two days to spare.

'All present and correct, right? Storm in a teacup, right?'

'I have never been fond of tea,' Hilary said.

1988–89

HOUSE AMID THE COCONUTS

1

In July 1988, after seven months wandering the byways of South-east Asia, Hilary met Craig Laurie in a tearoom on the summit of the three-thousand-foot peak called Penang Hill.

She had arrived on Penang Island the previous afternoon after a hot and frustrating trip from Trang in Southern Thailand. The coach had been crowded, the air-conditioning had broken down and by the time they finally crossed the bridge to Penang Island Hilary had felt as limp as a badly wrung-out dishcloth and was thoroughly fed up with herself. A woman nearing fifty on a pilgrimage to nowhere: where was the sense in that?

Now, a day later, she was squashed into another crowded space and asking herself the same question. She had been talked into making the half-hour train journey up the mountain by an English tourist whom she had met the previous evening, and was now bitterly regretting her decision. The train was packed. Jammed with twenty other people into a space the size of a lavatory Hilary had mislaid her companion somewhere in the mob. Hot bodies crushed her on every side and Hilary spent the journey staring at the back of a man's sweaty neck and praying the ordeal would soon be over.

By the time the train reached the summit she was in the mood to cut throats. She found Ruby Dyer, the English tourist who had battened on to her the previous afternoon. Thankfully she sucked fresh air into her lungs as she walked out of the station, only to find herself trapped in the midst of another crowd staring and exclaiming at the view of the city and coastline far below.

'Look at that, Hilary! Come and look!'

Ruby was enthusiasm on steroids but what Hilary wanted was not a view but a refuge, somewhere to sit in the shade, drink coffee and luxuriate in the cooler air of the hilltop.

'Let's keep moving,' she said.

And she did so, leaving an overweight Ruby struggling to catch up.

Miracle of miracles, Hilary found what she wanted in a colonial-style bungalow in its own grounds, approached up a steep gravel path. Beyond a hedge and old-fashioned wooden gate an expanse of shaded lawn was bordered by flowering shrubs and a table, to which a deferential waiter brought scones and jam, with real cream in a silver bowl and coffee for Hilary, a pot of tea for her companion. It spoke of a more gracious age and Hilary's clenched nerves began to relax.

Ruby, hot and flustered, departed in search of a Ladies while Hilary leant back in her chair, breathing the delights of solitude for the first time since her companion had homed in on her by the hotel swimming pool the previous afternoon, entangling her in the relationship with which she was presently afflicted.

During her Asian walkabout Hilary had turned her back on fancy hotels but yesterday had thought this one would do as a base while she looked for a small cottage out in the country where she could feel close to the earth. It was a relationship she had lost in recent years; only now was she beginning to rediscover how important to her it was.

A European man in his fifties came out of the bungalow, walked down the steps from the entrance and strolled across the close-clipped lawn towards her. He was tall and lean, with dark hair cut short and good shoulders, and was wearing a dark blue shirt and cream cotton trousers. He looked all together and purposeful and Hilary thought he might be interesting.

'G'day.'

Another Australian? Better still. She smiled up at him. 'G'day.'

'On holiday?'

'Sort of. And you?'

'You could say I'm on holiday all the time.' He grinned. 'I live here.'

That was interesting, too. He was surely too young to be retired. An artist of some kind? An international criminal?

'Why don't you sit down? I'm waiting for a friend,' Hilary said. It was only fair to warn him.

He smiled but remained standing. 'I saw her. I was sitting on the veranda when the two of you arrived. She looked a little flustered.'

'She was.'

'Where are you staying?'

'Batu Ferringhi. The Maharani.'

'Where all good tourists go when they die,' he said.

'And maybe some not-so-good ones, too.'

He laughed. 'We live in hope,' he said. 'Do you have a name?'

'Hilary.'

She was cautious about revealing her surname, especially with Australians. Hilary Brand had become famous – some would have said notorious – as one of the few tycoons who had walked away unscathed from the market crash that the previous October had left the battlefields of the financial world littered with the dead and dying. Skase, Bond, Rivkin, Connell, Holmes à Court and a dozen others were gone or seriously wounded. All had been much more famous than she but Hilary Brand had always been a private person who preferred to leave the headlines to others.

'Craig Laurie,' he said.

Ruby had emerged from the bungalow and was making her way across the grass towards them.

'I see your friend is coming,' he said. 'I'll leave you to it.'

A smile of the well shaped mouth, a flick of the hand and he was gone. Hilary watched him go out the gate and disappear.

'Who was that?' Ruby said.

'Some bloke passing the time of day,' Hilary said.

A pity he hadn't stayed. She had rather liked the look of him.

2

The next morning he turned up at the hotel.

The sun was barely clear of the horizon but Hilary was an early riser and had already been for a walk along the beach. Now she was breakfasting on the terrace and wondering what joys Ruby had dreamt up for today. A trip to Tanjong Bunga, perhaps. Take in the shops. Exclaim over brocaded cloth in an Indian store. Pick up a cheap memento or two to take home. Even the thought irritated her. The day before she had gone along with Ruby's plans but enough was enough. Now it was time to reclaim her life.

She would hire a car, explore the back blocks, see something of the country. Forget Ruby. There would be hills out there, patches of emerald paddy and coconut groves, tiny kampongs away from the coastal strip. That was what she wanted. You could keep the shops.

She paused in the act of buttering a croissant and there Craig Laurie was, as tall and trim as she remembered, his outline silhouetted against the morning sky.

Startled but pleased, she smiled up at him. 'I didn't know you were staying here.'

'I'm not. I came to look for you.'

A nerve jumped in Hilary's stomach. She finished buttering the croissant, added a dab of strawberry jam and took a bite. 'Why would you do that?'

'To ask if you'd like to spend the day with me.'

'Perhaps you'd better sit down,' Hilary said.

He did so. She saw that his eyes were the same dark blue as his short-sleeved shirt. Saw, too, that his sun-browned arms were strong, the flesh firm and well muscled. Again that dangerous nerve flipped in her stomach.

'Would you like some coffee?'

'Thank you.'

She raised her hand and the waiter came at once. She continued to eat her croissant, watching Craig thoughtfully. The smell of gardenias from the garden was very strong.

'Does this invitation include my friend?'

'Just you.'

'And how would we spend the day?'

'I thought a drive through the country. Get away from the mob for a while.'

'Why do you suppose I might want to get away from the mob?'

'You were at Brown's Restaurant on Penang Hill,' he pointed out. 'You wouldn't have been there if you liked crowds.'

It was an enticing prospect. And with this man...

That nerve was on overtime now.

'There is a waterfall in the hills,' he said. 'It has a pool at the bottom. By tropical standards the water's cool. Bring bathers; we could swim. Afterwards we could have lunch. I know a restaurant with an outside terrace. The owner will cook up something special for us if you can handle Chinese food.'

Hilary could handle Chinese food very well. And his suggestions fitted perfectly with her inclinations. And yet...

She didn't know this man. Caution was clearly called for; then she pictured the waterfall high in the hills, the water that by tropical standards was cool. She thought of Ruby brimming with bright ideas how they might spend the day. She thought, to hell with caution.

She said: 'Give me a minute to write my friend a note.'

3

The hills climbed skywards in many folds with bare rock on the higher slopes yet Craig's ute devoured the steepest climbs without hesitation.

Hilary saw no sign of human life yet the crowded pavements of the coastal strip were less than an hour away. No doubt Ruby would be cross at being abandoned but Hilary had no regrets. *Je ne regrette rien.* She had always been an admirer of Edith Piaf and her famous song.

They were off the bitumen now. His eyes watched the gravel road and his hands – strong and tanned, with fine hair on the backs of the fingers – were steady on the wheel. Hilary felt safe with this man. A thought came uninvited and potentially dangerous. How safe did she want to be?

The road climbed to a ridge, grey stone against a gentian sky. Beyond the ridge the way slanted steeply downhill with a wooden bridge at the bottom and Hilary saw the silver glint of water.

The tyres crunched on gravel as the ute drew to a stop just before the bridge. Craig switched off the engine.

'Now we walk,' he said.

They followed a narrow track beside the stream. The water ran fast, glinting over the stones. Craig went first, Hilary watching his back as she followed. The strong shoulders beneath the blue shirt. The seamed neck.

Frogs chinked in the thick grass and from time to time small birds flew in sudden flashes of variegated colours, too swiftly to be identified. The track drew a long curve through the bush. The voice of the water grew suddenly louder and Hilary saw they had come to the fall.

It was about fifteen metres wide and double that in height. The water flashed in rainbows of brilliant light as it fell into a rock-fringed pool before spilling over a lip and continuing down the valley. On either side of the pool the forest grew close, with trees leaning over the water. The sound of the fall was very loud and beyond it Hilary could see nothing but sky.

Craig stripped off his shirt and pants. His chest was flat and hard, exactly as she had imagined it. She had put on her cozzie at the hotel. She stood at the edge of the pool and looked at the water.

'How deep is it?'

'About four feet here. More in the middle.'

She made a shallow plunge, then stood with the water cascading off her. The water came to just below her breasts and was as cool as Craig had promised. She looked back at him. 'Coming in?'

'Of course.'

He dived in and surfaced beside her. They stood and smiled at each other before Hilary turned and swam up the pool until she reached the fall. The water crashed on her head but behind the curtain was an oasis of peace where the rock had been hollowed out over the centuries. She looked back through the veil of falling water. Even the roar of the stream was muted here.

Craig joined her. There was room for two if they stood close together. They stood very close indeed and Craig kissed her and she kissed him back. The kiss lasted a long time and all the while Hilary was asking herself what she thought she was doing.

It was a legitimate question but she knew it was already too late. There had been a time when she had sworn off men but that had been after the break-up with Lance. Eighteen years ago, she thought. My God! There had been one or two brief episodes since then but nothing of importance. Eighteen years, and now she was hungry for this man who had come so unexpectedly into her life and was thankful that her breasts were still firm, her body ten years younger than her age.

He caressed her upper arms and shoulders, pulled down the top of her costume and kissed first one breast then the other. She shivered not with cold but with heat as she leant against him. She held his head and pressed it to her. There. Oh God. There.

He stood back and smiled before kissing her mouth again. Her lips parted and she wondered whether her legs would be strong enough to hoist her out of the water when the time came.

'Shall we swim?' he asked.

She took a succession of deep breaths as she willed her heart to slow. She followed Craig back through the fall. They swam to and fro, splashing water over each other and laughing open-mouthed. Like kids, she thought, but so much more than that. Eventually they climbed out of the pool and lay on a rock shelf to let the sun dry them. The rock was warm beneath Hilary's shoulders, the noise of the fall once again loud in her ears.

She had wondered whether he would make love to her straight-away but he did not. They towelled off, got dressed and went in search of the restaurant he had mentioned.

The meal was as good as he had promised. After they had eaten, after Craig had thanked the smiling proprietor and paid him, they climbed into the ute and drove away, heading where she neither knew nor cared.

She wondered how often he had done this and with how many women. She wondered what he did for a living. She wondered who he was and why he had chosen to live in Penang. None of it mattered. The answers would come or not in their season. In the meantime he drove, she leaning back in her seat, eyes closed and heart thundering. It was then that he placed his left hand on her bare thigh. She put her hand on his and pressed it hard against her. While her senses swam, the engine hummed and the kilometres flew back.

4

Eventually they turned on to a side road that led past paddy fields where water buffalo were working, and Hilary caught glimpses of the sea between the trees. They turned on to a muddy track that ran downhill past more coconut palms and the occasional house raised on wooden piles above the ground. Indignant chooks catapulted beneath their wheels while women with shawled heads watched them from the shadows. A hundred metres past the last house the track ended. Craig switched off the engine, and they left the vehicle and walked down through the trees.

They came to a beach of yellow sand edging a horseshoe-shaped bay. Thirty metres back from the beach a house stood amid a grove of yet more coconuts. Red and yellow cannas grew in beds along the front of the house, whose wooden walls shone chestnut-coloured in the sun. This house too was raised on piles and had an arcaded veranda running along the front with a flight of steps leading up to it. The house was sturdily built and Hilary thought she had never seen a building more in harmony with its surroundings.

'What a wonderful place!'

'I like it,' Craig said.

'Does it have a name?'

'A Malay one. I decided to call it Rumah Kelapa.'

'Meaning?'

'The House amid the Coconuts.'

'Rumah Kelapa,' Hilary repeated.

The words flowed like honey on the tongue, the name and house yet more components of this day of endless wonder.

'Let me show you round.'

Hilary followed him up the steps to the veranda. From here she could see the entirety of the bay. At the far end was a point of land with the houses of another kampong showing through the trees. Three canoes were drawn up on the sand in front of them.

'The Malays called them koleks,' Craig said. 'They're handy for fishing or exploring the coast.'

The silence was absolute. Hilary thought this must surely be the end of the world or perhaps the beginning of paradise.

The interior of the house consisted of a succession of spacious rooms with glass windows through which the afternoon sun shone. The sunlight glowed on the wooden walls so that every room seemed to float in golden light. The furniture included large and comfortable easy chairs with plenty of cushions in brightly coloured Siamese silk. Persian rugs were scattered here and there. Wooden shelves crammed with books ran around the walls with more books in haphazard piles upon the floor. Books apart, everything was spick and span.

'A woman comes in twice a week,' Craig explained. 'She does the washing and ironing too.'

Every room had lofty ceilings from which hung broad-bladed fans.

'Although they are not really necessary,' Craig said. 'Since I had air-conditioning put in.'

'Where do you get your power?'

'Generators. They chew kerosene like crocodiles but make a big difference to your personal comfort. And the glass windows keep out the mosquitoes.'

Hilary walked out on to the veranda. Silence, like the house and trees, enfolded her. She observed the green vegetation, the red and yellow cannas, the blue sky and bluer sea, the sickle curve of yellow sand. She was conscious of Craig standing at her shoulder.

'It is more perfect than I could have imagined,' she said.

Two cane chairs and a round glass-topped table stood on the veranda. Craig gestured to them. 'I'll get us a glass of wine.'

She sat looking at the placid waters of the bay, the slatted leaves of the palms hanging in the still air, and wondered where she was going with this man. If anywhere. She smiled ruefully. She was not in the least tranquil by nature but now was prepared to wait tranquilly to see what the future would bring.

What it brought: a glass of white wine, flint dry and cold, with a round of Brie from which Craig cut segments with a broad-bladed knife. A meandering stroll along the beach. They watched the sun's red disc slide below the horizon. Lights began to flicker in the houses on the point. Waves shod with phosphorescence turned at their feet. Craig's fingers, interlaced with hers, were firm and warm.

Hilary thought, I have said nothing about going back to the hotel. Neither has he. What would she say if he said nothing? What would she say if he did?

They reached the end of the beach where the koleks lay on the sand. They turned back, Hilary's hand clasped as firmly as ever.

Perhaps he would drive her back to the hotel and leave her there. An end to the magical day and all its potential.

Did she want that? She did not. So would she stay, with all that implied? They were strangers; she knew almost nothing about him. Would she stay if the stranger asked?

They reached the house and climbed the steps. Since they left the waterfall he had not kissed her. Would he kiss her now? Would her soul fly out? He switched on the lights and turned to her. Beyond the windows the night was dark. Hilary could see her reflection lonely and wondering in the glass. She remembered how eager she had been for Sean Madigan, eager enough to marry him. Look how that had turned out.

She was older now, wiser and more cautious. But still eager. She wanted to eat Craig up. Be eaten up in her turn.

He was there. His lips were on hers. His hands were moving.

Yes.

5

She woke in the night with Craig asleep at her side. It was the dark of the moon and she could see nothing. Craig had said he did not like to sleep in air-conditioning and the windows were open with a mesh screen to protect them from mosquitoes. The slowly turning fan distributed its current of warm air. Hilary could hear waves stirring along the beach.

Their lovemaking had been all and more than she could have imagined. He had been gentle yet dominant, every nerve in her body responding as he made love to her. Really made love, as though love itself and not simply the act of love had been at the core of their union. She had heard herself cry out in wonder and at the last, after he had wound her nerves to their highest pitch so that they vibrated under her skin and every sinew of her body pleaded for release, she had felt a surge of fulfilment that had torn her and made her whole again, not once but again and yet again, and brought her in the end to the verge of grateful and unbelieving tears.

So wonderful. Such sanctuary and peace.

She imagined the stars beyond the windows. One hundred million points of light amid the blackness. She could have embraced them all, embraced everything. All was wonder and joy because she knew that after the barren months of seeking she had arrived at what might be journey's end.

She slept. When she awoke it was still dark but she sensed beyond the screened window the slow stirring of earth and sea as they readied themselves for the coming of the light. That was the true miracle. The coming of the light, the re-awakening of the dormant blood, the quickening of the spirit that proclaimed the wonder and joy of the coming day.

Careful not to disturb Craig, she slipped from beneath the sheet that covered her. She retrieved her shirt and shorts from the chair where she had dropped them. She put them on and went out to face the morning.

The sand was soft beneath her bare feet. Phosphorescence flashed in the slowly turning waves while overhead was the splendour of the stars. Hilary walked at one with the night. The jungle scent of the vegetation was a fecund presence in the darkness. Its mystery still had the power to beguile. She reached the point where the koleks lay unguarded upon the beach. There was a smell of fish and wood smoke from the houses beneath the trees. She stopped and stared at the sea. Conrad's Almayer stood at her shoulder but Almayer had been a lost soul. Hilary was not. She walked back towards the house. She was halfway when she saw a figure walking towards her along the beach. For a moment doubt flickered, then she saw.

'Good morning.'

'I thought you'd run out on me,' Craig said.

'No doubt you thought good riddance.'

'No doubt I thought nothing of the sort.'

It was a good, warm feeling. He took her hand and that was a good feeling too.

Above the eastern horizon darkness was giving way to the first pale birthing of the light.

'I thought maybe some coffee,' Craig said.

It sounded like a good idea.

'And afterwards…'

She looked at him, his features now faintly visible: the imperious jutting of the nose, the shadowed eye sockets. 'Afterwards?'

'Coffee has to be paid for.'

'You plan to put me to work, do you?'

'Something like that.'

'Best get on with it, then,' Hilary said.

And they did.

Later, after showering and putting on the same clothes because she had no others, after breakfast and more coffee, they piled into the four-wheel drive and drove back up the rumble-tumble track to the road and turned north towards Batu Ferringhi and the Maharani Hotel. Hilary went to her room.

The first thing she did was ring Sara's school and then Jennifer. Sara was in class and unavailable but she had better luck with Jennifer.

'I'm in Penang.'

'Are you having a good time?'

'Very good. I may stay on here a bit but I'll let you know what I decide. Could you please tell Sara for me? I couldn't get hold of her.'

'You sound different,' Jennifer said.

'How different?'

'You sound happy.'

Hilary laughed. 'Do I normally sound so grim?'

'I didn't mean that. But there's something...'

Now was not the moment for confidences. 'All well with you?'

'Fine.'

'Good. I must dash. My love to you both, as always.'

She hung up, packed her bag and wrote a note to Ruby Dyer.

Something has come up and I have moved out. I hope you enjoy the rest of your holiday.

Ruby would not be pleased but Hilary was not going to say she was sorry because she wasn't. She was full of joy because the prospect of life had returned.

She read the note through before signing it. *Something has come up...* How true was that? Even to think of it woke pleasurable tingles.

She left the note at reception, settled her bill and ran down the steps to the waiting vehicle.

'I thought I'd lost you,' Craig said.

'I had to ring my daughters.'

'To tell them you've found the love of your life?'

'I don't know that yet, do I?' She climbed into the ute. 'I shall need to buy some clothes,' she said. 'The ones I have are a bit raggy-taggy.'

'That's a disappointment,' Craig said.

'Why?'

'I wasn't planning on your wearing clothes.'

'Just now and then.'

'That's all right then.'

'I suppose you say that to all the girls.'

'Of course.'

'Shops,' Hilary said.

'Your wish is my command.'

They drove to a mall on Gurney Drive where there were shops aplenty. Afterwards they went back to the bungalow where she had another shower – the climate made that a good idea – and put on some of her new clothes and Craig drove her to the E and O Hotel for lunch.

The E and O was a relic of the colonial past with a strip of lawn and a low wall at the back, with the slow grey sea visible through the dining room windows.

While they ate they talked. They had made love twice already. They were lovers not only in the physical but every other way yet knew virtually nothing about each other.

Until now it hadn't mattered. There had been a shared awareness that precluded the need for greater knowledge. Now it was time to move on.

He told her he was fifty-three. He had been born in a posh Sydney suburb but had found when he grew up that a conventional civilian life was not for him.

'There were challenges in civilian life,' he said. 'But none that interested me.'

He joined the army straight from university. He had graduated in electronic engineering so they were keen to have him. It looked as though he could look forward to a stellar career in the military.

'Then I found I wasn't one for the military life after all,' he said. 'I should have known: I hadn't liked the boy scouts either. I had no thoughts on what else to do so decided I'd explore a bit. In the course of my travels I came here and loved it. I'd inherited a bit of money – enough to get by in a low-cost place, which fortunately this was – so I decided to stay. And here I am.'

'But what do you do?'

'A bit of consulting for local firms. Apart from that there are a thousand things to do. I walk, I swim, I go out with the fishermen, I read, I listen to music... You want me to go on?'

'You never married?'

Which was not what she was asking. Never mind the past. What she really wanted to know was whether he was married now.

'I never did,' he said.

'Why?'

He grinned. 'Never found anyone fool enough to say yes.'

Hilary looked at him and at the expanse of sea beyond the hotel windows, the distant shapes of vessels anchored in the roads.

'I like it here,' she said. 'Where I was before I came here was very beautiful too. But it didn't feel right.'

Craig watched her. He said nothing.

'I took a boat up the Mekong to Pakbeng, in Laos. There was a lodge for rich tourists and a temple in the hills with three golden figures beneath a cloth canopy. I thought it would be quiet. Sacred. It wasn't. The place was packed with tourists. I was a tourist myself so I couldn't complain but I felt we were treating the inhabitants like creatures in a zoo.'

'You were also providing them with an income.'

'I know. But it wasn't right. For me, I mean.'

'We have tourists, too. And Penang is a busy place.'

'I've only been here five minutes but I get the impression it doesn't seem to matter so much here. The tourists are just part of the whole. In Pakbeng they were everything. By being there I felt we desecrated the place. It was beautiful but I couldn't wait to get away. Penang is different. I think I could live here.'

Craig took her hand across the table. 'Then do that,' he said.

She watched him, feeling the pressure of his hand. 'For a week? A month?'

'Try forever.'

'You are serious?'

'Never more so,' he said.

Indeed it was a serious business. Commitment to the man meant, did it not, commitment to his way of life? She tried to imagine herself spending the long years in this place. She could not get her head around it. Craig was offering a romantic hideaway on a tropical island out of the storybooks. A wonderful destination for a holiday, but for life? Hilary was not willing to commit herself to that.

What she was willing to do was give herself time to enjoy this charismatic man with his wonderful house and a way of life that for a time at least was a siren song of enchantment. Turn him down and she knew she would regret it forever.

He was still holding her hand. She looked at him across the table.

'You do me great honour,' she said. 'Let's give it six months and see how it goes.'

Six months was good. She could handle six months. It would give her time but not too much. If at the end of it she wanted to take it further and he was still willing, so be it. Either way, by then she would surely know.

I shall dare the sirens but hang on to my lifeboat.

Australia was a million miles away but that night, waking briefly in the slow pre-dawn hours, she remembered the cut and thrust of her business life and knew, even as she drifted back to sleep, that the chains of the past were not so easily broken.

LOOKING LAZY AT THE SEA

1

It was evening. They had been together six weeks and were sitting in easy chairs on the veranda of Rumah Kelapa. It was warm and still and the glasses containing their drinks were beaded with moisture. The sun's lower hemisphere was an inch or two above the horizon, its image shimmering and distorted like a reflection in a pool. It was a breathless moment of failing light and the cicadas were setting up their nightly chorus in the undergrowth.

'What were you doing before you left Australia?' Craig asked.

'A bit of this, a bit of that.'

'That really spells it out,' he said. 'But it's not important. I get the Australian papers, you see.'

She looked at him.

'I've known from the first,' he said. 'Where is Australia's missing millionaire? Brand Corporation boss seeks redemption in the mystic east. Has Hilary a secret lover?'

She didn't know whether to laugh or scream. 'Why didn't you tell me?'

'I assumed you didn't want to talk about it. I believe in privacy, you see.'

'I never thought... I must speak to the girls.'

'Why?'

'What must they think, reading crap like that?'

'You speak to them every week,' Craig said.

'But –'

'Have they ever mentioned it? Do they sound bothered?'

'No –'

'They aren't children. They are women. Give them some credit.'

He was right, of course he was.

'The media comes up with such nonsense,' she said. 'It's one of the reasons I've always wanted to own my own television station.'

'But you never have.'

'Not yet.'

He drained his glass. 'Ah…'

'Why ah?'

'Because you said not yet. I was beginning to hope you had forgotten about the world out there.'

'How can I possibly forget it, or the girls? But one thing staying here has done for me: it's put things into perspective. There was a time when business and the market were the only things that mattered to me. To succeed, beat down the opposition, overcome the obstacles… When you start with nothing that's important.' A self-deprecating smile. 'I saw success in business as my highway to the stars. It *was* my life. Now I know it is only a part of it.' She reached across the table and took his hand. 'I won't lie to you: it still matters. But I am very glad we found each other.'

It was a commitment of sorts, but not enough. They looked at each other. She saw Craig lick his lips but his eyes were steady.

'I love you,' he said.

There. He had said it. He had unlocked the door and now Hilary found it easy to follow him into whatever might lie ahead for them both.

'I love you too.'

She had never thought to hear herself say such a thing again but she had. She felt a weight lift from her heart and knew her commitment to this man was not only soul-felt but forever.

Hands held tight to hands. Eyes drank.

The sun had disappeared below the horizon, leaving only a diminishing scarlet glow that was reflected in the undulating waves. The noise of the cicadas was tremendous. In near darkness they finished their drinks and stood up, the mood between them as tranquil as the darkening sea. Hand in hand they went into the house.

2

'It's time for me to take up the reins again,' Hilary said five months later. She spoke with conviction but there was sadness in her face that gave Craig hope, even when he knew there was no hope.

'Why must you? You're rich enough, surely? Why do you have to keep on working?'

'Business is what I do. I'm good at it and enjoy it, so it doesn't feel like work at all. Besides, it's not just a case of making money but of contributing. The creation of wealth benefits all society. If you doubt that you only have to look at how people live in countries that don't have it.'

'And where does that leave us?'

She walked to the window and looked out at the green stretch of lawn, the beds of red and yellow cannas blazing in the sunlight, the expanse of ocean beyond the casuarina trees. While he watched her back silently.

'Exactly where we are now,' she said. 'I shall come over here every year, if you'll have me. I'd like to think you'll come to Australia too. There's the telephone. There is this new email system everyone's talking about at home. We'll be able to communicate with each other every day.'

'It won't be the same.'

'No, it won't. But life is a compromise, isn't it? As compromises go, this seems to me a pretty good one.'

'You asked me once why I decided to settle in Penang,' Craig said.

'I'm not pushing you,' Hilary said. 'But whenever you want to talk about it, I'm listening.'

'Let me open a bottle of wine.'

He brought the wine and two glasses. They sat on the deck look-ing at the darkening sea and Craig talked.

When he had been in the army he had come across homeless children forced to scavenge like rats to survive.

'I saw them for myself. I'd read how children across the world, some as young as five, were being sold into what was effectively slavery yet nothing much was being done about it. After I left the army I decided to try and change that.'

The problem was, he said, that the sort of rescue operation he had in mind was an expensive business and governments were reluctant to hand out cash for anything but their own pet projects.

'If I had commercial backing they might agree to kick in some-thing but without it...' He shrugged.

'But why Penang?'

'Because the state government here said it would provide the land if I could come up with the money.'

'To do what?'

'To operate a home for damaged and runaway kids. So I thought: why not? I loved the place anyway. So I put down roots and hoped something would turn up.'

'And has it?'

'Basically, no.'

Hilary drank wine. The sea was almost invisible now and the dark sky was a chain of stars. She watched the lights of a vessel heading south into the Malacca Strait. 'Why didn't you tell me this before?'

'I was afraid you might think I was trying to bludge on you.'

'And now?'

'Now I know you better.' He laughed. 'Although I wouldn't say no if you agreed to help.'

Hilary thought, sipping more wine. 'My company has a policy of supporting worthy causes. Of which this is clearly one.'

He watched her. 'But?'

'Until now we have confined ourselves to Australian charities.'

'Charity begins at home?'

'Well, it does, doesn't it?' She thought some more. 'Let me mull over it for a while. Like it or not I am the custodian of other people's money. What sort of funding are we talking about?'

'As much as you can provide.'

She nodded. 'Let me think about it. I'll get back to you.'

'From Australia?'

'Yes.'

It was a sad day, one week later, when Craig drove her to Penang's country-style airport for the first leg of her return flight to Australia.

She collected her boarding pass and returned to where Craig was standing, a mariner shipwrecked amid a sea of faces.

'I love you,' Craig said.

'And I you.'

They had told each other that many times and it was as true now as it had been that first time but he shook his head, his face immeasurably sad. 'I hate this.'

She had locked her smile in place and would not let it slip. 'Think of it as a temporary parting.'

'I wonder.'

She gripped his hands in hers. 'I promise you. Unless you change your mind.'

'That I shall never do.'

Precious words. She carried them on to the plane like a priest bearing a chalice. Courage, she thought. That was the key.

1998

A NEW HORIZON

1

On Thursday 14 July 1998 Hilary sat in her office and stared thoughtfully at the man on the other side of her desk. He was young and his slender body trembled with barely controlled energy. He also had what she thought of as visionary's eyes, looking beyond the horizon at images only he could see. She had seen the same look in photographs of the arctic explorer Fridtjof Nansen and in icons of medieval saints but William Gainsborough was neither explorer nor saint; he was a scientist, a medical doctor who claimed to be working on a discovery that would revolutionise the treatment of cancer and other genetic diseases.

It was unusual for a man like Gainsborough to get to see Hilary at all; Janet in the front office screened out most of those who came hoping for funding for this or that project. They were many, most of their ideas ludicrous or unworkable or with no realistic prospect of commercial application or success, but this man, Janet had said, was different. He had come to talk about a sheep.

'Are you serious?'

'Just see him, Hilary. I get the feeling he's on to something but that'll be for you to judge.'

Hilary pondered, checking the gold Patek Philippe watch that had been Craig's gift to her. 'I'll give him five minutes,' she said. 'Ring me after that, remind me I have a board meeting.'

It was a game they had played ever since Janet had joined her five years before.

Within a minute William Gainsborough was in her office. At first sight he could have passed as a teenager with his blond hair falling in a soft wave over his forehead but it turned out he was in his early thirties with an impressive track record and degrees from a number of important universities. He had worked as a research assistant, most recently with Ian Wilmut at Scotland's Roslin Institute, and now was heading up a laboratory in WA.

'You want to talk to me about sheep?' Hilary said.

William laughed. 'Maybe one specific sheep.'

Hilary found the faint Scots accent as attractive as the man but she had no time for games, verbal or otherwise. She made a point of glancing at her watch. 'Explain.'

'Dolly the sheep was the first mammal to be successfully cloned from a single adult stem cell.'

'I remember reading about that. But if you're planning to clone human beings I doubt I can help you. The ethical concerns –'

'Are huge,' he said. 'I am well aware of that. I doubt it's possible in any case, given our present state of knowledge. I am talking about something entirely different.'

No looking at her watch now. 'Continue.'

'Our present research relates to the study of genetic diseases for which there is presently no cure. Within twenty years, possibly less, I believe we could be looking at the eradication of all forms of cancer, birth defects and Alzheimer's Disease, to say nothing of the damage to tendons and ligaments in the human body that at present account for over a quarter of this country's disability cases.'

'You said we *could* be looking,' Hilary said. 'What's the snag?'

'What it always is,' William Gainsborough said. 'Money. Or the lack of it.'

'You are hoping that this company will fund, or help to fund, the research you are discussing?'

'In a nutshell.'

'Then, in a nutshell, the answer is no.'

He hadn't been expecting that. 'No?'

'Not at this point. I take it we are talking of a great deal of money?'

'But the benefits –'

'Just answer me, Dr Gainsborough. Are we or are we not talking of a great deal of money?'

'It depends what you mean by a great deal.'

'Tens of thousands? Hundreds of thousands? Millions?'

'It is very hard to estimate –'

'No. I'm sorry. This won't do. Give me a straight answer or go.'

The phone rang. She lifted the receiver. 'Ask them to wait ten minutes.'

'I thought you'd find him interesting,' Janet said.

'Perhaps.' Hilary replaced the receiver. Her eyes dared him. 'You were saying?'

'I am not prepared to put a figure on it but it will be substantial. There is need for specialist equipment...'

'We are talking millions,' Hilary said. Putting the concept out there, flat and undeniable, so they could both see and acknowledge it.

'Perhaps. In the long run.' He spoke reluctantly, his accent stronger now. 'Research of this type is very expensive.'

'You have costings? A specific proposal?'

He looked at her helplessly.

'We are a commercial organisation,' Hilary said. 'Not a charity. We donate money to certain charities but we have shareholders, a board of directors. You know what they will say if I go to them with a proposal like this? They'll ask what's in it for them.' It was a harsh thing to say but she chose the words deliberately. Standing on the frontier of new knowledge required huge courage. She needed to know whether this man had the guts to fight his corner. 'What am I supposed to tell them?'

He stared back at her and his eyes did not waver. 'Tell them there is a fortune to be made when we make a breakthrough.'

'*When* you make a breakthrough? Don't you mean *if*?'

'I mean when. It will come; I am sure of it. The truth is there; it is just a question of putting our finger on it.'

'And you are confident you can?'

'If we have the funding.'

Hmm.

'And you say there is a fortune to be made?'

'We're talking about a procedure. A technique. It can be patented. A joint venture could be set up between Brand Corporation and my research laboratory. And yes, there is a need for this type of treatment all over the world. Think of it: a simple injection rather than invasive surgery, a high percentage of total cures… The demand will be immeasurable.'

'Commercial benefit from pure research? There are some won't like that.'

Gainsborough laughed scornfully. 'They can go hang.'

'And the risk of failure?'

'It's there, I'll not deny it. But I would say the risk is small.'

'There is another problem,' Hilary said. 'You have come to me with a proposal I am not competent to assess. I would need independent advice from an expert before I could even think of taking your idea to my board.'

'No!' Gainsborough said. 'That would not be possible.'

'But you must surely see it is essential.'

'There are no experts: that is the nature of original research. In any case I could not permit it. You must understand, Ms Brand, this is my lifetime dream and my fortune. I have staked everything I have on this. Premature publication of my findings and I would lose control of the project. Call me selfish if you wish but I am not prepared to risk that.'

'But how else am I to judge the merits of what you're telling me?'

Impasse. They looked at each other across the desk. Then Gainsborough sighed. 'I apologise for wasting your time.'

He made to stand up.

'Wait.'

Hilary was still watching him but in her mind another image took form: of an old woman sitting and looking vacantly at the sea while the nurse did what little she could to comfort her. An old woman who in her mental incapacity had been unable to recognise the safe return of her long-lost child.

Poor soul doesn't know which side is up any more.

'Dr Gainsborough...' Hilary spoke slowly. 'You say this research may help to cure a range of genetic disorders?'

'Aye. I have no definite proof for you but I am confident that is what it will do, yes. There is no limit to its potential.'

'My understanding is that Alzheimer's is a genetic condition for which there is at present no known cure. Is that correct?'

'The condition is attributed to at least seventy per cent genetic factors; and yes, at the moment there is no cure.'

'But to which your research, if successful, may find the answer?'

'It is too early to say for certain but I believe it may well do that.'

She felt a jar in her gut and recognised it at once for what it was: a feeling of excitement both indefinable and undeniable. She had felt it several times in her life: when at sixteen she had made up her mind to run away from Pattinsons' farm; the decision to head west; opening her own real estate agency in Perth; the never-to-be-forgotten day a decade earlier when she had committed herself to Craig Laurie. Now she had the feeling again, the sense that she was standing on the threshold of something important, perhaps even life changing. In this case for her, for the company, for humanity at large.

'I must have some independent assessment of your work. You cannot realistically expect us to provide funding purely on trust: neither business nor life works like that. But I understand your concerns. Leave it with me,' Hilary said. 'Give me a contact number and I'll get back to you within two days.'

2

She convened a board meeting for the following morning. Her financial director came to see her at once and he was not pleased. If Robert Clarke had a pet hate it was having his plans disrupted at the last minute. He had lined up meetings with the company's banks to finalise the funding arrangements for a new multi-tower development in Cairns and the idea of having to rearrange his schedule was enough to give him indigestion.

'Damn it all, Hilary, it sends such a bad signal to the banks.'

'They'll get over it,' Hilary said.

'What's so important, anyway?'

She explained briefly, knowing he would be against the idea. Robert's tidy mind abhorred what he called chaos and the idea of funding medical research would seem to him chaotic in the extreme. Sure enough:

'It's ridiculous! We're in construction and the media. What do we know about medical research?'

'We know nothing,' she said. 'Maybe it's time we changed that.'

He looked at her as though she'd lost her marbles. 'It's a hare-brained idea. We should stick to what we're good at.'

'Tomorrow morning,' Hilary said. 'We shall discuss it properly at the meeting tomorrow morning.'

3

Hilary looked around the boardroom table.

Vivienne Archer; Martha Tan; Desmond Bragg; Robert Clarke. Faces she knew; faces she trusted; faces that in some ways she loved. But she was under no illusions. All of them were business people, their senses finely tuned to what was profitable and what was not. If she were to persuade them to explore the concept of what William Gainsborough had brought her yesterday she needed to do a selling job on them. And perhaps on herself too.

She spelt out what William had told her: how the opportunity existed to earn vast profits while involving the company in a project that could be of great benefit to humanity.

As she spoke she watched each face in turn: Vivienne with the calm expression that hid her inevitable anxiety; Robert, stiff-backed and disapproving, frowning at the writing paper on the table in front of him; Martha watchful; Desmond Bragg doodling on his pad, seeming not to listen to a word but in reality, Hilary knew, taking it all in.

She finished her spiel and waited for comment.

'Medical research,' said Robert Clarke. As though Hilary had suggested marketing the Black Death. 'We have no expertise in medical research. Why didn't this man,' promoting his opposition to the proposal by pretending he couldn't remember William Gainsborough's name, 'go to one of the big pharmaceutical companies like Pfizer or Merck?'

'I asked him that. He said he wanted to keep the project in Australia.'

A sniff. 'Very commendable. Unless of course he's tried them already and they turned him down.'

'That is possible,' Hilary said. 'But not relevant at this point.'

'Not *relevant*?' It was possible that Robert's outrage was genuine; he had never been a pioneer.

'We are talking of the concept here,' Hilary said. 'Only that. If we believe there is a possibility of this being a worthwhile investment I believe we should investigate it. Obtain the best available advice; check out the financial implications, the costs and possible rewards; look at the legal implications.'

'We are talking genetic modification,' Vivienne said. 'Some shareholders might not be comfortable with that.'

Hilary said: 'This board has been appointed by the members to represent their interests commercially and financially. It is not our function to be the guardians of their souls.'

'And if they sell?'

'Then they sell.' Her eyes moved to Martha. 'Any thoughts?'

'I am in favour,' Martha said. 'Provided we are satisfied on the scientific side.'

One in favour; two – the most conservative members of the board – against.

Desmond said: 'You say this bloke was involved in that Dolly the sheep business?'

'That is what he told me. Should we go ahead we would of course need to confirm that.'

'That was one of the greatest public relations coups of all time.' Desmond rested his stomach against the edge of the boardroom table. 'Provided the science makes sense I think we should go for it.'

Two yes; two no. Hilary's casting vote would decide.

'We'll give it a go,' she said.

Robert's mouth was a disapproving line in his pale face. 'Subject to our obtaining satisfactory evidence scientifically speaking.'

'Of course. I shall get back to you all on that.' Hilary stood up; the meeting was at an end. 'Back to the treadmill,' she said. 'Martha, I'd like a word.'

It took less than a minute; she stood and watched Martha's back as she hurried out. A million bucks, she thought. Funny how things worked out. It didn't seem that long ago when a thousand would have been too much, ten thousand riches beyond measuring. Now everything depended on what Martha could find out. Then a decision, one way or the other, would have to be made. And that, as always, would be down to her.

She would not have had it any other way.

Ten hours later Martha was back.

'The time differences held me up,' she said.

'But you spoke to them?'

'Oh yes. I spoke to them all. Four people William Gainsborough has worked with in his career.'

'And their verdict?'

'Unanimous. Very, very talented, they say. If he has confidence, they seem to think there's a ninety per cent chance he will succeed. That was what his professor at university told me. I also spoke to

Professor Wee in Singapore. He knows Gainsborough. Not personally but his work. Professor Wee concurs. William Gainsborough is
a winner: those were his words.'

It was what Hilary had hoped to hear. 'Good. We'll go for it
then.'

'Beauty!'

Hilary smiled. Martha's voice still had echoes of Asia but she
had picked up the Aussie idiom too. Sometimes it created an odd
combination.

'Beauty!' Hilary agreed.

2000

A DOOR INTO CHINA

On Saturday 27 May 2000 Hilary Brand went into her office for a meeting with Willard Rice, CEO of Premier Tractors. Premier was the major manufacturer of earthmoving equipment in Australia with a significant investment in Asia, China in particular.

Willard had not been happy about coming into the office on a Saturday but Hilary had heard a rumour that Premier was in trouble and therefore it was for her to say where and when they would meet.

'Ten o'clock in my office. The only time I can manage, I'm afraid,' she told him. 'And I'm tied up the rest of the week. In any case, a confidential chat is best held when no one else is about, don't you find?'

So, like a lamb which by its expression was hoping to avoid the slaughter, Willard Rice had turned up. Ten minutes late, to prove to himself he was still the man, but Hilary was patient about that. The point was he had come and at her bidding.

'Coffee?'

Hilary had it ready but with no biscuits, chocky or otherwise; hospitality had its limits. No offer of a comfortable chair, either, although the office had several. She poured the coffee and sat behind her desk and smiled at him.

'Willard, you are looking well.' It was a lie and they both knew it. It was why she'd said it; Willard Rice was by way of being an old enemy. He had been a prime mover in a consortium that some years ago had hoped to mount a takeover of Brand. He had failed but she had not forgotten. 'How can I help you?' she said kindly.

He tried to box around the subject, saying how marvellous business was, how the sky was – or could be – the limit, while his eyes swithered this way and that like greased ball gearings. It was a kindness to cut him short. Hilary made sure he saw her look at her watch.

'I don't want to press you,' she said, pressing him, 'but I have another meeting in twenty-five minutes.'

So at last he came to the point. Premier had agencies all over the country. They also had a very big one in China, a smaller one in Southeast Asia...

'You're telling me you're stretched,' Hilary said.

Well, yes. Temporarily that was true. 'Cash flow is a problem for us all,' Willard said.

Hilary had had her share of problems in that area but not for some years now. 'It all comes down to planning, doesn't it?'

Premier's planning was impeccable, he assured her. Absolutely. Well, he would say that, wouldn't he?

'That's good,' she said. 'So what's the problem?'

China was the problem. Language was a hurdle. There was lack of skills on the ground. Technicians were inadequately trained. China was chewing up cash like a ravenous wolf. Which in turn was impacting on Premier's operations in Australia. In New South Wales in particular.

Hilary poured herself a second cup of coffee. She wasn't sure about China but New South Wales might be a different story. Now they were coming to it.

'What is the problem in New South Wales?'

Again it was a question of cash flow. Inadequate premises; inadequate training facilities for salespeople and mechanics; a question mark over the quality of management.

'You're telling me it's a mess,' Hilary said.

Willard Rice winced. 'Nothing that can't be put right with adequate resources. It could be a gold mine but –'

Hilary deliberately hardened her voice. 'But isn't. It's a mess and you want me to sort it out.'

'I was thinking perhaps a joint venture –'

After her experience with Haskins Gould Hilary was an all-or-nothing woman. Joint ventures in Hong Kong were an unavoidable fact of life but in this case she wasn't willing to be saddled with Premier's management inadequacies. If she couldn't claim one hundred per cent possession she didn't want to know. But she smiled at Willard and said she would get back to him.

After he had gone she sat pondering current plans and future developments. And wondering, as always, how Craig Laurie was doing so far away. For over twelve years she had contrived to spend time with him regularly; they exchanged emails on a daily basis and phoned each other several times a week. Her breasts burnt with remembered kisses, the children's home was going great guns, but there were many days when she asked herself whether they would ever get together again properly. Would they greet the dawn together, lie beside each other at night, smile into each other's eyes across a café table, take leisurely walks along the beach side by side?

She had promised herself – and Craig – that when the moment was right it would happen.

'Permanently?'

'Permanently,' she said.

She had meant it absolutely. But it was hard to imagine when; it would take something drastic to jolt her out of her present life, the hustle-and-bustle wheeler-dealer world she had made her own. To go and sit on a tropical beach? It was indeed hard to believe, yet a significant part of her mind could imagine nothing better. When the moment was right.

In the meantime, what was she going to do about Willard Rice and Premier?

On Monday she discussed it with Vivienne Archer. She had already made up her mind but as her number two Vivienne had the right to know and – who could say? – might have some useful input on the subject. But when they talked they found they were in complete agreement: they wouldn't touch it with a ten-foot pole.

'Don't we have enough problems without taking Premier's on board as well?' Vivienne said.

Hilary's thinking precisely.

'It could be a door into China,' Vivienne said.

'Maybe in a year or two's time,' Hilary said. 'But never in a joint venture. We don't know how bad their real position is. If it is really bad there may be something in it for us, down the track.'

'You mean take them over entirely?'

'Why not? If we let the fruit ripen on the vine –'

'It may fall off into our lap?'

'Exactly.'

So there, for the moment, they left it.

2004

HYENA IN AMBUSH

Physically he was a giant and knew better than most how to use his size to intimidate the world but, as he stood at the window of his thirtieth-floor office with its views over the harbour and the city that he was still determined to make his own, Haskins Gould felt twice the size he was.

Back in 1987 Hilary Brand had thought she'd ruined him. He'd introduced her to the world of shopping malls, he'd made her rich and in return the bitch had turned on him. He'd survived – no thanks to her – and now payback time was coming. Not long now and he'd be in the position to do to her what she had failed to do to him.

He'd started to play the market in the 1970s, shortly after the initial success with the Majestic Mall. At first he'd used money his father had lent him, money he'd promised to repay. Somehow he'd never got around to doing that and the old miser had moaned but only for the form of it: he'd never had any real need for it.

He'd done well – brilliantly – until the crash in '87. After the bust-up with Hilary he'd had to sell up almost everything he owned; things had looked grim for a while but he was resilient – by God he was! – and soon he'd turned to other games.

He moved to Zurich, where he found a mentor in Selwyn Glass; with him he learnt to play the market like a violin. Like an orchestra of violins!

Play was what it was. The world was a casino. He won often; occasionally he lost; the thrill of the spill took hold. He was never one to let the law stand in the way of excitement; many times he chose to do something illegal rather than within the law because that added to the thrill. He became addicted. He drew like-minded men to him. The helter-skelter became his vehicle of choice, up and down, up and down. By the time the 90s rocked around he had several bank accounts in Zurich and the Bahamas, all in the name of nominees.

They were the cowboy years. Takeover followed takeover and soon he was making money by the truckload. He'd liked everyone to know it too; he still did. Showing off was part of the deal; a low profile was for the birds. As he used to say to his many girlfriends, if you got 'em, flash 'em around. His parties were legendary; one of them aboard his motor yacht *Ariadne* had set him back over a hundred grand.

Ariadne was a work of art. Silk drapes on the walls of the master suite, gold taps in the bathrooms and the latest TV bimbo in his bed. Sometimes two. 'When you got it you share it,' he'd told one of his admirers. He had a Rolls Royce and a Lear jet, a Ferrari and a house in Bellevue Hill that had cost him a couple of million. When in Zurich he took a suite at the Hotel Storchen with terrace and views over the river; in London it was the Dorchester's Harlequin suite. When he travelled on business he left his bimbos behind but wherever he found himself fresh meat was always available to a man with his connections.

Oh yes. Life was the biggest birthday cake you ever saw and soon he'd be enjoying the cherry on top.

Hilary, take a bow.

He picked up the phone.

A BUSINESS OPPORTUNITY

1

On Tuesday 10 February 2004, twelve days later than the day initially proposed by Wong Chee-Weng, the three musketeers arrived in a bitterly cold Beijing. Andrea Chan, who Hilary told Sara had impressed her enormously, came with them.

They were met by an anonymous official, very young and smartly dressed, and a chauffeur-driven limousine half a mile long – thankfully heated – that drove them to their hotel. Hilary stared out of the window. It was her second visit to China's capital; she had been here seven years earlier as member of a trade delegation and was interested to see what changes had taken place since.

They were many and impressive. There were crowds of pedestrians muffled against the cold; bicycles still wove this way and that down the streets but there were many more vehicles; tower blocks were rising behind the one- and two-storey shopfronts that lined the street, each with Chinese characters in glossy red or gold above the entrance. A seething city, its pulsing energy evident even through the glass of the limousine's tinted windows.

'I feel like stout Cortez,' Hilary said.

'What's Cortez got to do with it?' Sara said.

'Keats's poem,' Hilary said. *'Staring with a wild surmise...'*

'*Silent upon a peak in Darien?*' Sara said. 'Wherever that was.'

'Maybe Panama?'

'Yellow fever and the canal.'

'No canal in Cortez's day,' Hilary said.

The two Chinese women might have been watching monkeys at play.

'Don't mind us,' Sara said. 'We're just crazy.'

And closer than we have been in our lives, Hilary thought and was glad it was so.

The driver was using his klaxon to clear a way through the weaving bicycles.

'Not as silent as all that,' Sara said.

'But the surmise is certainly there,' Hilary said.

'Exciting but scary?'

'Exactly.'

Hilary was excited by what she suspected might be one of the major opportunities of her business life. Even with Martha and Andrea to back her up China remained an unknown quantity but she had always relished the challenge of the unknown.

She sat back in her seat while the car continued along the highway into the city, where sunlight was gilding the upper windows of the skyscrapers that had already been completed.

The hotel was impressive. It stood in manicured grounds at the end of a tree-lined drive and Martha said it was undoubtedly the finest in Beijing. 'Maybe in all of China,' she said. The vast foyer was several storeys high, with bowls of orchids everywhere and walls lined with gilt statues of legendary figures, western as well as Chinese, at least double life-size. Staff ran to collect their bags.

The official came with them to the reception desk. After they were booked in he told them they would be collected from the hotel at four o'clock that afternoon and taken to meet Mr Wong and someone called Mr Li, the man they suspected was Mr Wong's boss.

Hilary remembered what Martha had told her. 'I deeply regret but that will not be possible,' she said.

The official frowned. He had a naturally stern face, which might have frightened many but Hilary was not one of them.

'The flight,' she said. 'So foolish but the long journey has exhausted me. Please give Mr Wong – and of course Mr Li – my profound apologies and suggest that ten o'clock tomorrow morning might be a more convenient time.' How sweetly she smiled! 'If that is possible?'

'I shall inform Mr Wong and let you know,' the frowning official said.

An hour later Hilary had a phone call in her hotel suite. A woman's voice. 'Tomorrow afternoon at four,' the voice said. 'Is convenient?'

'Thank you. That will be very good.'

'A driver will collect you,' the woman said.

Hilary was glad. Business games or not, she *was* feeling tired, though nothing that a good night's sleep wouldn't cure.

You're sixty-three, she told herself crossly, not ninety-three. But it made no difference to how she felt. The girls – no doubt politically incorrect but that was how she thought of them – suggested they should brave the freezing conditions and go for a walk around the extensive grounds but Hilary looked at the snow lying in patches beneath the bare winter branches of the trees and cried off.

'It'll do you good to get out after sitting so long but I'll stay. I have some work to do.'

So she had but she didn't do it. It was the first time she could remember when she had allowed her body to dictate terms to her mind but she lay on her bed and dozed and the hours passed. They had dinner in the luxurious dining room.

'You are feeling all right?' Martha said anxiously. She was the only other person to know of Hilary's heart problem – that nonsense, as Hilary thought of it – but even she did not know of the caution Dr Chang had given on her latest visit.

'Never better.'

And it was true she felt much improved for her lazy afternoon. A good thing, she thought. She suspected she'd need all her wits about her for their meeting the next day.

Martha and Andrea ordered the meal, discussing each dish in excited Cantonese before coming to a decision while Hilary watched. What a find this Andrea was. Brave, principled and smart. Good-looking too. They didn't come much better than that. We shall have to find a position for her, Hilary thought. I'll talk it over with Martha after I've seen how she handles herself over the next few days.

They went to bed early; despite her lazy afternoon Hilary slept the clock round and felt much better for it. In the morning the girls decided they would like to go shopping. Hilary did not join them but got the hotel to organise a car to take her to the Beijing museum and art gallery, where she made a beeline for the ceramics section on an upper floor. There she stood for a long time before an early Soong vase, wondering at its grace and simplicity, the purity of its glaze and line.

So beautiful, she thought. There was something almost holy about its silent perfection.

They met back at the hotel for lunch, when Hilary dutifully admired the loot the others had brought back from their shopping expedition: Andrea a pair of shoes in what might be but probably was not crocodile skin; Sara a jade brooch for her sister and a splendid silk scarf for Hilary; Martha odds and ends for friends back home.

'Have a good time?' Sara asked her.

'Very good.'

She remembered the Soong vase but for reasons she did not comprehend was unwilling to mention the feeling it had given her, that to be in the presence of such beauty was like a promise of eternity.

They ate sparingly and at four o'clock the car was waiting, with the same official in the front passenger seat.

Hilary smiled at them. 'Here we go.'

They were driven into the city and to the underground car park of an office block overlooking the vastness of Tiananmen Square. Uniformed attendants sprang forward to open the car doors and they were escorted to a lift and up to a suite of offices high in the building.

The silence of the reception area seemed to insulate the suite of soberly decorated rooms from the frenetic bustle of the city outside the building. A young Chinese woman, smartly dressed, was working at a desk. She did not look up as the official who had brought them up from the car park ushered them into an inner office. He gestured for them to sit; they did so and he went out, closing the door behind him.

If the intention is to impress the overseas visitors to the Middle Kingdom, Hilary thought, the authorities are doing a good job.

While they waited she looked around at the room, which she assumed must reflect the status of the man whom they had flown to Beijing to meet. It was expensively furnished but there was nothing personal about it: the only photographs were studio portraits of President Hu Jin-Tao and Premier Wen Jia-Bao. Nevertheless she thought the silent room gave a hint of his personality: a man of power who watched and listened, revealing nothing of himself. She smiled. It would be interesting to see whether the real man matched her sense of whom and what he was.

An inner door opened and two dark-suited men entered the room.

2

Mr Li was not tall but had square shoulders and a strong neck. Hilary thought he looked tough.

He came across the room, smiling and hand outstretched.

'Ms Brand, how good to see you. You have recovered your health, I hope?'

'Thank you. I am well.'

'I trust you enjoyed your visit to the museum?'

It came as a shock but was perhaps not surprising in light of everything she had heard about China. Mr Li's genial smile was still in place but he clearly wanted her to know they had been keeping an eye on her, as they no doubt did on all foreigners.

'Thank you. It was a wonderful experience. Chinese ceramics are the envy of the world.'

'Thank you, thank you.' He beamed, still holding her hand; she allowed herself to hope it might be a genuine smile but there was no way to be sure.

'And this is your daughter?'

They were all sitting around a long table: Hilary and the girls on one side, Mr Li and Mr Wong on the other. Hilary remembered Sara telling her how impressed with Mr Wong she had been yet in this company he was clearly outgunned and so far had not opened his mouth.

Mr Li smiled at all four women but when he spoke it was to Hilary. Boss to boss. Hilary, remembering Dr Chang's words, thought that was something she would have to change now, while the relationship had not had time to cement itself.

'I am delighted to welcome you back to China, Ms Brand.' His English was accented but fluent.

'Thank you,' Hilary said. 'I am delighted to be here and to have the opportunity to see for myself something of the remarkable progress your country has made since my previous visit.'

You smooth-talking creature, she thought. Of course it was all part of the game – the golden-voiced diplomat and the hard-bitten businesswoman – and she had been good at it and for almost half a century had played it to the full. She would miss it, she knew, but knew too that if she were to have a future now was the time she had to move on.

'I should make it clear that I am here now more as an observer than a participant.' She gave Mr Li her merriest smile. 'It was Ms Tan and my daughter, assisted most bravely by Ms Chan, who unmasked the criminal activities of the Lennox brothers. Ms Chan first disclosed their wrong-doing and assisted in bringing them to justice. Ms Chan and Ms Sara Brand obtained the evidence we needed to incriminate them and it was Ms Tan who urged that we should take steps to assist Mr Wong in keeping this most regrettable episode confidential between the Brand Corporation and the authorities here in China.'

How was she doing? She dared a glance at the two Chinese men on the other side of the table who continued to watch her, their faces expressionless.

'So you see,' she said, 'I have been no more than an observer in this matter. Now is the time for me to step aside and make way for the next generation. I shall of course assist in every way I can but I thought it right to clarify the position at the start of our discussions.'

'China had a very great emperor during the eighteenth century,' Mr Li said. 'He too talked of retirement. He even had a palace built for the purpose but never lived there. When the time came he found he could not let go of his power.'

'But I am not Emperor Qianlong,' Hilary said.

For the first time since Hilary started speaking Mr Li smiled. 'You are familiar with the Qianlong story?'

'If we are to do business together, as I hope, it is important that we know something of each other, is that not so?'

'That is a true saying,' Mr Li said. 'With knowledge comes understanding. If we do not know each other how can we be friends?'

'We on this side of the table have much to learn from China and welcome the opportunity to learn it, as comrades and equal partners in the future. But that is a task for the next generation. I have other plans for my retirement. I am very serious about this. Brand Corporation needs fresh blood, fresh ideas if it is to continue to grow.'

'Renewal is important to every country and organisation,' Mr Li said.

'As Chairman Mao wisely pointed out,' Hilary said. Although whether the Cultural Revolution was really such a good idea was another matter.

'Many western businessmen think it is their role to instruct us,' Mr Li said. 'Do this, do that… What is your opinion?'

'I strongly disagree with that way of thinking. If we have an opportunity to become involved with China it is my hope that we shall learn from China at the same time as we provide any assistance in our power. I would regard any such arrangement as a partnership between equals, of mutual benefit to both.'

The young woman from the outer office came into the room. She crossed to Mr Li and spoke in his ear. Mr Li nodded. 'Miss Fang has reminded me I have another meeting. You will have to excuse me.' He stood. 'I believe this has been a most valuable discussion,' he said. 'Your car will take you back to your hotel. I hope you are finding it satisfactory?'

'Thank you,' Hilary said. 'It is most satisfactory. And we appreciate the opportunity to have had this discussion with you and Mr Wong.'

3

Wrapped up to the eyes against the Beijing cold, they were walking in the hotel grounds, away from any bugs they all knew might have been concealed in their rooms.

'What happens now?' Hilary said.

'We wait.'

'How long?'

'It could be a long time or it could be tomorrow. There is no way to know.'

'As long as it takes?'

'Exactly.'

They went back into the welcome warmth of the hotel. They were barely through the doors when a member of the hotel staff came and spoke to Hilary.

'Comrade Li's office has been on phone. We explain you were out and they say will ring again.'

'Could they have come to a decision so quickly?' Hilary said to Martha as they walked to the lift.

'It is surprising. No doubt they will tell you when they phone.'

The call came ten minutes later. It was nothing to do with business but to invite them to join Comrade Li and a private party at the Beijing ballet that evening.

'As Ms Brand had expressed an interest in Chinese culture.'

'We shall be delighted,' Hilary said. 'Delighted and honoured.'

'A car will collect you at eight o'clock,' the caller said.

'I guess this is one time we should be punctual,' Hilary said to Martha. 'What should we wear?'

'The grandest clothes we have.'

Thank goodness Hilary had come prepared with a full-length Versace gown that looked like a million dollars and had cost almost as much.

It was a splendid evening, the ballet a sensational mixture of gracefully swaying figures, colourful gowns and variegated lights, and was followed by a banquet at what they were told was one of the capital's most prestigious restaurants, where they were served by beautiful young women wearing traditional dress.

'Very pricey,' Martha Tan murmured appreciatively.

Certainly the food was excellent. The only mention of business came at the evening's end as Mr Li assisted Hilary into her car.

'You were serious when you spoke of retirement?'

'Absolutely. I am willing to be involved in any discussions if you believe that will be helpful but my daughter and Ms Tan will be overseeing any future operations.'

'Thank you for your candour.'

'I thought it best that you should be told at the beginning. And thank you for a truly delightful evening.'

Two days later Martha and Sara returned from a meeting with Mr Li and his advisers to tell Hilary that the Chinese government was terminating its agreement with the present Premier Tractor management. From now on Brand Corporation would be supplying China with earthmoving equipment and the technical back-up to ensure that proper maintenance standards were observed. This time it was Sara who spoke for both of them.

'We told them that if Premier Wen's vision of developing the rural areas was to be realised it would necessitate a huge investment in infrastructure. Ideally this would mean graders and diggers in every town.'

'And the maintenance?'

'We suggested we should supply technicians to work with Chinese mechanics. They would learn the language as they went along and would assist local teams to gain the necessary expertise so that the life of the equipment would be extended as far as humanly possible.'

'Mutual help and teams working together,' Hilary said. 'I like it.'

'So did Mr Li.'

'What do you plan to do about Premier Tractors?'

'Without the China operation I doubt they're viable. I think we should be able to take them over without too much of a problem.'

'Good. But I think you should let Vivienne handle that. She has a lot of experience of takeovers and I don't want her to feel left out. She can teach you a lot over the next two years.'

'She will be the CEO,' Sara said. 'It is best that she should handle it.' A pause. 'Martha raised another matter with Mr Li. Pretty much out of the blue, I would say.'

'Strike while the iron is hot,' Martha said.

'Tell me.'

'I chanced to mention our involvement in genetic research. Very casually, you understand. This a matter of considerable interest in China.'

Hilary gave her a sharp look. 'You didn't mention Gainsborough's name?'

'Most certainly not.'

'But you think Mr Li was interested?'

'Oh yes.'

'He said so?'

'He said nothing. But we shall hear from him very soon.'

'You sound very sure.'

'Oh yes. It is the China way.'

'Dear Martha,' Hilary said. 'Where would we be without you?'

All in all it had been a hugely successful visit.

'The start of something truly great,' Hilary said as the Airbus flew south. 'I am proud of the pair of you.'

It was an odd feeling, all the same. She had chosen her course and would stick to it, though the sidelines had never been her preferred place. But I am not Qianlong, she thought. I have said I will step aside and I shall. In fact as well as theory.

Her thoughts turned to the future, full of golden promise, and also to the time, sixteen years earlier, when the focus of her world had changed and Craig Laurie had come into her life. From now on, she thought, Craig will *be* my life.

Now the decision had been made she couldn't wait.

'Are we finished here, then?'

'For the moment.'

'Then let's get home. I've a thousand things to do.'

'So have we all,' Sara said, 'Top of my list: interview for Channel 12 with Emil Broussard.'

BREAKING THE WALLS

1

It was late. Melbourne was a city that never slept yet when Jennifer came out of the hotel and kissed Martin passionately for one last time after what had been an evening of kisses, when she climbed into the taxi he had summoned and headed home, the streets were relatively quiet. Not to be wondered at, at two-fifteen in the morning.

Not that it mattered. Davis was away in Brisbane and as so often before she had grabbed the chance to fly the coop and spend the evening in Martin's arms.

That was the way they did it; Martin drove down from his mountain eyrie in the Dandenongs and they met at the hotel that after their first visit they had christened their assignation house. They seldom left the hotel room for fear of being seen by someone who knew her. Instead they smuggled snacks in and, giggling like naughty children, picnicked naked on the bed, gobbling rolls and ham and cheese and luscious fresh tomatoes and potato salad that she had picked up in the local supermarket.

A dozen times Martin had sketched her like that, naked and smiling on the rumpled bed, hair tousled and cheeks flushed, a plate of food in her lap, the magic of his talent shouting that this was a woman who loved and was loved and who, unmistakably, had just made love with all the passion in her soul.

And it was true, it was true. Every time they were together Jennifer was transported into a place she had never dreamt existed and, knowing that this man had the power to take her there, was all the more eager to be guided, roused, tantalised and ultimately consumed in the furnace of their shared desire. She was redeemed, Venus rising from the foam, as Martin repeatedly told her.

'What a job Botticelli would have made of you!' he said, his pencil already at work.

Later she looked curiously at this latest sketch. 'Are my breasts really as good as that?'

'They are the queen of tits,' he assured her, and kissed them both to prove it.

'Leave him,' he said each time they were together. 'You know you can't stand him.'

'One day,' she said.

'When?'

'Soon.'

She was braver than she had been but to walk out demanded a level of courage that for the moment was beyond her.

She had been overweight with a discontented mouth and haunted eyes; now she was transformed into a child freshly minted, for the first time transported to the land of love. Any man with half an eye would have recognised the signs but Davis never looked at her, so remained oblivious.

Now, as the taxi drew to a stop outside the house, she repeated to herself what earlier that evening she had told Martin.

'Very soon I will leave him.'

She opened the door, walked into the house and stopped midstride. There was a silence about an empty house that was unmistakable; she knew at once she was not alone.

Her blood paused in her veins; she listened, holding her breath; she watched the shadows from the corners of her eyes. The living-room door creaked as it swung open.

Davis said: 'Why are you so late?'

Shock was a drumbeat in her head. She thought: I am going to have a heart attack; I am going to have a stroke, fall to the floor, scream… While the sweat sprang icy cold beneath her clothes.

'You said you were going to be away so I went out.'

'Where?'

She dared not look at his eyes. 'I was at Tessa's.'

'Until two o'clock in the morning?' He stepped close to her; she sensed the air between them vibrating with his fury. 'You are lying.'

She would have been less terrified if he had shouted at her but his voice was low, venomous, dangerous.

'I am doing no such thing.'

The lie was risky, her story easily disproved, but she thought he would not risk the humiliation of ringing Tessa to find out. And at this hour? No, he would not do it. So she defied him.

'Why are you behaving like this? And why aren't you in Brisbane?'

Maybe the shock had sharpened her loathing; certainly she heard it in her voice and thought Davis must as well. Perhaps now the moment had come. Perhaps they had reached the point when after all the years of lies only the truth would do.

And he hit her. Not on the face, where a mark would be seen, but with his clenched fist deep into her belly.

Her breath fled. She was dying for lack of air, falling on the floor at his feet and fighting to draw breath while he stood over her. Through the pain she felt the shock and first hot fury of hatred but also, behind the fear and loathing, an awakening sense of triumph.

This was the catalyst she had needed; now she would be brave.

But only if she survived. Which was by no means certain as Davis Lander dragged her up by the hair, the pain excruciating, and hit her again and then a third time so that she cried out with the last of her breath and he turned from her and walked away, leaving her broken and helpless upon the floor, still fighting for the breath that his blows had driven from her body.

Through her pain she heard Davis say: 'You needn't worry. I won't touch you in any other way, ever again. I wouldn't demean myself.'

She had grown used to his psychological cruelty but had never expected this. She had never thought Davis a violent man but now realised that neither she nor her husband had understood the first thing about each other. The pain was terrible; she felt that physically she was no more than a husk of what she had been only minutes earlier, yet the humiliation was even worse.

When finally she crawled to a chair and, drawing up her legs, succeeded in clawing herself upright, she knew that staying in the house was out of the question. But where could she go? It was a quarter to three; Martin would be on the way back to the Dandenongs and out of contact; Mother and Sara were in Sydney; phone Tessa and she would dine out on the story for evermore. The ugly truth was there was no one she could turn to.

Acting on her own initiative was a new experience but she shrugged that off; determination had dispelled her old uncertainty. She knew that never again would she spend a night under Davis's roof.

Aching all over, barely able to stand, she wasn't up to driving. Luckily she had money in her purse and her credit card. Every step was agony but somehow she got to the phone and rang for an all-night taxi.

She waited outside the front door until it arrived, climbed painfully in and told the driver to take her to the hotel she had left barely an hour before. Oblivious to the concerned glances of the night staff, she booked a room.

'Are you all right, madam?'

'I am fine. Thank you.' Her voice sounded frail even to herself. 'No, I have no luggage.'

Not even a toothbrush or change of underwear.

Somehow she reached the room. She locked the door and leant against it while the room swirled about her. Summoning her last reserves of will she poured a bath, let her clothes fall where they would and managed to half-climb, half-fall into the hot water. She lay there, afraid she would pass out, while her body roared with pain.

Soaping herself was out of the question; even to touch her ribs or stomach was agony. She lay and soaked until the water began to cool. For a while she doubted she could get out of the bath but somehow she managed it. Gritting her teeth she patted herself dry; she looked at herself in the bathroom mirror. Already the bruises were purple blotches on her white skin.

I'll be a pretty picture in the morning, she thought. She got to the bed, lay on it and drew the bedclothes over her. Delayed shock seized her and she began to shake, the movement so violent that even that hurt. I hope he's done no serious damage, she thought. But whether he had or not, she would have to wait until morning to find out. At least for the moment she was safe. The shaking eased; even the pain eased a little provided she did not turn or move. She slept. Or at least passed out.

It was light when she woke. For a moment she did not feel too bad but as soon as she moved pain flared like a forest fire. Every part of her ached: even her neck and arms, which Davis had not touched. When she crawled out of bed she could not stand at first. She crawled to the bathroom and, inch by inch, clinging on to the door post, she levered herself upright. Her torso was black and when she looked in the mirror it was an old woman who looked back at her from the glass.

The question now was what she should do about it. She daren't tell Martin. Do that and Martin might kill him. Not that Davis didn't deserve it but she didn't want Martin getting into strife. Instead she did what she had done all her life when trouble threatened: she picked up the phone and rang Mother.

'I'm in trouble, Mummy...' After years of silence, now the words spilled out.

'He did *what?*'

'Three times! He hit me three times –'

'Are you all right?'

'I'm bruised and sore. But I'm all right, yes.'

'Where are you?'

'In a hotel in St Kilda.'

'Does he know where you are?'

'No.'

'Good. Now tell me: why did he hit you?'

'I was late getting home. He was supposed to be in Brisbane but the trip was cancelled and –'

Again Hilary cut her off. 'How late?'

'Very late.' It was hard to get the words out.

Silence for a moment. Then, voice decisive, Hilary said:

'You are having an affair, aren't you? An affair with Martin Gulliver?'

Jennifer gulped, sweat on her face. She did not answer.

Now Hilary's voice was razor-sharp. 'For God's sake, Jennifer! I'm on your side, OK? Were you with Martin or weren't you?'

A whisper: 'Yes.'

'Does Martin know what happened?'

'No.'

'Make sure you keep it that way. Now: stay put and don't worry. I'll handle it. I shall arrange for a doctor to give you a check-up.'

The thought of anyone seeing her like this threw Jennifer into a panic. 'There's no need for that.'

'There is every need. We need to make sure you're all right. And we may need a witness in case Davis disputes your version of what happened.' There was no arguing with Mother; there never was. 'What else do you need?'

'I've no clothes. Not even a toothbrush.'

'Money?'

'Not much. But I have my credit card.'

'Then this is what we'll do...'

Jennifer listened. When her mother had finished she put down the phone, knowing that the weight had lifted from her shoulders. Thank God for Mother, she thought.

Ten minutes later she had a phone call from Brand's Melbourne office, someone called Irene.

'Tell me what you need and your size. I'll bring out some clothes for you, toothpaste and brush. Anything else?'

2

In Sydney Hilary sat and thought, her face like stone. Finally she lifted the receiver. It was ten o'clock; if Davis wasn't in court he should be in his chambers by now. She did not need to check the number; with her phenomenal memory she forgot nothing. And, in this case, forgave nothing, either.

'Hello?' His lawyer's voice: lofty, a little patronising. 'Who is this?'

'Hilary Brand.'

Silence. Only for a second but it registered.

'And how can I help you?'

Loftier than ever now, giving nothing. We'll soon change that, she thought. 'It is not a question of how you can help me but what you are going to do.'

'I beg your pardon?'

'You beat up my daughter last night.'

'I most certainly did not.'

Such indignation!

'You beat up my daughter and I am warning you. You ever lay a finger on any member of my family again and I shall destroy you. You hear me?'

'I assure you, Hilary –' Not quite so lofty now.

'I haven't finished. You will grant my daughter an immediate divorce. You will pay her half a million dollars –'

'Don't you dare threaten me –'

'As they say, it is not a threat, Davis: it's a promise. Your assets must be worth well in excess of a million dollars. More than two, I would guess. I think half a million would be reasonable, in the circumstances.'

'Now you listen here –'

A fly buzzing; she ignored it. 'You will not see her or speak to her again, ever. You will clear out of the house long enough for her to retrieve whatever personal items she cares to keep, if there are any. You will make the settlement. You will not impede the divorce. If you do these things you will have no more trouble from me. If you do not, I *promise* you, Davis, you will have more trouble than you know how to handle.'

'Planning to have me roughed up, are you?'

'That is more your line than mine.' She paused for a moment to give her next words greater effect. 'Does the name Juanita Santos mean anything to you?'

'I don't believe it does.'

Defiant to the last: it was a quality she might have admired had she not detested him so much.

'I find that surprising. I have in front of me a report from a private enquiry agent. With dates and photographs. Entering the St Vincent hotel in the city. Leaving it four hours later, again with Ms Santos. A room booked in your name. Many more instances of the same. Do I need to go on? Or remind you how your head of chambers might react to what I can assure you would be a huge scandal? What would Mr Hawthorn have to say about that?'

'But that's blackmail.'

'Terrible, isn't it? Terrible, I tell you.'

Over the years Hilary had learnt how to speak with maximum impact; now Davis's voice was of a man shaken to his boots.

'What do you plan to do?'

'Provided you behave, nothing. Neither Jennifer nor I will mention it to a soul. I've got a photographer with her at the moment. She's badly bruised so the pictures won't be pretty but we won't share them with the media unless you try and fight us. If you do, I will make it my personal business to destroy you.'

She phoned Jennifer ten minutes later. 'It's all sorted. I trust you will be happy with the arrangement I've made.'

'What arrangement?'

'I am talking about an arrangement whereby you have swapped your husband for an immediate divorce and half a million in cash. But not a word to anyone, now or ever. That was my undertaking.'

'Davis will never agree to that.'

'He's done it. It's over, Jennifer.'

'But how…?'

'Never mind how. Just accept that it's done and be very, very thankful.'

'I am. I can't tell you how much. Will I really get that much money?'

'If Davis knows what's good for him.'

'Martin will be over the moon,' Jennifer said. She was pretty high in the stratosphere herself.

'I'm sure he will be. But I'd give it a week before you tell him.'

'Why?'

'It might not be a good idea for him to see how badly bruised you are.'

'No,' Jennifer said. 'I want him to know. To know now. Can you let me have some money?'

'How much?'

Jennifer told her. 'I need a car,' she said.

'I shall expect you to repay me.'

'Of course.'

The first thing Jennifer did was buy a brand-new two-door Honda sports car, pillar box red. It gave her an odd feeling to have money to spend and know that Davis was not waiting to damn her extravagance. She was free. It was like picking up a Get Out of Gaol card.

The second thing Jennifer did was drive up into the Dandenongs. Martin's place was on a ridge at the end of a steep track, a wooden house with a complication of rooms spread across a hilltop. It was completely isolated amid vast forest trees yet with views extending, it seemed, forever.

She knew she would have to be careful with Martin. He was big and strong. He was slow to anger but extremely protective of her and his anger, when roused, was like Vesuvius on a bad day. He was more than capable of taking Davis apart. That she must prevent yet he had to know what had happened.

'Softly softly catchee monkey,' she said as she bumped up the rutted track.

His ute was there. She parked behind it and climbed the steps to the entrance. Her feet echoed on the boards as she crossed the deck and went into the house. All was still. His studio was out the back. She went through and there he was.

And there, after all the wasted years, was she.

She couldn't help it; when he tried to hug her she winced.

'What is it?'

'I'm a bit sore.'

'Sore? Why?'

'I want you to listen to me,' she said.

A pause. His jaw clenched, but he was careful to keep his hands soft on her shoulders. 'What's he done to you?'

He wanted to see what damage had been done but she would not let him.

'I said listen to me. I mean it. Listen!'

'Tell me.' Nostrils flared; big hands clenched.

'Davis never went to Brisbane after all. He was there when I got home. We had a terrible row.'

'Did he hit you?'

'Listen…'

'*Did he hit you?*'

'Yes.'

'I'll fix the bastard.'

His rage was black and terrifying. At that moment she knew he would kill Davis Lander if he could get his hands on him. At all costs she had to stop him before he did anything stupid.

'I said *listen*.' Careless of her own pain she was shaking him. Luckily she had worked out in advance what she had to say. 'Don't you see? Davis has done us a huge favour.'

Martin was not listening. 'Take off your shirt!'

'No.'

'Take it off! I want to see what he's done to you.'

'I haven't finished talking! Now: *listen to me*!' Escaping from Davis had done more than release her physically; it seemed all her inhibitions had vanished too. 'Davis has agreed to give me an immediate divorce and a cash settlement.'

'I don't care about the cash.'

'It will be nice to have. And I am free of him. Don't you see? Free of him!'

'Why would he have agreed to that?'

'I don't know. But Mother spoke to him –'

'Your mother spoke to him? You told her before you told me?'

'Because I was afraid you'd kill him and I didn't want to lose you before we had even got together.' There were tears now, a mixture of joy and pain unlike anything she had experienced before. 'By hitting me he gave me the courage to do what I should have done long ago.' Now was the moment. Careless of the pain she held him close, tearful face upturned. 'Please forgive me for keeping you waiting so long.'

A huge sigh from the heart. Now Martin too was close to tears. 'Forgive you? Good God, there is nothing to forgive. I love you, Jennifer.'

'And I love you.'

And that, now they had finally come to it, was everything.

Later:

'I don't care if it hurts. I want you. Want you now.'

And presently, diffident yet determined:

'Perhaps, if we do it this way…'

It was amazing what you could do when you set your mind to it.

IN LIMBO

It was a strange time. Hilary couldn't settle. She could neither walk, sleep nor think. All the processes of mind and body seemed frozen in the limbo between her past and future lives.

To be there and not there, to sit in her chair behind her desk in her office and to know that power was slipping away... The knowledge that this was the course she had chosen and that she was right to have done so should have made the process easier but did not. There were days when the notion made her sick with apprehension.

She had not phoned Craig. Every day she told herself she must but every day she found excuses not to do so. This agreement must be finalised, that problem resolved. The truth was the prospect of phoning him terrified her. For so many years they had talked of the future, their future when they would be together at last. What if in that time the dream had become the reality? What if when he was faced with her imminent arrival he changed his mind and did not want to go ahead? *She must phone him.* She did not.

She knew she had to do it. No one was pushing her but everyone was waiting. It was bad for the senior staff who did not know where they were. Worse, it was bad for the company. Also she had told Mr Li in Beijing. It would never do to say one thing and do something else. She had to do it.

She sat up all night on the terrace of Cadogan Lodge. She stared at the light-dimpled waters of Sydney Harbour, the movement of marine traffic to and fro, while for the hundredth time her mind roamed over her past adventures: the battles she had fought and won, her many triumphs and occasional disasters. Morning came with a scud of rain. Mrs Walsh brought her a cup of coffee, asked about breakfast. The thought of food nauseated her. No, she said, she would have nothing. And still she sat.

At eight o'clock she phoned the office, said she would be in later. She had no appointments but not to go would create a vacuum. She did not think she could handle a vacuum. Not today.

If not today, then when?

At ten o'clock she took a deep breath, blinked her gritty eyes and walked into the house. She sat at her study desk and picked up the phone. She waited a few seconds, listening to the pounding of her heart. She dialled.

Swimming beneath the waterfall. Her first sight of Rumah Kelapa. The sickle curve of the sandy beach. Home?

Seven thousand kilometres away the phone lifted.

'Hullo?'

Craig's voice.

'It's me. I was wondering…' She swallowed and went on. 'Would it be all right with you if I came home?'

Silence. She had said it and could do no more. She could not even breathe.

'Come home as in visiting?' Craig said. 'Or to stay?'

She barely had the courage to say the words. 'To stay.'

She heard a gust of air into the phone as he breathed out. 'Thank God.'

There were tears then and sobs and an unwinding of all the tensions of recent days. None of it mattered, neither fears nor doubts nor delays. Now there was only joy and the certainty that the right decision had been made and that the future was bright.

'When?'

'Give me a week,' she said.

'Don't you dare change your mind.'

'I won't. I definitely won't.'

She hung up and went through to the kitchen.

'I am going for a swim, Mrs Walsh. When I get back I shall have a shower and then if you can arrange it I would like one of your big breakfasts with sausages and bacon and tomatoes and sauté potatoes and three eggs.'

'And toast?'

'Of course. And butter and marmalade. And a pot of your best coffee.'

'You are feeling better?'

'Mrs Walsh, I am feeling on top of the world.'

How true that was. How very, very true.

TERMINUS

1

There was a board meeting scheduled for that afternoon. The other directors did not know it yet, but this would be the last meeting with Hilary in the chair. She looked around the table. Andrew Lyle heading up the construction division; Desmond Bragg media and public relations; Martha Tan co-ordinator of China operations; Vivienne Archer CEO in waiting; Robert Clarke finance; Sara Brand, Vivienne's deputy.

A good team; maybe even an outstanding team. She was leaving the company and its shareholders in strong hands.

Each director reported in turn. Construction was booming both here and in Asia; the Hong Kong operation looked like being its most profitable ever; Channel 12 was leading the media pack and Desmond's team had done a fabulous job in raising Vivienne's public image.

'I think there is something else we should be looking at,' Sara said.

Hilary looked at her. 'Which is?'

'I think we should be considering the future.'

'In what way?'

'Most newspapers have launched online versions of themselves and Netflix has been sending out DVDs on demand for years.'

'And so?' Protective of his turf, Desmond looked displeased.

'It means we have to accept that eventually the internet will challenge not only our news services but the rest of our content.'

Desmond opened his mouth but Hilary's raised hand stopped him. 'What are you suggesting?'

'I think we should bring in an internet expert to make sure we stay ahead of the curve.'

'Desmond?'

'I think it's worth exploring,' he said.

'Vivienne? It'll be on your watch.'

'I agree with Desmond.'

'Then I'll leave the three of you to work something out,' Hilary said. 'What's next? Martha?'

Martha explained it was too soon to have significant feedback on the new China operations but the heavy equipment wharf at Tianjin, the Yellow Sea port south-east of Beijing, was already well under way and work had begun on the maintenance and repair workshops so things over there were looking good.

'I expect us to contribute something to the group's bottom line by next year at the latest,' she said.

Which would be miraculous if true.

The group's finances were strong, with no danger of the cash-flow crisis that had destroyed Premier; Sara was learning the tricks of the trade from Vivienne and would soon be taking a more prominent role; and Andrea Chan would stay in Sydney for a year to get used to the company's ways and after that would probably become Martha's deputy, based in Hong Kong. But that would not be Hilary's decision.

'All in all a very satisfactory performance,' she said. 'I congratulate every one of you. I have one further item I wish to bring to the board's attention.' She took a handwritten letter from the folder in front of her. She looked at each face in turn.

'Today is my last day of active service with the company. I now table my formal letter of resignation from the board.'

There was a murmur from the team seated around the table. Everyone there had been aware that the moment of her departure was coming, yet she knew in their hearts they had not believed it. Hilary *was* the company. They had all assisted in the process of creating it but she had been the motivator, the person above all others who had provided the will and inspiration that had moulded Brand Corporation into the organisation it had become.

Her departure would make a monumental difference to the group and the future of every person here. Or would it? Once the initial shock had worn off she thought things would go on very much as they had before. Fresh blood would bring fresh ideas and fresh growth. The process was already happening; Sara, Martha and the absent Andrea Chan were the new generation. Under their leadership she was confident the company's future was assured.

She smiled at them all now. 'Over the years many of you have smiled behind my back over my enthusiasm for poetry but I make no apology for quoting a famous line now. *The older order changeth, giving place to new.* Tennyson knew what he was talking about. It is the way of the world and, for Brand Corporation, the way into the future. That is what matters. Never mind the rights and wrongs of the past, the triumphs and disasters. The past has gone down the river and we can do nothing about it. It is the future that matters, only that. Therefore I do not intend that any of us should waste our time eulogising over past achievements. Where will the company be in twelve months' time? Where will Australia and the world be in a year, ten years, twenty years? That is what matters, to make Brand as profitable as we can, because without money you can do nothing. But let it be a source of good in the world, not of oppression. That is where our minds should be focused always. There will be no fancy dinners, no speakers spouting nonsense. As of today I am out of here and that is all there is to be said about it. I thank you with all my heart. I love you all. Goodbye.'

Hilary Brand smiled at them for the last time. She closed her folder and stood up. Walking tall, she strode in silence from the room.

2

Once again it was not as simple as that. The dramatic gesture was all very well but there were still a thousand things to be done, letters and documents to sign, an announcement for the press (very short) and a somewhat longer one for the staff; she had to approve the paragraph in the annual report that would cover her departure. There were endless loose ends to be tidied up.

'One thing I regret,' Hilary told Vivienne.

It was the day after the board meeting and they were sitting in what was now Vivienne's office.

'Or will be,' Hilary said, 'as soon as I shift my bum out of here.'

'What regret is that?'

'The fact that our investment in medical research hasn't paid off as I thought it would. It has taken years longer than I anticipated. But I hope you will continue to support it. Everyone believes the breakthrough will come and this is partly what I meant yesterday when I was rabbiting on about the company being a source of good in the world. I have every faith that research will pay off eventually and it would be nice to think we had been there all the way through. It would be enormously profitable too, of course. But that will be your decision.'

She signed all the papers. When she had finished she was a director of nothing; it was an odd feeling. 'Like taking your clothes off in public.'

'Done that, have you?'

'Not yet. But there's always a first time.'

Although there had been that one time on the beach in Penang, a night of the full moon and of a total eclipse...

But she would not go there, except in her memory and her heart.

'Come and have lunch with me,' she said.

A NEW LIFE

1

The last night: a watchful time of shadows that came and went, teasing the darkness, of voices calling on the wind. Of memories: explosions it was impossible she could remember yet did; a woman's voice screaming *Nasty little brat!*; the ocean vast and unknowable – *Here be dragons…*

Other images: steps along the highway she had followed all her life.

Instinct drew her from her bed. She stood at the window and looked out at the spreading waters of the harbour, a nail-paring of moon, a scattering of stars.

I am saying goodbye to the past, Hilary thought, but more importantly opening the door to the future. That was where she should be looking, at the house called Rumah Kelapa and the man who would be her home and refuge. Seven hours to Singapore, two more to Penang.

Vivienne had offered her the use of the company jet but she had turned it down. 'I shall be back with real people now,' she had said. 'I'd better get used to it.' Even flying first class there would be the promiscuity of the departure lounge, of having her ticket and her person checked by officials, of bumping shoulders with strangers.

It would be a challenge – she had got out of the habit of being ordinary – but this was the life she had chosen, walking at Craig's side on secluded beaches, eating in noisy food courts, crossing roads between a tornado of roaring scooters. She would listen entranced to the sound of bells from domed temples; she would observe passing parades for marriages and the dead. She would be happy in the arms of the man she had loved for sixteen years, at home at his side and in his bed.

A consummation devoutly to be wished, as Hamlet had said.

She went back to bed and to memories of two recent conversations.

2

'Mother...' Jennifer's voice. 'We wanted you to be the first to know.'

Hilary's breath caught in her throat. 'Tell me...'

'We're having a baby.'

'Well, you didn't waste much time. That's wonderful, darling. When is it due?'

'Next January.'

'I'll be in Penang.'

'Do you have to go?'

'Yes, my dear, I do. But I'll fly down for the birth if you'd like me to be there.'

'Of *course* I want you here.'

Hilary hung up. What marvellous news, she thought. The company's future and now the family, both secure. How lovely. We live in a truly wonderful world.

But the next message was not so good.

Sara's voice was so sad that she barely recognised it. 'Hilary...'

'What on earth is the matter, my darling?'

'Emil is dead.'

'What?'

'Millie got the message this morning.'

They had been expecting to hear from his agent to finalise terms for the interview. Now this.

'How?'

'Suicide, apparently. He'd told me he was dying. It seems –' for a moment her voice broke '– it seems he decided to speed up the process.'

'Did he leave you a message?'

'Yes.'

She didn't say what it was and Hilary knew she mustn't ask.

'How are you feeling?'

'I'll get over it, I suppose. In time.'

'You loved him,' Hilary said.

'I thought I was over him.' There were tears now. 'I was wrong. It's not easy.'

'It is never easy.'

Hilary hung up. Love, she thought. The ultimate gift, the ultimate blessing, but it was a gift with a dagger in its fist. Thank God for Craig, she thought. Thank God we found each other in time. Otherwise – who knows? – I might still be pining for Lance Bettinger.

COMING HOME

1

She had come a day earlier than they had planned and there had been no one at the airport to meet her. She had done this deliberately; she wanted to get into the skin of her new life before being reunited with Craig because once with him she knew she would be able to think of nothing else.

After the clamour of the airport she had taken a taxi, which was now bumping down the muddy track towards the house. Hilary had been this way a hundred times yet now looked at it through fresh eyes, no longer as a visitor but as someone whose future was intimately linked to every branch and leaf, each cicada singing in the shadows.

She had travelled light and chose to carry her bag down the slope through the trees. She saw the golden horseshoe of the bay in front of her and turned her head and saw the house and kicked off her shoes and walked towards it across the sand. The house was silent and she thought Craig must be out – that was the risk of arriving unannounced. The sliding door was open, though. She climbed the steps to the wooden deck and went indoors.

She stood inside the doorway. Silence; the house did not know her. She put her case down. Beneath her feet a floorboard creaked. Somewhere a clock ticked. The feeling of an empty house was unmistakable. Yet the sliding door had been open, Craig's vehicle in its usual place beneath the trees. He could not be far away.

She went back on to the deck. The breeze slatted the leaves of the palm trees; the fishing koleks were working in the bay. The sea watched.

'I shall wait here until he comes,' she said.

A figure was walking towards her on the sloping sand of the beach. It could be someone from the kampong but she did not think so. She waited, conscious of her rapidly beating heart. Tall; upright despite his age. The confident stride of a man still in his thirties. Instead of – what? – sixty-nine. Both of them getting old, she thought, but with a lot of living still to do. She was determined about that.

The figure was closer now. There could no longer be any doubt about who it was. Not that I ever doubted, she thought. Not for a second.

Without conscious decision Hilary was flying, feet barely touching the wooden steps as she ran down them to the sun-hot beach. She ran across the sand, the years that had united and divided them about to bring them together again at last.

Never to be parted, her heart said. Never, never, never.

2

Casting herself adrift from her old life proved not so simple; the past was a thorn embedded deep in her flesh.

Her health, first of all. She'd told him what the Singapore doctor had said and they had organised to have a defibrillator in the house, in case of emergencies.

'I'm sure we won't need it,' Hilary said.

'You know what they say: hope for the best and prepare for the worst.'

'Yes, sir.' And kissed him.

When they drove into the city the first thing she did was to check the papers for financial news but most of the local press was painfully parochial.

'Don't they care what is going on in the world?'

'Of course not,' Craig said.

'Don't you?'

'Not much. That is the point of getting away from it all.'

'To get away?'

'Exactly.'

It made sense but she couldn't do it. Anxiety was a villain in ambush; it waylaid her on the beach, on the road into town, in bed at night.

'It'll come right,' she told herself. 'If I'd had any doubts I would never have left.'

She had plenty of doubts now. She had to restrain herself from phoning Vivienne Archer to ask how things were going.

She had promised herself that being out meant precisely that, but promises were one thing, keeping them something else.

Increasing tension and lack of sleep took their toll. One day, without warning, she found herself sitting in the living room, shaking uncontrollably, tears streaming down her face.

There Craig found her.

He did not try to jolly her out of it; mercifully, he did not tell soothing lies about how it would just take patience.

'I am taking you away,' he said.

'Where?'

'To an island I know.'

'What's there?'

'Nothing and nobody but there is a small house owned by someone I know. I'll borrow it from him. You will be able to sleep and be at peace.'

'And forget?'

'Pulau Chantek is the best place I know for that.'

'Is that the island's name? What does it mean?' Because he had told her that all Malay names meant something.

'It means Isle of Beauty,' he said.

'A good name.'

'And well deserved,' he said.

They left that afternoon; she had noticed in the past how quickly Craig could get things organised when he wanted.

He packed for them both, permitting her to do nothing. He went to the shops, came back with enough supplies to last a week. He arranged with a fisherman to take them to the island. He helped Hilary climb aboard the high-prowed vessel with the eye painted on the bow to guide the boat through seas both fair and foul. He did everything he could to look after her.

'I feel truly cosseted,' she said but was still shaking uncontrollably, as he saw.

'We'll soon have you there,' he said. 'Then all will be well.'

It was a new experience to be so helpless. She nodded but did not speak.

3

Hilary thought afterwards that Pulau Chantek, the Isle of Beauty, must have been conjured by magic out of the sea. The water was so clear it seemed she had only to reach over the side to pick pebbles off the sand yet Craig told her the sea was five fathoms deep at this point.

The deceptive depth was a fitting introduction to the island.

'Poseidon's palace,' she said.

Craig shook his head. 'Here it's more likely to be Sultan Mahmud or even Kala, although we would hope not Kala.'

It was the first time Hilary had smiled all day. 'It would help if I knew what you were talking about.'

'Sultan Mahmud was one of the ancient Malay deities associated with the sea,' Craig said. 'Kala was the goddess of shipwreck.'

'Definitely not Kala, then,' she said. 'We want nothing to do with Kala.'

Whether ruled by Mahmud or Poseidon, the Isle of Beauty was indeed a magical place, emerald green and steep-sided yet with beaches of golden sand against which the seas lulled quietly and a bay with a narrow entrance through which the kolek nosed its way, and at the end of it a sharp-roofed wooden house raised on stilts above the sand.

The fisherman cut the engine. In a silence so profound that it seemed to take over the world the kolek drifted forward until its prow rested gently against the beach. All was still.

Round-eyed, Hilary turned to Craig. 'I didn't know such peace existed in the world.'

'*Of the world yet apart from it,*' he said. '*Bowery hollows crowned with summer sea.*'

'Tennyson's island of Avilion,' she said. 'You could be right. Maybe it will heal me, at that. Although what King Arthur's got to do with Sultan Mahmud I am not sure.'

'Argumentative,' he said. 'I like that. It means you're getting better already.'

They carried the stores across the beach to the house. Like Rumah Kelapa, this was based on the typical Malay design, with a flight of steps leading up to a narrow deck with a padlocked door into the house.

Hilary rested her arms on the guard rail and watched as the kolek negotiated its way out through the entrance. After it had gone and the sound of its engine had died the returning silence was so profound it seemed to cradle her in its arms.

Yes, she thought, there is healing here. How clever of Craig to bring me to this place. But clever was too superficial a word; rather he had shown a profound sensitivity for which she would always be grateful. I love him, she thought. How I love him. She had believed herself in love before but never with the intensity she felt now.

This isle of beauty, she thought. This place of peace will make me whole.

There was no power and therefore no fans but on its knoll the little house caught the night time breeze and was cool enough. She had assumed they would make love but at first they did not; Craig left her to sleep and she did so for two days and two nights. He told her later that three times a day he had brought her papaya or *pisang mas*, the small sweet bananas of Malaysia, but she had no recollection of it. She had no awareness of anything at all but on the third night she woke before dawn and knew she was over it. She was alone; she got up and went bare-footed on to the deck of the house. The breeze blew from the east to keep the mosquitoes away, the night was ablaze with stars and the softly turning waves were bright with phosphorescence.

'If this be not paradise,' she said, 'then I know not what paradise is.'

She did not know whether anyone had ever said that but if they hadn't they should have done. 'And I have said it for them,' she informed the night. 'So there.'

'Is that right?' a voice said behind her.

She turned. 'Are you spying on me?'

'All the time. To make sure you're OK. To make sure you are really here and I am not dreaming.'

'I am here all right,' she said. 'And I am OK. Very OK. In fact…'

They looked at each other.

'It is not only food I am hungry for,' she said.

He smiled and stretched out his hand. 'Come,' he said.

4

They stayed on Pulau Chantek a week. It was a time of beauty and of peace. They explored the patch of jungle in the middle of the island. They swam. They walked naked on the beach. They made love: in the house, on the deck, on the warm yellow sand.

'Pulau Chantek,' Hilary said with pleasure. 'A place where we can be young again.'

'Pulau Aman,' Craig said. 'Island of Peace.'

'I must learn Malay,' she said.

He nodded. 'I'll teach you. Awak sangat chantek.'

'Meaning?'

'You are very beautiful.'

'Thank you. How do I say that in Malay?'

'Terimah kaseh.'

She shaped her lips around the words. 'Terimah kaseh. Why didn't you ever bring me here before?'

'It was a secret place for us to come when we were truly together.'

'As we are,' she said. 'I am here. I am with you. I am truly happy and we shall live forever.'

5

It was a new life and she a new woman. They went home to Rumah Kelapa – the house amid the coconuts was truly home now, as it had never been in the old days – and the tranquillity of Pulau Chantek went with her. Craig had a fortune in books, many of which she had promised herself she would read but never had. Now she did: the plays of Shakespeare, Ibsen and O'Casey; *Don Quixote* and *The Tale of Genji;* the novels of Dickens and Dostoevsky, Steinbeck, Faulkner and Greene; the poetry of Eliot and Thomas and Ferlinghetti.

In the evenings they listened to music together. At first she was hesitant.

'I know nothing about music.'

'Then now is the time to start,' Craig said.

LOVE AFFAIR WITH A DEAF MAN

1

Hilary had learnt over the years that Craig meant what he said. Rumah Kelapa had state-of-the-art hi-fi equipment. He sat her down and selected a CD from his massive collection.

'We'll start with something easy,' he said.

She listened with some apprehension but it was pleasant enough, which was a relief. She thought: I am sixty-three years old. It's probably fair to say I have made some small mark on the world yet this is the first time I have ever sat down to listen to serious music.

It was like seeing the sea for the first time.

'What is it?' she said.

'Mozart,' Craig said. '"Eine kleine Nachtmusik". A little night music. Mozart wrote it to accompany people eating their dinner.'

She was disappointed; she felt classical music should be more momentous than an accompaniment to clattering knives and forks.

'How do you like it?'

'It's OK, I guess.'

She didn't know what she had expected. Perhaps she had thought it might make her feel like Cortez in Keats's poem, gazing out at the Pacific Ocean; if so, she was disappointed.

'Tomorrow we'll try something a little more demanding,' Craig said.

The following evening they repeated the process but demanding was right; if the previous evening she had been disappointed by the music's easy accessibility this time it was a nightmare, her ears rejecting a cacophony without form or meaning.

'It's like being run over by a tractor,' she said when the music – *music?* – finished at last. 'You're telling me people listen to that for pleasure?'

'Ever since 1808,' he said.

'What is it?'

'Beethoven's Fifth Symphony.'

She shook her head. 'I guess I don't have the ear for it.'

Craig was untroubled. 'Of course you don't. But it will come. When your ear gets used to it.'

She didn't believe it and felt much the same when he played it for her again the next evening. 'This is a waste of time.'

But the third night…

He had been watching her. 'Are you getting the hang of it now?'

She was cautious. 'Maybe a bit.'

She thought afterwards that had been the start of what she later decided was her love affair with Beethoven. Other composers too but Beethoven first of all. She found it barely credible that a deaf man could have created such huge, majestic, orgasmic sounds.

2

'The vocal parts of the Ninth Symphony. What do the words say?'

'They're taken from "Ode to Joy", a poem by the German poet Schiller. What Beethoven has done is combine the secular with the religious.'

'Explain.'

'He is saying that true joy is only possible through union with God.'

'Are you a believer?'

'I believe in Beethoven,' Craig said.

'So do I. Therefore I suppose one must believe to some extent. In any case it shows what a human being is capable of achieving,' she said.

'With genius,' Craig said.

Which was true.

'You haven't done too badly yourself,' Craig said. 'You know what Beethoven said? "I will seize fate by the throat."'

'Seize fate by the throat?' Hilary said. 'I like that.'

'Given your beginnings I would say you've done that.'

All her life she had been wary of praise. 'It seemed the logical thing to do at the time. Any number of people could have done it.'

'Could have. But you did it.'

'Not exactly the Ninth Symphony,' she said.

'Probably Beethoven thought that was the logical thing to do.'

'Another step along the highway?' Hilary said.

'Like his Great Fugue: a vision of music's future.'

He had introduced it to her the previous evening.

'I'm not sure about this business of looking into the future. I've always felt if we could see the future we would do nothing.'

Craig smiled. 'Not long ago you prophesied we would both live forever.'

'But we both know that isn't true. All we can do is live each day as it comes. Treat every minute as a bonus.'

'Live life to the full?' he said.

'Another way of saying the same thing.'

'I wonder where we'll be this time next year,' he said.

'Living life to the full,' she said.

'Let's hope,' he said. 'But in the meantime…'

She knew that look. 'Living life to the full?'

'I thought you'd never mention it.'

Later:

'You reckon Beethoven did this?'

'Do you care?'

'Probably not.'

There were other ways to the sublime.

TOGETHER AT LAST

1

With music and reading, with long walks along the sandy beaches and a trip to the Cameron Highlands, where they rediscovered the delights of sleeping under blankets and, victims of the advancing years, chose only the less ambitious hills to climb before returning ravenous to the hotel, the weeks and months passed.

They spent a lot of time at the children's home in the hills. There were over a hundred residents now, with a permanent staff and full-time manager, but Hilary, being Hilary, liked to keep her eye on things.

Hilary stayed in touch with her daughters. At first, like an alco-holic sampling a cautious glass of wine, she had been nervous about making the calls: control was an addiction not easily broken and she wasn't sure how things would go, but they worked out well enough.

Jennifer sounded a different woman from the one she had always known: happy as the grass was green, as Dylan Thomas had said in one of his poems, and by now heavily pregnant.

'It's a boy,' Jennifer said.

'About time we had a male in this family,' Hilary said. 'When's it due?'

'Early January.'

'I'll fly down, like I said,' Hilary told her.

'That will be nice.'

'No trouble from Davis?'

'Not a word.'

'You planning on getting married?'

'Probably not.'

Living in sin, as the old-timers would say. Just like her mother.

The conversation with Sara was more businesslike, as Hilary had expected. Yes, things were going well. Yes, she and Vivienne were getting on fine. Martha was doing splendidly in Hong Kong. The new genetics laboratory was being set up under William Gainsborough's supervision on the outskirts of Shanghai. Profits looked like being ten per cent up for the year.

'That should keep the shareholders happy,' Hilary said.

'Why should you care?'

'Because I'm one of them.'

Sara made no mention of any love life nor did Hilary enquire; it was natural for a mother to be interested but when Sara wanted her to know she would tell her. They had always been a family for secrets. Probably most families were.

2

It was night and they were lying in bed before sleep.

'I want to do something special for my birthday,' Hilary said.

'Like what?' Craig asked.

'In all the years you've lived here you've never explored the hongs of South Thailand, have you?'

'I don't even know what they are,' he said.

'Of course you do. I mentioned them to you before.'

'You must make allowances for my great age,' Craig said.

'You are only six years older than I am so spare me your nonsense.'

'Tell me again.'

'They are sea caves on the islands and coast of the Andaman Sea. They are open to the sky, no way in or out on the landward side, and very beautiful. Mysterious too, some of them.'

'How do you get into them?'

'By kayak, from the sea. Some of the entrances are so low you have to duck your head and so dark it feels like burrowing into the earth. Once you're inside it's different. It's light and there are mangroves. Even monkeys in some of them.'

'If I want to see monkeys I can go to the zoo. Less trouble.'

'Don't be a spoilsport. They are romantic. I thought you'd like that.'

'I am all in favour of romance in the right place.' With one arm around her, his free hand gentling her breast.

'Given the great age you mentioned just now I thought that sort of romance might be beyond you.'

'If you insist on sleeping naked at my side...'

'I am a shameless hussy.'

'And all the better for it.'

A little later she said: 'You're pretty shameless yourself.'

'I thought you'd never notice.'

Dear God, she thought, I love this man more than I believed it was possible to love anyone.

Sleep then, fathoms deep. When she woke they shared a tray of coffee and biscuits in bed while they admired the golden morning light beyond the window.

'Lazy slut,' she said.

'Thank you very much.'

'I am talking about myself. It's my job to make the coffee.'

'You can make the next lot.'

She nibbled a biscuit, making it last. 'Shall we do it, then?'

'Do what?'

'Shall we pay a visit to the hongs of the Andaman Sea?'

'Would you like to?'

'Christmas in Krabi,' she said. 'What could be nicer? And then my birthday afterwards.'

'You'll be sixty-four,' he said. 'Too old to go exploring caves. By rights it should then be a case of an armchair in front of the fire.'

'In the tropics? That would be smart, wouldn't it? In any case it's not relevant. The way you misused me last night, I doubt I'd have survived had I been a day over twenty.'

'Misused?'

'Manhandled, rather.'

'That's better. It seemed to suit you at the time,' he said.

'I heard no complaints from you either.'

The funny thing was she did feel young again. In the shower she thought: Christmas in Thailand. What could be nicer?

SEASON'S GREETINGS FROM HASKINS GOULD

1

It was the middle of a hot Sydney afternoon, fifteen days before Christmas. The season of festive lunches was in full swing but Sara was no more a fan of the business lunch than Hilary had been and never went near Cavaliers if she could help it.

She was in a session with one of the accountants when Desmond Bragg threw open her office door and barged in. No knock, no apology: his indifference to basic courtesies had always exasperated her; she thought sometimes that was why he did it. She looked up from the spreadsheets plastered across her desk.

'We're busy, Desmond. Can't it wait?'

'Well now, Sara, I'm inclined to think it can't, no.'

He plonked himself down in a chair on the other side of her desk, a fat man with a fat smile. His eyes were red-veined; his breath would have fuelled a distillery but his mind, as Sara well knew, was a steel trap.

Sara sighed. 'Give us a few minutes, Alan. OK?'

'Sure, Sara.'

The young accountant gathered his papers and fled. Sara stared at Desmond.

'So what is so urgent?'

'I've just come back from lunch. You know, Sara, you should try it sometime. Amazing what you hear.'

'Why do I need to do that? You aim to tell me anyway.'

Desmond laughed. 'Well, that's true. I was talking with Micky Monaghan. Good man to know, Sara. Nobody's got their ear closer to the ground than Micky Monaghan. He told me something interesting.'

Desmond's ego required that Sara coax the information out of him.

'Which was?'

'He's picked up a rumour that Haskins Gould is planning a raid on Brand Corporation.'

'A rumour?'

'That's all it was. There may be nothing to it but I thought you ought to know.'

'Have you told Vivienne?'

His eyes met hers. 'I get the impression she has enough on her plate without bothering her with what may be no more than idle gossip.'

'If that is what it is.'

'Be interesting to know if it's true or not,' Desmond said. 'Any thoughts on how we might find out?'

Clearer than words, Desmond's action in coming to her showed he regarded Sara as the boss in waiting. Very well; she would act like the boss.

'There may be nothing to it but I doubt we can just ignore it. I'll turn over a few stones, see if I can find anything. And thank you for bringing this to me.'

Desmond knew a brush off when he got one. He raised a sardonic eyebrow. 'Next thing we'll be calling you towkay neo,' he said.

Sara gave him a cold look. 'I'll get back to you,' she said.

Desmond hauled himself out of his chair. 'Ladies man like Haskins?' he said. 'Hell, Sara, make him the right sort of offer and he might even tell you himself.'

With the door shut behind him, Sara sat and thought.

I was sure you'd know what to do… Yeah, right. But saying it and doing it were two different things. On the other hand what else had he said? *Make him the right sort of offer…*

I'd dance on the moon before I'd do that, she thought. It wouldn't work anyway. But she remembered what Hilary had said to her once.

You will come across situations where you can't do what you know must be done. When that happens get someone else to do it for you. That way you'll get the job done.

She thought about that for a while. Should she discuss it with Vivienne? Vivienne, after all, was the CEO. No, she thought. Vivienne wouldn't approve and there was no point troubling her conscience if there was no need, right?

She'd picked up a few dodgy contacts during her time with Channel 12. Maybe now was the time to use them. She picked up the phone.

'Lou Masters? Sara Brand. I need a favour.'

Ten minutes later she was talking to a woman who said her name was Dolores Morrison.

2

They met for lunch four days later at an upscale restaurant, chosen by Dolores, in Sydney's east. Sara had understood that lunch would be on her, as would the services she wanted Dolores to provide.

Dolores said she was twenty-three. She had a university education, an angelic smile and a way with her that Sara saw would be useful in her line of work. Dolores Morrison was demure in both dress and appearance but that was misleading because she was an escort and no stranger, she claimed, to industrial espionage. Sara's contact had said she was the best in her field and she needed to be, the fee she was asking.

Sara didn't quite blink but it was close. 'I'm in the wrong line of work,' she said.

'You want the best you have to pay,' Dolores said.

'So it seems,' Sara said. 'Obviously our arrangement is confidential. No word of it must get out.'

'A blabbermouth wouldn't last five minutes in my business,' Dolores said.

'Very well.' Sara looked thoughtfully at the young woman working her way through her *sole Veronique* and was heartened: no false fastidiousness with this one. It was possible she was being set up but doubted it; it wouldn't be in Dolores's interests to double-cross her clients. She decided to trust her.

'Does the name Haskins Gould mean anything to you?'

Dolores smiled. 'I like to keep up with the business scene,' she said.

'Very well. Then this is what I want you to do.'

She spelt it out.

Dolores listened intently while she worked her way through a large helping of strawberry pavlova, with cream. 'You need to keep up your strength in my game,' she said.

Sara could well believe it. 'You think you can do this for me?'

'Haskins has a name for being a stud,' Dolores said. 'So that part should be easy. But whether I can get him to talk about his business interests is another matter.'

'But that is the whole point.'

'I know that. And I could easily say yes of course I can. But I don't work like that. I mean, I can screw him half to death and ask him every question in the book but if he won't tell he won't. I can hardly torture him, can I?'

'And if I offer you a bonus if you can get it out of him?'

Dolores shook her head. 'That's part of the deal. Whatever he tells me I'll pass on but if he won't, he won't.'

Which Sara supposed was fair enough. 'OK. We'll give it a try.'

'How do I meet him?'

'The lord mayor's giving a reception in three days' time. I'll get you an invite.'

'Good. And it's cash up front,' Dolores said.

'Half up front, half afterwards,' Sara said.

'No trust, no deal,' Dolores said. 'Cash up front. And before you ask, I don't take credit cards.' She gave Sara her angelic smile. 'But lunch is on me.'

3

Watching from a distance amid the pomp and glitter of the reception, Sara thought that Dolores looked like a million dollars. Not surprising; the rates she charged, she was probably worth at least that. It was certainly an eye-catching outfit with more of Dolores on show than some might have thought appropriate, but Sara doubted Haskins would be too discouraged.

She'd been scared Haskins would not be there but he was. They even saw each other briefly in the crush and he gave her his best crocodile smile, the one with the glint of teeth, which she returned in full measure. After that she lost sight of them but was confident Dolores would track her man down; confident too that Haskins would react the way she wanted. After that… It would all be in the laps of the gods and Dolores Morrison.

The next day Dolores phoned. 'We've made contact.'

'And?'

'And I'll keep you posted. These things take time.'

Now Sara was the one being given a brush off. Nothing she could do about it; she would just have to wait until Dolores got back to her. She walked into the bathroom that adjoined her office and stared at her reflection in the mirror. She spoke aloud.

'Are you up to the job? Are you tough enough?'

The reflection told her nothing but after a minute she nodded. *Yes.*

Whatever she had to do she would do. And always, she knew, she would have Hilary to fall back on in case of need.

INTO THE HONG

1

The car delivered Hilary and Craig straight to the resort. It was dark, the underwater lights of the swimming pool welcoming in the tropical night. They had eaten before they boarded the plane so didn't go to the dining room but followed the porter to their room. It was immaculately clean, the huge bed neatly turned down. There were paintings and Thai-style artefacts on the walls. A floor-to-ceiling window looked out over the small town of which nothing could now be seen but the flare of kerosene lanterns in the stalls that lined the main street and the faint shapes of people walking.

'You want a drink?' Craig asked.

'No thanks. Me for a shower and bed.'

'Mind if I join you?' he said.

'Might be handy if I wake up and feel lonely in the night.'

'You think that's likely?'

'Tomorrow definitely. Tonight maybe not.'

'Snivel,' he said. 'Sulk. No fun going on holiday with you.'

Hilary patted his hand. 'Poor baby. Tomorrow I'll give you all the fun you want.'

Before sleeping, with Craig already in bed and the room lights switched off, Hilary opened the bedroom's sliding window and stepped on to the balcony. Lights burnt in the resort and down the hill. She heard the distant murmur of voices, a motor scooter drove down the road, but the faint sounds seemed to complement rather than disturb the silence.

Her birthday was a week away; she felt strong, younger than her years. She drew the warm air into her lungs, aware of what she had seen ten thousand times yet never seen: the peaceful reaches of the night. The stars bore her up amid their blazing fires and a gush of heat, rising from her belly to her head, extended to embrace the peacefully murmuring town, a woman's laugh, the incomprehensible vastness of stars and space. At that moment Hilary knew she was one with all things, no more than a particle yet significant because she was part of the whole and without her all creation would be diminished.

Unexpected tears came to cleanse her spirit and Hilary Brand was filled with gratitude for her life: all that had passed, all that was still to come. The night overwhelmed her in an embrace of unbearable tenderness. Eyes blurred, face wet, she was conscious of something that was close to worship. Overhead was a glittering tent of stars.

2

The next morning was Christmas Eve. They went first to the beach. Off shore were many islands, jungle clad, their limestone cliffs rising vertically out of the waves. There was a slight heat haze; in the shimmering mist the islands looked like galleons under sail. A single-masted white yacht was anchored two hundred metres offshore with a rubber dinghy secured to its stern. As they watched two men climbed into the dinghy and headed for the shore.

Further along the beach fishermen, bare chests and legs, were hauling their net. The net formed a semi-circle in the thigh-deep water. Two hundred metres down the beach another group of men had brought one end of the net ashore; where Hilary and Craig were standing a second group was now doing the same. There was excited shouting as the net was drawn closer to the sand. Hilary could see a growing agitation of the water. A fish leapt, brushing the top of the net, and with a flick of its tail escaped back into the sea while the net closed tighter on the fish still trapped within its diminishing circle. Finally the net reached the sand. Excited shouts from the fishermen as they ran back down the beach where the catch was leaping and splashing in the shallows. Within seconds the men were throwing the fish to a chattering group of women, who began packing them into open boxes. A young woman with a small girl at her side stood with a smiling face, begging a fish from one of the youngest of the fishermen. Eventually he pulled out a nice-sized one and tossed it to her. Her smile broadened delightedly. She shouted something in a harsh voice and snatched it up, hurrying away with her prize with the child scurrying after her.

Hilary and Craig listened to the ribald laughter and mocking words of the other fishermen.

'Want to try the same trick?' Craig said.

'Oh sure. That girl looked about eighteen.'

'So do you.'

'Don't talk nonsense.' But, absurdly, was delighted.

After the beach they explored the town. The two men from the yacht had drawn their dinghy up the beach and were now walking ahead of them up the main street. It was early yet already the stall owners were rigging awnings in preparation for the day. They stopped at one of them and drank strong black coffee before climbing back up the hill to the resort.

Later they rented bicycles and rode out into the country. They passed paddy fields and palm trees with the heat-hazed sea an occasional blue blink through the vegetation, and Hilary was reminded of the day when Craig had first driven her to Rumah Kelapa. She gave him a brilliant smile as they free-wheeled down a hill into a tiny village clustered amid a plantation of rubber trees.

'What a wonderful world we live in!'

They dismounted and walked through the village. Everywhere were smiles and hands held palm to palm in greeting. Without words smiles had to suffice and did, and Hilary had a good feeling about the villagers and their presence among them. A building flew the Thai flag and they heard the sound of children's voices.

'Must be the school,' Craig said.

The villagers offered them coconuts and the red-skinned fruit that in Malaysia were called rambutans. They gave them a handful of baht, not knowing whether they were paying too much or too little, then mounted their bicycles and rode on through the countryside.

Later they cycled back to town. They ate prawns and spring rolls at a stall and returned to the resort.

'Tomorrow is Christmas Day,' said Hilary.

She was lying in the bath, glass of champagne in her hand, while Craig sat and admired her. Later still, with her full co-operation, he made love to her again and she thought she would never grow weary of his attentions or of the man who made them.

3

Saturday 25 December. She phoned the girls and she and Craig exchanged gifts before going to breakfast: a bolt of silk for her, Zeiss self-focusing binoculars for him.

After breakfast they went for a stroll through the town but it was hot, the humidity climbing, and it wasn't long before they headed back up the hill to the resort, where they spent a peaceful day overlooking the pool from the terrace of their room with only a plate of chicken sandwiches for lunch.

The evening was a dressy affair. They had come prepared and at seven o'clock they went down to the decorated dining room, Hilary in an azure and silver gown from Armani and Craig in a sharkskin jacket he told her he had never worn since buying it five years before.

'It still fits you,' she said.

The resort had done its guests proud with champagne and candlelight and Christmas crackers and a lavish seafood buffet.

'Thank God it's seafood,' Craig said. 'This is hardly the climate for roast turkey and Christmas pudding.'

Hilary wouldn't have minded a traditional dinner but supposed he was right: even though the dining room was air-conditioned you still had to live with your stomach afterwards.

There was dancing with a three-piece band but they did not make a night of it; they had to be up early to meet the boatman who would be taking them to what they had been told was the most spectacular of the hongs, and to fit in with the tides they had to leave the resort no later than seven in the morning.

'Why so early?' Craig asked. 'This is supposed to be a holiday, for God's sake.'

'Because you can only get through the entrance for two hours either side of low water.'

'So we won't have long there?'

'Four hours should be plenty.'

They went to bed and slept the sleep of the just and well fed.

When they awoke it was Boxing Day. 26 December 2004.

4

They met the fisherman at the mouth of the narrow creek that emptied into the sea at the northern end of the beach where they had walked the previous day.

'There she is,' Hilary said.

The fishing boat had a sharply cambered prow and rode high in the water.

'It looks like a shark,' Craig said. 'Which I suppose isn't a bad thing. But how are we supposed to get aboard?'

There was only one way. Neatly uniformed children were passing on their way to school as Hilary and Craig waded thigh-deep through the waters of the creek to get to the boat and haul themselves up and over the side.

'I am an old man,' Craig said, water streaming off him as he sat on the thwarts of the open cockpit. 'I'm not sure I'm up to this sort of thing any more.'

'You poor old soul,' Hilary said. 'And you so active in other ways.'

'I fear I may be ruined for life.' But he was smiling as he spoke.

'You'd better not be,' Hilary said. 'I have plans for you.'

'I feel better already,' Craig said.

One of the crew hauled in the anchor and the boat turned its bows towards the sea. The sun came warm and strong and the land began to slide back past them.

It was a quarter past eight.

Hilary pointed. 'I see the fishermen are hauling their net again. That young woman is there again too. Probably she lives on the fish they give her.'

'I wonder what she has to give them in return,' Craig said.

'She probably doesn't have anything else to offer,' Hilary said.

There was a European family on the beach, the mother in a large sunhat, a child who was probably their daughter running ahead of them towards the water. Further along the beach other families were spreading towels, some children already in the sea. A ball was thrown; they heard shrieks of laughter; a dog ran cavorting along the sand.

The white yacht was still there and they passed close to its stern. The morning was windless, the air sultry, and Hilary observed a German ensign hanging limply from its staff, a Thai flag no bigger than a handkerchief mounted on the mast's starboard cross tree.

The two men they had seen yesterday were in the yacht's cockpit and now waved at them. Hilary waved back then realised they were trying to attract their attention. She spoke to the fisherman who slowed the motor. Only ten metres separated the two craft.

She shouted across at the two men. 'Can we help you?'

The taller of the two men called back. 'We were told this part of the ocean is called the Ring of Fire. We thought it must mean there would be volcanoes but we have seen none. We therefore ask ourselves why does it have this name?'

His English was good, his accent strong. He was very young, very German, very correct.

Craig answered him. 'There are volcanoes in Indonesia.'

The German laughed. 'Indonesia? So far? So we should be safe enough here, ja?'

'I hope so.'

'Thank you very much.'

'You're welcome.'

The engine picked up; they motored on.

It was eight twenty-five.

It was just after nine when they dropped anchor off the entrance to the hong. The tide was out and on either side of the entrance, dark and mysterious, they could see the line where the sea reached when the tide was full.

The fishing boat had a kayak, which the crew launched over the side. The captain issued them with life jackets and checked to see they put them on correctly. He nodded approvingly.

'This very wonderful place. Others have many tourists but here you the only ones.'

'Shall we see birds?'

The captain threw his arms excitedly into the air. 'Birds, mangrove trees, maybe snakes: many, many things.'

'Snakes? Not deadly ones, I hope?' Craig said.

'Oh yes, very, very deadly,' the man assured him.

'That's all we need,' Craig said.

They climbed down into the kayak and settled themselves behind the burly young man whose job it was to paddle them through the dark tunnel and into the snake-infested marvels beyond.

Nine-twenty.

A surly slop and surge of water marked the entrance but the boatman negotiated it safely and paddled on into darkness. The rock ceiling, low to begin with, became still lower the further into the tunnel they got. In the confined space the sound of the sea slopping against the rock walls was very loud. The kayak was barely moving now. Before long they had to lower their heads as far as they could but still from time to time felt the rock brushing gently against their hair. It was absolutely dark; Hilary could see nothing, had no sense of any movement or even of the rock pressing close about them. All she could hear was the movement of the water, the dip and splash of the paddle, the thud of her heart. She remembered

Dr Chang and thought what a great place this would be to have a heart attack.

Still the tunnel continued, a cleft in the body of the cliff that seemed to go on forever. Except that now there was a change: she found that she could see the faint outline of the paddler in front of her, the faintest shadow against the returning light. The outline became stronger and soon she could make out the walls of the tunnel, black and glistening with water. The passage must have changed direction because all at once the light came flooding, the entrance into the hong open before them. After the dark tunnel the brightness was dazzling. The paddler increased the speed of his strokes until they emerged into daylight. Her eyes growing accustomed to the brightness, Hilary looked wonderingly about her. They had entered a hidden garden surrounded by vertical cliffs of white limestone that rose hundreds of feet into the sky. Trees with smooth trunks clustered on the open ground between the lagoon and the cliffs while mangroves showed their tangled, snake-like roots in the shallows. Cycads grew high on the cliffs and the air was still.

'We've gone back in time. It's like I always imagined the Garden of Eden,' Craig said. He looked up as the branches were shaken far above them and pointed at a black face peering down at them from the shelter of the leaves. 'Monkeys!'

'I seem to remember a snake,' said Hilary. 'I don't recall any monkeys.'

'I guess Eve got into enough strife without monkeys,' Craig said.

While Hilary sat, staring and wondering. This is so good, she thought, so perfect. It is a sacred place and I am so glad to be here and see it with Craig, with my true love. It is like a glimpse of heaven and it is far, far better than I could ever have imagined.

She turned to the boatman who was grinning as proudly as though he owned the hong and all that was in it. 'Can we go ashore?'

He seemed to understand because he nodded and Hilary and Craig stepped out of the kayak and waded ashore.

It was ten o'clock as they stepped on to the dry land.

Hilary, eyes shut to hold the image and the wonder more closely to herself, thought: So this is it. We are here together and it is perfect.

There were birds in the trees, a flock of birds. She looked up in the hope of identifying them and at that moment they took off in a noisy chorus that circled over their heads before flying up and over the cliff tops and vanishing. A monkey chattered furiously.

That's funny, Hilary thought. Something must have alarmed them.

At that moment Craig said in a voice that was not at all like his normal voice: 'Something is going on.'

She looked where he was pointing. It was past low water yet the water level in the hong was still dropping. They stared at each other.

It was ten-fifteen.

TSUNAMI

1

In the two hours since the fishing boat had passed, the beach had filled up. Holidaymakers were everywhere: family groups with children playing; young couples oiling each other's backs; individuals strolling along the water's edge. The two Germans were working on their yacht. Along the road that bordered the beach bicycle salesmen had parked beneath the trees, hoping to attract customers to buy ice cream, fresh fruit, newspapers, sun lotion. In the town the shops were open, the cafés full of people eating a late breakfast; motor scooters whizzed to and fro; townspeople shouted cheerful greetings to one another; and in the main street flowers were being placed before portraits of the king at shrines set up in his honour. It was a hot morning and getting hotter; in the resorts on the edge of town the swimming pools were full. The sky was blue and there was no wind. It was the ideal day to rest and recover after what for many had been an over-indulgent Christmas Day.

Mrs Cornelia Mudge was one of those who had eaten too much. She had never been one to resist a second helping and Christmas – a Christmas in Thailand, what was more – had made it almost a duty to take the most of her opportunities. She wondered what her friends back in England would say if they could see her now.

About as different from Reading as it's possible to be, she thought. It had cost them a packet but had been worth every penny.

Husband Brian was lying at her side. He'd eaten too much as well and drunk his share and maybe more, but Christmas, this Christmas in particular, was special, wasn't it, and he would soon get over it. Daughter Sylvia was off somewhere but Cornelia Mudge was not worried. She wouldn't be far. Sylvia was only ten but as bright as a button; she was more than capable of looking after herself.

2

Three hundred metres from the beach in the wood-walled shanty she shared with four other families, Chailai Suttikul and her daughter Dao were at the charcoal stove, preparing their meal from the fish she had begged that morning from Kamnah the fisherman. She knew he fancied her; she liked him too. But would he protect and support her? He was young and men were fickle. She nursed a secret hope they might make a life together but she was already twenty years old, a widow with a child of three, and knew how little she had to offer. A body and a willing heart, but bodies were cheap and how could any man read a woman's heart?

Later she would pay a visit to the Tiger Cave temple and pray yet again to Kwam Im that the goddess should show compassion on her.

The fish was cooked. She took it off the fire.

3

Hans Bauer had gone below to examine the charts in preparation for their cruise down the coast to the Malaysian island of Penang when Rudi called out to him.

'Step up here a minute.'

He went up on deck. 'What's the matter?'

'Look at the sea.'

Hans looked; his eyes opened wide. 'What the…?'

Because the sea was barely there. The ebb was over an hour since; the tide had no business to be still going out but it was.

He jumped to the controls and checked the depth under the keel.

'One metre forty-five?'

It was impossible but there it was.

'Let's get out of here!'

Rudi gaped. 'What?'

'If we don't move we'll be aground.'

'But why?'

'I don't care why. Let's move it. Hurry!'

4

In the village Hilary and Craig had visited two days before life continued as usual. Goaded by small boys, water buffalo were working in the communal paddy field a short distance away. A narrow track led to a muddy beach where the children were sometimes sent to gather tiny clams and other shellfish. The tide had gone out almost half a kilometre, much further than usual, but the children were in school, the majority of the inhabitants were farmers and no one thought anything of it.

The school echoed with the shrill chanting of the pupils learning by rote as they recited the Ramakien, the national epic of Thailand.

It was ten twenty-nine.

5

On the town beach the tide had gone out so far the sea was barely visible. Children from holidaying families were prospecting a long way from shore, some with shrimping nets, checking pools of water for whatever fish they might find. The yacht was heading for the horizon when Sylvia came racing up to her parents, half-asleep on the warm sand. She started shouting well before she reached them.

'Mum, Mum...'

'What is it, dear?'

'There's something wrong with the sea.'

Cornelia Mudge was slow to move or respond. She tended to be tolerant of her daughter's alarms; Sylvia was always coming up with some crazy theory so her present excitement was nothing new. Added to which Cornelia was comfortable where she was and did not feel like leaping to her feet just because something had pressed her daughter's panic button.

'What is wrong with it, dear?'

'Look at it!' Sylvia's excitement moved up a notch. 'It's gone right out.'

'I'm sure it'll be back when the tide comes in,' she said.

'But it's gone miles! It's not just the tide. It's something different. We did it with Mrs Willis at school. It's what happens just before a tsunami strikes.'

Cornelia Mudge had only the vaguest notion what a tsunami was. 'Isn't that some kind of tidal wave?'

'That's right!' Sylvia was dancing in agitation; she reached down and shook her mother's arm. 'Get up, Mum! Get up!'

Cornelia saw her daughter was close to tears. 'Why should there be a tidal wave?'

'I don't know why! All I know is that when the sea goes out like this it's a warning. First it goes out for miles and then comes in really fast: fast as an express train, Mrs Willis said. And when it hits the beach the waves will be enormous, higher than the trees. They'll drown everybody if we don't get them off the beach.'

'Well, I don't know about that,' Mrs Mudge said.

But her husband was on his feet. 'Sylvie's right. There is something wrong.'

The tone of his voice made Cornelia get up fast. The sea had certainly gone out a long way; it had almost vanished. She looked around and saw groups of other people, standing and pointing. Mothers were setting off after children far out on the wet sand, screaming at them to come in, come in *now*. The bicycle salesmen had packed up and were heading into town, standing on their pedals and making tracks as fast as they could go. She could sense panic building.

Brian Mudge obviously shared Sylvia's alarm. With her beside him he was running from group to group, talking urgently to each in turn. It was obvious to everyone by now that the sea's behaviour was out of the ordinary and might well indicate that some catastrophe was on the way. Better safe than sorry, Cornelia said to herself, and began to gather their towels and other bits and pieces together.

She heard a distant sound, like thunder. She turned and looked across the mud flats to where the sea should have been and saw emerging from the horizon a line of white: a gigantic wave extended as far as she could see, boiling and growing larger with every second and roaring as it came. The sound grew rapidly, became deafening, and the speed with which the wave advanced was so great that for a moment it mesmerised her. She forced her legs to move. She knew they had to get away at once if they were to have any hope of survival. Waiting only to confirm that her daughter and husband were also running for their lives, she abandoned their possessions and fled. While the monstrous wave raced landwards, its crest higher than the trees, and its roar engulfed the world.

6

A friend stuck her head around the door of Chailai's hut.

'The tide has gone out a long way. People are saying there should be lots of pools where fish may be trapped. I am going down to try and catch some. Are you coming?'

Extra food was always welcome. 'Of course.'

'Bring a bucket.'

Chailai settled baby Dao on her hip and set off with her friend down the track to the beach where both women stood and stared in amazement.

'Hau!'

The sea was gone. Neither could think what it might mean, nor did they waste time wondering about it. The retreating tide had indeed left many pools and already there were people moving from one to the next, scavenging what they could find. The two women set out across the oozy mud to join them.

The pools nearest to land had nothing in them; others had already emptied them so the two women went further out. A boy ran past them with a big crab in his hands. The crab's claws waved frantically and the boy's face was bright with triumph. They saw the bent backs of women, their hands busy as they raked through the silt-lined pools, but there were plenty of pools. They walked on until they found one with nobody beside it. Chailai set the child down on the sand and began to search.

Tiny fish darted from side to side of the pool. They were hard to catch but little by little the two friends managed to trap them. The surface of the pool began to tremble.

'Could it be a big fish buried in the sand?' the friend said.

Again their fingers raked the bed of the pool, sending the sand swirling. They found nothing but the water continued to tremble, the movement much stronger than before. Chailai frowned; it was very strange. She stood to ease her back. For the first time she heard a rumble like the engines of the big trucks that sometimes drove through the town. And now it was not only the water in the pool that was trembling; the ground itself was shaking beneath their feet.

The two friends stared at each other. They had come further out than the other villagers and were alone on the shaking sand. And the noise was much louder now.

Chailai looked out to sea. Her hands flew to her mouth and she screamed. An enormous wave was roaring towards them. She ran and snatched up the baby. Her friend was screaming too, both of them running frantically towards the land, both of them knowing it was far too late. No way could they hope to outrun the roaring sea and there was nowhere to hide. They stopped, knowing that all was lost, clinging with their despairing arms wrapped about each other, eyes and mouths wide with terror, as the tsunami fell upon them.

7

The water smashed into the land with the force of a nuclear blast. Ancient trees, some over a hundred feet high, shattered like matchsticks. Food stalls vanished; those who had stayed to protect their property from looters vanished too. Wooden shacks were ripped apart. The splintered fragments were swept away with many of the occupants.

Running flat out, eyes wide with terror, Cornelia Mudge and her family escaped by inches, the foaming sea licking at their heels as, breath like fire in their chests, they reached higher ground and safety. An old man who had come on holiday to get over the recent death of his wife managed to escape with them only to die of a heart attack in front of their horrified eyes. Not everyone had got away from the beach in time and many died, lost in the tumultuous seas.

In the lower parts of the town even stone buildings were affected, flood waters head high smashing windows and doors and destroying all in their path: tables, chairs, old people and babies asleep in back rooms, shoppers, those eating or working in the cafés. Broken pieces of masonry fell from inundated buildings, crushing those beneath.

Outside town giant waves engulfed the village where Hilary and Craig had bought coconuts and rambutans. Fruit trees and paddy fields were destroyed, the water buffalo and their minders drowned; bodies were swept away or buried metres deep in mud. Of the peaceful village and its school only ruins remained but a car that had been travelling along the road when the first wave struck was found half-buried in mud in the place where the school had been. A few children survived, clinging to debris and being swept along in the torrent until they reached higher ground and safety, but most died with their teacher in the gutted school.

Far out at sea the Germans' yacht was trapped beneath the monstrous waves. Overturned, mast gone, hull torn open, it was swept back on the crest of the toppling wave to be shattered into fragments on the shore. The two young men were snatched by the sea.

At the entrance to the hong the fishing boat captain eyed the dropping sea levels and fired up the engine. He ordered the anchor brought in; within a minute the boat was motoring along the coast in an attempt to avoid being grounded by the retreating seas. He was apprehensive; as a child he had heard stories of the sea retreating only to return later, destroying all in its path. One kilometre from the beach he had his first sight of the wall of water roaring in from the horizon. With the engine already running flat out there was nothing he could do. The disaster of ancient legend had returned to devour the land. All he could do was carry on and hope to reach shelter before the waves struck. He knew there was no chance of it and was right. The tsunami caught and destroyed the vessel and everything aboard. The last thing he saw was the face of death as the massive wave devoured them.

8

In the hong the area uncovered by the retreating sea had doubled in five minutes. Hilary and Craig stared at it and at each other.

'What's going on?' Hilary said.

'No idea.' Craig turned to the boatman but from his startled expression it was obvious he knew no more than they did.

'Whatever it is I don't much like it,' Hilary said.

'You and me both.'

Not only them; chattering furiously, monkeys were climbing as high in the trees as they could go; crabs scuttled into holes among the exposed roots of the mangroves; the birds had not come back. And now the stony floor of the entrance tunnel had appeared out of the water.

'No way out even if we wanted,' Craig said.

'I have a hunch we picked a bad day to come here,' Hilary said. 'But there's nothing we can do about it now.'

There certainly wasn't. They inspected the trees and the limestone cliffs – just in case, Craig said – but the smooth trunks of the trees offered no handholds while even a skilled mountaineer would have a problem with the cliff faces. It was obvious there was no way out there.

'Why should we be thinking like that anyway?' Hilary said.

'Because what has gone out will undoubtedly come back. And if it comes back as strongly as I think it may…'

There was no need to spell it out.

'At least we are together,' Hilary said. 'That's what matters.'

They turned to each other.

It's a strange place to be if the worst happened, Hilary thought. Trapped in a hole in the earth with monkeys and mangroves and a young man they couldn't speak to as their only companions.

With the thought she saw a flicker of movement, a blink of gaudy colour amid the leaves. Her eye sought out whatever it was she had seen. For a moment she saw nothing, then the flicker came again as a butterfly with enormous wings, red and gold and blue, flew a few metres through the still air before coming to rest on a leaf far above their heads. She looked up but the brightness of the sky dazzled her and she saw it no more. No matter; she had seen its beauty and that was enough. She was with her true love and that too was enough. She turned impulsively and put her arms around Craig's neck. She didn't care that the boatman might be watching. Let him watch; let the world watch. She did not care that they were trapped and helpless.

Trapped they certainly were. They had already moved as far away from the entrance as they could, they had checked and rechecked the smooth trunks of the trees. They were both reasonably fit for their age but that was the catch. If they'd been in their twenties they might have managed it but at sixty-three and sixty-nine shinnying up smooth-trunked trees was impossible.

Yet she found she could accept the situation peacefully. What she had now was a moment of perfection and she was happy, so happy. Never mind what the future held; this was now and she wanted nothing more from life than what she had.

She tightened her arms around Craig's neck.

He grunted. 'You are strangling me, woman.'

But his arms were around her also and she knew that she was safe, that whatever happened to them nothing could harm them because they were united and would be so always.

We are going to live forever, her heart said. We shall do wonderful things. We shall be happy, so happy.

She felt a breath of air, a movement where before there had been none. She turned, seeking its source. Found it in the entrance tunnel: a faint breath growing stronger. A wind that started to blow with increasing force. Now with the wind came sound: the hollow boom of what had become rushing air, with another sound behind it, a murmur that within seconds had strengthened to a roar. It grew so loud that it was impossible to speak against it or even shout. Even to breathe had become a problem. And still the wind and sound grew and still there was no water inside the black-mouthed tunnel leading to the catastrophe that she sensed must be gathering strength beyond the rocky walls. The rock had begun to vibrate: faintly at first, then stronger, then violently.

And the water came. A dribble, a spurt, a flood, a torrent that hurled itself into the hong with the force of a hundred fire hoses. Hilary and Craig clung together, thinking of nothing, knowing they were one and would be so for eternity.

'I love you, Craig.'

She shouted the words, hearing their sound inside her head. Whether he could hear them she did not know nor was it important. The words were engraved on both their hearts and nothing else mattered.

'I love you, Craig Laurie.'

'I love you, Hilary Brand.'

Forever and ever.

The highway of her days took form behind her: the child, the adolescent and the adult, their days gilded with hope or darkened by despair but always climbing in humility and joy until, one being at last, they found fulfilment amid the glory of the stars.

And the full flood of the tsunami, compressed to even greater intensity by the tunnel through which it had forced its way, lifted them, their arms embracing each other, and hurled them with shattering force across the hong and into the limestone cliffs. Where they lay still, bodies entwined, faces serene, while the floodwaters rose to cover them.

CATACLYSM

1

The sun shone on the shattered town. Where palm trees had lined the sandy beaches only splintered stumps remained; boats had been hurled far beyond the high-water mark. Stunned survivors drifted like ghosts through the ruins while scores of unidentified bodies retrieved by frantic rescue workers lay in mass graves bulldozed out of the earth. Over all was a drift of smoke where cooking fires had been lighted by homeless locals camping out amid the rubble.

Sara sat in her office in the Brand Corporation building, her mind groping to take hold of reality, as she stared in horror at the images, each more terrible than the last, that came and went on the television screen. In a theatrically sombre voice the commentator was saying that in terms of lives lost the Boxing Day tsunami was one of the worst natural disasters in history. He was talking of tens, maybe hundreds, of thousands dead. Aceh, in northern Sumatra, had been the worst hit, but in Thailand thousands had also been reported dead or missing. There were reports of deaths in Sri Lanka and even as far away as South Africa.

Sara had heard nothing from Hilary. She'd had a phone call from her on Christmas Day but whether she and Craig had been caught up in the tsunami she did not know. There had been enormous problems getting through to the town. She had forced herself to control the panic that threatened to devour her and had told Janet to just keep trying, and eventually they'd made contact. Sara had spoken to the manager of the resort where Hilary had told her they were staying.

The manager confirmed that Ms Brand had been a guest at the resort but all he could tell her was that she and Mr Laurie had gone out first thing and not come back.

'You have no idea where they were going?'

'As they left so early I think it may have been to visit one of the hongs, but I cannot be sure as they did not tell us their plans.'

'How many hongs are there?'

'Hundreds.'

'And the boat they went on?'

'No one knows. Most of the fleet has been destroyed or is still missing. The search for survivors goes on and of course we have not given up hope –'

Sara could hear the exhaustion in the manager's voice, still trying to come to terms with the scale of the catastrophe.

'Thank you for your assistance,' she said. 'If you hear anything –'

'We shall inform you at once.'

She put down the phone. The television was still relaying its doomsday pictures. With sudden fury Sara snatched up the remote and switched it off but in her head the images played on unabated.

Like the resort manager, she would not give up hope but she was not stupid; if Hilary had survived she would surely have been in touch by now. No, she thought, the chances were not good. With no one knowing where she had been when the tsunami struck even the likelihood of recovering her body was remote.

All her life Sara had been independent in both mind and spirit. She had admired and respected her mother but never until this moment had she realised how much she loved her. She knew it well enough now; there was an emptiness in her soul she knew would never be filled.

It was a frightening business to be alone, to know that – barring a miracle – there was no one to whom she could turn in case of need. Hilary had moved on with her life but had made it clear before she left that she had not abandoned her; if Sara ever needed her she would always be there. There had been huge comfort in that thought. No longer; now she was almost certainly gone and the knowledge was a cold wind blowing through Sara's heart, already cold with missing Emil. Devastation… But she must not give way to grief; nowadays she had new responsibilities and must not, would not, ignore them.

'Think,' she told herself. '*Think!*'

Vivienne was the CEO and nominally in charge but she had been number two too long, conditioned to take supportive action but not to initiate. What was needed now was strong action to demonstrate that the Brand Corporation had the talent and will to rise above the loss of its founder and she was not sure Vivienne was up to the challenge.

She sat and thought carefully about what she had to do. If Hilary had been here what would she have done?

She got to her feet and walked thoughtfully about her office while she thought things out. Finally she went back to her desk and sat down.

DANCING INSIDE HIS HEAD

It was Boxing Day, nine o'clock at night, and in his multi-million-dollar apartment overlooking Circular Quay Haskins Gould switched off the television set and poured himself another drink. Standing in the middle of the living room he toasted his reflection in the mirror.

'Here's to you, Haskins!'

The malt slipped down so sweetly. So the witch was dead. Alleluia! He'd have danced if he'd been a bit fitter, a bit younger, but that didn't matter; inside his head he was dancing all the same. But wait, he thought. Let's not be too hasty about this. Now was not the time to get over-excited; now was the time for calculation. The witch was dead – he felt it in his bones – but he'd thought that before and been wrong. As a corporate raider he'd had a heap of experience and with Hilary out of the way and his spies telling him Vivienne Archer hadn't a clue what she was doing he had started making moves. Like everyone else in the game he kept a string of shelf companies with nominal capital and no real assets. He used them to acquire shares in companies that interested him, building up a holding that nobody knew he had until he was ready to move on his target. He liked to refer to himself as a lion in ambush and the image always gave him a thrill. For months now he had been using some of his shelf companies to build up his interest in Brand. Only in small lots – important to avoid setting off alarm bells – but enough small lots added up to a significant holding. By placing his acquisitions through a dozen companies he had been able to avoid informing the Stock Exchange. Bearing in mind the provisions of the Corporations Act, the authorities might not think much of the arrangement but what they didn't know couldn't hurt them, right?

He'd been planning a move on Brand since the beginning of the year, had even got his mate Anthony Belloc to make a pass at Hilary's idiot daughter. If Hilary had been seriously ill the share price would have been certain to crash, but he'd been unable to find out anything definite and the plan had come to nothing. It wasn't important. If Hilary really was dead it wouldn't matter either way but taking risks was one thing, committing commercial suicide something else entirely. He wouldn't put it past Hilary bloody Brand to come back from the dead so it would be wise to wait a few more days in case the search teams found her alive under the rubble.

It might mean delaying a week or two, maybe a month, but once he was sure she really was dead he would make his move. Taking over the corporation that he had helped her create! The corporation she had stolen from him! He would reclaim it, take it back from her estate, strip out its assets and leave her family if not destitute than at least driven out from the company that their mother had intended as her legacy to them. Leaving her reputation in ruins…

He laughed as he savoured that vision. A pity she wouldn't be there to see the destruction of her life's work, but never mind. What poetic justice that would be! He'd never been one for poetry but would be only too happy to make an exception in this case. You'd better believe it!

A voice larded with invitation came from the bedroom. 'I'm waiting, baby. You planning on joining me any time soon?'

He had taken one of his blue pills an hour ago: what a blessing they were! And now this woman he'd met at the lord mayor's reception – stacked but discreet, just the way he liked it – was waiting in his bed and by the sound of her panting for it. It wouldn't be right to leave tits like those lonely for long, would it? He'd heard that Hilary Brand had once said that Haskins Gould gave a whole new meaning to the word gross. Damn right he did! And proud of it!

He swallowed the last of his drink, put down his glass and moved purposefully towards the bedroom door. 'Coming right now,' he called.

Anything to oblige a lady! What a way to end the day!

PAYBACK TIME

1

Jennifer had been attending an exhibition with Martin Gulliver at the Australian Centre for Contemporary Art in Sturt Street when she first heard about the Boxing Day tsunami. She was sad – who wouldn't be? – but paid the news no particular heed. After the exhibition they went out for a meal and a glass or two of wine – the baby was due in three weeks but the doctor had assured her a glass or two of good wine would do no harm – and thought no more about the tsunami until they got home to find Sara's message on the answering machine.

Jennifer returned the call at once. It was past eleven but Sara was a night owl. In any case the time was irrelevant. Tsunami? Mother missing? The idea made her feel quite faint.

'Surely you're not saying Mother may have been killed in this Indonesia business?'

'It hit Thailand as well. The whole region. I'm saying she's missing. That's all.'

'But she will turn up, won't she?'

Of course she would. Mother was indestructible.

'I… hope so,' Sara said. 'But it's not looking good, Jennifer.'

'Have you spoken to the ambassador? Surely he will know? Mother's not exactly unknown, after all!'

'There are thousands of people missing, Jennifer. Tens of thousands. Some may be found alive but very few. Have you seen the pictures? The place looks like it's been hit by a bomb.'

But *Mother*...

'She'll be alive and well somewhere,' she said. 'You'll see: she'll be in touch in a day or two.'

She spoke aggressively, as though daring her sister to disagree. Sara did not. But:

'I hope you're right,' she said.

'What do we do in the meantime?' Jennifer said.

'We wait.'

'Perhaps one of us could fly up there? Normally I'd be willing to go, if you're too busy, but with the baby –'

'Of course you can't go,' said Sara. 'There'd be nothing you could do anyway. Except get in the way,' she added unkindly.

'Surely one of us ought to be trying to find her. How do we know the people up there are doing things properly? Perhaps they're not searching at all.'

'For heaven's sake, Jennifer, they've got professional search teams on the job. Why don't you take a look at the pictures on television? That might give you a better idea of the scale of what's happened. Whole towns have been wiped out!'

Jennifer was still thinking up a sharp answer when she realised Sara had put down the phone.

'I was only trying to help,' she said. 'I don't see why she had to talk to me like that.' She waddled across to her easy chair and subsided into it. With the baby due so soon, even the simplest things were hard to do and her temper was easily frayed. 'God! Now I know how an elephant feels.'

'What did she want, anyway?' Martin said.

Jennifer told him. 'If anything's happened to Mother I don't think I'll be able to bear it.'

Martin was all commiseration, telling her she must take care of herself. 'Don't let yourself get worked up. I'm sure she'll be found safe and well.'

'That's what I told Sara but she didn't seem to think so.' She clutched Martin's arm, looking at him with a tear-stained face. 'You're not just saying it, are you? You really think she'll be all right?'

'Of course she'll be all right.'

'I must go and lie down,' she said.

Martin helped her into bed, gave her all the cosseting and kind words he could think of and left her to get some rest. She gave him a brave smile.

'I won't sleep a wink,' she said.

2

Jennifer said that every night and every night, when Martin came to bed, she was snoring. He went back into the living room and turned on the television, the sound muted. He was just in time to catch the late news. He watched the pictures gravely.

He'd always had a soft spot for Jennifer's mum. Funny, when you thought about it. The artist and the tycoon… Not his type of woman at all, really. Yet he'd sensed she'd been on his side from the first. And recently she'd been buying some of his work, too. Nothing wrong with that. He'd turned down her offer of the curatorship but that had been because he no longer needed the money, thank God. And now she was caught up in this catastrophe.

He went and poured himself a whisky and sipped it thoughtfully. Judging from what he'd seen on the telly he didn't fancy her chances. If it turned out she was indeed dead he didn't like to think of the effect it would have on Jennifer, especially at the moment, but there was nothing he could do about that.

All that remained was hope.

3

It was the following morning and a public holiday but Vivienne was in the office. With Hilary missing and likely dead there were many phone calls and decisions to be made; Hilary had been out of the company for months but her name still carried its old magic and there would be some anxious investors and others whose nerves Vivienne would need to soothe, public holiday or not. She had prepared a list of those whom she needed to speak to and had come into the office to do it.

She was one third of the way down the list when financial director Robert Clarke stuck his nose around the door.

'Any news?'

Vivienne's hopes jumped momentarily but subsided at once as Robert shook his head. 'I rang your place but they said you'd come in so I came too.'

The way he spoke set Vivienne's nerves on edge. 'Any particular reason?'

'I heard a rumour at the Willis, Roebuck annual party just before Christmas. I thought you ought to know about it.'

Now Vivienne was more nervous still; Willis, Roebuck was the corporation's principal stockbrokers and rumours from that source were likely to be significant.

'Tom Willis was telling me there seems to have been some accelerated dealing in Brand stock.'

'Everyone's heard about the tsunami,' Vivienne said. 'The market will know Hilary is missing, probably dead. It's bound to have a huge impact on the share price.'

'Of course it will. But this was before the tsunami.'

'*Before* the tsunami? That's strange. What does it mean?'

Robert shrugged. 'Could be coincidence. Or someone could be stalking us.'

'A takeover? Surely not. Who could it be?'

'Tom has no idea. If there is someone, he's keeping his head down.'

'What do we do?'

'We monitor the situation. That's about all we can do.'

Vivienne watched him go out the door. A sense of helplessness engulfed her.

I had two years to go and not a care in the world, she thought. And now this. Why did Hilary have to dump this lot on me? I was pleased at the time: who wouldn't be? It tickled my ego. To be the big boss of Brand… It really meant something. What a fool I was. I'd lived beside her all those years but had never realised what being the boss really meant. I know now. Know, too, that the burden is too heavy. I look in the mirror every morning and see a fraud. I have the top job but know I am only going through the motions. The truth is I am not a top person.

Now Hilary was gone; Vivienne had seen the pictures and knew that not even Hilary Brand could have survived such a disaster. Here she was in Hilary's chair behind Hilary's desk in Hilary's office, responsible for the wellbeing of Hilary's company, knowing she was not up to the job and facing the daunting prospect of what might prove to be a hostile takeover bid.

Dear God, she thought despairingly. What do I do now?

4

It was mid-morning and Sara was sitting at her desk contemplating a depressingly large pile of reports and accounts when Janet buzzed her.

'There is a Dolores Morrison in reception, says she wants to see you.'

'Show her in.'

'Sit down,' Sara said with what she hoped was a pleasant smile. 'Do you have anything for me?'

'You could say so.' Dolores took from her bag a tiny metal object about half the size of a matchbox.

'What's that?'

'It's a voice recorder.'

'The smallest one I've ever seen.'

'The smallest one there is. Even so, it isn't easy to smuggle it into bed when you've no clothes on.'

Sara was intrigued. 'How d'you manage it?'

'You don't want to know.' She pressed what Sara assumed was the playback button.

The machine might be small but its sound was clear.

You're mighty cheerful tonight.

Who wouldn't be with a woman like you in his bed?

That's sweet. (Pause) My, you are a big boy, aren't you?

'Do I have to listen to this?' Sara said.

'Just wait. We're coming to it now.'

Thanks for the compliment, baby, but don't try and kid me. Something else has put that smile on your face.

You could be right.

So tell me.

Just now.

Careful, baby. Ooh, that's nice. Oh my!

Dolores reached out a hand and switched off. 'I'll fast-forward a bit.'

'I'm relieved to hear you say so,' said Sara.

'Par for the course,' Dolores said. She fiddled with the recorder and pressed the play button. 'Here we are.'

Well, something certainly fired you up. You going to tell me about it?

Why should you care?'

Baby, a man like you doesn't come along every day. Of course I care. I want to know everything about you.

'Put it to them right, men will tell you anything,' Dolores said.

I had the word today an old enemy of mine has carked it. Not before time, either. That one owed me a few, I can tell you. My oath she did!

What did she do to you?

Only stole my share of a company I'd set up. Helped herself to two million bucks of my money and did a runner just as the market crashed on my head. Now it's payback time.

But if she's dead..?

Now I'm going to get it all back: my share, her kids' share, the lot.

Any woman tried to cross a man like you got to be crazy. How are you going to do it?

Sitting silently at Sara's desk the two women listened as Haskins Gould, luxuriating in his companion's awed admiration, explained. Finally, after several minutes, Dolores spoke again.

This scheme of yours… Is it legal?

Who cares?

I can see you've got it all worked out. But I'm afraid it's all beyond me.

No reason for you to worry your head about that. You got other talents.

You're not such a slouch yourself. Want to show me?

Dolores Morrison switched off the machine. The two women looked at each other.

'I've done a report, too,' Dolores said.

She handed Sara a slender file which Sara read with increasing amazement. 'You really got all this out of him like that?'

'Not entirely. Even he wasn't mug enough for that. But he gave me some clues. I doubt he even realised he'd done it but they got me started. I poked around a bit and soon ferreted out the rest.'

'How?'

Dolores smiled. 'Trade secrets, sweetie.'

'Can I have the tape?' Sara asked.

Dolores shook her head. 'He'll know where you got it from. He'd send somebody after me. I can't risk it.'

'If I just make notes of what he's been doing? If I give you my word I'll show it to nobody else? Nobody at all?'

Dolores stared at her sharp-eyed and for a moment did not answer.

'My word is good,' Sara said.

The scrutiny lasted a few seconds longer then Dolores nodded. 'I believe it is,' she said. 'And you won't tell him how you found out?'

'No.'

Dolores nodded again. 'OK, then.' She looked at her watch. 'I've got to dash.'

'Oh?'

'Another client. If you're good at what you do there's always a demand, isn't that so?' She winked. 'I daresay you find the same.'

'I'll be a couple of hours with the tape, then I'll leave it in a sealed envelope at reception,' Sara said. 'You can pick it up whenever you like.'

She watched her go. Interesting life she must lead, she thought. She did not feel in the least judgmental about it but Haskins Gould was a different story. As far as that one was concerned, judgment day was coming down on him like an avalanche and she couldn't wait.

She listened to the tape again, making notes and somehow managing to avoid most of the pillow talk. When she was ready she picked up the phone.

'Get me Mr Haskins Gould, Janet. If you please.'

5

'I don't even know why I'm talking to you,' Haskins said, but cautiously: if Sara had nothing she wouldn't be on the phone now.

'Fern Robin,' Sara Brand said. 'Name mean anything to you?'

The blood paused in his veins; she had no business knowing about Fern Robin. Along with several of his other shelf companies it had recently built up a sizeable holding in Brand Corporation.

'Should it mean anything?'

'I would have thought it likely. Since you own it.'

'I certainly do not!'

'Of course you don't. Forgive me. Henry Ward owns it. And Henry Ward works for you, does he not?'

How the hell had she found that out?

'Let us run through a few more names.'

He heard, rage gathering, as the bitch from hell proceeded calmly and methodically to list the names of every one of the companies in which he had for several months been lodging the shares he had bought in Brand. They were all public companies and their records could be accessed by anyone but how could she have known to check them out?

But questions could wait. What mattered now was what came next. Against his every inclination he forced himself to listen to what Sara Brand was saying.

'Between them these companies control significantly more than twenty per cent of Brand's shares. Indirectly you control them all. Given the requirement of the act, I presume you have notified the authorities?'

Haskins Gould did not answer.

'Bearing in mind the trouble you've had with them in the past,' Sara said, 'I am not sure how they would react if it came out that you were once again in breach of the regulations. Assuming, of course, that you are.' He could almost hear her smile. 'My own feeling is they might come down quite heavily on you. If you really have broken the rules, Haskins. Yet again. And if they found out.'

He was in denial, unable to believe that for the second time members of this unspeakable family had cut the ground from under him. 'You can't prove any of this.'

That was the way: defy and deny, defy and deny.

'But you see I can,' Sara said. 'I have all the details I need. How else would I have the information I have just given you?'

Haskins had never been afraid of a fight as long as it was with words and not fists. Despite being Jewish he'd always had a soft spot for Dr Goebbels's cult of the big lie. He sat back in his chair, took a deep breath and laughed loud and long. In his time he'd spent days practising that laugh, a clever combination of contempt and tolerant amusement. It had got him off the hook more than once in days gone by.

'Information? Is that what you call it? Sorry, darling,' he said. 'You're on the wrong track there. That's not information. That's a fairy story. A nice one, I grant you. A sweet one.' Sarcasm was a blade. 'But it's bullshit, sweetie. You know how many people I got working for me? I'll tell you. Over a thousand. You saying they're not permitted to have their own companies because they work for me? Not to own shares? Attila the Hun: that who you think I am? Genghis Khan, maybe? In your dreams, darling. I'll tell you this for free. No court in the land would listen to your nonsense. Not for five minutes, Sara! Now stop wasting my time.'

Haskins had hoped that would have blown her out of the water but seemingly it had not. Her voice when she answered was as unruffled as a mountain pond. With a touch of ice on it too. 'You're the one talking bullshit,' she said. 'You and I both know what you're doing. I will say it to you only once: back off.'

'And if I don't?'

'You'll be looking at more trouble than you can handle.'

6

Sara replaced the phone hard on its stand. Take that, you bastard. She sat and considered the situation.

Point one. No question about it, the rumours were right. Haskins Gould was planning a move on Brand.

Point two. She had to stop him.

Well and good; no argument about that. But how? All she really knew was she had to act and act fast. If Haskins Gould got hold of Brand it would mean the end not only of Hilary's legacy but her own future.

Trouble was, what he was doing might be against the regulations but was not necessarily criminal, and stopping him would not be easy. Her only real evidence was the tape recording Dolores had given her but that would never stand up in court.

She phoned Channel 12 again, this time to speak to Aaron, an old friend on the financial desk, and Aaron told her what she already knew, that Haskins Gould was one of the biggest crooks in the corporate world.

'Sell his mother for a quid if there were takers,' he told her. 'Not that there would be.'

'Why's that?'

'She gave birth to him, didn't she?'

Which said it all, Sara thought, but didn't help.

'I'll tell you what you should do,' Aaron said. 'Make some enquiries in Switzerland.'

'But how? Swiss banks never give details of their clients' affairs, do they?'

'Speak to Günter Flüry at the Bernese Land Bank,' Aaron said.

'I've never heard of him. Anyway, why should he help me? He doesn't know me from a bar of soap.'

'But he knows me. And he hates Haskins Gould like poison.'

'May I mention your name?'

'He won't tell you anything if you don't. He may not, anyway. I can't guarantee anything. But if he's sticky, ask him to give me a bell.'

'I owe you one,' Sara said.

'How do you plan to settle the debt?'

Aaron had always liked her. She laughed. 'Let's find out what he has to tell me first, OK?'

7

Whichever way you looked at it, Haskins thought, it was a problem he didn't need.

Maybe he'd seen Sara Brand off, maybe not, but either way he couldn't afford to let the Stock Exchange boys get on his case. They'd come close to catching him several times in the past; nifty footwork had saved him but he was older now and neither his footwork nor his nerves were what they'd been once, when the market had been a casino and those upon whom fate smiled had made fortunes. He'd been one of the lucky ones; he still had millions in Switzerland that no one knew about. Where else would he find the funds to go after Brand? But this was his last big play; with age his appetite for the razzmatazz of the markets had dulled. He still wanted this final coup, though. What an exit that would be, to have the scalp of the Brand Corporation hanging from his belt! That would give him crowing rights loud enough to give Hilary indigestion even in the afterlife. Let's hope it chokes her, he thought.

But he'd have to move; now the bitch's daughter was in the know he couldn't hang about. He must grab all the stock he could; once he had the company the regulators could scream all they liked but it would be too late.

Time to throw caution to the winds.

8

It took a while, first phoning Günter Flüry in Switzerland, then waiting while he phoned Aaron in Sydney, then having to phone him again, but at last she got the information she needed.

'People will want to know where you got it from,' Günter said.

Sara looked at the notes she had made during their conversation. 'I have no information. I don't know what you're talking about.'

'And if the police ask?'

'I shall say it has nothing to do with me and I know nothing about it.'

'Good. Please be sure to keep it that way.'

By then it was nearly eleven o'clock and everyone else had long gone home. No matter, she thought, I shall speak to Vivienne in the morning. And say what?

It gave her time, both in bed and over breakfast the next day, to think where she was heading. Was Vivienne up to the challenge of taking Brand Corporation past Hilary's legacy and into the future? She sat and thought carefully about that. No, she thought. She isn't. It's not in her. Very well. Mind made up, she picked up the phone.

'Vivienne? It's Sara. I'll be in the office in an hour. I'd like to see you, if you're free.'

9

The discussion was amicable and brief. Vivienne would retain the title of CEO for the next six months but at the AGM would announce she was stepping down for health reasons. Sara would replace her officially at that time but Vivienne would retain her place on the board in an advisory capacity.

'Wouldn't you sooner I quit altogether?' Vivienne said. 'I'd be happy to step down tomorrow if you'd prefer.'

'I'd much sooner you stayed on,' Sara said. 'Your experience and advice will be invaluable. In fact I am not sure I could manage without you.'

Vivienne felt a ton weight had been lifted from her shoulders. She hadn't been so happy for months and it made her magnanimous. 'I shall be happy to help in any way I can,' she said. A thought occurred to her. 'Do you really think you've worked out a way to fend off Haskins Gould?'

'I think I have,' Sara said.

Back in her own office Sara phoned Aaron at Channel 12 and fifteen minutes later walked into his office.

'The other day you asked me how I planned to settle my debt to you.'

A hopeful look momentarily brightened Aaron's face. 'A dinner?' he suggested. 'A secret rendezvous afterwards?'

'Alas,' Sara said.

'You can't blame me for trying,' Aaron said.

'I would be disappointed if you didn't.'

Sara took two sheets of A4 paper out of her briefcase. The sheets contained a typed list of transactions: their nature, dates and the amounts. All the amounts were large; some were huge.

Aaron looked at the list, frowning, and then at Sara. 'What is this?'

'A record of Mr Gould's financial dealings in Switzerland over the last twelve months.'

'My God.' It might have been a prayer of thanksgiving, the way Aaron spoke.

'You think the ATO might be interested in this?' Sara said.

'Would they ever.'

'Let's be quite clear about this,' Sara said. 'You never reveal your source.'

'Indeed. And if you are asked any questions?'

'I shall say it is nothing to do with me and I know nothing about any of it.'

'Bully!' Aaron said.

'If I may suggest: perhaps both the television and the print media?'

'Consider it done,' Aaron said.

FLIGHT

'Shit and derision!' screamed Haskins Gould. His fist pounded the surface of his desk as he stared with outraged eyes at the headlines of the newspaper spread in front of him. 'I do not believe it. I do not fucking well believe it!'

He knew he had a name for being a foul-mouthed screamer. So he was. No doubt there were some who didn't like it. Well, they could lump it. His power in this city had meant he didn't have to give a damn what other people thought; he never had. It was one of his many strengths, along with a nose that could sniff trouble a mile off.

He had not sniffed this.

He couldn't sit still. He gathered himself, rose from his executive leather chair – hand-crafted in Germany to suit his bulk– and turned to the window behind his desk. His sausage-sized fingers clenched and unclenched as he stared out at Sydney. Circular Quay and the harbour with the Manly ferry carving its wake across the blue water; the frigging Opera House: not that he would be seen dead in there; the million-dollar view of the city sprawling thirty floors below him. He had been a major player in this city for twenty years, off and on. The city? Say Australia, rather. Say the world. He still was and was determined to remain so. This – whatever the sodding *Monitor* might say – was a hiccup, no more than that. All the same, some drastic action was needed, and at once.

He took a deep breath, squared his massive shoulders and returned to his desk. He snatched up the paper and glared at it, willing the story to disappear, but it did not. The inch-high letters screamed back at him as he knew they would be doing across every boardroom in the land.

HASKINS'S HORDE!
GOULD'S SECRET MILLIONS REVEALED

It was all there: the Swiss bank accounts, his dealings with Selwyn Raucher, the letters he had written – in confidence! – to the Zurich District Attorney's office. There was even mention of the suicide of a currency trader and the murder – *murder!* – of the wife of a wheeler dealer who it was alleged had links to Haskins Gould.

Some hiccup, he thought. And all of it – the embarrassment, the adverse publicity and likely trouble with the taxman – was down to *The Monitor* and its triple-damned proprietor. Obviously someone had talked and he would deal with them in due course, but that was for later; what mattered now was how to kill off the story or, if it was too late for that, to insulate himself against the possible fall out.

Lots of times the authorities had tried to corner him but every time he'd managed to dodge the bullet. Until now.

One thing was certain. Gaol time was not a proposition.

His brain was a boiling soup of contradictory objectives. He had set his heart on grabbing Brand Corporation; he couldn't grab Brand Corporation because without his Swiss funds that was impossible. He had to get to Zurich to take control of his various bank accounts and switch their contents to a safer jurisdiction; now the story was out he daren't go to Zurich and face questions from the hard men of the Swiss regulatory authorities. He must stay in Oz to clear his name; he daren't stay in Oz and risk having not only his assets but his passport frozen when the tax boys got on his case, which would assuredly happen within hours.

He had money in the States and friends in Mexico. He liked Mexico: the people were friendly, the living cheap and it had a warm climate. He knew enough Spanish to get by. Maybe Cancun, on the Yucatan Peninsula, he thought. The beaches were as good as you could get anywhere, the nightlife was hot and the senoritas hotter still. Or so it was said. He had mates who'd get his money out of Zurich somehow. For a steep percentage, naturally – nothing for nothing, right? – and it would take time, but that couldn't be helped.

Maybe it was time to call it a day, hang up his boots. It was a pity he wouldn't be able to nail young Sara Brand but in this game you had to know when to cut your losses. And besides, another day another dollar. Who could say what the future might hold?

He had ten grand in hurry money in his safe. He took it and stuffed his wallet. He went out, beaming at the receptionist. 'Going to lunch. OK?'

He knew she would have seen the headlines – the whole of goddamned Sydney would have seen them – but she showed nothing as he waved gaily at her and went out and down in the express lift to the parking garage in the basement.

Three hours later he was in the air, enjoying the comfort of his first-class seat and sipping a glass of free bubbly as the Boeing headed east across the Pacific.

AN END AND A BEGINNING

Three days later Sara received a call from the manager of the resort in Thailand, giving her the news that she had been dreading but had come to accept was inevitable. Hilary, definitely, was dead.

The boatman who had taken Hilary and Craig into the hong had survived. To the police sergeant who questioned him he explained that he had been standing to one side of the entrance tunnel when the water arrived – driven by the demon Mara and the evil daughters of Mara, he said – and so had missed the worst of the impact that had hurled his two passengers to their deaths against the limestone cliffs.

Protected by the sea goddess Mazu and being young and agile he had escaped the rising waters by climbing into the topmost branches of the tallest tree in the hong, where he had clung, expecting every minute to be his last. There had been monkeys in the tree with him but – praise to Mazu! – they had been terrified and had not attacked him. After several hours the waters had subsided once more and he had climbed down, barely able to believe he had survived.

He had gone to check on the two Europeans but had seen at once there was nothing he could do for them. He had found the kayak and paddle jammed in the roots of a mangrove tree. They had been damaged but were still usable by someone like himself, a masterful boatman –

'A masterful braggart,' the sergeant had said. 'Spare us your boasting.'

The boatman had ignored this – a wise man did not argue with the police – and later had led a party to the hong.

'Where are the bodies now?' Sara asked.

'Stored in the mortuary at the hospital,' the resort manager said. 'I did not know what you wanted to do, whether to have them repatriated or buried here.'

'I'll let you know,' Sara said and rang off.

Dear God, she thought, first Emil and now Hilary. At least Emil had left her a one-line message. *I have always loved you.* But from Hilary, whom she had loved and admired so much, there was nothing but memories.

She sat, clasped hands on the desk in front of her, staring at emptiness. She and Hilary had never found it easy to express their feelings to each other. There had been admiration, yes; respect, certainly, but the loving mother-and-daughter chitchat that others achieved had never been there for either of them. Too much alike? Too close to rivalry? Perhaps. But that had been only on the surface. Underneath the feelings had been there all right. The love. Affection. Trust.

There were tears now, welling uncontrollably, flowing in choking floods down her face. She got up. Making no attempt to stop the tears she walked to the picture window, resting her hands on it. She looked out, saw nothing but blur. She could have smashed the window in her grief.

Hilary dead, her love unexpressed. Too late.

The phone rang.

A half-dozen furious steps; she snatched it up. 'I thought I said –'

'Martha Tan,' Janet said. 'I thought you would want to speak to her.'

A deep breath. 'Of course. Put her through.'

'I am so sorry,' Martha said. 'I loved her too, you know. I truly loved her.'

'I know you did. I did too, but somehow I never seemed able to say it. I wish I had.'

'Not important,' Martha said. 'She knew. Always she knew.'

'You think so? You're not just saying it?'

'So much like you. How could she not know?'

More tears then, a tempest of tears.

Martha was crying too. 'She was like a mother to me too.'

'*Towkay neo*,' Sara said, remembering the nickname Martha had given her.

'Oh yes. Always the big boss. But she had a good heart also.'

It was as good a summary of Hilary's life as you were likely to get, Sara thought. 'She did, didn't she?'

It was obvious that Jennifer should be allowed to have her say but Sara was not sure of the wisdom of discussing funeral arrangements with her at this late stage of her pregnancy. She took a chance, phoned anyway and spoke to Martin.

'As we feared. It seems they died together, which I suppose is something. The thing is, can you break the news to Jennifer? She must be told, obviously, but with the baby due so soon... How is she, anyway?'

'She's fine. Worried, of course, and sick to death of lugging that ton weight around –'

'Who wouldn't be?'

'Exactly. But I'll try and break it to her gently.'

'I'm afraid the media is likely to be on it pretty soon. You may get phone calls.'

'That's easy. I'll leave the phone off the hook. Are you having her brought back?'

'No. I thought we could have a memorial service for her here when Jennifer is out and about again but they'll be buried together in the Protestant cemetery in Penang. They were happy there and it was their home.'

'Jennifer won't like that.'

'I know. And I am sorry it won't be possible for her to fly up for the funeral but this isn't about Jennifer or me or anybody else. It is what Hilary would have wanted.'

'When is the funeral?'

'The day after tomorrow.'

'So soon?'

'It's the tropics, Martin. We can't hang about.'

'Will you be going?'

'I shall.'

'I shall be sorry to miss it myself,' Martin said. 'But in the circumstances –'

'I understand. And I want you to do something for me.'

'Name it.'

'I want a painting of Hilary for the boardroom. So that people who sit there in the years to come will have something to remember her by.'

'Continuity,' Martin said. 'I think that's a wonderful idea.'

'You'll be having some continuity of your own in the near future,' Sara said.

'The company and the family and the future,' Martin said.

'And your paintings,' Sara said. 'With all that going for us how can our future be anything but bright?'

ONWARDS AND UPWARDS

The cemetery was old, with many ancient trees shading the stone monuments to the dead. Francis Light, founder of the British colony of Penang, was buried there. Traffic roared beyond the perimeter fence but beneath the trees it was still, the dead undisturbed. The air breathed reverence and Sara thought it a fitting place for Hilary Brand who, like Light, had done so much in her life and died prematurely. It was the right place for Hilary and the man she had loved, together in death as in life.

Sara had been unsure how many would turn up but the funeral at the Anglican church in Lebuh Farquhar was heavy with brass. She gave a brief eulogy. Vivienne Archer was in the congregation; in their absence they had left Robert Clarke and Desmond Bragg to mind the shop; Desmond had already set his gremlins to work on preparing a documentary on Hilary's life. Martha Tan had flown in from Hong Kong, the Australian High Commissioner from Kuala Lumpur. A representative of the Malaysian government was present, bringing a message from the prime minister that Sara read to the congregation. The manager of the Penang Children's Society and several of the children were there too, along with the many friends Craig Laurie had made over his years on the island.

The reception was at the E & O Hotel, which had plenty of experience in catering for both the living and the dead.

Afterwards Sara went back alone to Rumah Kelapa. In his will Craig had left everything to Hilary. Hilary's major assets – shares in Brand, her interest in a huge portfolio of properties around the globe – were tied up in various family trusts, but after several bequests to friends, retainers and charities, especially the Penang Children's Society, her personal assets were divided between the two girls: the Perth house and other properties to Jennifer, Cadogan Place to Sara. Because she hadn't known Craig's intentions regarding Rumah Kelapa it was not mentioned in her will but Sara had fallen in love with it at first sight and was determined to hang on to it, if necessary paying Jennifer more than its value to do so.

Now, as she climbed the steps and walked into the wooden house, it was like walking into her mother's heart. Here, withdrawn from the world, Hilary had spent the last months of her life with the man she loved. She had loved Craig Laurie for years; it had been her conscious decision to wait before joining him as it had been her conscious decision, when she felt the time was right, to walk away from the business world and what until then had been her life. What had prompted that decision Sara discovered only when she went through her mother's papers and came across a note from a Dr Chang at Singapore's Mount Elizabeth Hospital. Heart trouble… Sara would never have known it. Yet even then Hilary had managed her life; never had she been a woman who permitted life to manage her. No, to the end she had been in charge.

'I shall miss her,' she told the silent house. 'How I shall miss her.'

One by one she went through the rooms. The living room, large and welcoming, golden in the sunlight shining through the windows; the bedrooms; the modern kitchen and bathrooms: she felt Hilary's presence everywhere, sensed her moving through the shadows.

She walked out on to the deck and looked out at the beach, the sea beyond. At night she would see her walking on the sand with Craig Laurie beside her, the imprint of their feet erased by waves foaming creamy-white in the darkness.

The home to which Hilary had returned over the years; the home in which she had found safe haven at last, united with her love. Yes, it was good they were buried there on the island, side by side in the silent earth.

It would be a haven to which Sara would return from time to time. She felt good there, at home there. But not yet. Now there were challenges to overcome, opportunities to seize, the excitement of measuring herself against the future. The next day she would appoint an agent to look after Rumah Kelapa in her absence. She would ask Vivienne to take over the management of the children's charity; as soon as she had done these things she would return to the world she knew and valued, to the fullness of life and its challenges. She was booked on a plane heading south the next afternoon: to Singapore, first of all, then on the airbus to Sydney. In the meantime she had documents in the briefcase she had brought with her that she must read, decisions that she must make. Towkay neo, she thought. The job for which destiny had schooled her.

'Onwards and upwards,' she told the ocean. 'I can't wait.'

She turned from her contemplation of the sea and walked into the house.

AUTHOR'S NOTES

As with my earlier books, *A Woman of Courage* is a work of fiction, and the characters and the incidents it contains are the product of the author's imagination. However, Hilary's childhood story is based on historical fact. For many years the British authorities sent children to Australia and Canada, with smaller numbers going to the then Rhodesia and to New Zealand. In many cases the authorities lied to both children and parents, claiming the parents were dead or the children had been adopted in the United Kingdom. In many cases children arriving in Australia were abused unmercifully by those to whom they were assigned. This disgraceful process continued in diminishing numbers until the 1960s.

The homes named in the text both in England and Australia existed although the administrators mentioned are fictitious. At the age of fifteen most girls in the homes were, as happens to Hilary, sent as domestic help to various parts of the country.

The only known Opie portrait of Lachlan Macquarie is in the State Library of New South Wales. The one mentioned in the text is invented for this story.

Myxomatosis did not reach the Pattinsons' area until after Hilary had moved on.

The property boom in Western Australia took place much as described.

The stock exchange crash of 1987 proved the downfall of many entrepreneurs and others.

Premier is an imaginary company, but China purchased large quantities of heavy earthmoving equipment at the time this story is set.

The hongs of the Andaman coast exist as described.

As is well known, the Boxing Day tsunami killed hundreds of thousands of people, including several thousand on the Andaman coast of southern Thailand. The fictitious character of Sylvia Mudge is based on a real child with some knowledge of the tsunami phenomenon, who warned of the coming disaster and by so doing succeeded in saving many lives.

ACKNOWLEDGEMENTS

I am pleased to acknowledge the invaluable advice given me by Ian Thwaites, Assistant Director (Services) of the Child's Migrant Trust, during my research into the conditions to which migrant children like Hilary Brand were exposed during the 1940s and 1950s.

As always, it gives me huge pleasure to thank Selwa Anthony, my agent and friend, for the unstinting help and encouragement she has given me over the years and whose contribution to the present work has been monumental.

I am also grateful to my editors and the magnificent team at Harlequin.

Thank you.

ABOUT THE AUTHOR

J.H. Fletcher is the prize-winning author of seventeen novels, published to both critical and popular acclaim in Australia, Germany and the UK, as well as numerous short stories and plays for radio and television. He was educated in England and France and travelled and worked in Europe, Asia and Africa before emigrating to Australia in 1991. Home is a house on the edge of the Western Tier Mountains in northern Tasmania.